Déjà vu

ALL OVER AGAIN

DISCARD

LARRY BRILL

Black Tie
B O O K S

Published by Black Tie Books
Austin, Texas

The Library of Congress has catalogued the trade paperback edition as follows:

Brill, Larry
Déjà vu All Over Again / by Larry Brill – 1st edition
LCCN: 2018905240
ISBN: 978-0-9960834-1-6

Printed in the United States of America
First Edition
10 9 8 7 6 5 4 3 2 1

Visit our website: www.larrybrill.com

DEDICATION

This is for all the great teachers out there, especially English teacher Mrs. Betty Lou Gillette who long ago encouraged this foolish dreamer to keep writing because some day...

Déjà vu
ALL OVER AGAIN

CHAPTER ONE

Bitch-Slapped but Unbowed

Considering all the ways life had bitch-slapped Nate Evans silly over the years, he thought it a minor miracle he hadn't gone ballistic long before the Air Force dropped a bomb on his home.

But then ballistic was a relative term. Did conking a military officer on the noggin with a five-iron count? He knew he wasn't a violent person so, yeah, in retrospect, it probably did. What does the military call that? Collateral damage. That's what the officer was. Just collateral damage. Still…

"This shit ain't right," Nate mumbled.

He sulked through the debris a good twenty yards from the burned-out shell of the mobile home he rented on an acre of prairie grass up the hill from Santa Barbara. The siding was equal parts rust and paint, and it leaked like a sieve when it rained, but it was all he had. It was the first Saturday of December, and that morning's explosion scattered the odds and ends of his life across the yard. It took a random act of God and the U.S. military to show him the apocalyptic mess it had become. And if anybody knew a thing or two about creating apocalyptic visuals, it was Nate Evans. In thirty years as a screenwriter, a Hollywood hack-for hire, he had written them into a dozen movie scripts. Apocalypse was a guaranteed blockbuster storyline every summer.

Strands of Nate's long gray hair, swirling in the breeze from the ocean, blew across his face. They smacked his nose and stuck to his lips. He tried to spit them away, but they only stuck to his tongue and tasted like Irish Spring soap. Out near the road, but inside the fence line, an Air Force lieutenant who had driven from Edwards Air Force Base stood talking to Sheriff's Deputy DiCarlo. The fire investigator from Santa Barbara County circled around to the back of the trailer. He didn't have much light left; the sun lingered over the Pacific's horizon like a rubbernecking tourist trying to get one last look at the horrific scene of an accident.

"Move along. Nothing to see here," Nate told the sun.

He toed a small golden trophy, blown off its base and out of his living room to this spot in the driveway. Mt. Hamilton High School, San Jose, California. Spirit trophy, class of '79. He sighed. What a waste. His yearbook had been on the same shelf. Now it was splayed facedown in the dirt a step away. Most of the pages fell away from the spine and landed with a thump at his feet when he picked it up. Nate tossed the cover aside, spinning it like a Frisbee. He picked up one of his golf clubs that had been blown out of its bag he kept near the door and used it to poke at the mess, all random stuff, nothing worth resurrecting. A computer mouse here, a scrap of wall with a vintage poster from an obscure movie still attached there, a coffee mug, and the fuzzy dice from his first car. They were covered with soot. Would he find anything worth salvaging once they let him inside the trailer? Did he even own anything worth salvaging? *Not likely.*

Then he found that damned lunchbox. It was a child's metal lunch-pail from the sixties with a rounded lid, illustrated with smiling faces of the cast from the TV show *Lost In Space*. Nate had come across it in an antique shop right after his divorce from Valerie went final five years ago. He bought it because it perfectly fit his state of mind at that time. Lost in space. He had filled it with photographs and letters from his twenty-five year marriage, his wedding ring, and the final divorce papers. He burned the contents and kept it as an urn for the ashes of a dead relationship. It was heartbreakingly funny at the time.

Nate leaned on the golf club for support, staring at the back end of the trailer where the bedroom survived. That corner still had its walls but swayed like a punch-drunk fighter ready to drop at the first breath of a serious wind. He set the lunchbox at his feet. It wasn't even singed. He could almost taste the resentment welling up and coating the back of his tongue. Why the fuck, out of all the memories he had tucked away in nooks and crannies of the mobile home, had the most painful part of his life been the only thing to survive intact?

Nate kicked at the dirt, his shoe catching on a DVD case. *Peggy Sue Got Married*. He had a bazillion movies in just about every corner of the little trailer. He had seen this one almost that many times. God, what he wouldn't give to go back and relive his high school days like Kathleen Turner did. The world made less sense when he was a teenager than it did now, but it was the last time he had been truly happy. Now all he had was a failed marriage. Failed career. Failed life, basically.

Nate pushed the head of the golf club into the dirt and leaned on it with both hands while he closed his eyes. A thin smile creased his lips. If he only wished for it hard enough, he might transport himself back in time. Raw desire with a tremendous imagination was a powerful thing. He could do it. He was almost there. Almost…

He thought of a girl named Cooper. The Coop-ster. Coop-o-rama. Julie to everyone else. "Jules," when he was alone with her. She had popped into his head now and again over the years, and she always made him smile. After Nate caught Valerie in bed with a junior partner from her law firm, it was Jules who came to him in the middle of many sleepless nights to soothe him. She assured him she would never have done a dirty deed like that, and she reminded Nate he should never have let her get away back in high school. Now, he used her. Jules had become his favorite go-to memory whenever he was down. Where was she today? His heart took him back in time to be with her, and a nano-moment of peace hugged him for the effort. Focus, boy. Almost there…

Then he opened his eyes. "Rats."

No surprise. Nothing had changed. A wisp of smoke rose from the charred rubble that had once been his home, like the incense from mass, an offering to some unseen God. The offering didn't work.

"Christ on a cracker, give me a break."

His belongings were still scattered everywhere. His life was still a shambles. This wasn't Hollywood. He didn't have a near-death experience like Peggy Sue to take him back in time. He didn't have John Cusack's *Hot Tub Time Machine.* Heck, he didn't even have *Mr. Destiny's* angel, Michael Caine, and that flick sucked pond scum.

Why couldn't life allow him a do-over like that? A mulligan. He wasn't bonkers, at least not certifiably. He knew this because he sometimes questioned his sanity, and that was proof. Everybody knows that only crazy people never question whether their elevator goes all the way to the top floor. No, he knew the difference between the dream and reality, but his heart badly wanted to go back and fix his life. His mind, knowing it was impossible, shrugged and indulged him. The daydreams started hitting him more often after he turned fifty and life in his rearview mirror looked prettier by the day. Sometimes they snuck up on him, but most were deliberate. It was pain management. He would conjure up memories, real and imagined, complete with conversations. High school, and those days with Julie and friends, became his way of finding a safe place to go when he felt blue. It didn't necessarily mean he was a few bricks shy of a load. Did it? The nostalgia and fond memories usually made him feel better. Usually.

Today they jilted him. They only reminded him of what should have been.

The Air Force officer headed his way, stopping to snap a picture with a pocket camera and dictate observations into a mini voice recorder. Pennybacker or Pennymoocher was his name. Nate couldn't recall after the way the officer grudgingly shook his hand with a mumbled introduction. This PennySucker guy treated him like an inconvenience.

"Now, Mr. Evans, tell me where you were, what were you doing, and what exactly did you see prior to this alleged explosion?"

Alleged? "Does this look like alleged?" Nate waved an upturned palm across the yard. Exhibit A.

The officer's silver nametag said Lt. Prettypenny. "Just to keep the record straight."

Nate had spent most of the day answering questions for the sheriff's deputy, the fire crew chief, neighbors, and strangers who stopped by the front gate, and the investigator who was still making notes at the far side of the yard. He was tired of this.

"Went to the shed on the other side of the driveway to get more kindling for the wood stove I use to heat the trailer," he told the lieutenant.

"Heading back when I heard a whistling sound. Looked up. Big-ass bullet-shaped thing falling out of the sky." Nate imitated the sound while making a diving motion with one hand before slapping it hard in the palm of his other one.

"Crazy bang. Must have gone through the roof on the far side, near the propane tank. Stunned. Saw one of those military drones flying over the hill thataway. Sucker was sputtering and it was wobbling a lot. The bomb must have come from it. Hell yes, I'm sure. Started for the front door when... *Kablooey*. Knocked me on my ass. Shit raining down all over the friggin' place."

He told the officer that the fire investigator dude had hinted—nothing official, but just between us boys—the projectile might have severed the gas line from the propane tank and the wood stove touched it off.

"That's pretty much it," Nate concluded.

The lieutenant asked him more questions as if probing for a flaw. Yes, it was a drone. Yes, Nate would know one if he saw it. "It was one of those Predators. I know that for a fact. Most likely the MQ-1," he added to impress the officer. It didn't work. Nate recognized the aircraft from his research for a movie script years earlier. He had written the hijacking of a Predator drone into a spectacularly unsuccessful story about computer nerd vampires raised on video games who got their hands on military stockpiles in an effort to take over the world. *Hellfire: A Love*

Story never caught on. But then, few of Nate's scripts ever did. He did sell it to an independent producer and made enough money off the movie option to cover a few months rent on the trailer that, now, was no more. The producer hadn't done anything with the story other than send him a small check each year just to keep the rights to make a film out of it someday. It was always someday with Nate's scripts.

He could sure use a decent sale like that now, even if the story got eighty-sixed after he cashed the check. He had gone too long between projects. So long, in fact, his agent had stopped returning Nate's calls. Some called it writer's block. Nate called it being creatively constipated. The words were stuck inside somewhere, making him even more miserable.

"Odd thing, Mr. Evans." The Air Force officer signaled for Nate to follow him. "It's rare to see this level of damage."

"This kind of thing happen a lot for you guys?" Nate was sorry when he said it. It was a feeble attempt at humor. It carried more sarcasm than he wanted but less anger than he felt. He wasn't sure the lieutenant deserved it, but somebody sure as hell did.

The lieutenant ignored him. Prettypenny was young, tall, and thin, and probably not stooped like a vulture as Nate saw him. He shrugged and passed the buck. "I am only the IAO—initial assessment officer. Someone higher on the chain of command will have to order up an investigation. Or not. What you think you saw will be considered."

Or not. Nate's anger was rising. "Give me a friggin' break, okay? This is my life here."

"I understand." PennySucker surveyed the mess and then laughed, "I'd be upset, too. It wasn't much of a life."

Not much of a life?

"Just kidding," PrettyAssSomething said. He quickly dropped the smile. The officer left Nate fuming there, telling him that nothing would get done until he filled out the appropriate papers.

Not much of a life? That son of a bitch. Where'd he come off with saying something like that? This was no joke.

Nate's head started to throb and the muscles in his neck tightened. He raised the five iron in his hand. Never had his swing been as pure as it was right then on the Nate Evans Memorial Greens front nine. He knocked the smile off the ceramic gnome near the driveway, head and all. The plastic pink yard flamingo absorbed a brutal fairway blow with a dull thud. It bounced three times before dying at the base of the concrete stoop to what had been his front door. He shanked a can of diced tomatoes back toward the kitchen, but he got no distance whatsoever from the glass picture frame that shattered on impact. Nate stooped and picked up his black Magic 8 Ball. He flipped it over and read the fortune that floated to the surface of its belly.

Outlook not so good.

"Damn straight." He tossed the ball up into the air and then clubbed it on the way down. The Magic 8 Ball soared over his ruined mobile home and nearly hit the fire department inspector. He glared back at Nate through the opening that should have been Nate's living room wall.

"Fore!" Nate yelled.

Then he spotted his next target. He hurled the club with all his might in the direction of Lieutenant PrettypennyPants. It was an Olympic caliber hammer throw, soaring high into the early evening sky. The golf club rotated with a slow, graceful backspin and fell to earth with only slightly less precision than the bomb the Air Force had dropped on his house. But then, for a weapon that only cost $89.95 (on sale at Golf Jockey) compared to the hundreds of thousands of dollars the military spent for its payload that day, accuracy wise, the five-iron was a much better return on investment.

The club came down grip end first and clipped the officer on the back of his head, knocking him to the ground. The metal blade of the five-iron made a glorious ping when it dinged the hood of the lieutenant's standard-issue sedan.

Nate grinned. *Asshole in one.*

God! That felt good. He should have smacked the shit out of something years ago. It wasn't enough. He was searching for something else to whack, smash, clobber, or otherwise maim when Prettypenny scrambled to his feet and marched at Nate.

Sheriff's Deputy DiCarlo was quick. He diverted the Air Force officer by grabbing and spinning him so that momentum carried them back toward the deputy's patrol car. As he looked over his shoulder at Nate, DiCarlo jerked his head in the direction of the road. And that's how Nate wound up twenty minutes later sitting on a rickety stool swapping lies with a bunch of rednecks.

Swapping spit with a bodacious barfly.

Picking a fight to preserve her honor.

And getting the snot beat out of him by a biker with a beaver mullet at Ginny's Church of the Holy Brew.

CHAPTER TWO

Holy Brew, Batman!

Ginny's was a dump. The kind of place in the middle of nowhere, smelling of cigarette smoke and stale beer, that gave dive bars respectability. It was the perfect place for Nate to lick his wounds from that day's disaster at his trailer. Three weeks before Christmas and the tired strings of holiday lights that lined shelves behind the bar twelve months out of the year depressed him more than usual.

The regulars called it simply "The Church." They were an odd mix of those who favored leather chaps, shaggy beards, tattoos, do-rags and hogs (the Harley kind), who hung out with the rednecks in the area who favored sweat-stained John Deere caps, hogs (the eatin' kind) and looked after the local ranches owned by city dwellers who found federal farming subsidies a great tax gift from Uncle Sam.

Ginny's had been a real church once upon a time. Several of the wooden pews served as benches along the wall opposite the bar. Nate had witnessed many a patron who, driven to his knees on the dance floor when the setting sun streamed through the stained glass above the entrance, were touched by divine inspiration and, in holy joy, ordered another round.

"How-dee. I'd like to get her nekkid wearing nothin' but a pair of mouse ears."

"Show a little respect, will you?"

Nate flicked a pretzel stick at his best friend, Woody, who was leering at a woman at the opposite end of the long bar. It was Nate's fault. He was the one who started it by mentioning how much she resembled Annette Funicello. Annette the post-*Mouse Club* beach babe. She had Annette's dark hair, dark eyes and an Ivory girl complexion with tiny lips and a full figure. Nate tilted his chin down as if studying his beer while he raised his eyes to watch her. She'd strolled in wearing tight jeans and a sleeveless blouse with a high, banded collar from somewhere out of the sixties. He guessed she was nearer to forty than his vision of Annette, but she was a great knockoff of every boy's favorite Mouseketeer.

"You're right. You're goddamned right," Woody said. He removed his sweat-stained Dodgers cap and placed it over his heart.

"Gentlemen, a moment of silence, please."

"May she rest in peace."

"Amen."

They clinked the necks of their beer bottles, and Nate felt a familiar pang of lust for the Annette of his past with her pair of large, beautiful, soft, round...mouse ears. She owned the hearts of an entire generation of boys like him.

His eyes darted to Annette Knockoff's left hand. No wedding ring. Some guys were breast men. For others, their first look dropped to a woman's butt or legs, while others started with a smile or the eyes before working their way down. Nate went directly to the ring finger before even considering whether he had a right to ogle a lady. Guys cheated on their wives. Wives cheated on their husbands. But what low-life, pond scum sucker would do it with another man's wife?

The kind who had diddled his wife, Valerie, that's who. That's how he wound up divorced after twenty-plus years. She had a wandering eye, along with other parts of her body. He had an overdeveloped sense of trust, along with denial that enabled her until the proof was too clear even for him to rationalize away. Nobody gave a rat's ass about the husband. Like Nate. So he swore he could never do that to anyone. Someone had to have a little respect for the other guy, especially if the wife didn't.

Annette Knockoff caught him gazing at her. She smiled. Nate ordered a shot of courage.

"What kind, hon?" Ginny asked. She had a voice that was pure gravel from two packs a day, white hair piled high on her head and her eyes let you know, in no uncertain terms, that you were boring her.

Nate considered his finances. "Cheap."

The old woman shook her head, disgusted. "Bottom shelf, coming up."

The beauty at the end of the bar not only had Mouseketeer written all over her, she had the same dark hair, high cheeks and mischievous eyes as The Coop-ster. He basked in the glow of a two-fer. Two shots of Julie Cooper memories in the same day. At least he wasn't standing in the debris of his life this time. He had made a few feeble attempts over the years to find Julie on Facebook and Google. She had married not long out of high school, he knew, but he couldn't remember her husband's name and that made his search futile. It was just as well. Finding her online, and finding she was still happily married, would only confirm he had no business wanting to see her again. Thinking of Julie while sitting on a barstool always called for a second shot.

"What if?" Whiskey and regrets always led him to ask that.

"What, what if?"

"What if you could go back to, say, high school? I mean, you know how your life turned out, right? So if you could go back and do it over again?"

"Stupid question," Woody replied.

"Frickin' stupid," the redneck on Nate's left said, although Nate hadn't asked him.

"Who wouldn't?" That came from the geezer on Woody's right.

All along the bar, the vote was informal but unanimous, life would be better, richer, more perfect if they got the kind of mulligan in life that you could on the golf course. A do-over.

Nate stole another glance at the woman, threw back his head and tossed down the rest of his whisky, hard, certain he was falling in love. He thumped the glass on the bar and exhaled slowly.

"Thanks for coming, Woody. And thanks for putting me up for tonight."

"No problema. Mi sofá es su sofá."

Woody had been his dorm mate in his first year at a state college just outside of Los Angeles. Nate had a baseball scholarship and interest in film studies. Woody had an interest in coeds and played in a rock band to meet girls. Thirty years later, he was still making music.

He jerked his thumb toward a table where two guys who blew in with Woody were playing a dice game with one hand while slugging beer from a bottle in the other. "Me and the boys are headed to this party down the hill tonight. It's gonna be an outrageous event. You should come along."

Together they were a band called Woody Wood and the

Peckerheads. The Peckerheads were famous for three weeks when their "yodel rap" song "Swillin' and Chillin'" went to the top of the country-western charts. With rap lyrics and a hip-hop beat featuring a slide guitar and fiddle, Woody's song about pimping a ride in his pickup with his bitch (a hunting dog named Ho) developed a cult following over the years. Yodel rap flamed out faster than a cheap Roman candle on the Fourth of July, but it was enough to make Woody some serious bling, and the band was still a favorite at county fairs and Indian casinos.

Woody said, "I still can't see you bopping the shit out of that military dude the way you did. That just ain't like you."

"Yep." Nate nodded. The more he thought about it, the more he was pleased with himself.

"I am impressed, Bubba. Being a pussy liberal and all."

"That hurts. And you are so wrong. I am not all that liberal."

"Okay. Just a pussy. I bet you can't remember the last time you took a swing at somebody."

That stopped Nate. Whenever it was, it had to have been serious, because Nate had anger issues. Not trouble controlling his anger, generating it. Nate accepted the fact he was too nice for his own good, but what could you do?

Then Woody ventured into an inconvenient truth. "Okay, maybe you ain't exactly pussy material but I can't imagine nobody else who'd catch his wife doing another man and then spend so much time trying to fix things until *she* walked out on *you*."

"Yeah, well, I've done stupider shit than that."

"Gave it your best shot. But you still should have beat her to the punch, you know?"

Nate did know. After seven months of intense marriage counseling, he surrendered to the obvious. He waited for her to get home from work on a Friday with his bags packed and ready to walk, rehearsing how to break it to Valerie in a way that wouldn't hurt her too badly. He was still waiting around midnight when she sent him a Twitter message to say she wouldn't be coming home at all. She couldn't respect any man who would put up with the crap she had pulled. Divorce papers to follow. The marriage ended with a Tweet.

"At least you got a great story out of the deal," Woody said. He didn't look at Nate. He studied the label of his beer bottle instead.

"Best damned thing I ever put out there." It was. Somewhere between Valerie's late night tweet and the final divorce degree, he opened a vein and poured his heart and soul into a beautiful script of heartbreak and love gone sour. Everybody, including his agent and an Acadmy award winning producer who bought the rights for a gob of money, said it was the best thing they had ever seen.

Nate barely had time to cash the check for the first installment—a pittance of the total with a promise of more to come—when the producer disappeared with the rest of Nate's money. Also missing: Six million dollars from major investors in the project. They went to court and won the right to hold Nate's story hostage until they got their money back.

Nate hadn't written a useful word since.

He watched Annette Knockoff. The stool next to her was empty.

"Twenty bucks says you ain't got the guts."

"What guts?"

"You've been eyeing that cutie over there since we got here. Twenty bucks says there's no way in hell you'll man up and pitch her."

Any other day Nate would have rationalized his way out of putting the moves on her, but that night he was a man with nothing to lose. Valerie, the ex-wife from hell, and the Air Force had made sure of that. He was tired of letting life push him around. By God, he would do it.

"Bet. Twenty bucks. This is the new Nate Evans you're talking to pardner. M.O.A. Man Of Action. I'm going to invite her to your damned party." The woman didn't look like the sort who would accept an offer to go off with a bunch of strangers, but what the hell; he had a PhD in rejection.

"Well?"

He hesitated. Then, fueled by alcohol and fatalistic bravado, he stood, hitched up his jeans and sauntered over to the woman like the cool and smooth Richard Gere-like character in his script *Cocktails for Kittens.*

"All night I've been wanting to tell you I would buy you a drink just for one of your smiles." It was a line straight out of his script.

Her name was Irene and she smelled of jasmine perfume. She was a hairdresser and worked in a shop north of town. They were only three minutes into what was shaping up to be a warm conversation when the door banged open.

"Irene, you ain't supposed to be here. I get home and where's my dinner? Ain't on the table."

"Hey, Phil," Irene said with zero enthusiasm.

Phil was a mountain of a man with deep red hair, buzz-cut on the sides but full on top with a mullet down the back of his head so that it looked like a squirrel had climbed up there and died. He had cut off the sleeves of his shirt to show the tattoos that covered both arms from wrist to neck, and the requisite redneck goatee, unkempt and bushy—it made you think he was in the middle of swallowing a small cat.

Nate watched Irene brush her bangs aside with her left hand, reassured that he hadn't been mistaken. There was no ring. Had it gone MIA? Recently? Deliberately? Possibly in the minute before Irene walked into Ginny's?

Phil tugged at her arm and turned toward the door. Irene shook loose but fell back when he slapped her, and Nate rushed between them to stop the big guy.

"Keep your goddamned hands off her." They could squabble all they wanted, but he couldn't stand a man getting physical with any woman.

"Fuck off, you little wimp. This ain't none of your business. And if you ever touch my girl again, I'll wipe the floor with your sorry ass."

Irene hissed at Phil, "I'm not going back. I'll get there when I get there." She didn't need him, and then, as if to prove it, she did a whirlwind survey of prospects in the bar. As she locked her eyes on Nate, a chill ran through him. Life did that sometimes. It put you in the wrong place at the wrong time. Before he knew what hit him, Irene planted her lips upon his and began drilling with her tongue, more eager than a rookie surgeon hot on the trail of a rogue tonsil.

As California earthquakes went, it wasn't more than three-point-five on the Richter scale, but the roar Phil let loose rattled the rafters and shook the floorboards. He grabbed Nate by the hair at the back of his neck and pulled him out from under the woman. He pushed Nate to clear some space and create room for a brawl.

Shit. The day started out as a disaster; no reason why it shouldn't end that way. Nate straightened himself. He threw back his shoulders and planted a finger in Phil's chest.

"Take your best shot, Fuck Face."

"Bring it on, you wimp."

The crowd had stopped yakking and moved closer to get a better view. Someone cranked up the bar's eight-track tape player: AC/DC's "Highway to Hell." Perfect. A goddamned fight anthem. So instead of addressing the big guy in front of him, Nate stretched both arms with his palms out like an actor ready to make his bow for the audience.

Then Nate, recently converted Man Of Action, raised his voice over the music. "Damned straight. I *am* a wimp. And I will kick the ass of anyone who says I ain't."

He wheeled. The good news was that he got in the first punch. The bad news: it wasn't nearly enough.

CHAPTER THREE
Suicide in One Hundred Forty Characters

"So much for being a Man of Action," Nate moaned.

"Dude! That is some righteous discoloration of the cranial covering." Nate couldn't see which of Woody's Peckerheads said it.

His left eye wouldn't quite focus as he tried to ice the bruise above, below and to the side of it with a chilled bottle of Sam Adams. Nursing a beer and nursing his wounds from the beating he'd taken in the bar, Nate sat on a faux boulder next to the faux waterfall of a pond in back of a mansion belonging to someone in the faux übercool class of Hollywood. Woody had said the owner was most definitely rich and most likely industry connected. Nate didn't want to be there, but he had nowhere to go. That simple fact made his head throb even more. Besides, he was in debt to the Peckerheads, and after his fight with Phil, he wasn't about to fight them when they decided he needed a party to cheer him up more than he needed to go straight to Woody's place and recover.

"I'll go get something to fix you up," Woody said. He had a fox-like grin that Nate could see even with his damaged eye. "Don't piss anybody off while I'm gone."

Nate's vision started to clear. The patio made up the ground floor of the property, with three stories of mansion stacked and stretching into the night sky over a sheer rock wall. Minglers ignored a jazz guitarist and his partner, their music simply adding to the buzz of white noise. Most were drawn to an open hospitality tent set up at the base of the patio wall. One of the Peckerheads told him that Ruffles, the Pekinese star of the hit TV series Murder, She Barked, was holding court under a blaze of video lights. Nate got to his feet and wandered over to join the audience. Ruffles' owner and co-star, Mary Grant, stood next to the dog. She played a quirky spinster sleuth named Mary who solved crimes with the aid of her Pekinese private-eye pooch on the show. Woody had wrangled an invite to the party because the Peckerheads had done a ten-second cameo as a lounge band in the latest episode.

Three cameras strategically placed around the tent pointed at the mutt in a chair with Ruffles' name stenciled on the backrest. The scene was lit from every angle. One of the minglers told him the cable TV show, Entertainment X-S, would be recording an interview for a show to be aired the following week.

Nate climbed a flight of steps that took him to the first floor of the main house, and he entered through a sliding glass door, stepping into a game room. Pool table. Foosball table. Huge flat-screen television sets on every wall where there wasn't some kind of modern retro impressionistic painting or photographs of notable Hollywood characters. He found Woody in the kitchen, one more flight up.

"So whose house is this?"

"Hell if I know. Somebody who knows somebody I don't. Does it matter? Look around you. This place has more beaver than an Oregon rainforest." Nate flinched. Crude but it did capture the ratio of starlets to mere mortals in the party crowd.

Woody took Nate by the arm, steered him to the sink and dumped wine out of a glass sitting there. He filled it with water. "This'll cheer you up. Guaranteed."

He handed him a rolled paper capsule about the size of a horse pill. "Ecstasy, as pure as it gets. Watch." Woody took the glass of water and tossed the paper ball onto the back of his tongue. He gulped the water until the glass was empty.

Shit. If life was going to hell in a handbasket anyway, he might as well enjoy the trip. He popped the capsule into his mouth and down it went. When he finished a second glass of water, he gave Woody a shrug. "Okaaaaay." He didn't feel anything.

Woody tapped the back of his wrist and told him to give it time. "Takes about half an hour. But you'll be feeling it. Trust me."

Bodies filled all the rooms on that main floor; Nate and Woody navigated around various couples and cliques. They stayed together until Woody spotted a tall blond pouting near the stairs that led to yet another level of the mansion. She was as rail thin as a fashion runway model and cursed with large eyes and a sharp beak that made Nate think of an owl.

"Try to get laid," Woody said. He took inventory of women in the room like a starving man at a buffet. "That shouldn't be too difficult here. And the ecstasy? Man, everything you're feeling, multiply it by four."

"Everything?"

"Yeah. Everything." Woody steered toward the blond.

Nate snatched a glass of wine from the tray of a waiter hustling across the room. In due time, he eased into a small group, some guy and three women he was trying to impress.

"You know Rob Castle?" the guy asked. "He was in a couple of movies. I forget which ones. Yeah, I had to work him over real good."

He bared his teeth and ran a finger across them. "We did his implants all along the front. What, you think those things are real?" Nate watched the man's eyes drop to measure the breasts of the woman in a scoop neckline blouse on his left. Nate looked at her left hand wrapped around a glass of wine. Wedding ring. *Run away.*

When her cleavage let go of his attention, he said, "I'd give you my card, but I can see that none of you ladies need help. You all have great smiles. I'm a dentist,"

"Like, dentist to the stars?"

"That's me," he replied. "But I do a bit of acting, too. That's really where my future is."

Nate snickered a bit too loudly. After all, that was the future for everybody in the place. Acting, writing, producing. He had been there. Sadly, the future was always the future and never the present. He eased away as one of the women acknowledged him with a nod, and he saluted her in turn with a wink and raised his glass. A slight smile turned into the tiniest scowl on her face. God. He had forgotten about the bruise over his eye. It must be hideous. In fact, everyone was staring at it.

Next he noticed a line of bass from the sound system thumping the room. It was enough to shake the walls and rattle even the dentist's perfect molars. Did someone suddenly turn up the volume on the music? He eyed the stairs on the far side of the room where Woody was fingering the curls of the blond owl. Nate hadn't seen anything resembling a master bedroom so far, so it had to be at the top of the stairs. He hoped it was cooler up there. This room, filled with bodies sweating their egos, was hotter than the devil's skivvies in August. The artwork decorating this level suggested a feminine touch. Pillows on the couch, embroidered with pictures of kittens, had tassels at the corners. That meant there was a woman of the house, and not just any woman but one who knew how things should look, including, he was sure, her own appearance. There must be makeup on the property, and that meant a way to cover the bruise that now had everyone's attention.

Oh, he was brilliant. He had never felt so smart. He had never *been* so smart. Was it the Ecstasy? Some said the drug brought on mental clarity, but he knew that only your average three-toed sloth would have needed pharmaceutical help to connect the dots that led him to the master bathroom upstairs. And he was no sloth. Not tonight. He was brilliant. Just ask the smartest man in the room if you doubted it. Wait, that was him. Oh, well, take his word for it.

"Bingo-rama."

Not one. Not two, but three deep drawers in the bathroom vanity. They held enough facial creams, body lotions, concealers, highlighters and implements of beauty construction to outfit an entire chorus line of Vegas showgirls. But too many choices made him want to cry. His bruised eye teared up and he lowered his chin to his chest.

"Try the Harvest Wheat," a voice said. Nate tried to ignore it before he realized it wasn't just in his head. He was leaning against the vanity with his back to the door cupping a bottle of tan liquid in his hands. In the mirror he saw the smallish woman he had saluted downstairs. Her hair was half-blond and half-electric-blue and she was peering around his shoulder making eye contact with him in the mirror. She circled to face him, and then she giggled. "Are you stoned?"

She wore dark-rimmed glasses that perched on an upturned pussycat nose; their lenses were the size of teacup saucers and dominated her face. She was the most beautiful girl he'd ever seen in a plain Jane sort of way. Nate fell in love with her instantly. He wanted to take her home and cuddle the night away.

Dopey, he said, "It's a little new to me, I haven't done...Ecstasy before." He lowered his eyes to follow his right hand as it dug into the pocket of his jeans and pulled out the second hit Woody had provided. He seemed to be moving in slow motion, but instead of a drunken blur, his hand, the bathroom, the light, that god-awful watercolor on the wall over the towel rack signed by Aunt Kitty and the woman all had a peculiar sharpness he marveled at. It was like seeing everything in 3-D when, in reality, it was.... well, reality *was* 3-D. "I have some to share if you'd like."

Once upon a time, he didn't need to get drunk or high or get a girl drunk or high to wind up in bed for incredible, mind-blowing, soul-sharing, hearts-beating-as-one sex. At least, that's how he remembered the sex back then.

"Molly? Oh, I love that. But...another time, maybe? I was leaving and just came up here to get my coat and bag."

"I came up here to get some makeup. I tangled with someone, or something, that I shouldn't have this evening. I must have been scaring the natives downstairs, wandering around the party like something out of one of my movies. What's your name?" he asked.

She told him it was Marci, and she had done a stint at the makeup counter at Macy's in Fresno. She had Nate sit on the toilet while she rummaged in the vanity drawers. "Movies, huh?" You wouldn't happen to be a producer or somebody important, would you?" She used a foam square to apply thick beige liquid from a bottle. Nate shook his head and Marci quickly clamped her hand on his jaw.

"Don't do that."

"I'm just a writer," he said.

"Me, too. Like, what do you write? Anything I know?"

"Nothing you've heard of. But it's a living." If you liked living on the meager payments for stories that never got produced. He would save that information for their second date.

She asked him his name. "You're right. Never heard of you. There. That's better." Marci gave him a thumbs-up and went to the bed to scrounge through the pile of coats. Nate followed and asked about her writing.

"It's a little complicated. It's paranormal historical fiction romance with futuristic themes."

"Totally get it," Nate said. He had no clue what that was. "It's sort of like..."

"It's like *Twilight* meets Jane Austen on Mars."

"Exactly. That's how I'd pitch it, too."

It was the kind of thing that would have made him puke if one of his students had tried it back when Nate still had the teaching gig at the community college. Creative Writing 101. But on that night, for some reason he couldn't fathom, it sounded perfectly plausible.

"It's got a murder mystery in there, too."

"Why not? Sounds like a winner." He turned and opened the sliding glass door to a narrow balcony overlooking the ocean. Damn, he was burning up. He was high but what the hell. He needed fresh air. The ocean breeze was a godsend. Buzz from the party rose from well below and mixed with the harmony of the distant surf. He leaned on the balcony railing. The patio of the mansion where Entertainment X-S had set up the interview tent for Mary Grant and Ruffles the crime dog was three stories of house and a rock wall below him. A good leap, he mused. "Your story. Maybe I could read it over for you and give it to my agent for a look-see."

"Really? Oh, that would be so totally awesome."

Marci stood in the doorway and pulled a white stationary box out of a large backpack. The box was heavy with manuscript. "This is it, huh? You brought it with you?"

"Just in case, you know."

"Well, it worked. I'll pass it along to my agent." He smiled knowing it wouldn't do much good. His agent, Jack Hewitt, constantly threatened to drop Nate and was only available occasionally when Nate called. Only the steady drips and drabs of royalties, for which Jack took his fifteen percent cut, kept their relationship on life support.

"I really appreciate it," Marci said. She leaned up and kissed him on the cheek.

Nate slipped a hand to the small of her back and pulled her body close while gently brushing his lips against hers.

"I hope you don't, you know, want me to, well, you know. Fuck you so you'll read this."

Actually that hadn't occurred to Nate. Though given the situation, it should have been at the top of his to-do list. Bartering his Hollywood connections would be the quickest way to get Marci in bed. If that was a possibility.

"Besides, you remind me of my grandfather. He's cool like you and all. But I mean, that would be weird, right?"

"Of course."

She left him the manuscript, gathered her coat and stopped at the doorway. "But, you know, if you *had* expected me to put out to get you to take this to your agent..."

"Would you have?"

"Yeah, maybe." Then Marci fanned herself. "Christ, I should have taken the X. It always makes me so horny."

She was gone. That hurt. He couldn't get laid even if he paid for it with a legitimate agent hook-up, the most valuable kind of coin in the Hollywood universe.

"Fuck me." Beads of perspiration dotted his forehead. He wiped them off and flicked them away with a finger.

He looked to the stars and flipped off God. "Fuck you, too." He started to cry and then stopped. What was going on? He started to scream and then stopped. He stomped the concrete patio floor and wrapped his arms tightly around his sides, throwing a fit like a child. His skin tingled like a bad sunburn and he was dizzy. The Ecstasy had kicked in but it wasn't working. Wasn't it going to protect him from feeling all this shit? He didn't have an answer and that drove him ever deeper into depression.

He couldn't get a woman to love him for even a few minutes. Worse, he couldn't get a wife to love him in twenty-something years of marriage. Moonlight danced on the ocean and anger squeezed his soul. He had spent his life letting other people and circumstances run the show. In fact, he thought if anyone made a movie of his life, he would only have a bit part, a character who didn't even have a name in the final credits. Schmuck number one, it would say. He tracked down his phone and hit the speed dial. Valerie answered after the sixth ring. She must have recognized the caller ID, Nate supposed, and struggled with whether to answer or not.

"I got a question for you."

"Nate, you sound like you've been drinking. I am going to hang up if that's the case."

"Worse, I've been thinking."

"I hate it when you do that. You should know better."

"Valerie, listen to this." He climbed on the low, adobe wall around the balcony and balanced on the outer edge. It was time to become the hero of his own tragic story. "Wife, have you ever wondered what it sounds like when you kill somebody?"

"Nate, what in the world are you talking about?"

"This is what it sounds like." Nate did his best Superman leap into space.

He regretted it immediately.

Not for what was about to happen; he could die with that. It occurred to him that this would make a killer (pun intended) of a movie scene, the greatest scene he had ever come up with, and now he'd never get the chance to write it. It was a touching, Oscar-winning bit of cinematic emotion. *Dialing for Death*, starring Nate Evans. Produced by Nate Evans. Directed by Nate Evans. Given the chance, he would shoot the scene in slow motion very much like this, and text on the way down instead of calling Valerie. Maybe a Twitter post. A two-hundred-eighty-character suicide note. Very cool.

CHAPTER FOUR
Déjà vu

The dream came to Nate when he was still in his mother's womb. Try as he might through years of random reflection, he had no other explanation. It had always been with him. Even at fifty-five, it was the most vivid of any memory in the bank of his brain.

The Girl stood three steps above him framed by the large oak door at the entrance to their elementary school. She wore a plaid jumper of navy and gold over a white blouse with a broad collar. And on the short white socks at her ankles? A tiny blue ribbon bow dressed the fold at the top above shiny black shoes. As The Girl smiled down at him from her concrete pedestal, she fingered the stem of a single white carnation in one hand. Her other hand rested gently, for balance, on the black metal railing that drew a line leading up to the door and served as a minor, but not insurmountable, divide between them. And it was there that Nate professed his undying love for The Girl. She owned his heart. She would always have his heart. He told her so.

"You're the one I love, not anyone else."

What did that mean? Whenever the dream escaped into Nate's consciousness, the words were the same. He was too young to understand them, but those were the words he used. He knew that much and he knew how it made him feel.

Squooshy.

And warm.

Like a handful of macaroni and cheese.

The dream was so natural he simply took for granted it was part of who he was, like the tiny birthmark behind his right ear or having large feet that he'd never quite grow into. For the first six years of his life, he gave the dream no more thought than to accept its existence. The dream hid in some recess of his soul as he grew from a chubby rug rat into a precocious little human. He didn't notice it through his formative years as he learned to talk and connect dots of comprehension, to make sentences and express feelings. It surely was there in the background as his emotional neurons clashed and sparked, clinging to one another for survival, shaping into a personality. Nate never fully understood its significance until he was much older and much wiser.

At age six.

Nate recognized The Girl the moment he saw her in the flesh for the first time. Déjà vu didn't come calling with a simple tap on the shoulder. No. Déjà vu lifted Nate by his scrawny shoulders and tossed him with all its might into that familiar dream onto the sidewalk at the bottom of those steps in front of the school on the day he started first grade. He didn't know déjà vu from Scooby-Doo, but he knew for certain he had been there before. He had lived that exact moment. There he was again with those words on his tongue.

Déjà vu. Nate wouldn't learn it had a name for years, but no matter. On that day, he only knew it wasn't a dream after all. He felt it. He breathed it and it smelled like, well, it smelled like Girl. It was all there.

Trouble breathing? Check.

Sweaty palms? Check.

Heart pounding in his throat? Check and double check.

And those words "You're the one I love," they danced on the tip of his tongue sweet as the first lick of ice cream. Nate knew he would say those words to her.

Déjà vu. The sensation was a fact even if its cause, its very essence, was a mystery that scoffed at every psychologist, philosopher, paranormal expert, MRI-toting brain scientist, reincarnation disciple, wino and wacko with a theory about it. You couldn't get déjà vu; it got you. Some believed it was nothing more than wishful thinking of an overactive imagination. Buddha might suggest it was one of our past lives nudging the present. Regardless of whether the sensation was a random clash of memories and desires, a spark of loose wires in the brain or past lives visiting the present, if déjà vu ever needed a poster boy, Nate came to believe it picked him, and it picked him that moment in time when he was six.

He had dawdled the morning away on the first day of first grade. His mother rushed as she dropped him at the curb and pushed him toward the front door. She had given him a single white carnation, a gift for the new teacher. He paused at the bottom of the steps, turned and waved to his mother as she climbed into the car and drove away. Nate sucked a bit of the cool September air and studied the tips of his black dress shoes, below the cuffs of his new brown corduroy pants. That was part of the school uniform at Saint Christopher of the Cross Catholic School. Chriscross Elementary to those who hadn't confessed the sin of irreverence to Father Dean and done penance for excessive whimsy.

Nate was scared and excited, nervous and filled with the wonderment that only the promise of adventure could offer. A ten-foot-tall nun in her black habit, gathered at the waist by a belt of rosary beads, held open the front door and clanged a hand bell. She called to the stragglers. *Stop loitering. Come inside. Grow up and get educated. It's time.*

Nate was lost in absorbing the moment and scarcely felt the awkward bump that caused his world to stop.

The Girl had raven, wavy hair to her shoulders and dark brown eyes that twinkled like Fourth of July sparklers whenever she laughed. Through the years, she would laugh easily and often when Nate was around. That day, in first grade, The Girl was just as he had dreamed, right down to her smile. It was a toothy smile with a shadow of a gap between the front two and a mouth that was thin on the corners with full, round lips dead center.

The Girl knelt down and picked up Nate's white carnation that had fallen to the sidewalk. When she stood, he was certain she had recognized him, too. Her eyes were wide until shyness forced her to look away. The nun clanged her bell. The Girl skipped up the stairs. At the top, she paused with one hand on the railing. Nate waited until she turned so he could say the words that had been with him since birth. But The Girl did not turn and smile down upon him as he expected. She passed by Sister and disappeared into the building still clutching his carnation. That wasn't the way things ended the first time this had happened, though he couldn't recall a definitive end to his first encounter with The Girl.

The difference confused him only enough to pause before he bounded up the stairs and down the hall after her with the aid of a stern but kindly cuff on the back of the head from Sister. A few minutes later, after being led to their desks in the classroom, each one tagged with their first names printed in big block letters on a strip of paper taped to the top, the students took turns standing and introducing themselves to the teacher and to the class. The Girl sat at the head of the second row, and Nate sat two students behind her in the last desk. When it was her turn, The Girl stood, tugged at the sides of her skirt and toed the floor. Her voice was soft but determined, and from three desks away, Nate heard her tell all the world that she loved him, too. Her exact words?

"My name is Julie Cooper."

CHAPTER FIVE
Julie Cooper

The light filtering through the blinds was weaker than any tenth grader's alibi for cutting PE. Julie Cooper-Finch wouldn't have to put up with any of that nonsense today. It was Saturday. The sun was barely up; she could go back to sleep if she wanted. She sighed and smiled. The best part of sleeping late was the joy of being awake enough to enjoy it, like *she* was the one playing hooky.

She scooched under the blanket toward the empty side of the bed, reaching for his pillow. Nope, not there. She wished he could have stayed through the morning to wake up with her. Noooo, he would rather spend the day scratching his privates, stroking that big aluminum bat he named Suzie Blue after his first wife, hanging with his teammates, swearing and spitting. To him, the game was more important than a morning of extra cuddles. After all, as he had explained in a tone she thought was far too serious the night before, the last softball tournament of the year only came around, well, once a year. This one was all the way out in Modesto, so he had bounded from bed at oh-dark-thirty to meet his team, the Master Batters, at their home bar, where they would be carpooling out at sunrise. His loss.

So Julie hugged the pillow against her breasts and buried her nose in the flannel pillowcase with Christmas penguins running amok across the white fabric. The penguins wore the residual scent of his cologne as if it was their own. Eau de penguin. She let it seep into her nostrils. Musky with a hint of tropical breeze, his cologne left a faint aftertaste in the back of her throat that reminded Julie of her father's Old Spice. God, it was nice to have a man back in her life after all these years.

As for the sex, that had snuck up on Julie the first time after dating Russell casually for several months. Sex was better now than she remembered. But then it had been so long she didn't like to dwell on the few-and-far-between relationships that failed over the years since her husband was pummeled to death in a tragic car washing accident. Her friend Carla urged her to play hard to get with Russell. After all, he was a bit of a mystery at the high school in San Jose where they all worked, and she had not been the only single woman Russell had flirted with. That was all done now; Julie won him over. Besides, what did Carla know about dating these days? She'd been married to Larry forever. Carla wasn't the one who lost her husband only five years into their marriage. Carla wasn't the one who had to give up on love for nearly thirty years while she raised two kids alone and put them through college. Carla wasn't the one who had to worry about cobwebs *down there* as she marched into middle age without a partner. Carla? Pfshh.

Julie tried to roll her eyes at the thought of Carla's advice. A layer of crust kept the left one glued shut.

"Jeez Louise." She'd forgotten to take out her contact lenses, distracted by their sex last night and not wanting to break the spell of spooning with him afterwards. Julie licked her thumb, wiped it along the lid of her left eye and then pried it open. She staggered into the bathroom, squinting in a way that made everything appear as if she were looking through a white plastic shower curtain. She removed the contacts and started them soaking, brushed her teeth, grabbed a terry-cloth robe from its hook on the back of the bathroom door, and snatched a pair of black-framed glasses from the dresser as she headed to the kitchen. After the disappointment of waking up alone in bed without Mr. Right, what she needed now was a date with Mr. Coffee.

"Awwww, that's so sweet."

A yellow and cherry-red chrysanthemum leaned like a leering sailor to greet her from a water tumbler next to the coffeepot. She didn't need to look to the table on the opposite side of the kitchen. So what if he merely snatched it from the arrangement sitting there and left it in a more obvious spot to start her day? The flowers came from a planter on her patio. This one flower was meant just for her.

Outside the window over the sink, the sky was turning California winter blue and the Eucalyptus trees along the back fence were being pushed around by a light breeze. It was the first week of December; Christmas would be here before you knew it. At least the Master Batters wouldn't get rained on. She pulled the grocery list from under a magnet on the refrigerator door and settled down with her coffee. Maybe she could convince Russell to come by for dinner on Tuesday, maybe Wednesday. She could cook spaghetti and they could share a bottle of wine. Julie added pasta, wine and sauce to the list. She left space between items in case she needed to add more, arranging them in the order she would find them as she pushed her cart up and down the aisles starting in the produce section and ending in paper products on the far side of the store. In neat block letters, she added one more item to the list of things on the drug/hygiene aisle, below dental floss.

ASTROGLIDE.

Five years post-menopause, a little feminine lubricant was a handy thing to have. Now that she knew she needed it, better to have too much on hand than run out. That would be a wonderful complication to avoid. Things had gotten serious in a good way. What a difference a year made. Carla depressed her last year with one of her observations that Julie was headed down that pothole-filled road, the one you took when you devolved into a snippy, crotchety, pathetically single cat lady. Never mind that Julie had no cats. Yet. Carla was sure it was bound to happen if she didn't find someone. Loneliness and the fear that it would become a permanent state had grown since her youngest, Daniel, finally graduated from college and moved out of the house to put his art degree to use, designing headstones for a cemetery monument company in Oregon. He married a lovely gal and they had a son whom Julie had seen exactly three times since Daniel moved away. Carla was the one who turned her concern about growing old alone into a matter of life or death. The more she worried about Julie, the more Julie worried.

She was in front of the open refrigerator door, searching for ideas about what she could add to the grocery list, when the phone rang.

"Tiffany," Julie said. "Happy Saturday, hon."

"My, you're in a good mood this morning, Mom. Is *he* there?" Her daughter giggled.

Since she had started seeing Russell, Tiffany had taken way too much interest in the relationship, and she danced around leading questions in search of some salacious tidbit without coming right out with what she wanted to know. Julie knew the drill because it was much the way she had pestered Tiffany about her sexual activity when the girl was still a girl. Mom had a right to know. A daughter? Not so much.

"Can you keep an eye on the little doodle for me over lunch today? Joe's working out of town and Heather, Heather, Brittany and Agnes need a girl's lunch out."

"What about Heather?" Julie asked. "She couldn't make it?"

"Nah. Her band has a gig next week. Trust me. They really need the extra practice."

Julie's daughter collected girlfriends named Heather the way Ruby Burton, Julie's latest sophomore reclamation project, collected detention slips. Tiffany ran through a string of Heathers in middle school and high school before settling into this group of stay-at-home moms. In order to keep them all straight, they referred to each other as H1, H2 and H2-point-0. The last one got that nickname for being a weepy lead singer in an all-female group that specialized in blending old-time torch songs with the sound of pop groups from the 1970s. They called themselves the CandleABBAs.

"What about the boys?"

Tiffany said her twins were headed to a friend's house where they would sleep over. "Just in case lunch runs a little, uh, long."

Julie was sure it would. "You'd better bring Morgan's pajamas just in case. And yours, too. In case lunch runs a little, uh, *too* long," she mimicked.

It was shaping up to be a good Saturday. Any Saturday with her little jewel of a granddaughter was a great Saturday. Julie poured herself a second cup of coffee after the call and stopped to smell the chrysanthemums. She knew the single flower he left for her wasn't any sweeter than the bunch, but this morning it just seemed that way.

She passed the dining room table on her way to a hot bath and tried to ignore the stack of files that called to her. She promised Russell she would make some progress on the presentation he needed for his job interview with the school board. Russell was the principal at Mt. Hamilton High, but if things worked out as he planned, he'd get a promotion to assistant superintendent. Russell was an organizational guru, great with spreadsheets, and she admired his skill with facts and figures, but sometimes he had trouble expressing the significance of his data in a way that didn't cause eyes to glaze over. He asked her to write the presentation. She promised to make it sing if it would help win over the board.

Julie liked her job. She was an assistant principal and counselor at Mt. Hamilton High. It was the same school she attended back in the seventies. She'd been working there fifteen years after spending her life moving through a series of low-paying clerical jobs and raising her family. Being back at the school where she graduated felt like going home again, spending her days in a familiar environment with low risk and high comfort.

She headed to the bedroom and paused when she noticed her purse had been moved on the credenza in the hall. Her lipstick had fallen to the floor; a comb and several pens were scattered on the table-top. Her wallet peeped over the lip of her purse like a nosy neighbor at the backyard fence. An envelope with his scribble sat on the edge of the credenza next to the purse.

Thanks for dinner, he wrote. *A little short of cash this morning so I borrowed. I'll catch you up on Monday.*

Julie sighed. She took the glasses from her face, nibbled on the right earpiece and squeezed her eyes shut. She calculated the number of ATM machines that had to exist between San Jose and Modesto. Only a million more than a couple, she guessed. She checked the wallet. Well, at least he had left her a dollar. A single dollar.

"I'm sorry," she apologized to no one in particular, but two years of dating and a few sleepovers when the stars aligned and they both had the time, energy and inclination for sex were all a good start to a permanent relationship, but that didn't give anybody the right to ransack a woman's purse. Nope. Shouldn't dating be easier when you were in your fifties than it was at twenty? No, check that. How would Julie know? Dating at nineteen was how she wound up married and pregnant. Not in that order.

At least she got Tiffany out of that deal, and then Daniel before James died two years later.

Julie laid her glasses on the credenza and crumpled the envelope in both hands, squeezing the annoyance out of her. She was about to drop it into the trash when she inspected it again. Then she tugged at its corners, flattened it on the tabletop and tried to press the wrinkles away with the palm of her hand. The envelope held this month's PG&E bill. She needed that. She couldn't even throw the darned thing away yet.

CHAPTER SIX
Plan B

First thing Monday morning, Julie rapped her knuckles on the wall at the edge of Russell's office door at Mt. Hamilton High. She paused only long enough to shoot him a smile and a cute little wave. The Master Batters had won a game in Saturday's softball tournament, a major accomplishment considering the way the season had been going. She wished she had been there to see it. The problem with winning Saturday was that the team spent the night in Modesto in order to get crushed and eliminated Sunday. He was in a sour mood, and he took a rain check on spending Sunday night with her when the team got back to San Jose. It shot any hopes she had of spending quality time with him, but he promised to make it up to her with dinner Monday and would let her pick the restaurant. That guaranteed it wouldn't be pizza and beer at a sports bar.

"Let him take you to that new vegan vegetarian place *Chez Tofu Del Mar*," her friend Carla said later in the faculty lounge. Carla wore a knee-length red Christmas cardigan with snowflakes over black slacks. She had one foot on a stepladder and the other on the counter next to the microwave in order to tack a banner of red and gold cutout letters on the wall that read *Happy Holidays*.

"Why would I want to go to a place like *Chez Tofu*? I don't like tofu."

"Who does? But it will tell you how serious he is about the relationship. Any man who would buy dinner without whining at a place where it's super expensive and they don't have steak on the menu, a place where the portions are tiny and look more like art than food, so that you wouldn't ruin the dish by sticking a fork in it even if you didn't mind the taste—a guy who would do that for you—well, I'd say that's true love."

Julie laughed. "You may have a point. Maybe I should learn to like tofu." She helped her friend climb down, and together they stood and admired Carla's effort.

Carla Almeida was one of those cute little bundles of energy no bigger than the smallest freshman. If not for the crow's feet at her eyes, the pesky strands of gray in her hair that was otherwise the color of finely toasted pizza crust, and wrinkled skin from too many hours out in the California sun as a teen, she could easily pass for one of her science students. People who met her for the first extended time were frequently torn between wanting to wrap her in a big, loving hug and squashing her underfoot to stamp out so much perkiness.

"Now that we have that done, here. Take one of these." Carla held out a small wicker basket. It was full of red envelopes. As part of her self-appointed duties to be campus morale officer, Carla instigated, organized, supervised and browbeat stragglers into participating in the annual staff Secret Santa gift exchange.

"No. Not that one," she said when Julie dug into the pile to pull an envelope from near the bottom of the basket. "Take the one on top."

Julie reached for another.

"Uh uh," Carla said. She rocked the basket from side to side, swirling the top of the pile, chasing Julie's fingers as they reached for one envelope and then another. When Julie got a smile, she took the envelope she was destined to have.

"Not much secret to this Santa game if you are going to set everybody up."

"I don't know what you're talking about," Carla said with a straight face. Then she admitted she was tempted to play favorites for one or two friends who could benefit from some Santa hanky-panky.

"Meaning me."

"I wasn't the one who turned fifty"—Carla deliberately ran her hand over her lips to muffle the second digit of Julie's age—"last week."

"Thanks for reminding me." Sarcasm aside, Julie didn't mind another birthday so much. Russell had broken their standing agreement of not dating on a school night, stopping by with a bottle of wine, a romantic comedy DVD, popcorn and a pair of earrings that were prettier, more stylish and more expensive than she'd expected. If only he hadn't brought up the fact that she was three years older than him. He thought he was being funny, and he was, the first time, but when he brought it up for a third time, it was as funny as a funeral.

Julie opened the envelope and read the name on the card inside. She closed it with a shrug and the kind of resignation that comes with finding out, what a shock, your lottery numbers had failed to hit again.

No jackpot today. Not even from her best friend. Still, the name on the card held a certain amount of intrigue for all the wrong reasons.

"I smell a setup."

"You bet your tush, toots. That's what friends are for. Besides, Seth Naylor is a good guy. No harm there. He teaches music. You used to play piano. You love sports. He's a good sport. He's available and you're…"

"Dating Russell. And don't start with me."

"Yeah, yeah. I don't know what it is, but I just won't trust Mr. Festerhaven to make an honest woman of you until he says 'I do.' I'm starting to think you should have a backup plan."

"And so now I suppose I'll be getting a Secret Santa gift from Seth?"

"No, I left that one up to fate. If it happens, well…"

Carla wouldn't admit to rigging the gift exchange. "Why couldn't you fix me up with Russell? That would be the logical thing, right?"

"There were a couple of problems there. First, he thought that, as the principal, he shouldn't have to take part in something as silly as this. Second, he'll be getting you a Christmas gift anyway. If he doesn't get you something special like something you could wear on your ring finger, you should start exploring your options."

Julie said, "The real surprise will be if anybody *but* Seth gets my name."

"You could do a whole lot worse, lady. I should know."

"God. Like that insurance guy. Wayne?"

"Hey, I apologized for that, didn't I?"

"It was sweet of you to buy that life insurance policy just to get him to agree to a date. But you, lady, are certifiably crazy."

"That's okay. I cancelled the policy when things didn't work out."

"You know what's really sad? He wasn't the worst guy you've tried to set me up with."

"So we've had a couple of losers. But let's face it; the pool of available men is getting pretty shallow. It's not easy and you're not young anymore."

Julie answered her by sticking out her tongue, but Carla had a point, and it cut more than Julie was willing to show. Yes, she wasn't young anymore. She was aging faster than ever, and the prospect of growing old alone, something that was a mild dread in the light of day, could too easily morph into terrifying premonitions on those nights when she had trouble sleeping. Alone. Russell might be her last, best chance to avoid that.

And she loved him. He was whip-smart with a dry sense of humor, handsome enough and knew what he wanted out of life. And he wanted her. Bonus points for that. He'd charmed her socks off the first day after he became principal at Mt. Hamilton High. He was hard to resist when he turned on the charm. Julie couldn't.

Staff trickled in; teachers checked their mail slots and swapped greetings with the other faculty members within their individual cliques, trading snippets of gossip and the latest war story from their classrooms. They picked up paperwork, grabbed a quick cup of coffee and got waylaid by Carla's basket of Santa cards next to a plate of brownies in the center of the faculty lounge.

"It looks like Santa's little elf has been busy this morning." Rosilla Hernandez made a show of holding up the red envelope she had pulled from the basket.

Beverly Myers and Barbara Unger, English and English II teachers, gave them a nominal wave as they passed on their way to the refrigerator with their lunches in hand and a serious conversation in progress.

"She actually had the nerve to say she didn't think I needed dessert, right out loud. The whole restaurant heard her. It was totally embarrassing. It's not like I'm exactly fat, you know." Which was true in the mind of a big-boned woman approaching thirty who had shopped the full-figure women's rack at Macy's for years. "I hate her."

"She is such a bitch," Beverly said.

"And even if she does think so, my date was sitting right there. She practically called me a fat cow in front of him. I hate her."

"Barb, that is so unfair. She is such a bitch."

Julie glanced at the clock as she and Carla left the lounge. She still had a few minutes before settling down to work. They walked past the counter that separated staff desks from the foot traffic on three sides of the common area, and out the double glass doors to a courtyard between administration and the school library.

Mt. Hamilton High was typical of the single-story campuses built by the school district in a mad dash to keep up with the wave of baby boomers in the sixties. It was ninety-eight percent dense concrete and two percent character. California prisons had more charm. The library sat in the middle of the campus, a concrete box of a building inside a square. Classrooms faced the library on each side, long and low, like walls that shielded the campus from the outside world. Only the east side of the library had any charm, gussied up by a tile pool not more than a foot high—square, of course—that gurgled with water from a small fountain in the middle.

Carla leaned into Julie as they skirted the fountain. "Speak of the devil." She stopped and dropped her book bag on a metal bench.

A large black tuba case made its way along a wall on the far side of the quadrangle, weaving like a drunk trying to stay inside the boundaries of the walkway. Seth Naylor had it wrapped in his arms and peered over the top. Then he raised the case and dropped his bald head to the side to confirm he was still in his lane of traffic on the path.

Carla said, "Options. In case Russell turns out to be just another failed experiment, and I'm still not feeling the love in spite of your rosy outlook, you need a Plan B. Everybody should have a Plan B. At the very least, Seth could be your Plan B."

"Plan B?"

"Here's my theory," Carla explained. "Everybody should have a backup for their relationship. Someone who is Plan B in case, in case... Well, let's say that Larry gets crushed by a runaway ice cream truck tomorrow. I mean, I love him and I'd be crushed, too. I wouldn't bring a date to the funeral, but it's comforting to know that sooner or later I could turn to the guy who's my Plan B."

"Carla. That is so cold."

"If you had a Plan B in place when James died, you wouldn't have spent all these years raising kids on your own. And you wouldn't be starting over at this stage."

"Right," Julie said, unconvinced. "So if Larry is your Plan A, who's *your* Plan B?"

Carla waited until a cluster of kids passed and then put her hand on Julie's shoulder. She stretched up to get close to Julie's ear. "George Clooney."

Carla rocked back on her heels, laughing until Julie rapped her knuckle on the top of her vertically challenged head. "Hey." And then she started laughing again.

Julie asked, "How come you get George Clooney for Plan B, and I get Seth Naylor?"

"Because I've got Larry. For better or worse, you know? He's a good Plan A, but get real. Until you get our Mr. Festerhaven to commit, you don't have a Plan A yet. Start small and who knows? You might have Brad Pitt for your Plan B some day."

"Ladies." Seth set his tuba on the sidewalk in front of him. It wasn't lost on Julie that he acknowledged Carla with a nod and her with a thin, shy smile. "Mrs. Finch." Julie could have elbowed Carla for the look she gave her.

He reached into the pocket of his windbreaker and handed them both a single sheet flier. "Just a little reminder about the holiday concert on Friday. It should be a fun time. It would be nice if we had a good turnout."

"Sorry to hear about your grandma," Julie said. "I mean, the song. I heard Mr. Festerhaven put the kibosh on playing the 'Grandma Got Run Over by a Reindeer' song."

Seth sighed. "Yes, well, I guess it wasn't quite appropriate. Especially after how upset he got when we wrapped up the halftime show at the game against Oak Grove with 'Tears in Heaven.'"

Poor Seth. He had really struggled to regain his footing since breast cancer stole his wife from him, and the music department's performances had taken a decidedly darker tone. It made Julie appreciate all the more what a rare marriage Carla had. She liked to think she and James would have had one of those lifetime marriages too, but she gave up thinking about what might have been long ago.

Carla picked up her bag and said brightly, "Great. Julie, let's catch up at lunch. Come on Seth, we're both headed this way."

Seth struggled to balance the tuba, and as they turned away, Julie heard Carla say in a loud voice, "So, Mr. Naylor. Have you ever thought about having a Plan B?"

CHAPTER SEVEN
Julie's Plan B

The Wednesday before Christmas, Julie turned up the collar on her wool coat, shivering while she stood in front of the Happy Yen Mini Mart and Texas Barbecue store. The Weather Channel had forecast that morning the high temperature would be two degrees warmer in Fairbanks, Alaska. Brrr.

She had her hands deep in the pockets of her coat as she swiveled her head, waiting for inspiration. With her right hand, she fingered the piece of paper that could hold the key to her future. Or not. She considered the license plate number of the car parked two spaces over in front of the store. It didn't sing to her. Neither did the price of gas on the digital sign out front. She pulled the scrap from her pocket.

Ten? She made note of that on her walk to the store. The house at 1010 Bailey Avenue had the prettiest Christmas light display in the neighborhood. It was an omen.

One? Easy, that was her birthday a few weeks back. She could play that number until New Year's Day.

Over coffee that morning, Carla had mentioned she had spent most of Sunday organizing her closet and came up with thirty-one shoes. Not pairs of shoes. Carla's inventory included seven different orphans with no mate. Thirty-one shoes seemed too odd to ignore.

The final score of Sunday night's Forty-Niners' game provided two numbers, thirty-five to twenty-eight. The Niners won, for a change. It would be bad luck to use the numbers when your team loses, though Carla had been rooting for Dallas because their quarterback had become this week's Plan B if her husband, Larry, developed a fatal case of gingivitis. Now Julie needed just one more lucky number. She sighed. Inspiration was not stalking her outside the Mini Mart.

"Evening, lady. I'm feeling lucky for you tonight. Thirteen million. It is a very lucky number."

Julie stopped. She waved a finger at the short, weathered Vietnamese owner behind the counter. "Mr. Nguyen, you think every night is my night."

"You see. One day I will be right. Go on. Try lucky thirteen."

Julie went straight to the California Lottery kiosk at the rear of the store. Shelves there were neglected and held an odd assortment of items collecting dust. A yellow bottle of Pennzoil reminded Julie she had gotten an email from her mechanic. Her Ford was due for its regular oil change and service. She would ask Matt at the garage about the pesky ping the car had started making. She drew a breath, pulled her lucky pen from her purse and filled in the circles on a lottery slip, pausing when she needed the final number of the six picks. She scanned the store until her eyes came back to the bottle of oil. 10-40? She already had the ten. Pennzoil was talking to her. She filled in the number forty bubble.

"No number thirteen," Mr. Nguyen said when she handed him the ticket. He tsk-tsked her as he fed the slip into the lottery machine.

God, no. Number thirteen was never going to make it on Julie's lottery ticket. Her husband, James Finch, proposed on a Friday the thirteenth after she learned she was pregnant. She'd been nineteen and working a summer internship at her father's accounting firm. James was the junior-most associate, a paper pusher at the company there, six years older than Julie, who never did enough to earn a promotion. He had an air of life experience as if he had already done it all and there was nothing left that would shape him, and he doted on her in a way no boy—no man—ever had. He did the honest thing when they learned she was pregnant, and they were married. Four years and two babies later, on a thirteenth of June, James Finch was whapped to death at the Suds Up! Self Car Wash.

James and three friends were returning from a bachelor party that involved bottles and bottles of Coors Light, shots of tequila, and naked women at a bar in Sunnyvale. On the way home, they decided to wash five years of caked mud from the groom-to-be's Bronco in order not to embarrass the bride-to-be on their wedding getaway. So they pulled the Bronco into the bay at the car wash around two in the morning. The spray of the water hitting the windshield during the pre-soak mode triggered something in James' bladder. By the time the mechanical arms of the wash spewed soap all over the vehicle, James' kidneys were crying in pain, so he tried to escape from the passenger seat intent on watering the first bush he could find in the shadows. When his shoes hit the soapy floor of the wash bay, James slipped, fell to his knees, and was assaulted by the huge water-spitting, spinning ball of bristles and cloth strips that pinned him to the body of the SUV. The coroner recorded it as a drowning death. The killer brush slipped off its track, impeded by the victim, and stopped moving while continuing to spin and beat him senseless. They told Julie the pummeling lasted almost an hour while the rest of the party dozed in the cab of the Bronco. Before removing the body from the scene, the medical examiner commented to police on the extraordinary hygiene of the scrubbed corpse.

The number thirteen might be modestly unlucky for most people, but it rejoiced in tormenting Julie every chance it got. Nope, it wasn't going to make her lottery ticket in this life or in that great auto wash in the sky.

"If that doesn't do it, Mr. Nguyen, I don't know what will," Julie said.

"I miss you when you win and no need me anymore. Usual tonight?"

Julie nodded. "Yum."

He went to a stainless steel warming oven at the far corner behind the counter and beyond the deli case full of chicken wings, warmed-over brisket, pizza slices, burritos and rollers of fossilized hot dogs beneath heat lamps. Mr. Nguyen saved the fresh, choice meats in his oven for his best customers.

That was Julie's Wednesday routine, one lottery ticket and half a roast chicken. It was also her Saturday routine. One ticket with a side of chicken. If she really wanted to splurge, she might get some potato salad, too. She had been playing the game as long as she could remember. It was an indulgence, and reckless when she'd been a single mother counting pennies and juggling bills to make ends meet each month. Money was no longer the problem it had been when the kids were growing up, but she hadn't lost that sense of guilty pleasure that came with setting aside a few dollars each week for herself. How many times had she ignored the better, more practical ways she could spend that dollar? Julie was nothing if not practical in most aspects of life. But that was the point. Carla thought it was a pathetically amusing way of Julie letting her hair down. "This is wild and crazy?" she teased. "Hold me back."

Julie liked to rationalize each dollar invested could win—after all, *somebody* was going to win, it might as well be her—but she never told her friend that the lottery was as much Julie's Plan B as any fantasy that George Clooney or an NFL quarterback might ride to Carla's rescue. And at only a gazillion-to-one, Julie figured her odds were better.

CHAPTER EIGHT

Nate's Fifteen Minutes of Fame

The video of Nate's plunge and near demise was an overnight YouTube sensation. Woody pissed him off by pointing out that more people had seen the video in the last three weeks than any movie project Nate had, or was likely to, produce. That was the beauty of their relationship. Whenever Nate was down and out, he could count on Woody to kick dirt in his face.

TV Star Survives Deadly Fall.

That was the headline on the YouTube page, and they weren't talking about Nate. His leap had interrupted Mary Grant and Ruffles in the middle of their television interview for Entertainment X-S. All the cameras set up for the segment had been recording and captured the scene. Nate hit the canopy of the media tent, and it billowed inward, breaking his fall before a seam gave way and he dropped the final six feet with a thud. He landed on Ruffles.

"This is a major hoot," Woody said. "We're getting close to two million views."

He tapped the screen of Nate's new iPad. After he survived the leap, Nate spent Christmas recovering at his older brother's house.

David was an insurance agent in La Jolla, and the tablet was David's present to him. For three weeks, he vegged out in front of the television and binged on *It's a Wonderful Life* in an effort to heal his spirit. Now it was almost New Years Day; it was time to move on.

"Remind me to kill you later," Nate said.

Nate and Woody leaned against the bumper of a U-Haul rental truck parked next to the battered shell of his mobile home. They were taking a break from packing up everything that had survived Bombing Day. Progress was slow because Nate had one arm in a sling to help his broken collarbone. There wasn't much to pack. Even though he'd rented the smallest truck, his belongings wouldn't fill half of it. The mobile home, rusted and ratty to begin with, appeared to Nate as if it had been beaten into submission and begged to be put out of its misery. Since he had only been renting the trailer, the landlord would get the lion's share of any settlement with the government, and even most of the furniture had been there when Nate moved in. There was little to call his own.

Nate tugged on the collar of a coat he had borrowed from Woody. The air was thick with ocean fog and mist, colder than a politician's heart, and it compounded the stiffness in every part of his body. He lost his balance and fell back against the bumper.

"Forget what I said about killing you later. Let me do it now and put you out of my misery." He took a swipe at Woody with his good arm. The contusions deep in his chest made it nearly impossible to breathe.

"I told you I was sorry. Dammit. How was I to know you'd have that kind of reaction to the X? I was just trying to get you feeling happy again, but you heard what the doctor said. Who could have known, right?"

The doctor gave him a royal holier-than-thou lecture when he delivered toxicology results that came back positive for Ecstasy. Nate had to lie and say he didn't know where the drug had come from—it was a big party with a lot of people he didn't know. He said he hadn't intentionally swallowed anything stronger than alcohol. He didn't think the doctor bought it and was surprised when he asked if Nate had been suffering from depression or anxiety.

"How's your life right now?" He said suicidal thoughts were common in depressed people, and while Ecstasy was known for enhancing positive emotions, it could also exacerbate all the negative ones that came with being down.

"Right now, I couldn't get any lower," Nate had told the doctor. "But I've never had a suicidal impulse. Ever." Woody, who was sitting in a chair in a corner of the hospital room at the time, vouched for him.

"That boy ain't wired for suicide, Doc. Trust me."

Now, Woody avoided looking at Nate and said, "Sorry. I didn't know that thing about how it might mess with someone as messed up as you were that night."

Nate was hunched over trying to catch his breath. He nodded to the trailer. "What? You didn't think I might be suffering a little bit of stress that day?"

"I was just trying to pick you up after that big guy beat the crap out of you at the bar."

With a new year coming, the black cloud that covered him was unlikely to dissolve with the simple turn of the calendar page in a couple of days, but he knew he had to escape. He was desperate for a place to curl up in a fetal-like ball and hide until it was safe to show his face again. For the past three years, his life had been like a Whack-a-Mole carnival game, someone or something always waiting to bop him when he poked his head out of the mole hole. Enough of that. He was going to run away. Back to the last place where he felt good about himself. And he wasn't going to come out until he could feel that again.

"Two million views, huh?" He took the tablet from Woody. Nate had to admit it was a finely edited twenty seconds of movie. He had scripted a couple of never-produced commercials that didn't have all the storytelling elements in this one bit of YouTubeosity.

Cue ominous music.

Wide shot of hero dog and Spinster Detective sidekick.

Chaos. Sound of ripping canvas dubbed over.

Zoom in on hero's face. Slow motion he looks up, confused.

Unidentified Falling Body obscures view of scene.

Ominous music swells to a doom-like crescendo.

Cut to a closeup of the body on the floor and from beneath it, a furry dog's paw reaches toward the camera, straining and twitching before going limp.

Dissolve to paramedics pushing a gurney carrying the hero through the grief-stricken crowd and into the ambulance.

Closing shot: Ambulance drives away, headed for the Happy Hound Veterinary Hospital. The camera stays on shot until the emergency lights are a fading blur in the night.

Whoever edited it from the Entertainment X-S video did a good job. His own ambulance ride to the hospital made only the local TV newscasts and had a shelf life of twenty-four hours. Coverage of the Ruffles' hospital vigil, with the crowds placing candles and sympathy cards on the sidewalk, singing prayers, providing breathless reporters with quotes about how Ruffles had impacted their lives and wishing him a speedy recovery, lasted three days longer until the doctors could assure everyone that Ruffles was out of danger. They doubted, however, that he would ever act again.

Nate attempted a smile. "It's not everybody who gets to watch their life flash before their eyes over and over. And over again. It's like sitting through reruns of a really bad sitcom."

Woody chuckled. "A rerun of something you probably wrote." Then he held up both palms. "I know. I promise. I'll remind you to kill me later."

Nate ordered him to pack up the cardboard boxes with stuff they had salvaged from his bedroom and tuck them in with the other boxes in the back of the truck. He went to its open rear and surveyed what they had already packed. He could have hitched a trailer to his car easily enough but had to sell the Honda to pay the medical bills. Then he went to the shed in search of any remaining items he might want to take with him. He walked gingerly and stumbled over a dumbbell next to the workout bench next to the door. He wouldn't need that, for sure. The shed stank of dust, mold and neglect. He went to the corner and rummaged in the clutter there, pulling a backpack from his camping gear. His baseball glove was there, lovingly oiled to protect it from age and the elements. He held the leather to his nose. The greatest smell in the world. As a kid, he'd slept with his baseball glove and still had trouble passing by the sporting goods section of a Target or Big-5 store without stopping to sniff the mitts. Now *that* would be a good point in life to return to if he could ever invent his fantasy time machine and get the do-over he longed for. The scent of cowhide took him back and brought a smile. Julie Cooper would laugh at him if she walked in and caught him. She'd laughed when he'd revealed his mitt fetish to her one day as they sat in the bleachers after a high school ballgame. He glanced over his shoulder, just in case she showed up. That made him smile, too.

Oh, well. He reached into several dusty and neglected cardboard cartons stacked against the wall and pulled out bottles of vitamins B, C, and liquid D and L, HGH anti-aging supplements, antioxidants, mental-energy-boosting ginseng powdered drink mix and aloe-laced skin-rejuvenating lotion. Dozens of boxes filled that corner of the shed with more products than he could keep track of. Ordered over the Internet, some were never opened. Although Nate's gray hair was still thick and full and long enough to brush his shoulders, he had a year's supply of Rogaine there, too.

The pills and potions, the powders and lotions piled up during a two-year effort wasted trying to patch things up with Valerie after her affair with Skippy. Of course, Skippy wasn't his real name; he couldn't bring himself to call the guy by his real name, and it fit since the Skip-ster was about half Valerie's age. Nate worked hard to be young again. He was too stubborn to let the marriage die without a fight. In the end, all of their counseling sessions and all of his self-prescribed fountain-of-youth cocktails couldn't make Valerie love him. It simply delayed the inevitable. Now, he couldn't remember what half the supplements did, but he tossed a handful of each into the backpack.

He was about to flick off the light when he was stopped by one last thought. He moved a weed whacker to the side and shoved the mower away with his foot in order to reach a heavy box set on the floor apart from the rest. He opened the flap on the carton. Oh, yeah. It was ten bottles toward a full case of Jack Daniel's Old Number 7. He had col-lected the whiskey, each bottle a Christmas gift from David through the years. It was the expensive stuff, and Nate had been saving them for the party he would throw when one of his orphaned stories actually made it to the screen. Sometimes you needed a true friend like Jack to help you forget your troubles. Nate tucked one bottle of whiskey into his backpack with the other drugs. He had survived and now all he wanted to do was escape. It was going to take a hell of a lot more than a good bender to do it, but he was tired. He was tired of letting fate and other people drive the bus. That's how his life had veered out of control and he ended up wrecked in a ditch, wheels pointing at the sky and spinning uselessly. He lingered over that metaphor; he liked it. It seemed about right. Getting his life back on the road might be possible; knowing where to go after that—that was a bitch.

CHAPTER NINE
Send in the Clowns

The whole idea of running away to join the circus was long passé by the time Nate, as a kid, might have considered it an option. The morning before New Year's Eve, as he stood on the porch with a finger paused at the doorbell of the house he grew up in, it was as if he had just run away *from* the circus.

"Well, well, well. Your mother said you'd be falling out of the sky soon," his father cackled. "And vy-ola, here you are." He leaned his forearm with faded tattoos against the half-open door waiting for Nate to ask permission to enter. Nate came prepared; he thrust the virgin bottle of Jack Daniels at his old man. He had saved it for this confrontation; it was part peace offering and part toll.

"I'm fine, Charlie. How you doing?"

"Woke up this morning. All my body parts in good working order. Functioning on autopilot. I don't hurt much. I'm looking forward to a proctology exam this afternoon, so I couldn't be happier."

His father hadn't aged much through the years of Nate's infrequent visits home. Charlie was a big reason he stayed away. He'd looked like he was pushing eighty when he was fifty. Now that he was pushing eighty, he looked his age. Bald across his liver-spotted crown, a bulbous nose over thin lips, Charlie had once been six foot something and cut a handsome figure when he was young, though now, with a slight stoop, he seemed smaller but hardly frail for someone his age. Nate hoped he inherited his father's good genes without much else in the DNA garden taking root.

"Since you're here, you can put your stuff in your old bedroom. You *do* remember where that is, don't you? Second door on the right." Charlie walked away, clutching the whiskey to his chest. To say Nate had a distant relationship with his father was the kind of understatement only the sadistically coy could appreciate. His father had disappeared before Nate turned two. He would show up unannounced from time to time, during a layover between the jobs he chased in Alaska, Australia, and other parts of the world, working as a bush pilot. When times were good out there, he'd sent money home to the family. But those checks were as unreliable as his promises that he'd be home soon. For years, Nate blamed himself, convinced he ran Charlie out of the family simply by being born and being a burden the old man didn't want. When he realized he had nothing to do with Charlie wandering off, he tried to pretend his father didn't exist. Other times, he lied, like when he told Sister Agatha, his fifth grade teacher, that his father had died hunting elephants in South America. It didn't get much sympathy and earned him a trip to confession with Father Dean.

During one layover, on his way from a job in Wyoming to Texas, Charlie stayed long enough to impregnate Nate's mother with his baby sister, Krystal. Twelve years later, he came back for good, timing his arrival for Nate's high school graduation. No surprise, Charlie got the date wrong and missed the commencement by a month, just as he'd missed every other significant moment in Nate's life. He never forgave the old man.

Nate stood in the doorway to his old bedroom. It was hard to tell from peeking inside that he had ever existed. An ironing board and a basket of laundry sat in front of the window next to a rocking chair and a stack of paperbacks where his dressing bureau used to be. The closet was filled with stacked plastic storage bins. The only reminder that Nate had once lived in the room was a three-peg hat rack hanging on a wall where his little league baseball cap and his high school graduation tassel collected dust. He was determined to reclaim the room. That was essential.

"Your mother's out in the backyard with her friends," Charlie said as Nate wandered into the living room. "Wednesday is Tai Chi." He pointed by extending one finger from the hand wrapped around his glass of Nate's whiskey.

"They do this every week?"

"When they get some good weather like this, yeah."

"Hey, Mom," Nate called out.

"Out here, honey."

He was only halfway through the screen door when he pulled up and turned his head away. It was a sight that would burn forever in his memory, and not in a good way. Never had he seen so much sagging flesh in one location.

Nate's mother stretched and leaned forward slowly in a classic Tai Chi form facing her group of five gray, blue, and orange-dyed-haired women. Each woman had shed her clothes, and modesty apparently, and followed Regina Evans' movements.

"Inhale, ladies. This is my son," she said while staying focused on some point, distant and straight ahead. "Exhale."

The woman in the rear corner of the group dropped her arms and turned. "Is that little Nate? Hello, Nate."

"Mrs. Wilkus?" Nate averted his eyes to the opposite corner of the yard, but not before catching a full frontal glimpse at his once-upon-a-time next-door neighbor.

"It's good to see you, dearie. Say, why don't you join us? We could use some manhood here." The other ladies snickered.

"Enough of that, Max," his mother said. "Ladies, stay focused. Honey, we'll be done in a bit. There's juice in the fridge if you're thirsty. I'll fix lunch when we're done."

"I don't see why you are so shocked," his mother scolded him later over an avocado and cheese sandwich. What he wouldn't give for a slice of ham right then. He plucked a green grape from a stem on the side of his plate and popped it into his mouth.

"You don't come home every day and find naked women dancing around your backyard."

"Well, you might if you'd come home a little more often," she sniffed.

"Frankly, Mom, it's not a sight I want to get accustomed to."

"You may as well get used to it if you're planning on staying here any length of time at all." She smiled. "Which brings up the question, dear, just how long are you going to be with us?"

Nate doubted that forever would be a good answer. He didn't know. He had no real goal beyond hunkering down. It wasn't the first time he started a story without knowing how it would end. Moving back home was his first act. How could he tell his mother that "now what" was not part of his thinking?

"I'm not sure," Nate said. "I won't stay a minute more than you'll let me get away with."

Regina paused and poked at her sandwich, untouched on the plate. He braced himself. *Here it comes.*

"So how is Valerie these days?"

Not bad. He had been home two full hours before she asked. "How should I know? You'd have to ask the guy she moved in with." He certainly couldn't tell his mother that he had a ten-second conversation with Valerie during his leap from the third story of a mansion and that she sounded as solid as ever. Valerie had sent him a text message before he got out of the hospital. She and Lester had heard what happened and wished him well.

Lester. Nate was certain the live-in boyfriend's name had been Bill or George or something very vanilla. By now, whatever his name was, he must be last year's flavor, replaced by a *Lester.* "Mom, it's complicated. You of all people know that. But let's not talk about Charlie, okay?" Whenever he pressed her about why she stayed with his dad, she'd roll her eyes. It seemed to her such a silly question.

"I didn't. He was never here, so I never needed to leave him."

"But you always take him back."

"Of course. He's such a free spirit. I love that."

And that explained it all.

As they sat across from one another at the kitchen table, she said, "Your problem is that you should have married a nice girl instead of a lawyer, of all things. I told you that was trouble. Look at David. I love your brother dearly, but I hear he's been donating to the Republicans again."

Nate sat in silence, picking at the grapes and ignoring the

sandwich. He hated avocado.

"Have you thought about a job?"

"No."

"Are you going to think about a job?"

"No."

"You should do something. We could use another pair of hands at the shop if you want to earn a little until you find yourself."

Ah, yes, the family business.

It was a logical offer, just as it had been a logical career choice for Regina. She'd dropped out of Berkeley to sell flowers in Haight Ashbury during the sixties. Through the years, she had been a life coach, a children's librarian, a yoga instructor and the director of community theater, until she found her true calling in multi-level marketing selling a line of hemp products. She was the Mary Kay of hemp beauty supplies and clothing. The moment California gave the green light to medical marijuana, long before legalizing it recreationally for the average Joe, Regina used her contacts and marketing skills to set up shop within walking distance of the San Jose State campus. The High Society Wellness Clinic was born.

Then Nate's little sister, Krystal, joined the business. Krystal had built a reputation as a glass artist for years, but her work really took off when she began blowing bong art. She sold high-end, handcrafted glass pipes and bongs for hundreds of dollars a pop on her website. Just to round things out, Charlie was put in charge of the retail inventory at the clinic and, euphemistically speaking, quality control over the pot they sold.

How David escaped the greening of the Evans clan, Nate didn't know. David was considered the white sheep of the family and, by Evans family definition then, an outlier to his hippy parents. He suspected that, in their souls, they believed Nate had sold out to Hollywood, though they gave him a pass because he did it for the sake of his "art." They must have felt being a starving artist indicated his intentions were pure if not the outlet for his creativity.

"Well, you certainly can't sit around and do nothing," Regina said. "That wouldn't be healthy. Think about it."

"I don't think my future is in retail," Nate told his mom.

He preferred not to think about his future at all.

CHAPTER TEN

Ring-a-Ding Ding

On New Year's Eve he sat on his bed in his skivvies. He ignored the gluten-free eggplant-and-mushroom casserole his mother had left in the refrigerator for him, stole the key to his father's Chevy from its peg near the back door and had made a run to Burger King. He hoped Charlie wouldn't mind that he borrowed the family car without asking first. Regina and Charlie were ringing in the new year at a Native American powwow on the summit of Mt. Umunhum, the western peak of the Santa Clara Valley. Regina went to reconnect with Mother Earth with the help of an Aztec shaman she followed on Twitter who organized the event. Nate suspected Charlie went because he hoped to score some peyote.

Nate bobbed his head to Aerosmith singing "Dream On" through the headset clamped over his ears and sang along with Steven Tyler's falsetto repetition of the title line while he scribbled random words and drew crude cartoons on a yellow legal pad. He ripped the page out, crumpled it and tossed the ball of paper to the floor where it landed among dozens of crumpled doodles, random words, thoughts and dreams.

"Yeah, whatever."

He wanted to shut down his brain but it wouldn't go quietly so he stretched out on his bed with a notepad and a pen to see if what spilled out might give him some direction but came away with nothing to show for the effort. His plan for getting his shit together didn't stretch much beyond returning home and hunkering down until he pulled out of the funk. Tomorrow. Maybe the next day or next month, sooner or later. Whenever was soon enough.

He leaned back against the bed's headboard and stared at the ceiling. How hard would it be to find a copy of Raquel Welch's famous fur bikini poster from the movie *One Million Years B.C.?* He had tacked one to the ceiling when he was twelve and spent his teen years waking up to Raquel every morning. What a great way to start each day. What else could he do to recreate the room he'd had as a teenager? Wouldn't that be a kick? Such good times he had back then, and once again he took inventory of his favorite points in his life he would relive if he had a chance.

"I'm not obsessed, right?"

"I'm what you might call a nostalgist. A retro-naut."

That's how he had once explained it to Woody. Maybe someday, if Lady Muse ever returned, he might write that into a story. He tapped the pen against his teeth. He'd call it…

He'd call it *Mulligan.*

He pulled the yellow pad onto his lap, still hampered by having his left arm in a sling, and he began to write.

Our hero, uh, Nate. *Our hero Nate, mid-fifties, ruggedly handsome in an aging baby-boomer sort of way, is beaten down by life. No wife, no home, no job, no prospects, he survives a suicide attempt and takes refuge from the mess his life has become by moving back home with his parents, lovable but ditzy former hippies.*

Stumped. Where it would go from there? Maybe it was a shitty idea; it wouldn't be his first and hardly his worst. Either way, it wouldn't go anywhere without a leading lady. That kind of story required a Meg Ryan, Julia Roberts-type love interest. There were only three significant leading ladies in Nate's past. Julie, the girl who got away in high school, his wife, Valerie, the girl who crushed his heart like an empty beer can and didn't even bother to put it in the recycle bin, and Eppie Johnson, the girl who, to Nate's vivid imagination, altered the course of history.

Prom date Eppie.

Epiphany Alice Johnson to those who risked a serious verbal smackdown by using her given name. If Nate needed a scapegoat for why he'd failed to marry Julie Cooper and live happily ever after, it would be Eppie. But he never wanted a scapegoat. He knew it was his own damned fault. No scaping to be done, just one goat there.

Julie was the girl Nate and two-thirds of the senior class absolutely knew he was going to ask to the prom, but he wound up going with Eppie instead. He heard Julie had gone so far as to buy the gown she never got to wear and that tears ensued. Months later, she said she had forgiven him, but Nate never forgave himself.

He looked at his watch. It was an hour before midnight and he had a date, sort of. Ring in the new year. Ring-a-ding ding. Nate friended Eppie Johnson on Facebook once upon a time and checked her page occasionally, but hadn't reached out to contact her in years. Life had become embarrassingly shitty and the thought of whining about that in public was something he didn't want to vomit on anyone.

Eppie, on the other hand, was a blabbermouth, cheerleader,

rabble-rouser and star of the social media universe. From her grand-children's birthdays to her recent hysterectomy, no detail was too personal to share. She hadn't changed a bit, smart and wickedly irreverent, still living in San Jose, where she'd raised three perfectly above-average children and headed up the Human Resources Department at their old school district. Since nobody from their apathetic graduating class could generate enthusiasm for a real reunion, Eppie had taken it upon herself to create a Facebook group of former class-mates on the site. Randy, George, Pattie Clarke and the Waggoner twins. Eppie had a bevy of former classmates among her legion of followers. It seemed to Nate that she had kept in touch with so many and had what he imagined was a thick, digital dossier of gossip to track the status of everyone.

Now it was New Year's Eve and she had set up a virtual video party on Google Hangout to celebrate. By eleven thirty, he had put on a clean shirt, combed his long, gray hair and pulled it into a neat pigtail. He even shaved before he settled into his father's leather Barcalounger with an iPad tablet on his lap, its camera pointed at his face and a tall floor lamp three feet in front of him and a quarter-angle to the left in a Speilberg-esque attempt to light the picture properly. He hadn't spent all those years hanging around movie sets for nothing. Eight faces in individual boxes with various backgrounds filled the screen.

"Oh, my God. Evans, you scuzzy hunk. What a surprise," Eppie said when he saw his own face pop up on the screen to join the oth-ers. Since everyone else had been in touch through Eppie's Facebook group for a few years, they took turns catching him up. Nine class-mates sharing their past thirty-plus years, mostly for his benefit. Most of them, like Eppie, still lived in San Jose, or near enough that they could have held this little party in person. Nate got a twofer from Gerry and Shirley Summers. They married right out of high school, and, still married, they wrestled with the web camera on their computer so that first one and then the other was featured on the screen, kibitzing when they were not.

For his part, Nate deflected questions with vague answers about his stalled career as a Hollywood scriptwriting legend and glossed over the years he'd spent teaching English at the community college to fill in the gaps between sales. Married? Divorced. Yeah, been there. Done that.

Teasing and banter continued through the stroke of midnight. The talk took them on frequent trips down memory lane. Nate got a glow from the journey.

Remember who had the coolest car?

Remember how Lisa Lyttle and Bobby Hurst went steady all four years at Mt. Hamilton High and everyone thought they'd be the first to get married? It turned out Bobby was totally gay.

"Bobby Hurst? Quarterback and captain of the football team Hurst?"

How about Senior Cut Day? Half the class came down with the flu and tried to get better by spending a day at the beach.

And how, if you were a pretty girl on Allen Schmidt's good side, you could go into the Dairy Barn when he was working and get a milkshake just for a smile.

"If the boss wasn't looking."

Nate settled deeper into the chair. The living room hadn't changed much, so familiar and so comfortable as if he had returned to a place that was as close to a cocoon as an adolescent could have. Nate absorbed the scene; except for the disconnect by conversing online instead of in person, he could be seventeen again. Once again, his imagination tickled him.

"What if?" it asked.

So he Frisbeed the question he had put to the geezers at Ginny's Church of the Holy Brew weeks earlier.

"If you could go back, back to high school, and do it all over again, would you?"

The score was three for, two against, and one "What, are you kidding? It was the worst time of my life."

"In a heartbeat," Nate answered when they turned the question on him before his brain went into overdrive.

Holy shit! How hard might it be to recreate those days? He could do that. He would start with finding a copy of the poster of Raquel Welch to hang again on the ceiling. The more he thought about it, the funnier it got. It wasn't a long-term solution, but recreating his youth, at his age, would keep him distracted for a few months until life stopped beating him like a redheaded stepchild. It would be a giggle and he hadn't had a good giggle in forever.

"Okay, guys," he said. "Something's come up. But let's get together soon, maybe we can throw a real party just like we used to. Eppie, I'll be in touch."

He flopped down on his bed with his notepad and began scribbling with more focus this time, plotting how he would recreate those days. Or, rather, how his fictional character Nate would do it. He used his own miserable life for the backstory and his dream of getting his mulligan for Fictional Nate's motivation. The plot thickened.

He would write out a plan of action in a story form and then act it out. Script first, and then perform. It seemed more coherent than a simple "to do list" that he was likely to ignore. That was his story *Mulligan*, script your life before you live it. If he had done that the first time he wouldn't have been such a screw up. It was obvious now, he was just one of those people who needs a dress rehearsal.

By God, he hadn't felt this good in a long time. Tomorrow would be New Year's Day and things were turning for him. *Mulligan.* Maybe he would get an honest-to-God usable script from it, send it to his agent or anyone else who might be interested in something like *Grumpy Old Men* meets *Back to the Future*—minus the Delorean time-travel hot rod. Well, maybe not. Who cares? If it didn't amount to anything? Hey, there was nothing wrong with living in the past—as long as you stayed in the present.

CHAPTER ELEVEN
Auld Lang Syne, Jules

"Wow. Julie, you look fabulous."

Larry Almeida stood on Julie's front porch with a sappy grin. "So good, in fact, if I wasn't a married man, I'd eat you up right here and now."

Carla elbowed him before she passed Julie at the door. "Keep that up, Larry, and you won't be married much longer." She reached up and gave Julie an air peck on the cheek. "Happy New Year, Julie. Ignore my hubby but you do look great."

Julie nodded, trying to take the compliments lightly, all the while blushing inside like a schoolgirl from head to cherry-painted toenails. She felt beautiful and she wanted to shine. It was nice to know her bedroom mirror wasn't the only friend to tell her so. She was happy with the way she looked and happy with the way she felt. It was a full-body sort of joy that touched her just about every way she could imagine. Russell didn't always notice the times when she put on her Superwoman outfit and makeup, shedding her practical mom and school administrator persona. Carla liked to needle her, suggesting she do it more often. Maybe she was right.

Russell dropped a hint about how much he was looking forward to tonight and that it could be special. It was odd the way he said "could be special." It lacked the coy inflection someone used as an exaggerated hint meant to tickle a person with anticipation. There was no teasing in his voice, but one of the things about Russell she loved was his direct nature. Seldom was there any guesswork involved.

Unless he was getting ready to propose.

That would fall into one of those times when the playful Russell came out and left her guessing. The anticipation was romantic in its own way. So while Russell didn't always notice when she put a little extra effort into her appearance, if he missed the signs tonight, there was no hope for him. If he was going to propose, and she was going to accept, she wanted to be dressed for the part.

Carla led the way to the living room. "That dress. Isn't it everything I told you it would be?"

Julie ducked her head and smiled. Carla had dragged her to half a dozen consignment shops from Los Gatos and Menlo Park all the way up to San Francisco to find the perfect dress for that night's New Year's Eve party. Julie couldn't justify paying full price for designer labels, so the compromise was to find an outfit that was gently used but guaranteed to knock a boyfriend's socks off. She had approached Carla's dress safari with guilty skepticism before she fell in love with a silk China blue number that she pulled off the rack at one of Carla's favorite stores up in San Francisco, an out-of-the-way consignment boutique in the Nob Hill section of "The City."

"Where else are you going to find a two-thousand-dollar Vera Wang outfit for under two hundred dollars?" Carla asked when Julie dithered. It wasn't until after Julie got home that she noticed the label was that of a designer named Velma Wong, and not the designer of movie stars and first ladies.

"So? Wang. Wong. Nothing *wong* with that. It looks great on you," Carla replied when Julie pointed it out to her.

Julie glanced down the length of the dress to the hem at her knee. "It does look good, doesn't it?" She admired the expensive Jimmy Choo sandals Carla had talked her into. The shoes cost more than the dress and lacy undergarments she bought combined. Though after getting the Wong Wang, Julie did a Google search to confirm that her Choo shoes weren't a knockoff as well.

Carla performed a pirouette in the middle of the living room. "Besides, who reads the labels? No one's going to notice or care that this little outfit is a Don Karan original."

"You mean *Donna* Karan."

"Nah. This was designed by Don. I think it's her brother. All that matters is that we look good. Right?" Carla completed her outfit with a cheap, WalMart-grade plastic headband. It was covered with glitter and the year 2018 carved out of the crown. She adjusted it with her hands, swiveled and asked, "So tell me, does this tiara make my butt look big?"

"Of course not," Julie replied.

"Good answer."

"What butt?" her husband asked.

"Bad answer."

"Trick question," Larry said. "If I say no, you won't believe me. If I say yes, I'm sleeping on the couch tonight. Can't win. Say, Julie, is that champagne in that ice bucket on the table there?"

"Yes, it is," she laughed. "I want to save it until Russell gets here.

But I have some wine in the refrigerator if you'd like."

When they settled in again, Julie said, "I can't remember the last time I was up at the Mountain Winery; it's been years. I have *really* been looking forward to this."

"And not just the party, I assume." Carla gave her husband a wink big enough that you couldn't miss it from a block away. "So you think tonight's the night?"

"Carla, you're the only one who thinks so. Really now. Sometimes I think if he doesn't propose, you'll be more disappointed than I will."

"Can we take that as a yes?" Larry said.

"I doubt he will with the two of you gawking at us in public."

"Julie, that's exactly how he would do it. When have you known him to ever worry about who's watching what? He'll just bull ahead as always, oblivious to everything else," Carla said.

Larry corrected her, "No, hon. I think you meant to say he would be focused. Focused on Julie, here, swept up in her beauty and so overcome that nothing would distract him from declaring his love. Am I right or am I right?"

Julie blushed. "Can I clone you? Carla, can I clone him? That was a much more romantic way of putting it."

"See what happens when you pull an IRS auditor away from his computer? They have this pent-up romantic energy. I swear, most days Larry thinks nothing is sexier than a faulty tax form."

The conversation drifted off to small talk and mindless bits of time-killing observations while Julie checked her watch every five minutes and Carla and Larry exchanged glances as the evening got later. Julie dialed Russell's number, but the call went straight to voice mail. Twice. Finally she suggested the couple go to the party without her.

"We'll catch up with you there." And then Julie apologized.

Carla Almeida, Queen of Snark and Patron Saint of Sarcasm asked, "You don't think he got the dates mixed up, do you? I mean, it's only New Year's Eve. Easy to get that wrong on the calendar."

"Something must have come up. You know what's going to happen. Russell will show up two minutes after you're gone. So we'll be a little late. But if you leave now, you can still make it in time for the dinner. Don't let this spoil your fun."

Three hours later, she opened one bleary and bloodshot eye and focused on the champagne bottle barely a foot from her nose. She was on the sofa. The bottle was on the coffee table. Both were lying on their sides, horizontal and empty.

She reached down and picked up the champagne cork from where it had fallen on the carpet, rolling it between her thumb and forefinger slowly in front of her eyes before flinging it halfheartedly at the television. In his run up to the rocking stroke of midnight in Times Square, Ryan Seacrest was interviewing some underdressed and overly painted singer. Or maybe she was an actress. Maybe she was a comedian. She could have been a hotel maid or a sales clerk at a beauty supply store for all Julie knew. Thank God the sound was muted. The digital clock in the corner of the screen counted down the time. Twenty-three minutes, seventeen seconds to midnight.

Julie wiped her fingers across the corner of her mouth where she had drooled after nodding off and then sat up to check her cell phone. No call. No text. No Russell. What had happened? This wasn't like him. Something important must have come up. Or…vague visions of car wrecks infiltrated her thoughts. She fought them off. *Nonsense.*

The room spun gently like the last slow movement of a carnival ride before they opened the gates to let everyone off as she made her way to the bedroom to undress. She didn't like what she saw in the mirrored double doors to her closet. Rumpled and rejected, she had such high expectations for a fun evening with friends. Instead she was ringing in the new year with Velma Wong, Jimmy Choo and Two-buck Chuck—knockoff designers and cheap wine. Not much of a celebration. Oh, not to mention Victoria's Secret. Carla had goaded her into something fancy. At least that was justifiable, Julie reasoned, considering the possibilities of the evening. But as she tenderly removed the black lace, she couldn't understand how in the world she had let her daughter, Tiffany, talk her into the bikini wax to go with the sexy underwear. Tiffany hadn't been to blame for that much pain down there since the day she was born. In fact, childbirth was a piece of cake. And at Julie's age, bikini wax? Really? Well, for sure Russell wasn't going to see it.

After slipping into sweat pants and a flannel top, Julie stood in the living room with a small glass of Listerine-spiked water, alternately dipping a toothbrush in the water and working it in her mouth, while she watched the television countdown to midnight. Less than ten minutes to go. The doorbell rang. Julie set down the glass and picked up her phone in case she had to call 9-1-1. Then a heavy hand pounded on the door. She approached it cautiously and peeped through the security hole. Julie could make out Russell's thinning patch of hair on the top of his head. He was leaning with one hand against the door with his chin resting on his chest.

"Julie, I made it. Let me in, honey."

She was glad she hadn't turned up the volume on the television. She could ignore him. Better to let him think she hadn't been waiting on him all night. Julie resisted the temptation to open the door just for the satisfaction of slamming it in his face. She leaned with her back against the door and slid down until she was sitting on the floor. Her phone pinged an alert.

Where R U? Russell texted.

Julie waited what she thought would be a reasonable amount of time. *Not home. Where are you?*

Russell replied he was at her place and asked why she wasn't home.

Julie: *Party. Remember?*

Russell slapped the door, causing Julie to flinch and spit out the toothbrush that she had tucked in the cheek of her mouth. The aftertaste had lost its minty flavor and now coated her tongue with something closer to rubbing alcohol. He swore loudly and Julie was glad she had the door between them. It wasn't much, but for all Russell knew, they could be miles, instead of inches, apart. Silence. Then her phone pinged again.

Russell: *Had beers with buds wa ching football.*

Russell: *Sooners won. Boomer Sooners!!!*

Well, la-de-da!

Russell had done his undergraduate work at the University of Oklahoma, and even after living on the West Coast for so many years, he still bled red for the football team. But they had a date. A special date, he'd indicated.

Russell: *Lost track of time. My bad.*

He misspelled every third word, a drunk slurring his text. *Sorry,* he typed three times in a row. Back and forth they went. A lover's quarrel separated only by a few feet, a wooden door and billions and billions of bits of computer code shooting like caustic stars in cyber space. Julie and Russell sniped at one another in rapid-fire text messages.

Bitch.

Bastard.

That stopped him. There was a long pause between messages. Julie took the moment to scroll through the exchange. God, it stung to see how juvenile it had become.

Finally, Russell: *But we WON. Come home n tell you all about it. Said this would be a special night. Boomer Sooners!*

It might have been special to Russell, but it did nothing to ease the hurt inside.

Russell: *Bsides. I have a present for you.*

No. He wasn't going to propose via text. She could count the number of times she had seen him out of control on one hand. Actually, two fingers would do. Both involved sports and alcohol. He was rock solid and predictable every other day of the week, so she couldn't imagine he'd Tweet a marriage proposal and prayed that he wouldn't be that insensitive when she asked: *What is it?*

She stood and watched him through the peephole in the door. Russell had stepped back, just off the porch, and was little more than a shadow playing with something in his hand. She could open the door and confront him. She had let the charade of distance go on too long. He was standing only a few feet away, and she was in no mood to accept his engagement ring no matter how much he tried to make it up to her. Then again, maybe it was better to let him stew and see how long it took him to go home while she took a day to collect herself before they talked this out.

Russell: *Present. Scored two tickets to Super Bowl. You and me.*

That's it? The big surprise was the Super Bowl? There was no appropriate text response for that. Crushed, she was such a fool. A teardrop rolled off her cheek and plopped onto the face of the phone in her hand. Russell had gotten her hopes up. Carla had gotten her hopes up. Julie had gotten her own hopes up that he was going to propose. Maybe he wasn't serious after all. She hated herself for falling into the trap of thinking otherwise.

Russell lingered on the porch and she ignored him until he left. She shut off the television, doused the lights and sat in the dark with her head in her hands. She might have set a new record for gullibility. In the history of all the relationships between men and women since the beginning of time, had anybody ever been so stupid as to suffer through a bikini wax for a stupid football game?

Happy New Year.

CHAPTER TWELVE

Skateboarding Through Life

Recreating the best year of his life was going to be trickier than Nate thought. Over the month since he dreamed up the idea on New Year's Eve while video chatting with Eppie and the gang, he managed to make progress. Living at home and decorating his bedroom to approximate the way it had been back in high school was the starting point. Recreating other parts of those years required looking at the big picture and compromising on the details. So he made a list with two columns.

What had made him happy in his senior year of high school? That was one column. Conversely, what had made him sad that year? That was the second column. All he had to do was maximize the activities in column A while correcting the screw-ups he had listed in column B and he'd get his life's mulligan.

Everything back then revolved around school and his friends. He liked school. Column A.

Dating. Definitely on the A list.

Playing baseball. He was captain of the school team.

Trips with friends to spend long summer days on the beach.

Milkshakes at the Dairy Barn.

The B list wasn't long and included items that would be not only prudent to avoid but impossible to recreate. Like the hickey he got from Rhonda "Hoover" Willows on a date at the Capitol Drive-In and TP-ing Kevin Howard's house for some reason Nate could no longer recall.

Some items were perfectly doable but created a conundrum's conundrum for putting it into practice.

Things like skateboarding.

"So, dude, how old is he?"

Nate barely heard the question. He stood scanning a wall full of skateboard decks with eyes that had glazed over from an overload of choices.

"Who?" he asked the voice behind him.

"Your grandson. And how long has he been skating? You're gonna blow him away getting him something like this. Birthday?"

The clerk smiled at Nate from one corner of his mouth. He wore a light gray Old Navy knit cap and a black T-shirt with a red Rolling Stones tongue and lips on his chest. He was so thin Nate could imagine him hiding easily behind one slat of a picket fence. With a wispy moustache and goatee, he was a character right out of a *Doonesbury* comic strip. Zonker was in the house.

"Nah, this is something for me."

The clerk laughed. "No. Seriously, dude."

"Yes. Seriously. Dude."

"Wick-ed."

Nate told him he had a skateboard as a teenager and wondered what it would be like to try again after all these years. How could he explain to a kid like this that he wanted to feel like a kid himself again? "I thought it might be fun to see if I could still handle a skateboard without killing myself after all these years."

The clerk said his name was Jason. "Are you sure you wouldn't be better off with a starter board at WalMart? Costco?"

That was his conundrum. It was a matter of principle. In high school, he didn't have the money to buy the kind of high-end deck that the cutting edge kids on wheels were getting, the kind he would have given his left wheel for. So recreating that part of his life meant compromise. He could stick to his principles and go cheap, or he could pull out the credit card and upgrade his life this time around.

Seriously, dude? Like there is anything to think about?

"I like that one," Nate said. He'd have to bite the bullet and live with the fact that he had more money than a reasonable teenager of his disposition could spend in a year. He could treat MasterCard like the allowance his mother had given him, at least until he found a job.

He circled the store, shopping the walls hung with skateboard decks, to make sure nothing better stole his heart. He thrust his hands into the pockets of an extra-large Hollister brand hoodie that he soiled, ripped and cleaned the newness out of with four cycles through the washing machine with a throw rug from the kitchen. He wore baggy cargo shorts and had switched from tighty-white skivvies to boxers in order to have a couple of inches showing above his waistband and had a Hurley logo ball cap backwards on his head. His dress was another concession to the times. If he was going to be cool, he had to dress the part. Thirty years earlier, cool was bellbottoms and polyester. That shit was goofy enough the first time around.

It turned out Jason owned the shop along with two other stores on opposite sides of the valley. His voice was tired. Nate heard in it the weight of disillusionment. He suggested the soon-to-be skater magnate didn't sound very happy.

Jason grinned. "It's turned into such a business. It's a much bigger deal than I imagined. Or wanted. I'm not the CEO type."

"I hear you. Growing up is a bitch. I really don't recommend it."

Two hours later, Eppie Johnson gave him grief as they moved along a path in the Japanese Tea Gardens for being, in no particular order, a baby, immature, emotionally stunted and pathetic in too many ways to count because he refused to grow up.

"And frankly, you're creeping me out, Evans."

With one fluid push, Eppie Johnson rolled a step ahead of Nate and spun her wheelchair to cut him off at the pass. Nate pulled one hand out of the pocket of his sweatshirt, bent and pinched a pink snapdragon at his knee, avoiding her eyes. With a soft pop, it opened and spread its petals as if it bloomed to greet him. "You think I'm wiggin' out?"

"Look at how you're dressed. That answers that."

Nate admitted he might have gone overboard. Sure, disco was dead, but letting his shorts sag from below his waist had him constantly grabbing the belt, paranoid that they would fall off his drooping butt to the floor. He wasn't sure how the boys did it. Tomorrow, he promised Eppie, he would dial back and be a little less grody.

"Did you just say *grody*?"

"Right on."

"Whoa. I think we just crossed some kind of perverse line here. It's weird enough that you want to live in the seventies, but do you have to talk like it, too? You are absolutely insane." Eppie spun and wheeled her chair in the direction of a gazebo on the other side of a bridge.

He jogged forward laughing, took the handles of her wheel-chair and pushed her up one side of the arched wooden bridge over a stream in the heart of the garden and let her roll free down the other side. "I'm trying to have some fun with it."

"And how long do we have to put up with this shit?"

Nate wasn't sure. Until he got *his* shit together.

"You are pathetic, Evans. F-ing pathetic," she said. Then she added, "But that's okay; you can't help yourself. You were born pathetic. It's part of your charm. And you are nothing if not pathetically charming."

Nate had become her pathetically charming pal the day Eppie first rolled into Mt. Hamilton High their sophomore year and threw a book at him when he rudely tried to help her up the handicap ramp. She had been in a wheelchair since she jumped off the train trestle over Coyote Creek on a dare the summer before seventh grade. If she had only landed two feet to the left, she would have missed the lone sandstone rock just below the surface.

"Thanks, but get lost," Eppie said that day.

"Just trying to help." Nate moved around to face her and then ducked when Eppie chucked her student handbook at him.

"You throw like a girl." Nate thought she was cute. She was only a few pounds over slim, had long blond hair with a bit of strawberry that draped to her waist and more freckles than stars in the night sky. He told her she could be real cute if she would smile.

"Cute is not my style. And I'm warning you right now, neither is pity."

"Cool beans." He decided right then it would be his mission to make this girl smile a few times before they graduated even if it meant aggravating the snot out of her.

Nate wheeled Eppie to the edge of the gazebo and sat down on the lip of its floor next to her. Foot traffic was light for a late Saturday afternoon. The winter blooms were colorful, but they were as sparse as visitors. Nate and Eppie had the garden to themselves. As they talked, he placed a hand on the armrest of her wheelchair. Just as naturally, she laid a hand on top of his. Life had softened her, though he would have been disappointed if she had lost her sharp tongue and the wisecracking shots she took at him. She was content. Who could ask for anything more?

"You sound happy with the way things turned out," he said. "But have you ever wondered what life would be like if you hadn't jumped off the train trestle? Wouldn't it be great to go back and do it differently? Maybe pick one thing to fix? That's sort of where I am right now."

"Didn't we have this discussion once upon a time?"

They had. One starlit night in a vineyard clearing, they'd stretched out on a blanket and pondered the meaning of life. How much had her answer changed over the years?

"Sure, I'd like to walk like everybody else, but everybody has regrets of one kind or another that handicap us. Some big and some small. My legs are mine. Yours is you think too much. At least lately," she added.

"It wouldn't be the first time."

She said, "You can dress the part. You can talk the part. You can do all this stuff you've been doing and pretend you're seventeen again, but sooner or later, you'll have to quit it and get back to reality."

"As soon as I find a reason, I will," he said. He winked at her. Then he told her about his list of things to replicate. "I'm making progress on that."

"And where is Julie Cooper on that list of yours?"

"What do you mean?"

"She's on the list somewhere. You wouldn't be you if she wasn't there."

Was he that easy to read? "I gave up on that long ago. I poked around online and couldn't find her." Maybe he was searching in all the wrong places. Unlike Eppie, Julie Cooper was nowhere to be found on Facebook, LinkedIn, Google, Instagram, Snapchat and every other social media site. She wasn't even in the crystal ball of a fortune-teller he had come across at sunset near the Santa Monica pier one day. Twenty bucks. He should have demanded his money back.

"I don't suppose *you* know where she is?"

"Sure. Doesn't everybody?" Her sarcasm was unmistakable. "I'm a little surprised it's taken this long for you to bring it up."

"You brought her up," he reminded her.

Eppie put the tip of a finger between her teeth. Thinking or teasing him with her silence, he wasn't sure which.

"Well? Are you going to tell me? Because I don't know how to get in touch with her."

"That's because you're a doofus."

Nate was in no position to argue that.

Eppie said, "I can help you out, but promise me you won't screw it up this time."

CHAPTER THIRTEEN

But...But...But

The problem with putting a girl on a pedestal was that it drove a boy at any age into tongue-tied foolishness, the kind that made him overthink even the simplest task, like asking her to the senior prom. When he was seventeen, that turned out to be an affliction worse than a serious outbreak of zits. He'd fretted nearly a month over finding the perfect time and place to pop the question when procrastination, a noble heart and Eppie came between him and prom night with Julie Cooper.

It was a classic case of thinking too much and doing too little because Nate wanted to make this more than your average, run-of-the-mill, once-in-a-lifetime, happily-ever-after prom date. He dreamed how it would unfold, tweaking a detail here or a comment there. He had been working extra shifts at Albertson's, where he bagged groceries, so he wouldn't have to scrimp on a tux, corsage, dinner and after-dance party. None of it. First class all the way. Plus now he had enough to take Julie to a nice restaurant on Friday, where he would ask her to go with him to the dance. And then, holding her during a slow dance to some song that would become "their song," he would sweep her off her feet. He'd ask her to go steady, and they would leave their child-hood behind together, hand in hand. The relationship would grow and would ultimately end up…where? At seventeen, he was looking for-ward to finding out. Yep. He had it all planned.

These things were on his mind as he walked across the Mt. Ham-ilton High campus on a beautiful spring day. Steve Miller Band was playing "Fly Like an Eagle" in his head. "Do da da-do do." He sang the bridge when he stopped to perform a smart little shuffle, head down and watching his feet on the concrete path. Oh, Julie was going to like that move. He would practice it a few more times and refine it before the dance. The Nate Date Shuffle, he'd call it.

He stopped in front of a sign hanging on the library wall remind-ing students that senior prom was less than a month away. Buy tick-ets now. At least he had done that part already. Debbie Caldwell and her twin sister, Denise, were leaning against the wall near the sign. Debbie and Denise were A-listers and didn't bestow their attention on just anyone, but he got along with them okay. Debbie was most likely to wind up prom queen, while Denise appeared to be a shoo-in for being voted most popular girl. Or maybe it was the other way around.

Nate walked down the corridor to his locker. Joanne Traveras, another A-lister, and two other girls—A-list by association only—were giving Eppie serious grief. Their boyfriends crowded Eppie on either side, willing to be led around by their dicks and showing off for the girls by taunting Eppie.

"C'mon E-*Piff*-any. Get up and dance. Show us some of those Cripple Disco moves."

Nate shouldered his way into the group. "Let go and leave her alone." He pushed the boys away from the wheelchair.

"Stay out of this, Evans." It came at Nate in stereo, the bigger of the boys and Eppie Johnson both warning him off.

There were threats and name-calling and insightful exchanges like "Oh, yeah?" And "Yeah. So there." There was just enough shoving to make everyone feel good about himself, and then Nate rolled Eppie away. He was as surprised as anyone that the confrontation almost turned into a fistfight and by how much he wanted to bop those creeps. That wasn't his style, but then, even Sheriff Matt Dillon had to shoot the bad guys on *Gunsmoke* every so often.

Nate was headed to baseball practice after school when he saw Eppie sitting at the far end of the student parking lot, waiting for her mother to pick her up. He stole behind her and touched her on the arm. She spun her head, recognized him, and then wheeled around away. It was like a dance where she kept her back to Nate no matter which way he dodged. He had seen her eyes at that first glance and asked her if she was crying.

"I'm not crying." She wouldn't face him. Nate stopped chasing her so that Eppie could safely dry her eyes without being obvious. She sniffed.

"I didn't think you were. I know you don't cry," he said. But he knew what he saw, and he was starting to get angry all over again. "If I had those clowns ganging up on me, I guess I'd feel weird about it."

"I don't give a shit about them."

"Me, neither."

Eppie said it started because Joanne was upset Eppie was blocking her locker and it was taking Eppie forever to get out of her way. Then somebody brought up the prom and they started making fun of her. Eppie let them know that Principal Conklin had told her that morning that she had been chosen prom queen.

"I was supposed to keep it a secret. The prom committee picked me, poor pitiful cripple that I am, so they could feel good about themselves. Conklin said he only told me because they wanted to be sure I was *going* to the prom."

"What did you tell him?"

"I didn't. I was going to tell him no tomorrow. But when those bitches got all snotty about how I couldn't possibly go to the dance because… Well, things got worse."

"That's when you dropped the prom queen news on them, I'll bet." It was a sure bet. "Good for you."

"Are you kidding? Now I *have* to go. It'll be all over the school by tomorrow and embarrassing if I don't. But I don't have a date. I won't be able to get a date. Now I can't even tell Mr. Conklin no thanks."

Nate dropped to a knee, put his elbow on the armrest of Eppie's wheelchair and propped his chin on the palm of his hand. On the far side of the parking lot, his teammates were lollygagging on their way to the practice field. Coach was going to make him run laps for being late. He stayed by her side, not sure what he could say.

It was a long time before she said, "I hate them. I hate this school. I hate this wheelchair and especially I hate proms."

"I hate it when you feel this way." Nate knew it was a lame response and that it didn't sound the least bit funny like he had hoped, and he wished he hadn't said anything at all. Eppie was sad, so Nate was sad. He'd give anything not to feel sad.

"I didn't need to be pitied by those assholes on the committee. I didn't need to be reminded that prom is one more thing I'll never get to do because I'm in this *fucking wheelchair!*"

Eppie didn't try to hide the tears that welled in her eyes this time.

"So why not show them up and go to the dance? I mean, you can move to the music in your own way. I'll bet guys would dance with you. I know I would."

Eppie stared at him. *So that's what they mean by looks that kill.* He shifted his eyes away to avoid getting burned down to his soul by her glare. "So go. Why not?"

"Why not? Evans, you're a real dork. What am I supposed to do? Everybody will be there with their dates like you and Cooper, and I'm supposed to go by myself and sit there all night, waiting until you can squeeze in one dance or two with me? And if nobody else does, that's my whole night. Big whoop. No thanks."

"Then we'll get you a date."

"Leave me alone. Now I hate you, too." Eppie tried to roll away, but he stuck a foot out to block a wheel. Frustrated, she said, "Who do you think you are? You'll *get* me a date? I don't need your help *getting* me a date."

So maybe that was the wrong way to phrase it, but Eppie did need his sympathy. All he needed to do was plant the right suggestion in the right ear. He could think of a couple of perfectly reasonable guys who were too shy to ask a girl out, guys who were fun enough and, more importantly, respected him enough to listen to him. He could convince them to ask Eppie to the dance and wouldn't embarrass her when they got there.

Eppie pushed with all her might, finally getting the wheel over his toes. He grabbed the handles and tugged to slow her down. "I didn't mean get you a date, like, you know, it would be hard. Like I said, I'd take you to the dance myself—wheelchair and all." That is, if he weren't going to the prom with Jules instead, of course. That was understood. She understood, right?

"Are you saying what I think you're saying?"

What was he saying? What did Eppie think he was saying? He didn't know, so he said, "Sure."

"Evans, you're not doing this just because you feel sorry for me, right? I thought you were my friend."

Nate turned Eppie so that they were face-to-face. He was making a mental list of several unattached boys he could hook Eppie up with for the prom, starting with Mark O'Leary, the class valedictorian. He was pretty cool when he didn't have his nose in a book, and did a hilarious imitation of Principal Conklin when he loosened up.

"You know I'd never do it because I felt sorry for you. No, I know better than that."

Eppie searched his eyes. "Okay then."

"Okay." The feel-good excitement after standing up for her and staring down the bitchy girls and their asshole boyfriends was back. Nate Evans to the rescue.

"Okay, then. Evans, I'd be happy to be your date for the prom." When Nate was slow to respond, Eppie said, "That *was* what you were asking, wasn't it?"

Not at all. But he swallowed hard and said, "Sure, it'll be a blast." Then he thought about Julie, and something really gross rose from his belly and grabbed him in the throat. And it didn't taste so good.

"Great." Eppie did a slow circle in her chair and rocked her shoulders to music in her head. Nate had spent enough time with her over the last three years to see that, for someone who spent so much time showing so little emotion, the girl could beam when she wanted. Too bad she kept it to herself. The good feeling slowly returned. Nate the White Knight.

Eppie asked what he would do about Cooper. Everybody knew he was going to ask her.

"But I didn't ask Julie, did I?" Technically true. How was he going to explain it to her? Maybe she would understand that he had gotten caught up in the moment. He could deny it and Eppie could pretend, but it was a sympathy date. Maybe he could make it up to her afterwards. Maybe, but he was in deep doo-doo. He hoped Eppie would come to her senses and turn him down. Someone was going to wind up with a heartache, but watching her wave her arms over her head and smile, as happy as he had ever seen her, he decided it wasn't going to be Eppie.

Nate knew he didn't have a clue about what he was doing but tried to convince himself this would be fun. When Eppie's mom pulled up in their station wagon, he bent down and kissed her. He intended it to be a quick, nothing-special peck on the cheek, but she leaned into his face, and her lips followed his as he pulled back. It made for a lingering kiss, like a kiss that meant more than it did. He glanced over at Mrs. Johnson, who was scolding them with her look, but Eppie shrugged and smiled.

The whole scene left Nate unsettled for many reasons, but mostly because, as thrilling as it was to kiss a girl, and a pretty one like Eppie, all Nate could think about was Julie Cooper. And as he waved at Eppie one last time, it occurred to him that he had just kissed a girl he never intended to date and screwed up the chance to kiss the girl he wanted most.

CHAPTER FOURTEEN
What Would Dr. Rachel Do?

"It occurred to me…"

Julie cringed. "I hate it when you say that." She had her back to Carla and poured coffee into two large mugs at her kitchen sink. Carla usually followed up that phrase with something that made Julie think about things that were best left unthought. It was three months after the New Year's Eve debacle with Russell.

"It occurred to me on the way over here that the kids in our freshman class the year you and Russell had your first date are probably all married with kids of their own by now."

"Come on. Don't be silly. It hasn't been that long."

"Okay. So they're getting ready to graduate. How about you and Russell? I think that puts an interesting perspective on how long your relationship has been dragging out, though, don't you?"

"Interesting, yes. That's about all."

Carla slid a book across the kitchen table as Julie set the coffee in front of them.

Dr. Rachel, Dating Coach. "Dating coach?"

The Fifty Dumbest Things Women Do to Ruin Relationships. Carla tapped the title. "She has one for every decade. This one is for women fifty-plus. And we're obviously not talking dress sizes here."

Annoyed, Julie looked down on the book. "Do you really think I need this?" It wasn't a question; it was pure rejection.

"It was either this or set up an intervention like they do with alcoholics. I thought you could use some expert advice. I still can't wrap my head around the fact that you're going to take Russell back."

"It's been three months. Look, Carla, that whole New Year's Eve mess? I'm over it and so should you be. Besides, he's been sweet and apologetic. And he's been trying really hard to make up for it."

"He stood you up on New Year's Eve."

"I explained that already. He was a little tipsy and he lost track of time." He was drunk, actually, and in retrospect, Julie blamed herself for being too angry to take his car keys and keep him from driving home.

"And you didn't even get your ring out of the deal."

"And he was so excited about getting the Super Bowl tickets."

"Not as exciting as getting an engagement ring."

"He apologized."

"He should have proposed."

"You're the only one who thinks so." Julie shook her head.

"After he got your hopes up and all."

"*You're* the one who got my hopes up. I know better than to listen to you. I don't know what I was thinking."

"You were thinking that if Russell doesn't move in with you, some cat would. And then another and another until you're up to your tush in whiskers and fur balls."

Only Carla could get away with a comment like that, tapping into her uneasiness about growing old without someone to share those years with, and make her smile in the process. But Julie knew there was more truth in what Carla said than she would admit to anyone else.

"We needed the break, that's all," she said. "It was a good thing. It gave us a chance to evaluate where we're going, and it made me realize how much I missed him."

They'd had a fight on New Year's Day and it left her with a grudge she held longer than the line of cars trying to get onto the Bayshore Freeeway at rush hour. She'd avoided bringing up that she had expected a marriage proposal, but she couldn't make him understand how much he hurt her. He accused her of overreacting but didn't bother to put up a fight when she told him she wanted a break, and that made her hurt worse. Then, after time began to thaw the frosty truce that followed, he was back.

Russell sent roses on Valentines Day when she told him she had something "better" to do than a dinner date with him. Vindictive? Maybe. Cautious? Definitely. "Better" was a day at the aquarium in Monterey and dinner alone on Cannery Row. It hurt when she leaned back in her chair, took stock of the other customers and accepted the fact that she was the only person in the restaurant with a table for one. That was when she knew being a couple with Russell reminded her how much she wanted someone male in her life again. Working near him each day and going home alone most nights reinforced how lonely she had been before they had begun dating. A girl could only do so much with Ben and Jerry's Chunky Monkey and binge-watching *Downton Abbey*. The only good thing about it was that, with Ben and Jerry on her hips, she had taken up jogging again.

Russell shocked her when he gave her a little gift to pass along to her daughter, Tiffany, on her birthday. That was sweet. What kind of guy remembered your daughter's birthday? A good guy who missed her. That was important.

Carla said, "And that's another thing. Why is it that whenever you don't have time for Russell, he goes out of his way for you? He turns sweet. And he sure has been persistent. Like the harder he has to try, the better he likes it."

"He's sweet most of the time. You just never get to see it. So I think it's time to patch things up. He's taking me to dinner at the Grandview tonight. Romantic, don't you think?"

Carla started to say something, thought better of it and pushed the dating book in her direction.

Yellow sticky notes clung to pages throughout the book. Julie flipped through them. Carla said, "I marked a few things that got me thinking. You'll recognize them. They are so you."

"There must be two dozen or so here."

"Only eighteen, actually. But out of the fifty dumb things women do, that's not too bad. If this were a midterm, you'd flunk in a good way. Unless I decide to grade on a curve, in which case, we have a problem."

"I don't have a problem."

"Page twenty-three, if memory serves me. You have a problem," Carla said.

Julie snapped the book shut. "Well, it's easy for you to read this and say 'Oh, that is so Julie.' You don't know what it's like to be single at our age. You've been married for thirty-something years."

"She has three whole chapters about that. But right now I don't have time to fix myself. We have to fix you first. This is your life I'm messing with."

"Messing is right," Julie replied, though the way Carla's eyes twinkled, it was impossible to be annoyed.

Julie opened to a page Carla called to her attention. According to Dating Coach Rachel Rowan, PhD, she, Julie, needed more spine.

Guys are simple; unfortunately the good ones don't just fall out of the sky. Even if they did, they'd get lost on the way because they won't stop and ask for directions. Regardless, don't be afraid to give your guy a gentle nudge so he knows where to go.

"I'm not certain Russell is the nudgeable type."

"If he is, I'm sure you'll find a way to do it. I have faith. And you need to start with dinner tonight."

"Let's get through the school year," she repeated. She stroked the cover of Dr. Rachel's book and mused. She might have time to get through a chapter or two before Russell picked her up for dinner.

Chapter three, page twenty-seven. Julie lay on her back that night and stared at the ceiling of her bedroom. Did it apply to her? Did she even care? What would Dr. Rachel say? She snuggled her head deeper into her pillow while she tried to form images in her mind's eye from the patterns in the popcorn ceiling. The moon was full and glowed brightly around the edges of her window blinds, illuminating the room.

Chapter three, page twenty-seven. Dr. Rachel warned that one of the most common of fifty stupid things women do at her age was to treat sex like finding an oasis after wandering for years in the desert. She wrote:

The trap that mature women fall into is that they are too quick to trade a few minutes of OMG! for years of Aaaargh!

She went on to advise Julie to take enough time to get it right. She hadn't planned on a sleepover. Maybe it was the full moon. Maybe it was the way Russell wrapped his arms around her and nuzzled that erotic spot behind her left ear at her door when they returned from dinner. It was a spot she didn't know existed until he came along. Maybe it was the way he looked at her and lied about how good she looked even though her neglected hair badly needed a cut and color. Maybe it was his words or his touch, but whatever the reason, by the time the night was late and they were wrapped in each others arms on the couch, there was no way she would let Russell go home without a fight.

She needed more *OMG!* in her life.

Julie swiveled her hips and got out of bed. She went to the window and raised the blinds. The light bathed her naked body and she felt warm and loved. And happy. The man in the moon must have known; he winked at her as if they were sharing a secret. What did Dr. Rachel know? Russell was too calm, too stable ninety percent of the time to be an *Aaaargh!* kind of guy, and she loved him for that. He said he was too boring for his first wife, and his second marriage was an impulsive mistake that he wasn't going to repeat. So Dr. Rachel would be pleased to know that they would go into it with eyes wide open.

"What are you thinking?" She loved the sound of his voice. It was deep and soothing as a back rub.

"Not much," she answered. "Just enjoying this." She turned toward the edge of the bed, where he took her hand and guided her to sit next to him. "What about you? What are you thinking?"

"Hawaii."

"Hawaii?"

"What would you say to spending a week or ten days together in Hawaii as soon as school lets out?"

She would say, "How fast can I pack?" It was the kind of trip she always wanted, a trip she would have taken long ago if kids and jobs and commitments and finances would have let her get away with it. The most exotic trip she had taken in thirty years was to Disneyland (twice) when her kids were little. The only trip out of state was two weeks in the car on a drive with her mother and the children to Yellowstone. The closest she had come to a tropical vacation was the distance she could swim out from the beach in Santa Cruz.

"I'm not sure I can afford a trip like that," she said. It wouldn't be prudent, but it would be fun. It could be romantic.

"No problem. I've wrangled a speaker's slot at the West Coast Region's Secondary Education Leadership Workshop. They're holding it in Maui this year. Imagine that. I'll be on a panel with Superintendent Fox, and the school district is footing the bill for the stay."

"How did you manage that?" She really didn't care. It sounded a lot less romantic when he put it that way.

"I'll be tied up for a few days with the conference. I thought we could stay on for a few more and snorkel, do the luaus, sit in a beach chair and sip those little drinks you like with the umbrellas in them. And we could get to know each other even better."

"Better than what?"

"What better way to find out if we belong together twenty-four-seven?"

He tugged her hand and drew her to him. She lay down and put her head on his chest. It sounded practically romantic. Or maybe it sounded romantically practical. Either way, it sounded wonderful.

CHAPTER FIFTEEN
Back to the Future

Sit up straight.

Eat your peas.

Don't come home late.

Clean up your room.

You are not *wearing* that *to work.*

Being mothered was not the kind of life Nate considered when he ran away from his life in southern California to move back home with Mom and Dad at age fifty-five. It came with the territory. That territory being his old bedroom. When did a mother stop mothering? Probably never, he decided. Regina Evans even criticized him for the length of his hair.

It was too short.

"I miss those long locks, the way you used to wear it."

In a concession to the reality of getting a job and having to be an adult now, and after spending an afternoon with the latest *GQ* magazines, Nate went hip short cut with a flip-front that spiked up from his forehead. He had spent an hour, dazed by choices in the beauty aisle at Safeway, before rejecting the hair color choices just for men and went with a Lady Clairol chestnut flavor that, if the woman on the box was not lying, had the color of his youth. His first attempt was a dismal failure of the orange variety. Like any guy, if the box said let it set half an hour, Nate assumed twice that long would look twice as nice, right? So the second attempt ended in a shoe-polish look. In the end, he went to a stylist, handed her a picture from his *GQ* magazine and a box of hair color that had been pummeled out of frustration and revenge. "Do this."

Regina shook her head and asked him to let his hair grow out. "Just a little. For me? You look so, so Republican," she said.

"Mom. Everybody wears it like this."

She sniffed. "If you want to be like one of those nasty boys from *Fox News*, sure. What happened to that sweet little liberal I raised?"

He looked at his watch. If he left now, he could take his time and get to the new job easily. It wasn't much over a mile away. He had imagined this day a dozen times since Eppie convinced him to apply for it. He was dying to find out if reality could compete with his fantasy. He swallowed the last bit of coffee. Let the adventure begin.

Regina smiled and reached for her son with both hands. Nate steeled himself against the inevitable two-handed pinch of his cheeks and kiss on the forehead. Instead, she grabbed the ends of his tie not yet knotted and pulled it from around his neck. "You aren't going to wear that to work."

"What's wrong with this?" he asked the fashion police.

Charlie sat across the breakfast table from him and pointed with the crust from an unfinished piece of toast. He thought better of making a comment and shrugged.

"If I have to explain it to you, you're hopeless." His mother pointed to the design on the tie. "Really? The Three Stooges?" The contorted faces of Moe, Larry and Curly stared at Nate from the fabric his mother dangled in front of him with disgust. Regina marched to his bedroom and returned a minute later with his funeral tie, a solid black number.

"I like the other one. It kind of makes a statement," he said.

"And the statement is 'I'm a goofball so don't take me seriously.' But it's not that. You don't wear purple plaid and green paisley together. I raised you better than that."

"Okay."

"How in the world did you survive when you were teaching down there at the little college?"

"I guess they figured I was one of those eccentric creative types."

Fashion faux pas aside, Mother had advice on just about every subject since he moved back home. Many were familiar, things that he had heard forty years earlier. He would have dismissed them now as easily as when he was seventeen if not for the fact that, through the years, he'd learned, much to his surprise, that Mother had been right more often than not. He hated when that happened.

Curfews. "Mom, I'm a little old for a curfew."

"Not when you're living in my house."

Money management. "Mom, I can handle my own finances. I've been doing it for years."

"Here's an extra five dollars, dear. Just in case. You don't want to be at Starbucks and not have enough to pay for your date's espresso mocha latte, or whatever it is you kids drink these days. Suppose she orders extra whipped cream?"

"That's why God invented credit cards."

Regina handed him his brand-new backpack. She had made

him lunch and put a bottle of spring water in there with it. His parents walked with him down to the sidewalk. The sun was peeking over the top of the eastern foothills. It was mid-August and going to be a hot one, but mornings in the Santa Clara Valley had a way of teasing you with a promise of perfect weather all day long. He felt great. After years of being scorched by people and events he couldn't seem to control, he felt like he was wading into a cold swimming pool. Relief at last.

"Nate, I'm so happy you're up and about. You've been spending far too much time moping and just, I don't know, drifting. This new job will be good for you."

"I totally agree. I feel good, Mom."

"And aside from work, I think you should get out more."

"Or you could just get out," Charlie said. "It's been six months now."

Regina dismissed her husband with a wave of her backhand. "I was talking about finding a girl. A nice girl, this time."

"I was talking about rent," Charlie said.

Nate blinked and then looked at his mother. "But I offered. You said you wouldn't hear of it." He had made the offer when the settlement with the Air Force was a done deal.

Charlie scowled. "Funny, I don't remember having that conversation."

Nate's settlement with the Air Force wasn't much considering his landlord got the bulk of the money. It was pretty cut-and-dried. As long as Nate agreed to a nondisclosure clause, he got a lump sum for the loss of his personal belongings. It was a pittance, but enough to pay a few months' rent to Mom and Dad and enough to tide him over until he found a job. Now he was going to have a salary, and maybe get a life.

Regina changed the subject and asked, "Nate, do you remember Mrs. Garner? Dorothy Garner?"

He couldn't fathom where that question had come from. But then Mom perfected the ability to bring any unrelated distraction into a conversation with a question from left field. This was a woman who, on a trip to the Grand Canyon, stood at the roadside overlook, scanned the vast canyon and the Arizona desert above it and wondered why dolphins didn't come in different colors.

"They're all such a boring shade of gray, aren't they?" he remembered her asking. He was twelve at the time. Nate believed he had inherited some rogue attention deficit gene from his mother. The constant daydreaming it fueled was great for storytelling but had little use in all the other aspects of life.

"Mrs. Garner? No, I can't say I know who she is."

"You should. She was your fifth grade teacher. I bumped into her recently and her daughter is single. And I was thinking we could invite them over for dinner on Saturday."

"Mom, I don't need you to fix me up."

Regina was undaunted. "You haven't made any new friends since you moved back home. It might help you stop pining and forget Valerie."

Talking about serious relationships with your parents was a slippery slope, he knew, regardless of your age. You needed to provide enough information to satisfy their curiosity, but give them too much information and you opened yourself up for no end to parental appraisal, unwanted advice and criticism.

If only she knew. Valerie was just one more kick in the nuts out of so many. "Who's pining?" he bristled. "The divorce was five years ago.

I haven't exactly been a monk," Nate assured her. "I've dated plenty of times."

One was nearly serious. He thought about the months he'd spent with an actress finally coming into her own after slogging for a decade through a string of forgettable roles and TV commercials. He could relate to all of that, except for the success part. It was the longest relationship with a woman Nate had fit into his post-married life. Her name was Tina, and she went on to fame and fortune, and he went back to being rejected by the movie studios.

Regina said, "Honey, I'm thinking that it couldn't hurt for you to meet her daughter. I'm sure there's a nice girl out there who's right for you."

Nate didn't know if that was true, but he was making the effort to find out. Eppie told him how to find Julie Cooper. She told him the Coop-ster was single and available. And now he had a plan to see her again. Then what? Seeing her again could be a huge mistake. But even if that happened, it would definitively stomp out the nagging curiosity of what if. What if he had done more when they were young and not let her slip away?

"Okay, fine," he said. "Whatever. Invite them over for dinner. I'll try to clear my social calendar." The sarcasm was lost on his mother.

Regina smiled and raised her palms. "I'll call Dorothy tomorrow. A little wine, a little conversation, that's all." She gave him a final peck on the cheek.

Nate slung the backpack over one shoulder and admired his new set of wheels. He nudged the skateboard to get some momentum before he stepped on it, concentrating to regain his balance after a wobbly start.

Kick. Push. Glide. He rolled down the sidewalk.

CHAPTER SIXTEEN
Starting All Over Again Is Gonna Be Rough

"When he asked me to spend the weekend at the lake, I went out and found the cutest little swimsuit at Macy's."

"I'll bet you looked terrific in it."

"But then we wound up water-skiing with a bunch of his friends, and he spent the whole day flirting with some blond bimbo who came along and didn't even touch the water."

"Like you weren't even there. Barb, I keep telling you he's such a jerk."

"I hate him."

Beverly and Barbara motored past Julie when she slipped out of the administration office, their conversation tailing them like a wake on the water. There was freshness in the morning air despite the fact that they would likely have a sweltering start to the new school year. The summer break was short and sweet, though Julie had taken a lot of work home with her to get a head start. None of it got done in the week she spent with Russell in Hawaii. The scenery. The waterfalls and the flowers. The sand and the surf. It was the best vacation she could remember. Granted, Russell spent more time with Superintendent Fox and two other school board members than she would have liked. But once the conference was over, she had him all to herself. He seemed proud to have her on his arm at the social events, sometimes to an embarrassing extent when he introduced her to Fox and the others. He never left her feeling like she didn't belong. It was a far cry from the distance he had maintained on campus before the trip, and things got even better when they returned home.

It was the first day back on campus for staff. The students would follow in a couple of weeks, and she was going to enjoy the calm before the storm. She strolled across the quad that separated the offices from the library with a cup of Starbucks. Vacation was too short. They had a handful of new teachers; Russell had asked her to be part of the initiation committee, with the assignment to meet with the newbies and get them settled in to the campus. A blue jay flitted from under a crease in the overhang of the admin building to a live oak across from her and squawked, perturbed, no doubt, that Julie hadn't let him sleep in. By the time she got back to the faculty lounge, Carla was trying to salvage the icing on a cake she had brought for their first day back.

"It slid off the seat when I had to hit the brakes hard at Dunkin' Donuts. The guy in front of me at the drive-thru almost hit me with his rear bumper."

"He was backing up in the drive thru?"

"Not exactly. He was sitting there like he didn't even see me pulling up. Good thing I stopped in time. But we almost lost the cake."

Julie swiped a dollop of white icing that Carla had pushed to the edge of the plate and licked her finger. "Yum."

She went to the bank of mail slots in a shelf unit on the far wall, each one identified by the name of a staff member. There were only a couple of generic first-day forms there. It was too soon to get much. But there was also an intriguing small white card, folded like a pup tent and standing up and staring at her with a blank face. She unfolded the card.

Smile, the note said in manly block letters accompanied by a crude happy face from somewhere out of the seventies.

"I'm going to guess this didn't come from you." Julie held it out to her friend.

"Cute. And you're right. It wasn't me." And then as she finished patching the last dent in the cake with a flourish, Carla cocked her head. Without looking at Julie she asked, "So what did our Mr. Fester-haven do *this* time?"

"What do you mean?" Julie knew exactly what Carla meant.

Carla lowered her voice and motioned with her head for Julie to follow her to the coffeemaker on the far side of the room. "Come on. It's just the kind of thing he would do when he gets in trouble. Very nice, but really."

"He hasn't done anything that I know of."

"Preemptive apology. Otherwise, why the note? He must have done something and you don't know it yet."

"Psh. Don't be like that."

"Call me suspicious, but I think he's up to something. He's a man. If he isn't up to something now, he will be."

It was a familiar joke for Carla. Her playful cynicism where her husband was concerned was part of the reason she was so happily married all these years. You only had to watch Carla and Larry together for a few minutes to see there was a deep current of love and respect below the surface of their teasing. Julie envied her.

Russell's secretary stuck her head in the door. Mr. Festerhaven was asking about the enrollment retention file that Julie knew was buried in her desk's in-box. She tucked his sweet little surprise note into her pocket and waved at Russell as they passed his office. It barely registered with him.

"So how is your day starting?" she asked when she returned with the file he wanted.

"Couldn't be better. But ask me again in an hour." Russell smiled.

She handed him the file. "Mr. Festerhaven."

"Mrs. Finch," he nodded.

Julie reached into her pocket and pulled out the smiley note. She stepped up to the edge of the desk and he asked, "And how is your day starting?"

Julie swished the note card in front of him.

"It's starting out great. How could it not? This was a nice thing to find in my mailbox first thing this morning."

Russell glanced at it. "Hmm. It isn't mine. Who's playing morale fairy this morning? Mrs. Almeida again? It's usually her."

"Nope. I asked her. Besides, that's not her handwriting."

"Not mine, either. Though I wish I *had* thought of it. It's nice."

Julie's eyes narrowed. He might be spoofing and she told him so.

He inspected the card again and then gave her a dismissive scowl. "Do I look like the kind of guy who would sign something with a little smiley face thing like this?"

He had that right. It was a mystery.

"I'm sure you'll figure it out. It must have been meant for someone else and it got into your mailbox by mistake."

That must be it, though it irked her that he could dismiss it as a mistake so easily, as if nobody might go out of their way to make a friendly gesture like that for her. Julie took the card and used it to strum the fingers of her left hand. Why did the note feel familiar? It was déjà vu without the déjà or the vu.

Russell's eyes darted past her and he raised his eyebrows.

"Oh. You're back. Great timing." As Julie turned, Russell added, "Mrs. Finch, this fellow says he knows you. Julie, Mr. Evans here is taking over the freshman English class and Creative Composition for the visual arts."

Goodness. She swallowed hard.

"Nate, Julie here will be leading your teacher orientation this afternoon."

Something clutched in her throat. The curly, long brown locks were gone, and the face was sculpted gently by age but still had a boyish character of someone unaffected by worries or the demands of adulthood. That would be Nate to a T, she thought. If there had been any doubt at all, it disappeared with the goofy grin and the casual circular wave he gave her while leaning against the door.

"Surprise."

"Boy. Well. Wow. Nate Evans."

"Julie Cooper. Cooper-Finch. Finch, is it?"

"Nate Evans. Wow." *Quit saying that.* "Wow. So many years. Here you are." Oh, that was a brilliant response. Julie drove her hands into the pockets of her slacks and rocked back on her heels.

"It's good to see you again, too, Julie. Mrs. Finch, I mean. I guess I'll have to get used to that."

"Freshman English?"

"And he's going to take over Mr. Larsen's creative writing for the seniors," Russell said. "I thought it might be good to take advantage of his Hollywood experience. Fiction in the arts."

"Experience? I've sold a few things, so I suppose that counts. Any blind squirrel with a laptop and Microsoft Word can get lucky in Hollywood once in a while. But who knows? Things have changed so much, what with YouTube and all that, I might learn a thing or two from the students. I have to say, it's ironic. I didn't know what a magnet school was until somebody explained it to me recently. On top of all the regular high school subjects, you guys have a whole special curriculum for film and theater arts, stuff that I can actually teach. Right here at the school where we graduated. Ironic in a cool sort of way."

"Ironic." She could have been blindfolded and she still would have recognized his voice. It was unnerving after all the years spent worlds apart. Nate looked deep into her eyes as he talked and Julie feared she was blushing. She felt like they stood there without saying anything for a century.

"Good. We've established the irony of it all." Russell broke the spell. His eyes shifted from her to Nate and back before he said, "Okay. I've got a lot to do this morning. It's nice that you remember each other and I'm sure you two have a lot to catch up on. I'd love to hear all about it. Later."

Nate laid a hand on her arm after they moved into the hallway and then withdrew it quickly with embarrassment. He apologized. "Sorry. Flashback. Me and you here on campus. For a moment there it was like we never left."

"I see you cut your hair," she said.

"I see you kept your smile."

He held his gaze on her. Once upon a time, she would have

glanced away when he did that, too shy to stare him down. This time she didn't flinch. *You flirt*, she thought, though she was glad he said it.

He stepped back and looked her over from head to toe. "It's so good to see you again."

Julie shrugged with her palms up. "In the flesh."

That caused Nate to pause. He was still smiling, but the warmth evaporated. He reached out and took her left hand. "Whoa. Look at this." It was theatrical, a simple statement overplayed. It was her ring he noticed. He turned her hand one way and then the other as the diamond captured the light from the fluorescents. She couldn't tell, was he admiring or assessing it?

"Isn't it sweet? Russell." Julie nodded toward the principal's door. "I'm still getting used to the idea. We got engaged last weekend."

CHAPTER SEVENTEEN
The Fountain of Puppy Love

It was twelve thirteen on Friday, and Julie paused at the corner of the library. She leaned forward, sneaking a peek into the fountain quadrangle that sat between the library and the wall of lockers outside the English classrooms.

Yep. He was there. Nate sat at a metal picnic table on the opposite side of the fountain, where he had spent every lunch hour that first week. She ducked as if afraid he might see her. As if it mattered. *How silly is that?* She held a three-by-five notecard in her hand. It had been folded in half and set in her mail slot that morning so that it was sitting up, waiting for her with its blank face forward.

Happy Friday, it said on the inside. An anonymous author had taped a penny above the words: *For your thoughts.*

They were more than a week away from the return of the student hordes, and the quad was blissfully silent except for the fountain that gurgled like a small mountain stream, echoing off the canyon of concrete school walls around it. Even from a distance, she saw his eyes pop open wide as she stepped from the shadows and around the corner of the library.

"Just sitting here like old times," he said.

It was odd having Nate around, but it was fun, too. He was still handsome, enough to warrant a second look and a smile from more than one of the women teachers. Julie hadn't noticed but Carla swore it was true. She wouldn't name names except to say she overheard a certain potty-mouth English teacher who was almost young enough to be his daughter make a suggestive comment about Nate to her close friend, who was also from the English department. No surprise there. Barbara Unger didn't seem to care who she told she would chase anything in pants if she chose to do so. Sadly, she never seemed to catch one.

Nate had always been easygoing, quick with a smile or a joke, and she suspected it wouldn't be long before he was the new best friend of everybody who passed through the faculty lounge. That was Nate. As for her, if wrinkles were a way to keep score, she was beating him by a mile. He must have had it easy out there in the real world. She was happy for him. She had commandeered a long table in the faculty lounge a few days earlier to collate the latest three-page edict from the district that she would distribute to the teachers when Seth Naylor got him talking about his career in Hollywood. She got the pages all out of order as she eavesdropped and found herself comparing Nate's life to her own. He didn't brag. He didn't need to because his life seemed glamorous and successful. Seeing him again, especially here at their old high school, made it obvious she hadn't progressed beyond the campus they shared long ago.

Oh, and he was single and unattached. As if that mattered. It did not, though she found it intriguing. When she asked, he admitted he hadn't been immune to divorce, but who was these days? It was a twenty-year marriage; he had told her that much but little else.

"I think these belong to you." She handed him the two notecards he had planted in her mail slot and sat down across from him at the table.

"How long did it take for you to realize it was me?"

"When I saw you in Russell's office. Maybe it didn't sink in until the next day. The first day I was so surprised to see you again and forgot about the note. But when you left another one this morning, there wasn't any doubt. And that was before Carla saw you and ratted you out."

"The munchkin? Busted. She walked in but I thought I got away with it. I thought I was sneakier than that."

"You used to be. But it did make me think of the first time you did it. I assume you wanted to remind me."

Nate took the card, held it to his temple and closed his eyes. "Thirty-two, thirty-eight, fourteen. That was the combination on your locker our freshman year when I started sneaking notes in there for you to find."

Holy moly. "You remember the combination number? After all these years?"

"Nah. I made that part up."

She laughed. Yes, that would be too weird, but she had fallen for it.

"You caught me a lot quicker this time. I would have felt like an ass if you didn't make the connection to high school."

Nate's easy laughter drew her into reminiscing along with him about the close group of friends they had shared this corner of the campus with, friends who scattered after college and were now only faces familiar from their high school yearbook. It was a kind of sentimental, revisionist history that would lead you to think only good things happened back then. The concrete reflected daylight in a way that, today at least, was like a warm, white cocoon that comforted her.

"I'm developing a real bad habit," Nate said. "I've been walking over to the Dairy Barn every day this week, the way we used to do with Meg and Ben and everybody. Remember that? Hard to believe it's still there. And you can still smell the grease in the air, so thick you can practically wear it home."

"Funny. It's so close and yet I never think to stop by these days."

"Then come with me. We'll make it a field trip or something like that."

"Maybe we could do that sometime," she said. Then she asked him what brought him back home, generally, and to a teaching job at Mt. Hamilton High specifically.

For the first time, she saw his smile fade, though he didn't avert his gaze and there was something in his eyes she couldn't define. Disappointment? He thumbed the penny he had taped to the card in her mail slot that morning. Now he peeled it off and pinched it. "It's simple. I needed a change. Look around you here," he said as he waved his hand. "Does it get any better than this?" Then the corners of his mouth turned up, pushing the wrinkles at his eyes so that his entire face smiled at her. He held up the coin. *A penny for your thoughts.* He was playing a game, a mild version of Truth Or Dare that he invented. It had been their private game, played as teenagers when they were alone and deep into long, rambling conversations after a date or on a walk home from school. Now it was her turn. He handed her the penny.

"I can't tell anymore. I came back, oh, more than a dozen years ago for the job, and some days it feels like this is all I know. It may be all I'll ever know." She said it as she gazed at the coin in her hand. Nate took it back and rubbed it between his thumb and forefinger.

"That's not so bad if the memories are good. I love this place." He never took his eyes off her and handed the coin back.

"We had some good times," she said. "But I was never as enamored with high school as you seem to be. To be honest, I just don't think about those days that much. Only now and again."

She expected a joke, a dash of humor in case he was disappointed in some way. When he didn't pop off right away, she held the penny between them. Then she placed it in his palm. *Your turn.*

Nate patted the back of her hand and stood up. "I would bet there are more good memories than you remember remembering." He beckoned her to walk with him. He led her around the edge of the fountain. He told Julie he was thinking about how they dyed the water red after beating Piedmont in football their junior year.

"Oh, Lord. Not that." Although it hadn't crossed her mind since leaving high school, it was suddenly, surprisingly vivid now.

"Everybody was standing around; you were at this edge, I think. I grabbed you and threatened to throw you in."

She remembered how everyone had egged him on and how he'd leaned her over. "I almost lost my balance."

"But I had you tight. Pulled you back and let you get away."

"Let me? I shoved you and you fell backwards into the water."

"I let you get away with that, too. But then when you saw the principal, Mr.... Mr...."

"Conklin."

Nate gave her a sideways glance and winked. "Yeah. Conklin. Anyway, what *I* remember most was when you saw Mr. Conklin coming, you jumped in after me. And there we were, both flat on our backs in water up to our ears."

She watched the water stream from the nozzle in the center. It was a fun memory for sure. When she raised her head, his eyes were twinkling with his head tilted slightly to one side. "What? Why are you looking at me like that?"

"I'm wondering… What ever happened to that girl? The girl in the fountain?"

"I'm not sure what you mean."

"Fountain Girl. Where is she today?"

She wasn't sure how to answer. What did he want her to say? Was he disappointed in her? Maybe, and that was unsettling. "The usual place kids go, adulthood. She got married and had a family. Lost a husband. Raised the kids alone because what else could you do? Fountain Girl grew up."

Nate sighed, understanding yet amused. "You did a great job of it. But Fountain Boy? Fountain Boy, not so much. He'll always be a kid for better or worse."

CHAPTER EIGHTEEN
A Day at the Fair

By Sunday afternoon, the boy and girl were in trouble. The first plot twist, a roadblock for their relationship, happened right on schedule, right around page twenty of *Mulligan*, the script Nate was working on, the one inspired by a spark from Eppie, and one that had badgered him with daydreams and nightmares ever since. *Write me!* He had floated the story to his agent back in June.

An old fart, obsessed with the past, moves back home with his ditsy hippie parents and tries to recreate his high school days in order to woo the girl who got away.

His agent, Jack Hewitt, after ignoring the first three emails Nate sent with the idea and a few details, was unimpressed but encouraged him to keep at it until he came up with something decent. "Maybe it'll grow on me. Send me more if you get around to it."

Unfortunately, "more" was in short supply. He was too preoccupied with the reality of living the story to make up some fictional plot development in what would be the first act if he ever got serious about fleshing out a script.

It was Eppie who told him Julie was widowed, available and

working at their high school. As head of the district's HR department, she pulled strings to help him land the job there. He thought he'd be looking forward to a date with Julie by now, but life bitch-slapped him again. How else could he explain her getting engaged only one week, *one fucking week,* before he arrived on campus to commence wooing? It was so ridiculously cliché he couldn't have scripted it better. So that's what he did.

He finished typing the scene where the girl he named Julie flashed her engagement ring at the boy and gushed about how perfect her fiancé was, how perfect their love was and how perfect their future would be together. Then he attached the latest pages to an email back to Jack. Of course, none of the gushing had really happened, but he was disappointed that his chance to rekindle something with Julie was snuffed out immediately, before he could even find out if there was a reason to try. At least he had answered that nagging question of what if he had a second chance. So now he was going to write it the way he felt, and he felt like shit. That little chip of diamond on her hand taunted him each time their paths crossed.

It didn't help that he had wasted his Saturday evening entertaining his former grade school teacher, Mrs. Garner, and her single daughter, Edith, at his mother's blind date setup. Edith had pinged him with a text message Sunday morning suggesting they arrange a date sans parents because it was obvious they had so much in common. The girl was trying too hard, and that was just one issue. Nate figured the only thing they had in common was divorce. She went on and on about her ex's faults, and Edith listed every one of them for Nate over the course of drinks before dinner, dinner, dessert, a post-dessert nightcap and well past the time any reasonable guest would have left. By the end of the night, he pitied the husband, thought highly of him for choosing divorce over homicide and understood why she was still single.

When his mother asked how it went, he had a pat answer:

"Edith's not the right girl for me."

But that begged the question, who was the right girl? He flopped down across his bed and stared up at the poster of Raquel Welch in her prehistoric lion-skin bikini. He loved eBay. It had been a snap to find that poster again and put it up on the ceiling where it belonged. So, too, Luke Skywalker, who brandished his lightsaber on the wall near his desk. Getting his bedroom back to the 1970s was complete. His mother had unearthed boxes of junk he hadn't thought about in years. He picked the best memories and placed them strategically about the room. It occurred to him that if he indeed did find the right girl now, he couldn't bring her back here for a night of nookie. There was no way to explain living at home at his age to a woman interested enough in spending the night, let alone doing it under Raquel's critical eye.

In his disappointment, it struck him that while Julie wasn't available, she might, just might, be the only woman out there who would understand him enough to cut him slack on that front.

Later that afternoon, Nate sat in the shade of a tree at the county fairgrounds ignoring the corn dog in one hand and sipping a Coke from the other.

"What do you think about soul mates?" he asked. "I mean, do they exist? Does anyone really have one?"

"If they are the real deal, then why the hell did we invent divorce? Answer that one." Woody, with his cowboy hat tipped low over his brow, sat back against the trunk of the tree keeping an eye on his band-mates as they set up their equipment on the music stage. Woody Wood and the Peckerheads! Live at the Santa Clara County Fair! They had gotten a three-day gig.

Nate wrapped the nibbled-on corn dog in a paper napkin and set it aside for the next trash can he found. "What if you were soul mates with somebody, except she didn't know it?"

Eppie Johnson sat in her wheelchair on his left. "It looks like she didn't get the memo," she said. "Sorry about that, Evans. When I told you how to find her, I didn't know Cooper was engaged."

"How could you? It's a new wrinkle."

When Nate called her for a lunch date or drinks, hoping to talk through his discovery of Julie's relationship with their principal, she suggested Sunday evening, but Nate had already promised Woody he would hit the county fair to catch their act.

"Fine." She told him to meet her there. "We've been promising my youngest grandkid we'd take her. The hubby can keep an eye on the kids."

Now, he found himself sitting between the two people in his life he could turn to for advice. Woody and Eppie were both full of bullshit, but their BS usually carried more than a grain of truth, and they hit it off immediately. Shadows were getting long as the three of them sat across from the music stage on the edge of the livestock arena. Bells clanged and the sound of fun and games rode the breeze from the carnival midway in the distance.

"I got to thinking earlier today," Nate told them. "What if you have a soul mate but she had a soul mate of her own? Somebody different."

"Now you're talking. A soul mate ménage à tois. Sounds kinky. I like it," Woody said.

"Forget I said anything."

"Done. This is getting way too deep for me anyway."

Nate had never shared with anyone the dream, or the déjà vu that hit him the first time he saw Julie as a six-year-old. Now it had returned, stronger in some ways, triggered by seeing Julie on campus that first day back. He hated the cliché that his heart skipped a beat when he saw her, but something squeezed him inside. It was her smile that brought back the memory of his first grade déjà vu that refused to let go of him. Later, walking across campus together on their way to the new teacher orientation felt as if they hadn't grown up after all. If that wasn't soul-mateness, what was?

"But now she's getting married and I'm screwed."

They agreed it was a big problem. "Though not insurmountable, I suppose," Eppie said.

"She's not married yet," Woody added.

Not yet. It was technically true, but it was too close for comfort. His comfort. "She wouldn't be marrying the guy if she doesn't love him, right? So I have no shot. Not now."

Nate tapped his ring finger for Woody's sake and his friend nodded. Eppie, who didn't know the history of Nate's messy divorce and his aversion to diamond adorned married women, missed the sign.

That was his rule. He couldn't meddle no matter what because a guy didn't steal another guy's gal and a gal didn't steal another gal's guy, marriage or not. That shit just wasn't right.

Woody said, "Looks like y'all have a choice here. Either hang around, stand in line, wait your turn and hope this engagement goes south. Or..."

"Or what?" Eppie asked.

"I know a guy named Guido. We could arrange to have Mr.

Principal disappear. Dump the body in the bay, in the muck around Alviso. You take him out of the picture and you move to the front of the line."

Woody winked at him. It was a cheap shot between friends. Nate knew he deserved it. Guido. It was a character out of a third-rate mob movie and one, not coincidentally, he wrote. *The Mob and the Mongoose* wasn't even third-rate good, but he'd paid for his honeymoon with the option money he got selling it to Random Capers Productions. The studio never bothered to make the movie, and Woody joked that they must have buried the screenplay with Jimmy Hoffa's body. Neither had been seen since.

"So I'm wasting my time?"

"I wouldn't say that. You're writing again. That's a good thing. Stick with it. If nothing else, you'll get a story to sell out of it. That's not so bad." Woody stretched and stood. His joints creaked and cracked and he uttered a soft "ooph." He leaned an elbow against the tree. "You and I know the best stuff comes from here," he said, tapping two fingers over his heart. "This is the one that'll get y'all back in the saddle again. Put it to good use, partner."

"Is he a real cowboy?" Eppie asked when Woody went off to supervise the Peckerheads' setup crew. That crew was all of the band members but Woody.

"Not even. But he talks a good game."

Eppie checked her watch and suggested they start for the opposite side of the carnival midway, where her husband would be herding the three grandchildren through all of the rides.

Nate pushed her wheelchair across the ruts in the lawn until they reached a solid gravel path that led to the carnival midway. At that point she waved him away. She still wanted little help and zero pity. The crowd, or lack thereof, disappointed him. It was smaller and less engaged than he remembered. Even in her wheelchair, Eppie was able to dodge most of the foot traffic. He lurched, bumped by a couple of teenagers running along the midway. They were laughing, the boy tugging the girl while she hopped along behind him struggling to adjust one of her sandals.

"Sorry, mister," the boy said when he stopped. He put his arms around the girl's waist as she leaned against him and finally got her footwear in place. She looked up, he looked down, and they shared the cutest giggle. A nice kid, the boy waved another apology and looked at him as if to say, "See what I have to put up with?" No complaints, for sure.

Enjoy it while you can, kids, he thought as they bounded away.

Eppie asked about the story Woody mentioned and how it was coming along.

"It's not going anywhere right now. It started well; living at home, retro-fitting the bedroom, going to school every day and all that, it's about as close to making things the way things used to be as I could have dreamed up. Having Julie around makes a big difference. I think it's having someone from that same little slice of my life that makes it feel like I've gone back in time without really going back in time."

"Especially when that person is Cooper." She raised her hand and studied her fingernails, a nonchalantly obvious way to let him know she had his number.

"And I've got you to rag on my ass about her, just like before. So it couldn't be better." He swatted the air near her arm, a backhanded rebuke. Then he told her about sitting with Julie next to the fountain at lunch where the bench that had been "their bench" used to be. "Got these iron picnic tables around the quad now, no character at all and you can't carve your initials in them." He talked about walking across the campus with her where he could only imagine holding her hand with their fingers interlocked. "But since that part of the story ain't gonna happen, I guess I'll make something up." But his heart wasn't in it.

They stopped at a snack trailer, and Nate bought a couple of pretzels before they found a place to sit between the kiddie rides and the thrill rides. Eppie waved to her husband. He was standing near the rail of the bumper cars arena.

"I still have trouble imagining you with kids."

She held up two fingers. "Who would have thought? And three grandkids now."

"I'm surprised. You know, your injury and all. I didn't think it was possible."

"Everybody assumes that. But it is very possible. Though Sarah was a really difficult birth and I swore off any more after that."

Nate drummed his fingers on the armrest to her wheelchair and asked her if she knew pregnancy was possible when they were in high school.

"No way. The doctors said it'd never happen. Why?"

She had put on pounds over the years, and her face was wider than he remembered with big, round cheeks, but it was as full of freckles as ever. It made her appear younger than she was. She gave him a crooked grin.

Nate shrugged. "No reason."

Unconvinced, she said, "Maybe. Maybe not." If quiet reflection was possible in the middle of a carnival, it settled on them as they sat back to enjoy the moment and their renewed friendship.

She said, "Tell me, how serious do you think Cooper is about this fellow, the principal, Mr. Festerhaven, right?"

"Like I said, she's going to marry him. I'd have to say that's beyond serious. That's, like, fatally serious."

"I don't see it as fatal. Not yet. Now look at me. Back in the day, when we were whatever we were, not only did I think having kids was impossible, I assumed finding a husband was, too. Who'd want me? I spent a lot of years believing that, but then Will came along, late but better than never. So without getting all sappy on your ass, things always seem to work out even if it takes a while."

It was the most optimistic, sunny thing Nate ever heard from her. "But if you tell anybody I said that, not only will I deny it but I'll grate you into little tiny bits and feed you to the seagulls."

"Your secret is safe with me."

Eppie had mellowed through the years but managed to retain some of her attitude. It was a nice mix and he liked it.

"Seriously. What do you think I should do? I didn't expect to feel so down about this."

"I think you need to decide once and for all if you're in love with some made-up version of Cooper, the dream Cooper, and the real Cooper isn't what you want in the long run. Or if she really is your soul mate you keep jabbering about. Don't you want to at least know that?"

"Well, of course. But I certainly can't do anything that might screw up what they have. Not fair to her or to him."

Eppie told him that he should find out. "So you're going to put your tail between your legs and slink away. You're thinking about what's best for her. You're thinking about what's best for him. But think for a minute of what's best for you."

"To slink away like the dog I am?"

Eppie shook her head, disgusted. "Back in high school, the way I heard it, she would have done anything for you."

He knitted his eyebrows and his mouth twitched to one side. "She never said anything like that."

"She was too shy to tell you, and you were too stupid to figure it out. And that, my friend, is why you two never got together. So this time, if you think she is the real deal and not some fantasy you've cooked up over the years, you need to tell her, straight up. Yeah, straight up. Nothing ambiguous."

No way. What Eppie was suggesting rankled something inside him. Even though Julie wasn't married yet, he didn't want to be like the guys that hit on his wife and made it so easy for Valerie to cheat on him.

Then again, he was sure Julie would never do anything like that. They would both respect the ring, so he had a safety net. "Hell, she'll blow me off and probably hate me for even bringing it up."

Eppie told him he was supposed to be a creative guy. "You can come up with something that isn't rude. Gentle. Honest, but most importantly, leaves no doubt. Leave it up to her and see what happens."

"Suppose she tells me to get lost?"

"That's what I would do if I was her. But then I was never in love with you. Much," she added with a grin. "And what if she does prefer this other guy to you? You still have another option."

"And that is?"

"Guido, the hit man."

CHAPTER NINETEEN

Confession at the Dairy Barn

At the end of the first day of classes, the boy took the girl aside and revealed he had hidden his strong feelings for her since they were children. She realized she felt the same, and love triumphed.

Delete.

At the end of the first day of classes, the girl cried on the boy's shoulder looking for comfort after breaking up with her fiancé, and love triumphed.

Delete.

At the end of the first day of classes, there was no girl, no boy and no hope of getting them together.

Delete. Delete. Delete. Nate stabbed the button repeatedly in frustration.

He leaned on a fist in the light of his laptop on the desk in his bedroom, full of gloom as he stared at the pages on the screen, variations of scenes he had imagined and fiction he had committed over long nights leading up to the first day of school. It was almost midnight. The Righteous Brothers were singing "Unchained Melody" on the headphones plugged into his computer. He had a long iTunes playlist of melancholy songs for times like this. He opened his favorite scene, the one where, at the end of the first day of classes, word spread the principal was dead. He was bitten by a wild beaver while trying to take a selfie with the animal he had dragged from a creek on a weekend hunting trip. The girl, his fiancée, turned to the boy for consolation, and love triumphed.

"If only real life worked like that," he mumbled. He tried to come up with a way to sneak a rabid beaver into Festerhaven's office. *Oh, well.*

He leaned back in the chair at his desk in the corner of his bedroom and ignored the computer screen while his mind wandered to some spot where it looked back at him from an objective distance, intrigued by how his life and his fictional story were at the same intersection. If he had a shrink, she'd tell him that it was not only inevitable but also deliberate. He reached into the bottom drawer to the right of his knee and pulled a snack package of Fig Newtons from where he had hidden them underneath a handful of *Playboy* magazines.

His mother would have a fit if she looked there. The magazines served two purposes. First, they were from the 1970s like the one he stashed under his mattress as a curious boy. Nate hadn't had a peek at *Playboy* in too many years to count but lamented the end of the era when he heard the magazine decided to bounce nudes from its pages now. So he was preserving a bit of personal and cultural history. Second, if Regina found them, she would shake her head, disgusted with Nate's bourgeois taste, but might leave well enough alone and not discover the worse sin of Fig Newtons and Snickers bars hidden beneath them. All that sugar and processed food was totally unacceptable, and she would lecture him long and loudly about it. In Mandarin. Regina had taken up lessons in that language with passion. She thought it best to develop good communication skills early and be prepared for when the Chinese took over running the world from the US. She told Nate it was more than being practical, it was the polite thing to do.

Lacking the creative energy to make something up, Nate typed what had actually gone down at the end of that first day of classes.

He enticed Julie and several others on staff to mark surviving the first day of classes with a trip to the Dairy Barn after school. He hoped the principal, Festerhaven, would join them so Nate could observe the dynamics of Julie's relationship with him.

"Russell doesn't like getting too cozy with staff," she whispered when he asked why the principal laughed off Nate's invitation.

"He seems to be okay getting cozy with you." Nate gently pinched her arm, teasing, like two good friends sharing an inside joke. *It's what I would do.*

Naturally, Julie was the only one with his shared history to understand the significance of a group visit to the Dairy Barn after school. He was pleased she didn't let it pass without a comment. "This feels familiar."

It was a comfortable mix of folks that he found himself easing into. Carla, the science teacher, and Seth, the music guy, were there. Beverly and Barbara, the chatty twin sisters of different mothers from the English department, came along, as did Festerhaven's secretary and Ray, the black vice-principal in charge of discipline with a thousand-watt smile and biceps like a pro linebacker.

When Ray mentioned having gone back for his high school reunion that summer, everyone chimed in with stories of their own. Nate had come back for two, the ten- and twenty-year reunions. Julie said she had neither the time nor much inclination to attend either.

He couldn't resist posing the question, "Let's say high school is your fork in the road. One direction leads you right where you are today, and the other, well, who knows? Would you do things differently if you could?"

Carla said she might consider doing a lot of little things here and there through the years, "But I'd still be teaching. It's what I do."

Seth, the music instructor, said he would buy a guitar and join a rock band instead of taking up the tuba. "Maybe I would could've been a roadie for Journey."

"Wild," Nate said. And then he looked directly at Julie. "And you? Would you change your life?"

She never hesitated. "I wouldn't change anything."

"Nothing?"

"Because if I did, I wouldn't have my children. And I wouldn't have the grandchildren. I might have had different children, but I kind of love the ones I have."

"That," Nate had said, "is the perfect answer."

He liked these people, and they provided a lot of advice about everything from which office directives could be safely ignored to tips on engaging high school students without losing their respect. Out of habit, he caught himself making mental notes about them, characters he might later spoon into his *Mulligan* story.

He rejected offers for a ride back to campus, even though no one was headed that way. It was only five blocks; he would walk.

"I think I'll walk, too," Julie said. She had left her car at the school and caught a ride with Carla. It was a pleasantly surprising development.

"You know, I've never spent much time looking back, but you have a way of making the past out to be more fun than I think it was," she said as they walked out of the Dairy Barn. She circled the air with her finger. "This was certainly interesting."

They walked a route back to the school that took them down neighborhood streets lined with ash and maple trees. He asked about her children and the grandkids. Did she have any pictures? She told him she didn't want to be one of those grandmothers who believed everybody should be as interested in the kids as she was while she pulled her phone from her purse and then scrolled through several for him.

A block later, he asked about Festerhaven. "He seems a decent enough guy."

"He is." Try as he might, Nate couldn't find much to dislike about Festerhaven based on Julie's account. He listened closely to her words, the tone of her voice and the energy of her convictions, hoping for some chink in her fiancé's shining knight armor. He was successful, practical, passionate about sports but willing to suffer through a chick flick she wanted to see even if he didn't always manage to stay awake.

"A true Renaissance man," Nate said. "A man after my own heart."

She said he got along tolerably well with her family. "Though I don't think he likes the idea of being a grandpa." She added a snicker and slight shake of her head, amused by that.

"Yep. Sounds decent to me, lots to like there. But you left out his best quality, the most important one, in my mind."

"Really? And which is…?"

"He's in love with you. And in my book, that makes him damned near perfect."

Julie stopped and looked at him with wide eyes. It was a lightning-quick sense of wonderment that puzzled him. The fact that Festerhaven was in love with her was hardly a news flash, so that wasn't what he saw in her face. Maybe she had never thought about what another person's love in general, and Festerhaven's love specifically, said about her. Made her special. Maybe she was amazed that someone like Nate would think so. Maybe nobody had ever told her.

"Thank you for saying so."

The pause that followed was only a single heartbeat, but long enough that he was sure something passed between them. She was the one who flinched first and started walking again. He stayed behind. She turned, he knew she was watching him but he didn't mind. He closed his eyes and savored the moment.

"What are you doing?"

"Who knows if we'll ever share this feeling again? One thing I'm trying to get better at is taking more time to enjoy each moment, in case this, this walking with you again becomes nothing more than cool memory thirty years from now. I wish I had that kind of perspective when we were in high school."

Julie raised a thumb to her lips, nibbling on her nail thoughtfully. "I guess it takes years to appreciate a moment. It isn't special until then."

"Yeah, but I want it to be special now. Is that asking too much?"

"Yes, it probably is. But still, I'm glad you fixed it up for this little field trip, as you called it, getting a group together for milkshakes and sodas, of all things." She was watching her feet as she added, "And I'm glad you're back. You got me thinking about a lot of things, like what good friends we were and how it feels to have a friend like you again."

Nate never had a problem being a friend. Tried and true, someone who would have your back whether you deserved it or not. But if she thought of their relationship now as being just friends—that was friends with a little "f" as opposed to the big "F"—well, how the hell was he going to get around that? Back in high school, they had dated a few times but had never gotten serious because, as Eppie pointed out, he was a doofus who didn't tell her how seriously "in like" he was with her. Back then, he had plenty of time to tell her, an entire life ahead of them. But now, he was fifty-five and he didn't have time to be "just..."

"Friends?"

"Of course. What else would we be?"

Nate knew there would never be a better moment to make his case for better or worse. It was the moment he wanted. Even if she rejected him, she would know the truth, and he could live or die with that. He stopped on the sidewalk so that she was forced to turn and face him with the sunlight in her face. She raised her left hand to shield her eyes and the light set off a miniature fireworks display bouncing off the diamond on her ring.

He had perfected the fraud of hiding disappointment through the years, and Julie put him at the top of his game that afternoon by dropping the F word—friends—on him. "We could be *Best Friends*. Best ever," he said. Then he laughed.

They walked the rest of the way to the school chatting about things he paid no attention to. In his ear, he heard Eppie whispering over and over.

"You pussy."

CHAPTER TWENTY
Keeping Score

"Nate Evans, you are a stud. Let me kiss your big stick."

"Russ, if it wasn't for the sexual connotation in that, I'd be happy to oblige. Better if we just high-five. Maybe a chest bump?"

"Then let me buy you a beer, buddy." The Master Batters, Fester-haven's softball team in the over-fifty league, gathered around three tables they pulled together in the clubhouse of the softball complex. Whoopin' and hollerin' was the sport of the moment. You'd think they'd just won the World Series after knocking off the best team in their league for the first time ever.

"Thanks, Captain." Nate was sipping on a Pepsi. On most softball days, a beer would have been natural, but not today. Julie was sitting to his right. She had ordered a soda, and Nate didn't want her to drink him under the table. He leaned in as she checked the scorebook she had kept during the game. "I take it these guys don't win many games."

Julie smiled. She added up the totals for hits, runs, runs-batted-in on the bottom row. "Hardly ever."

"You'd never guess our Mr. Principal could let his hair down like this, that is, if he had any hair to speak of. Totally different dude away from campus."

"It's not just on campus. Trust me."

Well, if anyone would know, Julie would be his go-to resource on the matter. Festerhaven appeared much more relaxed away from school, but Nate still thought he was wound tighter than a girdle on a three-hundred-pound diva.

"When I got here, he was supervising the players during warm-ups like they didn't know how to stretch or play catch. He busted that guy over there —Mike?—for sneaking a beer before the game like he was coming down on one of the students. He takes this manager role way too seriously."

Julie disappointed Nate by defending her fiancé too quickly. "He can be a sweetheart, when the mood strikes him, and it does, I think, more often than he realizes. But he also has a competitive streak you wouldn't believe. When we win, he gets a little crazy. And when he gets to drinking and winning, well, things can get interesting." Julie said this with an air of amused tolerance.

It had been a month since their trip to the Dairy Barn and their walk back to campus when he'd declared his undying "friendship" for her. In that time, he had established ground rules for the relationship. Of course, Julie had no idea the rules existed. She would treat him like a good friend back from the past, and he would spend their time together trying to convince himself he was good with that. The problem was, it was getting harder to live with his self-imposed rules of engagement—hers to Russell. The trade-off was he got to spend more time with her than he might otherwise.

This teaching gig wasn't bad. The kids were a riot, and he found it easy to deal with them on their level. If he didn't have to run the classroom, he could have been one of them. And he liked the other teachers. They were becoming an extended family. Nate scored big with the principal when Julie told him he'd been captain of the high school baseball team, good enough to have snagged a college scholarship to a school in southern California. Festerhaven recruited him on the spot to join the softball team and jokingly threatened to make his life miserable at school if he refused.

Julie finished and closed her scorebook. "Not bad, Evans, for a rookie. Four for four, you're batting a thousand. You scored three runs, with five runs batted in. Five ribbies including the winning run."

"Ribbies? Ooh. I love it when you talk dirty to me." Nate jabbed her with his elbow and watched the rosy sunburn on her cheeks turn a shade darker while she avoided his eyes. Still, she giggled. That made him five for five on the day even though he wasn't going to score this time.

"Let's not mention to the Russ-ter that my scholarship only lasted that first year."

"I didn't know that. Too bad."

"That's what the coach said. He said I was 'too bad' to keep on scholarship." Ba-da-bump! He waited for her to laugh. "Actually, he asked me to stay on the team, but it was clear I wouldn't be playing much, so that's when I hung up my cleats and figured since I was already enrolled, maybe I should try my hand at studying for a change."

He didn't tell Julie that he intended to move back to San Jose and finish college close to home. The first thing he did at the start of summer break was go looking for her. It was Julie's mother who told him she had gotten married a month earlier. How crazy was that? Barely a year out of high school, nobody got married that young. If Nate had known she was that serious about a guy, he would have gone back to San Jose sooner, and he would have… he would have… What would he have done? Probably exactly what he was doing now, he lamented, letting the guy who stole her heart buy him a beer.

"Here you go," Festerhaven said. Nate took the bottle, raised it and sipped along with Festerhaven. He set it aside as soon as the captain of the Master Batters moved on to a group of players, wives and girlfriends who were standing closer to the bar.

"I'm glad they let me fill in today. Looks like your fiancé is having himself a righteous good time." Odd. Festerhaven seemed to be paying a tad more attention to a leggy blond in tight jeans standing next to him than the others. He touched her elbow for the third time in the last two minutes. Nate watched his hand linger a bit too long. No, he must be seeing things he only wanted to see. Still, who was her player? She didn't seem to be attached to anyone in particular though she had a wedding ring with a rock so big it must have been a strain to lift her left hand.

"Dream faster, Nate. She's taken," Julie interrupted.

"Huh?"

"Loretta. She's married to Aaron, the guy you replaced today. Aaron's out of town again. He's probably the best player on the team, but you are way better. At least you were today."

"It's nice that she came to watch the team anyway, even with her old man away. Now *that* is a fan."

"She always shows up even when her husband is traveling. And Loretta keeps score for me when I can't be here. Though I don't think she pays attention; the scorebook is always a mess and useless." Her brow narrowed as she watched them at the bar. Chink. Was that the faint sign of discord?

"Shouldn't you be over there having fun with the Russ-ster?"

"I don't think so. Russell is in his element and I like it just fine here."

So did he. Just friends, of course. Those were the ground rules. Besides, the principal didn't deserve to be stabbed in the back by a romance-killing interloper. Nate knew too well what it felt like to be on the wrong side of that blade. Oh, but how he'd love to hear Julie say, "Interlope me."

"I'm running late. I've got to go." Julie tucked the scorebook into her purse, and Nate snapped out of his dream. "Mom's birthday is tomorrow and we're going to have dinner and a cake at Tiffany's house tonight. I have to pick up the cake on the way home."

Nate stood up as Julie checked in with Festerhaven at the bar before she pulled him aside, just enough space for a private exchange. They were disagreeing about something before she surrendered and gave him a cute little peck on the cheek. Nate met her halfway to the door.

"I'm glad you came out to play today," she said. "Do me a favor? Make sure he gets home safely. He swears he's okay to drive, but promise me you'll take a bat to him and take his keys if he stays for one more round."

"Absolutely." He saluted her.

For someone in a hurry, Julie dawdled outside clubhouse, pausing at the top of the steps down to the parking lot. She looked back at the door like someone with misgivings about her decision to leave. Or, in Nate's mind, like someone who was jealous and worried about leaving Russell with the blond. She shook her head. It was subtle, but his antennae were up and running. She turned and he followed her to the bottom of the steps and toward her car.

"Carla and I were talking about you the other day. She thinks, *she* thinks you're just a big kid. In a good sort of way, and I told her you've always been like that. She has this theory that you rub off on people. Carla says you're contagious."

"Of course. You know, I never told you my middle name is Peter. As in Pan, right?"

"I did not know that," she said, playing along with him as if awed by the revelation.

"And how about you? Are you feeling young, youngish, younger, or whatever? Have you caught this bug I seem to be spreading?"

"No. I built up an immune system to you back in high school."

Nate stopped. It was a goofy little thing, but the whole day put him in a goofy mood.

"What?"

He stood there, listening to the music coming from the speakers bolted along the eaves of the clubhouse along the deck. "I thought for a moment they were playing our song. I was wrong. Come on."

"Wait. What song? We didn't have a song. We never had a song."

Gotcha. "Oh, Jules. It hurts to think you don't remember. You know our song. The one you said would always remind you of me."

He could tell there was a hint of doubt in her mind. "We didn't have a song. You're making that up."

"Of course I'm making it up. But trust me, if we did have a song, I would definitely remember it. Would you? I remember most every-thing about those days."

"Of course I'd remember a song. If we had one. Which we didn't.

You don't forget things like that. Not if they're important. Which they aren't."

"Jules, you're full of it. Every memory is important in its own way."

"For you, maybe, but I'm not stuck in the past."

They reached Julie's car, and she opened the door so that it became a barrier between them. She glanced at the clubhouse as if distracted by a vexing thought. He turned his head but saw nothing unusual. When he turned back, she was leaning against the door, grinning, eyes dancing, and Nate knew she was about to waylay him.

"All right, smarty pants. If every memory is so important to you, how about this? I'll bet you can't tell me the first time you kissed me."

Julie's eyes darted down immediately. "Forget I said that. I shouldn't have." She was embarrassed. She ought to be, after a sophomoric flirtation like that. It was, Nate thought, right in his wheelhouse. Ironically the answer was sophomore year and Nate could knock this one out of the park.

"Summer before sophomore year started. Susan Ross threw a party and we were slow dancing in the garage. We were dancing to…. Well, I'm sure it was our song, whatever song it was, and I kissed you right then. Right on the lips for the first time."

He watched her jaw actually drop in amazement, stunned that he not only pulled that one out but that he could do it with zero hesitation.

"I don't believe it."

"See?"

"I can't believe you don't remember. You are so wrong. Not even close, Nate. That was not the first time. You are so wrong," she repeated.

Nate searched her face; Julie was seriously smug and enjoying it. What had he missed? No, he had to be right. "Okay, if it wasn't that dance, and I distinctly remember a kiss there in the dark, what was it?"

But Julie just laughed at him and climbed into her car. She rolled down the window. "This was strike one. Two more and you're out." She left it at that.

His bladder was straining to hold all that soda on his way back to the clubhouse, so he headed straight for the men's room before he returned to collect FesterFace and head for home. The Master Batters crowd was woefully thin at that point, leaving the principal with the stragglers, Jim, the catcher, and his wife, and Loretta, the stunning blond in tight jeans—sans husband. Festerhaven was settling up with the bartender. It was time to go.

When Nate finished and went back into the bar, Festerhaven was helping Loretta out the door with his palm on her butt. He gave the room one last furtive look but didn't see Nate in the far corner behind the pool table. Nate waited three beats and then rushed to the door, poking his head out before walking the deck down to the corner of the clubhouse. They were in the parking lot now. He watched Fester-Stud lean his body, starting with his groin, against an obviously will-ing Loretta, pressing her back against the side of an ocean-blue BMW. It was a made-for-movie scene Nate could write in his sleep, the kind that had caused him more than one stiff night alone in bed. The couple shared a little sugar that involved hands, hips and, Nate assumed, tongues. Festerhaven stroked her throat down to and inside her blouse where it buttoned at her cleavage. Checking to see her bra was fit prop-erly, no doubt. Then she danced around the car to the driver's side while he climbed into the passenger seat of the BMW. The tires kicked up gravel as they took off, leaving Festerhaven's SUV behind, aban-doned one parking space over.

CHAPTER TWENTY-ONE
A Family Affair

From the ball field to the tub. Julie spent that Saturday giving her youngest grandchild a bath. Morgan was five, small but hardly frail. She almost got lost amid the floating boats and critters and soap bubbles. Julie scooped up a handful of suds and toyed with her, threatening to dab them on her nose, to the mixed horror and delight of the girl.

"Gramma, you're silly," Morgan said as she took soap bubbles that rose over the sea of bathwater like a thunderhead. She turned her palms out and pushed them toward Julie's face.

"No, Morgan is silly." Julie leaned closer and blew them back. Giggles all around. Julie stroked her cheek. Morgan had her mother's high, full cheeks and dark eyes, the same ones that Tiffany had inherited from Julie. The two older children, Tiffany's twin boys, were good kids and all, but this one was the light of Julie's life.

Tiffany had a cup of tea waiting for her when they wandered into the kitchen after bath time. Julie took it through the sliding glass door to the deck off the kitchen, where Tiffany's husband, Joe, was poking at the charcoal in a kettle grill. She squeezed his arm as she passed, but he was too intent on getting the coals in a perfect bed of heat to notice.

Thin clouds provided a veil through which a nearly full moon watched over them.

She joined her mother, who was leaning back in a cushioned patio chair with a blanket across her lap, warming her toes at a metal fire pit on the far corner of the deck. Mother was nursing a glass of rosé that Julie knew was seventy percent water with only a dab of wine. Though with one more of those, Mom would tell everyone how tipsy she was getting.

After talking about this and talking about that and talking about nothing at all, Mother finally asked, "How are things with your young man, the principal?"

"They're going well, Mom." It was the same discussion they had had only an hour earlier. And the day before yesterday. And the week before that. It wasn't that her mother was nagging Julie; age was stealing Mom's memory. Some conversations simply vanished as soon as they ended, as if they never existed at all. This was one of them.

"When are you going to bring him around so we can all meet him? He sounds nice enough."

"Mom, he was at my house. We had dinner together last week. Don't you remember?"

"Oh, so he was. I did forget," she said with some amusement. "These days are all running together, these days." Julie wasn't convinced. Mother refused to concede she was slipping.

"He wanted to be here this evening," she told her mother. No need to mention that softball and beer got in the way. It was probably better this way.

"I think he's good for you, Julie. I hope we get to meet him before the wedding."

"Oh, Mom."

She now had Russell agreeing to a wedding in early summer, after the school year, with the actual date still to be determined, though she would have preferred one over Christmas break. It seemed like a long time to wait but, for Russell, it hinged on when, not whether, he got hired as the new school district assistant superintendent. He was consumed with that, and while he was annoyed the school board was dragging its feet to fill the position, he believed the trip to Hawaii had helped cement his relationship with Superintendent Fox. She smiled. The two days she spent with Russell after the conference had done wonders for their relationship, too.

Tiffany came up behind them, handed her grandmother a new glass with ice cubes and a spritz of pink wine as light as the last minutes before sunrise, and plopped heavily into a third chair at the fire. "Joe's putting the burgers on; dinner's in a few. Are we talking about The Boyfriend?"

"I think this Mr. Russell fellow is good for her," her mother said. Then to Julie, "He seems to make you happy, and that's nice."

"He does. And it is," Julie said with a sigh.

Tiffany said Julie's mood had been even better lately. Julie asked, "When was I ever in a bad mood?"

"You know what I mean, Mom. You're, like, a bit more..." Tiffany searched for words. "Perkier. Peppier these days."

"Happier," Julie's mother offered.

Any other time, Julie might have been tempted to simply dismiss the idea, but given how that Saturday had gone, with its sunny skies, winning the softball game and giving Russell a jolt of joy that spilled over into camaraderie in the clubhouse that was a rare site for the

Master Batters, and especially getting the better of Nate Evans before she left, Julie was in too good of a mood to argue.

Tiffany called out to her husband standing over the hamburgers to check on the children. The sound of mischief was floating from the living room. Then she continued, "Let me give you an example."

"Okay."

"Last week when we came over and Joe spent most of the day fixing that rattle in your car? And you put your arm around him and told him what a good husband he is, and how much you appreciated that?"

"He fixed my car. Of course I was going to tell him I appreciated it."

Tiffany shook her head. "No, you said how much you appreciate what a good husband he is. When have you ever said anything like that?"

"I've never heard it," Julie's mother said. She was staring at the weak wine in her hand. "Goodness. I think I'm getting tipsy."

"Come now, Tiffany. You know I love Joe," Julie said. Though if pressed, she might admit love was a bit of a stretch. When the kids first got married, it felt as if Joe was stealing away her daughter, forcing Tiffany to choose between mother and husband. The daughter chose the husband.

Duh.

Once upon a time, Julie imagined Tiffany would have done better if she had waited. Joe was quiet and kind, a simple man and decent provider, content with his job in a motorcycle repair shop. In a word, he was everything Julie's husband had been. Competent. Boring. Safe. When she couldn't cry at James' funeral, Julie realized that instead of finding a soul mate, she had too quickly settled for a safe mate. She thought Tiffany had done the same. She was wrong.

The kids were madly in love and didn't hesitate to show it. It was embarrassingly cute at times. Joe adored her daughter. Julie wished she knew how that felt.

"Mine was a stinker," Julie's mother said to no one in particular. "But I loved him, too."

Julie raised her cup of tea and the three women toasted to all the good husbands everywhere. They might be few and far between, but these girls had snagged their share. The sliding glass door scraped open, and little Morgan ran ahead of her father onto the deck. He turned to the barbeque grill; she ran to Julie's side. Morgan wore her jammies and a plush panda hat that draped over her ears. "Daddy says dinner is weddy." She tugged on Julie's hand.

"I'm ready, too," Julie's mother said as she stood. Then, after two cautious steps, "Oh. I don't think I can make it to the dining room. I'm sure I'm half-snockered now."

"Mother, there isn't enough wine in that glass to get a hummingbird high," Julie told her.

"Really? Well. Then maybe I should have another. Tiffany, fix me another one, please. Just don't make it so strong this time."

Julie patted her granddaughter on the behind to scoot her into the kitchen, and then she looped her arm through Joe's as he heaped the burgers onto a serving plate. She leaned her head against his shoulder.

"Joe, in case I haven't said it enough, I'm glad to have you in the family. You make Tiff happy and that makes me happy."

"I try." He lowered the lid on the grill. Then he asked, "So what do you think?"

"About what?"

"I thought Tiff told you. Didn't she tell you yet? I got that promotion. Crockett gave me the news yesterday."

Julie followed him into the kitchen and turned her back on Joe as she slid the glass door shut. "The new shop in Texas? Your own shop. That's wonderful," she said. "I don't know what to say."

Actually, Julie knew exactly what to say. She wanted to tell him to turn the job down and that he couldn't possibly consider uprooting her family and moving them a million miles away from her. Texas, no less. First her youngest, Daniel, went off to college in Oregon and decided to stay. He had a great job as a graphic designer for a cemetery headstone company, but it didn't pay enough for frequent trips back home. Now Tiffany was leaving, taking Joe and the boys and little Morgan away?

"I'm happy for you, Joe. You certainly deserve it." Julie suddenly felt very cold.

Talk over dinner rarely strayed far from the excitement of Joe's new job and the impending move. It was a life-changing one for Tiffany and the kids and, to Julie's way of thinking, for the family being left behind. She got teary as she wiped applesauce from little Morgan's face, her big brown eyes twinkling at Julie. The darling was going to grow up without her.

Her eyes went from moist to weepy as she sat in her car outside Tiffany's house before leaving. She felt abandoned. Damn. They weren't even gone yet, and she already missed her family so much. Julie took out her phone and dialed Russell's number. His voice, recorded and telling her to leave a message, was no comfort.

"Call me as soon as you get this message," she told the phone. Thinking that sounded too foreboding she added, "It's not an emergency, but call me just the same. It doesn't matter how late. I'll be up."

She had sent him a text message earlier in the evening, before she got the good news about Joe's promotion that depressed her so. No response. Now he wasn't answering his home phone. Nate had promised to get Russell home safely. He probably went straight to bed. Julie left the neighborhood and headed for Russell's house. He might grump at her for waking him up, but she really needed a hug right now and a warm body to snuggle with and comfort her through the night.

But somewhere on the drive an irrational irritation steered her away. It was unfair that he wasn't there when she needed him, even if he didn't know it. That wasn't his fault, but she told herself if he had been at the dinner to begin with, she wouldn't have to show up at his door unexpectedly. Now she was lonely and miffed. Instead of driving to Russell's, she pulled into the parking lot of the Happy Yen Mini Mart and Texas Barbecue. She sat in the car and watched Mr. Nguyen through the storefront windows, feeling heavy, as if she had gained two hundred pounds and it was all pressing her into the seat of her little Ford. Tears trickled onto her cheeks.

Julie dried her eyes, steeled herself and went into the Happy Yen. It barely registered when Mr. Nyguen told her it was too late to buy a lottery ticket; the drawing had been an hour earlier. She walked out of the store with a pint of ice cream. At least she wouldn't have to share it with anyone, but then, that was the problem.

CHAPTER TWENTY-TWO

Carla Weighs In

"So is Nate your Plan B now?" Carla wanted to know.

"More like Plan Z, I would think."

Carla poshed that idea. "He's nice-looking. He seems smart enough and funny as all get-out. I like him. If you ask me, he's interested in you. If he wasn't in the running for Plan B, why did you kiss him?"

"Carla! I did no such thing."

"You thought about it."

"Not even. How many times do I have to say it?"

"Okay, you flirted a little."

That was closer to the truth. She hadn't meant it as a flirt when she asked Nate about their first kiss. It just came out, unchecked. It was childish, actually, and so unlike her. Carla made it sound as if the exchange was something to be embarrassed about. But when it came to blowing things out of proportion, Carla was Mount Vesuvius. If she was honest, she had asked the question without knowing the answer herself. She simply hadn't thought about it enough. She was shocked that Nate had so easily called up a kiss long forgotten even if she was convinced it wasn't the right answer.

It was Wednesday afternoon, and they walked along Los Gatos Creek late in the day. She wanted to think. She wanted to clear her head. The problem was every time she cleared it, Carla would fill her head with something else. It wasn't until the subject of her chat with Nate came up that she found herself marching and working up a sweat.

"I'm starting to understand why you were in love with him back in high school."

"I was never 'in love' with Nate Evans." She scratched quotation marks on the air with her free hand, then used a corner of the towel hanging around her neck to dab her cheek. They were only a mile down the trail. The way she was huffing and puffing, she was glad Carla was walking with her; it meant she'd have a good excuse to stop and turn at the park ahead. "Maybe I sort of had a *crush* on him, just typical teenage stuff."

"Right. Well, I like my version better. Can we slow down a little, please?" Carla wheezed. Julie pulled a water bottle from the small of her back, where she had tucked it into a waist pack, and took a slow, measured sip. Carla pulled even with her, asking exactly why they were there. "You asked if I wanted to go for a walk, but this isn't a walk. This is work."

"We haven't been getting much exercise. I think it may be time to start getting out on a regular basis again."

"Okay. But warn me next time. I'll buy some running shoes and wait in the car."

Julie stopped and toed a rock from the middle of the path. "I wish you'd let it go. We don't need to talk about him."

"Have it your way, Miss Snippy Pants. It's more fun needling you about Nate than watching you torture yourself over Tiffany moving away. I'm trying to take your mind off the worse of two evils. If you want to call flirting with him evil. I don't think it's so bad. No disrespect to Russell, of course."

"Well, Nate probably thought so. I think he respects Russell and the relationship we have." But she was having doubts. She worried he was avoiding her since the weekend. When their paths did cross, there was something she couldn't identify in his eyes, like a mixture of disappointment and pity. Maybe he thought her a silly fool. Maybe she deserved it. But if anybody would have had fun with the way she teased him that Saturday in the parking lot, it would be Nate Evans. Go figure.

He had apologized for letting her down and not keeping a closer eye on Russell to make sure he got home safely. But that wasn't it. Anyway, Russell had explained that away. He didn't drive himself home; he got a ride from one of the other players.

They started walking again and said little until they reached the park and stopped to rest on a picnic bench before heading back. She sat there and didn't listen to whatever Carla had to say. Then she asked, "Have you ever wished you could freeze time? Stop life right where you are so that nothing changes, and you don't have to worry about what's coming?"

"I might if I ever find myself lounging in a hot tub filled with chocolate and Brad Pitt right beside me with his hand on my knee."

"Ever since Tiffany said they were moving away…" She left it at that. The future had become unsettled. Nate Peter Pan Evans had her thinking a lot about the past, but Julie wanted to stay right there in the present. Then she would always have her daughter and her darling granddaughter. And she could savor the anticipation of marrying

Russell. If she could stop life in its tracks, she would keep her family nearby and enjoy the love she shared with Russell without having to deal with the overwhelming uncertainty that had gotten its grips on her. "I wonder if it will last."

"What will?"

"Things."

"I hate to see you like this. But you'll get through it. And I doubt it will be as bad as you think."

Sometimes she feared it might be worse.

They walked back down the trail in silence, keeping to the shady side under the spruce trees.

"Don't you think it's more than a little strange that this Nate guy from out of your past should show up where you work, the same high school you went to together?" Carla asked. "Poof. Out of thin air just like that. I think it's an omen."

"I think it's a coincidence."

"No. Coincidence is this guy you had *a crush on* comes back into your life at exactly the moment you suddenly want to get out and start jogging to get some exercise. Coincidence is this guy you had *a crush on* comes along exactly when you've started to worry about the way you're dressed. Coincidence is this guy you had *a crush on* comes along exactly when you decide it's been far too long since you got a new cut and color. I really like your hair this way, by the way, this shorter cut is just different enough to be different. That's coincidence, I guess. But I think it's an omen."

"An omen."

"Yeah. This guy you had *a crush on* in high school shows up at the exact moment you're about to marry someone else. That's an omen."

"For someone who teaches science, you are the most irrational person I know."

"So let's get into the math of probabilities if you want to. What are the probabilities of Nate showing up right now? Probably less than your chance of winning the lottery. That's a scientific omen."

Julie surrendered. "If you say so. But I don't like the way you keep emphasizing that *guy you had a crush on* like it was anything more than that." Carla was starting to annoy her, even if her chatter did keep Julie from thinking about losing her family to Texas. "You're not going to make me wish I never said anything about it, are you?"

"You know I will. It's what I do. But never mind. I still think the timing of all this is strange."

Exasperated, she asked, "What are you getting at, Carla?"

"Maybe it really is an omen. Wait. Today's Wednesday, right? Have you bought your lottery ticket yet?"

Julie said she planned to stop and pick up dinner and buy a ticket on the way home.

"Maybe the lotto is speaking to you. Maybe you should use numbers you know about Nate, like his birthday. You could use that for two numbers."

"How am I supposed to know what his birthday is? Or remember it if I ever knew it in the first place?"

"You could check his personnel file."

"Carla! I'm not going go snooping like that."

"No. Of course not. And you shouldn't. That's my job. It's February twenty-seventh."

"You are certifiable."

"Where's your spirit of adventure?"

"I left it back in the eighties, remember?"

Carla told Julie she was no fun. "Isn't buying those stupid tickets a lark anyway? I'm telling you, it could be an omen. You could use his birthday and your birthday, the month and the day. That leaves just two other numbers to pick."

When they reached the parking lot, Carla asked, "What kept you two from becoming a thing in school?"

It was a question that tweaked Julie. "Can we stop talking about Nate?"

"Okay. If it's a sore subject."

"Which it isn't." She should have expected this when she told Carla about the kissing memory flirt—it really *was* unintentional, she reminded herself. "There's not much to tell. We hung around with the same group at school. We dated a few times, nothing serious; he dated several girls. We went to the same parties and hung out with friends after the football games."

"But you had a crush on him."

"Like I told you, who didn't? He was that kind of boy everybody liked. And Nate liked everybody. Especially the girls."

"Oh. One of those. A heartbreaker, huh?"

Julie toyed with that thought. Things sure looked different now. "I don't think it was intentional. I think Nate was having too much fun to even realize it."

"So you're saying he was clueless."

Julie laughed. "Yep. Think of it this way. Nate is like a puppy that runs around being adorable and makes you laugh. He's affectionate, and just when he gets to your heart, he piddles on your shoe and goes off chasing after a rabbit. That's why he can't possibly be Plan B."

"Because he piddles on shoes."

"Because he won't stay around. One week we'd have a date and I'd get my hopes up, then I'd be mad at him a few days later because he would be taking some other girl out. I'd have a good cry and get over it just in time for him to ask me out again. Date. Rinse. Repeat. Let's go. I have some homework to do tonight. I have to find some way to spin something more positive from the test scores report. Russell wants something to show to Superintendent Fox. He's still lobbying hard for the assistant super's position, and the poor guy can't seem to put together a decent proposal without me. Or so he says."

"Yeah, and I have a lesson to prepare." Carla paused with her hand on the car door. "It's so disappointing, though. I was expecting some real sparks. I thought maybe you were sweethearts torn apart. Voted the cutest couple, queen and king of the prom, things like that."

Julie didn't answer. She wanted to get off the subject but, after another long pause, couldn't resist. "Actually Nate talked about going to the prom, but he asked another girl instead. She was the prom queen."

"Ah ha!"

"Oh, this is childish. I was over it like that." She snapped her fingers.

"Good. Now I don't have to like him. But like you said, it's hard to not like him. Still, I say buy a lottery ticket just the same. You never know."

Julie was still chuckling over the absurdity of Carla's suggestion when she stopped at the Happy Yen Mini Mart and Texas Barbecue and filled in the numbered bubbles on her lottery ticket. Nate's birthday. Her birthday. Then she looked past the naked fluorescent lights to the gritty ceiling.

"I did my part. It's up to you now." Then she filled in two more numbered bubbles on the lottery slip without paying attention to where the pen landed

Stupid?

Sure.

An omen?

Hardly.

But what the heck, they were as good as any other numbers. She couldn't remember the last time the lottery had come even close to her picks. They certainly weren't going to start now. Nate Evans couldn't change that.

CHAPTER TWENTY-THREE
Nate de Bergerac

Kick. Push. Glide.

By the following Monday morning, Nate was more depressed than ever. Things were totally effed up.

Kick. Push. Glide. He leaned and steered his skateboard through a slight curve and a mild slope down the sidewalk. Wobbly, he had to concentrate to maintain his balance. Skateboarding used to be second nature to him once upon a time; now his reflexes were slow, his balance was bad, and, worse, he couldn't do it fearlessly like he did as a teen. Fear and gravity were the greatest threats to competent boarding. He cruised down the street with a hand on the bandage that covered most of his chin, hiding the road rash he got from a face plant on the way home from school on Friday. Maybe it was time to buy an alternative mode of transportation. He could afford a car now. Granted, the starting teacher's salary didn't measure up to the allowance a couple of his students pulled down each month. But they were the exception at MHHS.

He had played two games with Festerhaven's softball team over the weekend. Only two weak hits along with two errors, a lackluster performance at best. He couldn't concentrate. Aaron, the husband of Festerhaven's throat-hockey partner, was there, and the way Loretta stayed near his side, you'd never guess she had a double play going with the principal. Festerhaven, for his part, was more attentive to Julie, and it put an extra spark in her day. Worse, Aaron turned out to be a decent guy and a great teammate and didn't deserve to have his world crushed if Nate ratted out his wife. Julie would hate him for tattling on her fiancé. They were two hearts he didn't want to break, even if it wasn't his fault. More to the point, it was none of his business. Nate wished he had Carla Almeida's brass ovaries, sex change notwithstanding. She considered everything her business, and he doubted she would find anything wrong with setting the record straight with all the parties involved.

Lean left. Lean right.

Kick. Push. Glide.

Stumble. Stop. Remount.

He rolled past two students on the sidewalk approaching the school. They were several feet apart, and he took them on like cones on a slalom course. He had his Giants cap on backwards and wore Panama Jack sunglasses and an oversized Hawaiian shirt. Somewhere in the nineties, he guessed, the dress code changed for teachers in the public schools. The fashion line separating the faculty and the students crumbled like the Berlin Wall. He had been such a dweeb showing up to class in a tie that first week. His mother approved of the laid-back look and gave him some of Charlie's old tie-dyed shirts from the sixties to wear. If he couldn't be the most respected teacher on campus, he would definitely be the coolest.

Kick. Push. Whoa! Steady, fella.

Nate stumbled off his skateboard as he took the corner at the end of a wall of lockers outside the English quad, pulled down by a strong hand.

"Mr. Evans. What do you think you're doing?"

"Oh. Hey, Russ. I mean, Mr. Festerhaven."

Two girls snickered as they stepped around the men. Nate had seen plenty of smirks from students as he wheeled each morning onto campus and the "what-the-iff#@?" looks from a couple of teachers. But a "what-the-eff#@?" look from the principal was not a good way to start the day.

"That sign over there that says no skateboarding on campus means no skateboarding," Festerhaven said. "Don't think you get a pass because you are faculty. You don't. If I could, I'd have you in detention and send a note home to your parents."

If only. Nate answered to his parents every day, and would as long as he went on living in their house, which could be forever at this rate. Sure, he could afford to move out, but that would ruin the fantasy he had crafted. He was determined to live with his parents at least through graduation in the spring to find out where this story, this life was going to take him. Another big plus, the bedroom at his parents' place felt safe and comfortable. He could understand why moving back home was all the rage with millenials these days. If Festerhaven knew that little fact, he might try to send a note home to Mom and Dad, so his threat wasn't entirely empty. Then again, Nate's mother would tear it up and toss it like so many of the disciplinary tickets he had gotten for rogue but harmless behavior as a teen. Mom believed a little civil disobedience was good training for the real world.

"In fact it is worse than if you were a student. Set an example and be an adult." Festerhaven frowned. The principal wasn't impressed with Nate's classroom attire.

FesterBoss had a good sense of humor when he wanted, though used it sparingly on campus. Maybe that was part of the job. He kind of, sort of, almost liked the guy and Nate could see why Julie attached herself to him even if he didn't deserve her. If only she knew... He tucked the skateboard under his arm and walked off, his conscience following close behind.

"He's a liar and a cheat," it hissed in his left ear.

"It's none of your business," it screamed in his right.

He had first period free, so he went to the music department. Seth Naylor asked him to drop in for a talk.

Nate sat down on a stool next to the music teacher's desk at the front of the room. He picked up a guitar and plucked notes, searching for the opening riff from "Stairway to Heaven." He knew it once upon a time.

Seth blushed as he turned his iPad so that Nate could see the picture on the screen. "This is Angela."

Nate leaned forward. "Angel Strings. She looks pretty." It was an unflattering selfie posted on the dating site called WinkConnection.com. Nate had never investigated one of those match sites before. He assumed this one was typical as he read the profile beneath Angel Strings' picture. Played the violin and cello. Worked as a therapist teaching music to kids with disabilities. Liked Mozart and Adele equally.

"It says she's looking for a guy who's not afraid to dance in public. That says a lot. You got any moves?"

"Uh, Arthur Murray Studios. It's been years. Does Salsa count?"

"I hear it's making a comeback."

He reached out with his thumb and finger to enlarge the picture. Angela had red hair pulled back with a wide-open Irish face full of freckles and eyes that, if you could believe the selfie, lacked color. She wasn't a beauty but, as Seth said, her picture wouldn't make you puke. No, actually Angela was cuter than that. He knew that sometimes love was blind, and sometimes it was merely cross-eyed. She had clearly captured Seth's heart. The most remarkable feature Angela had, however, was tiny lips that were quite off-center enough to give the impression she was perpetually perplexed.

He nodded and gave Seth a thumbs-up that provided a kind of validation. "Wink Connection dot com? I never considered you as the type to need help from a dating website. Does it really work as they advertise?"

"My sister found her husband on the Wink app. I'm going to be an uncle now," Seth said with a grin. He said his sister pestered him to give it a try and so he had exchanged online "winks" with a number of women over the past year.

"Did you ever meet any of them?"

"No. I couldn't do that. I mean, I could, but they always lost interest after we got past the winks and flirts and emailed back and forth a few times." He looked at the picture of Angel Strings. Nate thought it was a way to avoid looking at him. "I was hoping I could get your help. You know how to write things. You were talking about writing love scenes for your movies a while back, and it got me thinking. You must be good at it since you've had all that success."

Success? Hardly.

Seth went on, "Me? If it's not on the music scale, I can't write it.

Somebody else has to come up with the lyrics because words fail me. I'm lost. Totally clueless."

It really was that bad. Seth showed him an exchange with a woman called "Snooky Shoes." It was stilted yet rambling, and he was self-deprecating in a way that begged for pity.

"She blocked me from any more emails. You see, I choked. I was trying too hard because she could be the one. Stanford gave her an eight."

Nate asked what Stanford had to do with Seth's love life.

"Oh, some researchers have this compatibility generator online. You go there and plug in everything you know about somebody and what you know about yourself based on a questionnaire. Some of the dating sites do it with their own algorithms to find the perfect match. The Stanford research site is like their match computers, only on steroids."

"My first try was Snooky Shoes, her real name is Lisa, and she scored higher than anyone else after I plugged in all the traits I want to find in a date. But, like I said, I killed it with one bad email. That's why I want your help to keep from screwing it up with Angela."

Snooky Shoes, Angel Strings and computer-driven love; it was all very weird. "She's the perfect match. According to Stanford?"

"Nope. I didn't bother with that. I just know. And I didn't find her, she found me. She liked my profile picture." Seth showed Nate his profile page; the photo didn't have a face. It was a beautiful shot of fingers on the strings of a stand-up bass. MusicMan35. That was his online identity.

"MusicMan35?"

"My work. My age. Seemed to fit."

And then Seth handed him a flyer promoting an evening of jazz at the Renaissance Club at St. Pedro Square downtown.

"This you?"

"It's a little quartet. A couple of college buddies of mine and one's father."

"Are you guys any good?"

Seth smiled and nodded. "I think so. We practice a lot, but we've never tried to approach the clubs. This is our first one."

Nate checked the clock on the wall. The kids would be grateful if he was five minutes late. "I can see why you're jazzed, pardon the pun." He said he wouldn't miss their opening night, and then turned the conversation back to Angel Strings and finding true love.

"You know, thoughts and feelings about things," Seth said.

"Keep it simple. Compliment her about her interesting profile, you are impressed with the work she does, and you have a lot in common, and then suggest you meet up for coffee. Four simple steps and you got yourself a date."

"It's not that simple. Here, read this. How am I going to answer that?"

Nate could see his point. Seth had apparently asked Angel Strings to describe herself. The response was creative but weighed down by references to moonlit walks on the beach, the joy of finding a child's chalk hopscotch on the sidewalk, the smell of rosemary just before it goes into her pasta sauce, and music. A lot of references to music, which made sense given it was the common thread binding these two. Nate reread the email and couldn't decide if Angel Strings was as deep as Emily Dickenson or as shallow as a Kardashian on a good day. Ultimately he decided she was simply a hopeless romantic, like him. He could relate, just not in so many flowery words.

"It's really something."

Seth was up and pacing. He finally sat at the piano bench and poked distractedly with a finger on the keyboard. "I tried writing back, but I couldn't get it to sing. Not like she did."

That was an interesting choice of words, Nate thought.

Seth said, "I want your help. Write something for me just as good. But honest. Exactly how I feel."

"Your feelings, but my words? I'm not sure how honest that is. It sounds so very *Cyrano de Bergerac*." Talk about life imitating art.

"*Cyrano de Bergerac*?"

"Old story. Done a thousand times from Shakespeare to Steve Martin. A guy who is good at romance steps in to, let's say, woo a girl for a friend who's too lame or too ugly—no offense meant there—to do it himself. Think Steve Martin and Darryl Hannah in *Roxanne*. Janeane Garofalo did a chick version with cats and dogs. I even ripped it off myself for a plot one time."

Wrong Face, Wrong Time was still sitting in some studio exec's office long past its shelf life. Hmm, should he dust it off and try again?

"Well, if you've done it before; you can do it for me, can't you? It would mean a heck of a lot."

Sure, Nate felt it shouldn't be a problem, and he'd give it more thought than your average, run-of-the-mill Nate Evans script. Seth played a series of chords and a pretty little riff. He played as if his fingers had a mind of their own, unconcerned with the pressing issue of making a pass at a woman neither one of them knew. It was a tune that touched familiar emotional notes inside him even though he'd never heard it before.

"Okay," Nate said. "But promise me that if this works, you'll bring her to one of my Popcorn Thursday classes. I'm letting the kids bring dates now, for extra credit. Maybe I'll show *Roxanne*. Just for you. In fact, why not come by for the next one anyway? It's always the first Thursday of the month. We start at fifth period and kids get extra credit for staying an hour over to finish the movie. I'll have the popcorn machine set up. Movie and popcorn and soda. What better way to kill an afternoon after school?"

"What are you showing this time?"

"*Tootsie*. Dustin Hoffman. Jessica Lange."

Nate felt as if he'd been tossed into the teaching pool and left to sink or swim with little direction, so for his creative writing class, he simply did what came naturally to him. He watched movies. Now he assigned his students to write film reviews for credit.

By the time Nate left the music room, he had wrung enough of Seth's views on life, love and music to send a response to Angel Strings sure to intrigue her, as well as three different follow-up letters Seth could use depending upon her reaction.

That night he sat on his bed, not ready to sleep, wondering why he was alone at his age. He went to his computer. If you could believe the Internet, over a third of the singles in America were on one dating site or another these days. That was a boatload of lonely people. Seth had told him where to find the Stanford University compatibility website. He started filling in answers to the questionnaire. If there was a Julie Cooper clone, Nate hoped she was out there somewhere.

CHAPTER TWENTY-FOUR
Nate Pops the Question

Dustin Hoffman was marching down a New York City street in a dress and a wig when Julie slipped into Nate's classroom. She stopped at a table set up near the door, picked up a red-striped bag of popcorn and then sat down at a desk next to him in the back of the room. She stared straight ahead, her eyes on the movie that played on a screen in front of about twenty students. She didn't look at him as she silently offered him the bag with one hand while she snacked on the popcorn with the other. Nate took a handful, avoiding her eyes in return. Instead, he looked off past Seth Naylor, who sat on his left, to the window that he had covered with cardboard to darken the room. After the first Popcorn Thursday, two of his students painted a decent image of a theater marquee on the makeshift window blind. *Now Showing!*

Nate could recite every line from *Tootsie* by heart, so he spent the remainder of the movie watching her from the corner of his eye. He was happy to see her, of course, but why did he have this sensation of being trapped? It had been weeks since he'd watched Festerhaven ride off into the sunset from the ball field with another woman, and Nate still hadn't figured out what to do about it. He hadn't been avoiding

Julie, exactly, but he had stopped finding excuses to pass by her office or loiter in the faculty lounge at those times when he knew she was most likely to show up. He dumped on Eppie about his suspicions that FesterScum was two-timing his girl, venting his anger, but agreed that he shouldn't be the one to tattle on him. Not right away. Instead, she had pressed him again to make an honest pitch to Julie about how he felt and see what happened.

"Go big or go home."

Woody also got the story and had advised him in more than one email to "go all Guido on his ass."

Not a bad idea, except that Nate didn't have proof. Twice he found the principal alone, and he had opportunity to talk about work and sports and women and other manly pursuits. Nate hoped that by buddying up and sneaking in a deliberately random leading question, he might get some kind of admission, possibly a locker room screw-and-tell kind of brag, but FesterSnake deflected his attempts to get to the bottom of it.

Julie stuck around after the students had left for the day. Seth lingered, too, and fidgeted with growing impatience like someone waiting outside an occupied bathroom. They made small talk about the movie until it was clear Julie was in no hurry and would outlast him.

"Let's talk later," Seth finally said.

"I'm glad you came by today." Nate began to straighten up the classroom, pushing desks back into neat rows.

"It was fun. I'd never seen that one before."

That was appalling. "You've never seen *Tootsie*? You need to get out more."

"I'll see what I can do about that."

An awkward silence followed; they were like strangers at a dance, neither one knowing how to break the ice.

Finally, she said, "Is it just me? You've been a bit…" She searched for the words. "A bit distant lately. Ever since that little joke I played on you at the softball field lot last month."

"We both got a laugh. Forget about it."

He couldn't.

In fact, she had thrown him a curve. What was she thinking challenging him to recall their first kiss? It sounded like a flirt. It felt like a flirt. He wanted it to be a flirt. He couldn't let go of it, even if he denied it when she asked. In the days that followed, he ran it through his mind over and over like a favorite movie and fantasized about different ways it could have or might play out. He added it to the story he was writing, working so late into the night that he slept through first period the following day. Did she Like him? Not in a friendly, "just friends" way, but Like with a capital L. The kind of Like that takes a guy and gal to the next level, going steady, or whatever the adult equivalent was. Ultimately he convinced himself that just because he wanted it to be flirtatious didn't make it so.

"It's all good," he said to reassure her. He changed the subject and asked about her daughter's big move. "I heard she was going to Texas or some other Godforsaken land far, far away. Are you okay with that?"

"Not really. But I don't have a say in the matter. I'm happy for them, naturally."

She left it there. She was sad, and Nate hated it when people were sad. No, a better description was that Julie was blue. Blue was less problem-specific and more temporary, easier to fix. There was a quiet beauty in being blue; it had been captured by painters and filmmakers through the centuries and seldom failed to tug the heartstrings. He loved the way the fluorescent lights overhead added a yellow tint to her skin and highlighted her hair. The rogue strands of gray were gone and she had added just a few soft, pink highlights. It was a youthful statement that he adored. Although the corners of her mouth turned south, the little creases there that came with age pointed north, hinting that a smile would be back shortly. Julie was the most depressingly beautiful thing he had ever seen.

"Maybe that's the real reason I came by for the movie this afternoon. I was feeling a little down and I thought this would be a pick-me-up."

"Did it work?"

"Yes. It was fun. Plus, you're fun to be around because nothing ever bothers you. And you're so full of..."

"Life?" Nate said.

"No. Shit. Full of shit, but in a good way." Now the smile returned.

"I'm glad I could help." He picked up his backpack and his skateboard, flipped off the lights and held the door for her as they left. The autumn shadows from the library were long and cool as they skirted the fountain, walking back to her office. He stopped and pulled a coin from his pocket, closed his eyes and tossed it in the fountain.

"What did you wish for?"

"For somebody or something to pull you out of this funk you're in today." He wanted to volunteer for the job. It was tempting. He should have wished for someone to come along and resolve for him the static in his brain that was Julie Cooper-Finch and what to do about her. Someone who would take a fist and bang the top of his head to clear up the picture like he used to do to his mother's first black-and-white

TV. "Although I have to say, as funks go, you wear it well," he added. He turned to leave, but she stopped him, holding out a palm and using her eyes to turn his attention to the fountain. He pulled loose change from his pocket. Somewhere he had picked up a gold dollar coin, and he gave it to her.

"I'm not sure this one is worth that much, but here goes." She tossed it high into the air, and it landed only a few inches inside the fountain's rim. Just good enough.

"So what about your wish?"

She hesitated. "To be a little more like you. To have fun without having to schedule it. To not worry so much about things."

"The Julie Cooper I knew used to be like that."

"Me? Never."

"Yes, you. *Fountain Girl.*"

"Never heard of her." Julie chucked him on the arm. He got his wish; she was in a happier place now.

They turned away from the fountain and started down the path to the administration building. Did she just brush the back of his hand with hers as they walked? Was it intentional? They parted at her office door. She went to collect her things; he went to the faculty lounge to stall. Only a few stragglers were left on campus, and Festerhaven's office was dark. Good. He caught up with her as she was leaving the building and walked her to her car. It was a nondescript compact, rental-car white, clean as a whistle and probably paid off, he thought. A perfectly practical choice for a practical person. *Fountain Girl* would have put a bumper sticker on it at the very least, maybe hung a dream catcher from the rearview mirror.

"I've been thinking, wondering actually," she said. "A while back when we all went on that field trip to the Dairy Barn, you asked every-body if they would go back and change something if they could. But you never answered the question yourself. How about it? Would you?"

"In a heartbeat." He answered too quickly. Now he was trapped and would have to face the inevitable follow-up.

"So what would you change?"

"Oh, I'd say only a thousand things or so." He hoped it was sat-isfyingly evasive. "I've thought about some really good ones, but it depends on how far back you want to go to start over."

"Start over? So make it high school. That's what you're doing now, aren't you You are living high school, trying to start over?"

"What makes you say that?"

"Oh, I'd say skateboards. Spending every lunch in the fountain quad. Always talking about people we knew or things that happened back then. It's obvious. It's too obvious. Though I haven't figured out why you're playing this game."

Her eyes were wide and she was neither angry nor dismissive. She was puzzled and waited while he didn't answer, so he told her how life had been beating him like a redheaded step child for years and confessed that he ran away, needing a place to hide until he could get his act together. "I couldn't think of any place better. I suppose, if you want to know the truth, high school was some of the best years of my life."

He dropped his gaze and shuffled one foot. It was too honest for comfort. But, damn her, even when they were teenagers, she was the one girl he ever talked openly with, and she apparently had dusted off that magic. In retrospect, he wished they had spent more time necking and less time talking. It might make it easier to look her in the eye now.

"Did you know I was here when you decided to come back and

get this job at the school?"

She was trying to read him. He turned and stroked the fender of her Ford. His telltale face was why he never played poker anymore, a lesson he wished he had learned before dropping all the money he got for *Dog Days in Denmark* in a card game with the film crew on location in Amsterdam. The monetary hit was almost as painful as what they did with his script. Killing off a major character with a rubber chicken full of poisoned Jell-O was the only element saved from Nate's version.

"Not entirely, but that's part of it." Okay, he thought, that wasn't so hard. If there was ever going to be a time to fish or cut bait, to put up or shut up, strike while the iron was hot and all the other clichés that ran through his mind, the time was right. She watched him, waiting for more—pleading almost, he imagined—for him to say, "Yes, it was all about you." He was trying to find the words when Julie unwittingly gave them to him.

"All right. Now you're back in high school. What are you going to do about it since you have the chance? What's the big thing you would change?"

"Top of my list, huh?" he said. "Remember when we all went up to that swimming hole on the river on the way to Santa Cruz, that summer after graduation? That last get-together before I left for college?

"You had this new boyfriend and kept talking about what a nice guy he was and how happy you were. So naturally, I said I was happy for you to find someone like that. I remember telling you how much I hoped it worked out."

"It seems to me you practically said I should marry him. It sounded that way as I remember."

Nate asked what ever happened to that fellow.

"That was James. I married him."

"Oh. That guy. Well, the point is, all that stuff, all that crap I said was the last thing I wanted to say. Far from it. I was lying. I didn't know enough to tell you the truth."

She seemed unsure, like someone whose canoe had drifted into swift water, who feared there were rapids and rocks ahead. At the same time, she appeared to enjoy seeing him squirm. "Then what did you *really* want to say back then?"

"I should have done back then something like this: I would stop."

He did.

"I would look into your eyes."

He did that, too, putting his hands on her arms and turning Julie to face him.

"And I would say, 'Jules, if you really love the guy you're with, if this is the guy for you and forever, then go for it. I want you to be happy and that's all that matters.'"

"That sounds the same," Julie said.

"Yeah, but today? Let me say, if your guy ever gives you any doubt, any inkling, anything he does that is reason to think twice, like, oh, I don't know, cheating on you or just being an asshole in general, call me. I'll be right there to break his kneecaps. If for any reason at all, you want to consider options, call me. I guess what I'm saying is, I'd gladly be your first option."

"Oh, Nate. I'm speechless."

"That's okay. I talk too much for both of us. Always have."

She looked away. "I'm not comfortable with this. It is sweet, I'll admit. Flattering. You know the situation. Can't we be just friends? Don't spoil it."

Nate's skateboard was at his feet; he pushed it with the toe of his sneaker so that it cleared her car. He followed it, putting his back to her.

"I know the situation better than you imagine." He was angry now. Life had led him to this place and tricked him to love all over again, only to slap him silly. It wasn't fair. He had to leave before he said something he would regret. The truth about FesterCheater was on the tip of his tongue. He put one foot on the deck of his board, planning to skate away, but turned and faced her again.

"Since you asked, I didn't come back so we could be *just friends.*"

"Nate, I didn't ask for this."

"No, you didn't ask for it," he said. "You can't always get what you want. But you just might find you get what you need. Rolling Stones, 1969. Best song featured in *The Big Chill.*"

She called after him but he didn't look back. He rolled away with the song in his head. He could see the funeral scene from the movie as it played. How appropriate. And he thought if that was their relationship in the casket, at least this time it died a noble death.

CHAPTER TWENTY-FIVE
Yearbooks and Yearnings

By the time Saturday afternoon rolled around, Julie had mopped the kitchen floor even though it didn't need it. She had folded the clothes, gotten in a brisk walk, bought roasted chicken and a lottery ticket at the Happy Yen Mini Mart and Texas Barbecue, stared at the weeds that were starting to overrun her planter box in the backyard long and hard as if that would wilt them away, spent twenty minutes on the phone with Tiffany and left a voice message for her son, Daniel, in Oregon. Eventually she ran out of tasks she used as excuses to avoid doing the thing she wanted to do most. It had been on her mind since Nate left her in the school parking lot Thursday.

She went to the closet in what used to be Daniel's bedroom. The right side of the closet, behind the sliding mirrored door that seldom got opened, was stacked with different colored plastic storage bins. White bins were full of useful stuff. Blue ones belonged to the kids. Gray ones, under all the others, held memories. It was in the second bin from the bottom, right where she knew it would be. She pulled it out and walked her high school senior yearbook out to the living room, where she curled up on the couch. She meandered through the pages, spending time with the memories from some more than others. Some, buried deep by the decades, felt fresh again. Others teased her with things she should recall but created only vague and fuzzy feelings. She finally reached a page near the back of the book where the photographer got a camera-about-campus shot of her with Nate, yucking it up with friends on their bench near the fountain. Julie had leaned into Nate and bopped his shoulder with her head over some undoubtedly horrible joke he made. The photograph made it look like they were in love. A cute couple doing what cute couples do.

"Lord, the grief we took over that," she mumbled.

Seeing that picture again warmed Julie not unlike the way she felt as she studied it endlessly when she was seventeen. The photographer got it on an early spring day during one of those brief periods when Julie thought her friendship with Nate was about to go to the next level. Silly girl.

Then she finally got it. Seeing that picture again made her feel something she had forgotten, the feeling Nate was chasing. Sure, if she could make every day give her the kind of innocent joy they shared when that photo was snapped, Julie would want to go back and relive those days, too. She almost made it, too, near the fountain after Popcorn Thursday when their hands touched as they walked. The feeling raised her spirits then, and it was stronger as she sat there with the yearbook in her lap. She laid gentle fingertips on the picture. They were a cute couple.

Nearly an hour later, the doorbell rousted her from a dream. She didn't know when she had fallen asleep, but she woke on the sofa with the yearbook open and face down on her chest. She snapped it shut as she rose. That had to be Russell at the front door, and even though it was ridiculous to think he'd give the picture a second thought if he recognized them, she jumped up with a twinge of embarrassment, the kind that comes with discovering you left a public restroom dragging a foot of toilet paper stuck to the heel of your shoe. Guilt, maybe? Not at all, and she proved it to herself by leaving the book out on the coffee table instead of tucking it on a shelf.

Any vague sense of guilt evaporated when Carla breezed past her after she opened the door.

"You missed a great game last night. We only lost by three touchdowns this week."

"Sounds like an improvement, but I guess Coach Garcia isn't going to do any better than Coach Miles." She leaned out the door and scanned the street. Russell's SUV wasn't there. He had promised her that he'd stop by that afternoon. There wasn't much of the afternoon left.

"You seem healthy. Sound healthy. So what did you do on your sick day yesterday? It wasn't a sudden case of the flu. Have you got any iced tea?"

"I just needed a mental health day," Julie said. "I spent some time with Mom, finally straightened out my closet and took some clothes to Goodwill, ran errands, went to the mall. The usual things."

"Did you buy anything?"

Julie shook her head, so naturally Carla asked how long she spent at the mall.

"A couple of hours, three, maybe." She finally admitted most of that time was browsing with no purpose, wandering and thinking. "Then I came home and I didn't do much of anything after that."

They carried glasses of iced tea back to the living room, where they sat facing each other from the opposite armrests of the sofa. "What's going on?"

So she told Carla about what had happened and where they ended with Nate in the school parking lot on Thursday. "When I said it was a 'mental health' day, I thought it was the best way to avoid him while I sorted things out."

"It's not like you to avoid a good tussle. Especially when you're right."

But being right wasn't very satisfying, and after a restless night floating between the comforting nostalgia Nate inspired and annoyance that, no matter how good his intentions were, he might compromise her happiness with Russell, she called in sick Friday morning.

"So let me get this straight. Tiffany calls on Thursday, and you're talking. She says your mom isn't taking her medications again and you're worried about that. She mentions that Joe left for Texas to look at houses. Okay. Now you're feeling down about that. But instead of coming to me, your best friend, you go spend the afternoon with Nate at his little movie thing. I should be insulted."

"Yes, you should, but that doesn't work because you are impervious to insults. I've tried," she said between sips. "But I've cried on your shoulder enough. And I wasn't feeling all *that* bad. You've seen what he's like, so easygoing and upbeat; I just thought I could use a little Nate Prozac."

"Prozac, huh?"

"Oh, you know what I mean. You're the one who says he rubs off on people."

"And it worked?"

She nodded. "That may be part of the problem now. I was in a bad mood, and I couldn't think of anybody better to cheer me up. He has to stop making me feel good."

"That's bad?"

"It is if it comes between us. Russell and me."

"Just an observation; it's not working, *Jules*."

Her defenses were mounting, but her immediate comeback disappeared, derailed by the snide way Carla used the nickname Nate had given her. No one else called her that. "Jules? Where did you get that? No, I know where you got it. You've been talking with Nate? Tell me you haven't been talking to Nate."

"I haven't been talking to Nate."

"You're lying."

"Of course I'm lying. You told me to, so I did." Carla raised her eyebrows while simultaneously biting her lower lip. "That's what he called you when he stopped by my classroom yesterday asking about you. It must have stuck in my head. Kind of catchy. I like it. Jules. *Jules*. Can I call you that, too?"

She'd been had. Big-time. "You mean you came here knowing the whole story?"

"Not at all." Carla kicked off her shoes and propped her feet on the coffee table, sliding the yearbook to one side to make room. "Nate didn't say anything. He noticed you weren't at school and asked if I knew about it and if I knew why. That's all. Well, that and the part about having feelings for you and coming to me, as your best friend on whose shoulders you wouldn't bother crying, looking for advice on what you're thinking and what he should do about it.

"Tell me you're kidding."

"I'm kidding." She raised both palms. "No, I know, you told me to say it; I'm not kidding. Come on, that's what we do, or used to do when we were young and stupid and in love. When in doubt, ask the best friend and swear them to secrecy that you asked."

"But you're telling me now, so you're not keeping the secret."

"Yeah, I've always been bad about that, huh? At least he noticed you were gone. For the record, Jules, your fiancé, who should, didn't. At the football game? He was surprised you weren't there, and wasn't even aware you had taken the day off. Speaking of, where is he today?"

"He'll be here any minute. They had a softball game this morning, but I wasn't up to going."

"Avoiding him, too?"

"No." Maybe a little, she thought.

Carla had been toeing the yearbook on the table. She bolted and leaned forward. "Whoa. What's this?" She flipped it open with a smirk that was somewhere between a tsk and *you've got to be kidding me*. She said, "I suppose this is a little more of that Prozac you were talking about."

She moved next to Carla as she thumbed the pages straight to the back, where the class pictures were.

"Oh. My. God. Is this really you? What was that, a pixie cut? Your hair was so short."

Julie hated that picture with the short, short cut that seemed like a good idea at the time. It was an act of rebellion, she said. Her father hated it and she had cut it after he grounded her for getting a C in science. Everyone tagged Julie as one of the smart girls in school, most likely to succeed and least likely to have a steady boyfriend. Marked for life, why fight it? At the time, she thought it made her stand out as smart and, she hoped, sassy.

Carla pointed to another girl. Naturally it was the girl voted most popular in the class, big hair, movie star smile and all. "We called that Texas hair when I was growing up down there."

"You grew up in Idaho."

"Yeah, but the longest summer of my life was the week I spent with my grandparents in Dallas."

Carla pointed to a face on the opposite page. "Now this. This is the real giggle. Nate had twice as much hair as you did. Look at that. First chance I get, I'm going to scan that picture and make up a most-wanted poster for the office."

"He was kind of cute, wasn't he?" Julie observed.

"Still is. But who asked me?"

Julie took the yearbook and thumbed a few more pages. "Look at this one. Go ahead and laugh all you want." She turned it around for Carla and poked at a picture that took up a full quarter of the page.

"Is that really you? Wow. What ever happened to that girl?" Carla asked.

"Me?" First Nate and then Carla. Then Nate again. Was something so out of sorts that everyone kept asking that question?

"That's you in the psychedelic angel outfit, right?"

Carla spun the yearbook back to Julie and pointed at Julie, wearing wings and a tie-dyed caftan, dancing through one of the numbers from the spring play with Gina Fernandez and Wendy Davis. All the pestering lately had Julie wondering what had become of that girl, too. "It was the spring play. Nate and I played opposite each other as a pair of angels."

"Aw. That's cute."

Her own sixteen-year-old face smiled up at her from the page, and she felt a warm blush. "We even had a kissing scene." That was when Julie practically, no, actually, threw herself at him. Like the rest of their relationship, it derailed before they got up to speed. Nate had said he had a thousand different points in their lives that he would gladly go back and relive. Looking at that picture now, she understood. This would be one of hers.

CHAPTER TWENTY-SIX
Almost Heaven

It was in March of their senior year, rehearsing for the spring play, that they reached "almost heaven," as Nate teased her afterwards. It was awkward but thrilling at the time, and laughable once Julie got older, wiser and sex was no longer a mystery.

Mr. Thatcher wrote a play that combined elements of the movies *Heaven Can Wait, It's a Wonderful Life* and *Jaws*. The gist being that two angels, played by Nate Evans and Julie Cooper, were sent down to earth to redeem the life of a morally bankrupt fisherman before he got chomped by a great white shark.

The Saturday two weeks before the performance, Nate rode his bike to her house to rehearse. The angels, Roy and Rita, spent most of the play bickering like an old married couple over how best to accomplish their mission. It was Nate who convinced Mr. Thatcher to rewrite the end of the play so that when the feuding angels kissed and made up, they shared a real kiss. Not a big deal on stage, but in Julie's living room that Saturday, with her father off on a weekend motorcycle ride with the doctors and lawyers that made up his "biker gang," her mother doing volunteer work at O'Connor Hospital, and the house to themselves, it became something much more for a couple of teenagers inebriated by raging hormones. They worked comfortably through the first three acts; it was that final scene, the one that ended with the kiss, where they both pulled back on the first try as if doused with a bucket of cold bashfulness.

On the second try, when they reached the end, he paused before that kiss, looking into her eyes in a way that made her feel he really meant it. She melted when, on the fourth run-through, he cupped her face with both hands and kissed her gently, slowly, and it tasted of forever. She knew they'd be going steady before the afternoon was over. Until now, the only boy who tried to kiss her like he wanted more than just lips was Tommy Tucker at a party the year before. He slobbered and groped and that was plain icky.

They continued to practice all the way from the living room to her bedroom. She offered token resistance when his hands began exploring her body. She offered encouragement to his hands when he mistook that as a definite no. Before long they were naked; he was awkward and she was nervous. Julie had never done it before, she told him. He said it was his first time, too, sounding guilty, as if he was embarrassed to admit it, and Julie believed him even though Nate had a date with Margo Willingham once and Margo was not shy about being *that* sort of girl. Julie kissed him again and hoped he wouldn't notice she was trembling. She must be in love with him because she wanted to do it. If he wanted it so much, that must mean he loved her, too. More than Margo and any of the other girls he could have had sex with if he loved them.

And then, when the moment of truth arrived, when Julie expected she was about to experience trumpets blaring and angels singing, instead she heard: "Julie. I'm home."

"It's Mom." She pushed Nate; he rolled off the bed and landed on the floor with a thump.

"Dear, are you in there?"

He ducked behind the bedroom door. She leapt to the pile of clothes on the floor beside the bed, made it into her panties and was still fastening her bra when her mother opened the door just wide enough to poke her nose into the room.

"What in the world are you doing, Julie? Why aren't you dressed?"

She searched for a plausible excuse, knowing she was flushed from head to toe, caught more than red-handed. If her mother came into the room, they were cooked.

"Mom, can't I have some privacy?" She threw an arm across her slack brassiere as much to hold it in place as to show some sense of modesty. That stopped her mother, who asked again what she was up to. Nate, with only the door between him and her mother, pointed to the window behind her, held his nose and made a water motion.

"I was getting into my swimsuit."

And then her mother asked about the bike propped up near the front door. "Is that Nate Evans' bicycle?"

"Uh huh. He came by to rehearse for the play and we decided we'd go for a swim." *Lord, please let this work. I'll be good from now on.*

"Well, he had better not be in there with you," she said sternly. And then after a pause, she laughed. Of course she laughed. It was a silly notion. A good, respectable boy like Nate Evans, of all people. "I'm just kidding you, dear. Where is he? I want to say hello."

"He's in back already, I think. Mah-ummm," she whined. "Can I finish getting dressed now?

Before she closed the door, Julie's mother tsked, "That Nathan. He's such a nice boy. Honey, I'm glad you're seeing more of him these days."

She swung her eyes to where Nate was cowering behind the door, hands cupped between his naked thighs, and she laughed. "Me, too, Mom."

Julie bounded after her mother while Nate made a beeline for the window that opened to the backyard. She stuck her head out the bedroom door, fumbling with the front of her bra and stalling for time.

"Nate invited me to a party tonight. One of the other kids in the play. At their house. Can I go?"

"I don't think your father would approve. Are their parents going to be there?"

"Yes, they are. And Daddy's not here, so he can't really mind."

"That's not the point, young lady."

She heard the window click shut behind her while Mom said she would think about it.

Julie slipped into her swimsuit as quickly as possible, took two large towels from the linen closet and wrapped one around her as she ran out the door to the patio. She stopped in her tracks. Mother was standing only a few feet from the pool staring down on Nate, who was in the water and holding himself against the wall looking up at her with one hand shading his eyes against the sun's glare and one arm along the tile lip of the pool to hold him close to its edge. Mom was chuckling about something Nate had said as if it was the most natural conversation to have with your girlfriend's mother. Not the kind you'd have after she caught you naked in the bedroom. Almost caught. In heaven.

She tossed the towels onto a deck chair and jumped into the water next to Nate. Her splash forced her mother to retreat a step or two. After getting Nate's assurance that the party wasn't going to involve booze or drugs and that chaperones would be on the premises, Mom agreed to let Julie go as long as he had her home at a reasonable hour.

"Don't worry, Mrs. Coop. The last thing I want to do is get Julie in trouble," he said as the woman went back to the house.

"I can't believe you. Talking to my mother like that. You're naked."

"Yeah. Kind of creepy, isn't it?"

Nate kept his body turned away from her and apologized. When she asked what for, he said, "For being pushy. For wanting to…well, you know."

Julie laid a hand on his shoulder. "Me, too." She was disappointed and relieved at the same time. It had been stupid, but the way Nate looked at her, the way he touched her, she felt so ready. Now, after this near-miss, she was certain it would happen someday, but she couldn't tell Nate that. She wasn't a Margo Willingham kind of girl, no matter how much she wanted to be only a few minutes ago. So they agreed that maybe almost getting caught was a good thing, and taking their time would be better.

"But I will tell you this," Nate said. His eyes were dancing and Julie knew a joke was coming. "There isn't anyone that I would rather *almost* do it with than you. Almost."

He laughed and splashed her face. Julie sputtered with water running off her cheeks and chlorine in her nose. She splashed water back at him and kicked herself into the deeper end of the pool. Nate chased, reaching for her ankle. He reeled her in and, with both hands on her shoulders, gave her enough time to draw a deep breath before he dunked her.

Underwater and free of his hands Julie opened her eyes, immediately struck by one curious observation: Gosh, it seemed so much bigger in her bedroom.

CHAPTER TWENTY-SEVEN
The Gremlin

It was somewhere near Salinas, cruising up the highway that split acres of lettuce stretching to the horizon on either side of him in perfect rows like a green picket fence lying on the ground, that Nate felt the nervous energy from what he was about to do. He had the next scene for his life in his head now.

By late November the boy was convinced it wasn't just the memory of the girl he was in love with. He was in love with the woman she had become.

And he was desperate.

Sabotage.

The boy was about to become a Man of Action.

And Nate hoped to hell he could pull it off without Julie wanting to kill him.

He was driving home in a 1972 Gremlin he found on craigslist and bought from a guy in Flagstaff, Arizona, as one more step in recreating his life. It was a two-door hatchback just like the one he drove his senior year. Like Nate, the little Gremlin was rusty around the edges, didn't do hills very well, had trouble starting in the morning and an occasional exhaust problem. It was prettier and more reliable than the one he bought back in school with money saved up from summers spent cutting, boxing and hauling apricots along with the rest of the teenage labor at the orchards that covered the east foothills of the valley. He loved that first car. It wasn't much, but it was worth every nick from his paring knife, every splinter from the wooden trays he had to carry to the drying sheds and every sweaty hour under the summer sun running buckets full of apricots from the pickers to the pickups parked on the dirt road just beyond the trees.

Julie was on his mind on the Southwest flight down to Arizona. She had recovered from whatever it was that kept her from work on the Friday after he bombed using Eppie's direct approach and let her know exactly how he felt about her. He was convinced it was Nate flu because she refused to talk to him for nearly a week, and even then, not until the campus was deserted and they could meet in the open quad near the library, giving them privacy to talk in the protection of a public space. He sat on the waist high ledge that formed the base of the library building. She stood, shifting her weight from one foot to the other, close enough for intimate talk but maintaining an arm's length between them.

"I really like you, Nate, you know that," she said. "But let's not let things get out of hand." He nodded and parsed every word. She spoke softly, haltingly, and maybe it was just his imagination that she spoke without conviction. How much did she care for the fiancé? She never said, which left him to speculate that it could be a lot, maybe just enough that she didn't want to second-guess her decision to marry him, or somewhere in between. As much as he wanted to, he definitely could rule out "not at all."

As she talked, Nate decided "Friends" was not an option. He'd slink back to L.A. and love her from more than just an emotional distance before he would sit and watch her every day with that guy.

"Things will look different, you'll see." She was certain he'd find somebody else. "That's what you need. You'll find the right woman for you."

A replacement? A diversion? Someone who would make him forget Jules? Seriously?

That was the first tickle to his imagination on how to fix his Julie issue. After closing the deal on the Gremlin in Flagstaff, he spent the night in a Motel 6 munching on take-out pizza, sipping bottled water, and noodling over various scenarios ranging from logical but likely ineffective, to absurd and likely to lay waste to any chance he had of winning her back.

Sabotage. That theme nagged him worse than if his mother caught him with the mouthful of double meat pizza he was chewing. He wasn't the one who needed to find an alternative to love. Festerhaven was the one who needed an alternative to Julie, a distraction that would take him out of the picture. He thought about Seth Naylor's problem. The poor guy was still paralyzed by the thought of meeting Angel Strings in person. Nate had continued to woo her in Seth's name, and it was obvious that he had her falling in love with the guy—the version of Seth that Nate created. If he could work that kind of magic for one, could he possibly do it again? Staring at the ceiling, boxed in by the pea green walls of a cheap motel in the middle of nowhere, Nate decided that moment that he was going to try.

"You clearly haven't thought this through." Jack Hewitt said. He watched his barking rat-like terrier straining at the leash raise his leg and take a leak on a small cactus. Nate was exhausted and his agent's comment had him feeling pissed upon just like that plant the pooch watered. Jack had the dog's leash in one hand and a cigar the size of sub sandwich in the other.

They stood on the sidewalk outside Jack's condo on Van Ness Avenue under a palm tree that sprouted in a tiny rock garden between two concrete and stone staircases in front of the building. Nate spent seven hours and fifty-five minutes of the eight-hour drive from Flagstaff to L.A. thinking about his plot to win Julie back. He pulled in to a truck stop in Barstow for chicken fried steak at the five-hour mark and spent two more hours jotting a list of pros and cons, developing a plan of action before he called his agent and hit the road to Los Angeles. Even though it was Saturday, Jack said he could give him some time before he headed out to a "Grip and Grin" session at the opening of an artsy-fartsy movie. It was the kind that would draw some big players from the industry who liked to be seen in public supporting highbrow flicks they wouldn't waste a nickel on producing.

"The way I see it, you've got us to the mid-point in the second act, and…so what? We've stalled out. Something's going to happen now, right?"

"Sure." If his life really was a movie he now had a plot twist. He liked the irony of that. Nate shaded his eyes. The sun was going down behind the drab, milk chocolate stucco condominium Jack lived in. It was only two stories, but it was the largest building tucked between rows of narrow adobe duplexes with their front doors facing each other, a side wall facing the street, and separated only by concrete walkways as they stretched to the back of the lot. Jack's building was kept up well, but looked every bit its fifty years and not the glamorous kind of place people imagine when they think of Hollywood. It was in a pedestrian, low rent neighborhood that backed up to Paramount Studios.

"The story has some workable parts but I'm not sold on it."

"What do you like so far?"

Jack looked off and sucked on his cigar for what seemed like an eternity. "Well, act one, for instance. The hero going back to high school to win over the girl he lost forever ago will tap a few nostalgic hot buttons. Not original but who the hell wants anything really original these days? Too much risk. Then in act two we find out she's getting married, ala *My Best Friend's Wedding*. That's the crisis, not unexpected, but a comfortable turn of events that has us rooting for them as a couple. Mostly, though, I love the way you wrote the gal, Julie, is it? She's conflicted about the hero and in self-denial about the cheating asshole. She's a great character the way you've written her. I can see the audience relating to her, though I never pegged you for a guy who'd write a chick-flick like this."

That stopped Nate, wounded and badly misunderstood. "It's not a chick-flick." He thought for a moment. "Yeah, it's got rom-com appeal, but it's about the guy. It's his redemption I'm getting at."

"Uhm, I'm not seeing that. Feels like a chick flick. Where's my Man of Action you wrote on page twelve that stands up to the goon and getting beat up for it in the bar scene? Fifty pages in and all we got is this Nat guy, a pussy in love who doesn't do anything after the Julie character shuts him down."

There was that word again. Eppie's word. Pussy, she called him, and accused Nate of lacking a certain part of the male anatomy for not putting up much of a fight. "Normally, I'm on board with when a woman says no it means no," she told Nate after Julie sent him to

"Friends" detention. "But in this case? I'm not convinced. You're giving up too easily," she said.

"I like the way you've built the parallel stories with the guy—wasting his life away because he's a passive slacker just taking whatever shit life hands him," Jack was telling him now.

"Parallel to the girl's backstory," Nate said. "The single mom who is so devoted to her kids that she sacrifices her individuality to the point she's lost sight of the person she thought she would be."

"Right. And now their worlds collide after all these years. I'll buy that because the audience will buy it. But the way I see it, fifty minutes in you've got a serviceable setup and conflict, so do something that's gonna make this all worth the price of admission."

"That's not the point."

"No? Then why are you wasting my time?" Jack jerked the dog leash, pulling the mutt to a sitting position at his feet.

"Never mind."

Sure, Nate would kill to turn this escapade of his into something that would knock Hollywood on its collective ass, but how could he explain to Jack that was secondary to using the script to get his shit together? Nobody's going to buy the story—they never do—so sending pages to Jack was like working on a deadline. It forced him to keep moving his life forward.

"The way I see it, this guy either mans up and does something spectacularly risky or you're just wasting everybody's time. So what have you got for me? You got to have something, some cool twist in mind, right?" Jack stared at him, expecting an answer.

"You ever hear of Cyrano de Bergerac?"

The agent squinted, and it made the heavy bags under his eyes more pronounced. "Uh, the schmuck with the big nose? Something about pretending to be his best friend who was having trouble getting laid. I think Bill Murray did a rip off of it years ago."

"It was Steve Martin. But imagine: *Cyrano de Bergerac* meets *The Sting*."

"*The Sting*? Bob Redford and Paul Newman *The Sting*? Love that old movie."

Then Nate laid out how he was going to win Julie over or go down in flames trying. "I've already written it out," he lied.

Jack said, "*The Sting*. A bit intriguing. Who knows these days? Send me something clean. No promises. And, seriously, think chick-flick. I can sell that."

He tugged on the terrier's leash and turned toward the stone stairs leading to a second floor entrance over the condo's gated parking garage. He paused next to Nate's car in front of the gate so the dog could mark its territory on the Gremlin's front tire.

"Nice ride," Jack said. "Classic. Maybe you should think about putting it in the story too."

Nate spent that night at Woody's. By the third and final shot of tequila sitting across from each other in the living room, Woody started to accept that Nate had come up with the best possible solution to a rotten situation, even if he still thought it was too passive-aggressive.

"I can't sabotage them by ratting the fink out," Nate said while he sucked on a lime wedge. "Even if that works, nobody, especially Julie, is going to love the rat who does the finking even when he is finking out a rat."

"Damned straight there. She'd hate you because it's none of your bees wax." Woody scratched a spot on his recliner chair's arm like a bothersome itch in the vinyl. "Better if I really did know a hit man like Guido. But y'all know the Peckerheads will go up there, hold the guy down for you while you take a Louisville Slugger to his kneecap. If that'd do you right."

"No you wouldn't. But thanks for offering."

By their fourth and final shot, the idea sounded better. By their fifth and final final shot, it was awesome, couldn't miss and settled. Woody stopped on his way to bed, staring at Nate and grinning.

"What?"

"I am more impressed with you every day, Bud. First you whack a military dude with a golf club and now this. But I swear, never, ever in my life would I have figured you grow up to be a pimp."

"A pimp? Is that what I am? Nah. I'm a love facilitator."

"Is there gonna be sex involved?"

The answer made Nate uncomfortable. "I hope everything's resolved before it goes that far. That's the plan. But I can't rule out sex."

"Sure as shit sounds like you're pimping to me."

He waved at his mother stirring a pot on the kitchen stove when he got home a little after noon and ignored her greeting as he headed for his bedroom. Nate flipped the cardboard sign hanging from a hook on the door to the side that said No Trespassing. Not that it mattered; the reverse side said Keep Out except that his dad had run a marker through it and scrawled Fuck Off with a smiley face.

He reached into the desk drawer and pulled out a snack pack of Doritos from under the stash of *Playboy* magazines. He munched and thought, and spent the afternoon scouring the Internet for advice and tips, adding to everything he had learned when Seth and the Stanford compatibility computer introduced him to digital dating. After a scrumptious dinner of his mother's eggplant root, kale and tofu stew, Nate set up a new account on Wink Connection.

Vintage Rascal. He liked that screen name.

Vintage was a wink to his age and Rascal was an inspired choice because it was the kind of name women were intrigued by, or so he read in research from dating advice sites all afternoon. He was particularly drawn to one advice site by a Dr. Rachel somebody or other. He consulted the yellow pad next to his computer with keywords and hot-button phrases based on all the advice that he planned to put into his Vintage Rascal profile.

He posted a picture of himself with Festerhaven that Julie had taken after their big softball victory, hoping prospective dates would be lured into learning more. One expert advised surrounding yourself with "beautiful people" in profile pictures, leading prospective dates to feel beautiful by association. He hoped ladies might see Festerhaven as a handsome, fun sidekick, suitable for dating in his own right. The profile? That was all Festerhaven. Nate spun his personality in a way he hoped would attract a Stanford-rated ten, AAA, five-star perfect woman. Then all he had to do was convince the principal to go with a bird in the bush instead of the fiancée in his hand. It was dangerous territory. If it blew up in his face, there could be hell to pay. If Festerhaven behaved the way he should, and couldn't be tempted, then Nate would give him due credit and walk away without another word.

He let his imagination run to shape Vintage Rascal. Even though it was supposed to be Nate's profile, everything was in the mold of Festerhaven. Unreliable mood swings were now part of FesterPrince-Charming's interesting character. He wasn't competitive to a fault, just driven to succeed. He wasn't self-centered, but seldom let others distract him from achieving his goal. He wasn't oversexed—he was intensely romantic.

It was so much fiction, the kind of bullshit Nate wrote so beautifully, and he was so engrossed in typing, deleting and editing, he barely heard the first raps on his bedroom door. He lowered the screen on his laptop like a teenager hiding an Internet porn site from view. Shaking loose of such a knee-jerk guilty reflex was hard when you lived with your parents no matter your age. He waved his father into the room.

Charlie cocked his head, chewed on his upper lip and scratched a spot behind his right ear. He gave Nate a low grunt.

"We need to have a little talk."

Nate nodded. "Sure."

"Your mother thought this would be a good idea."

"Okay. I won't blame you. Go on."

"Your mother's a bit concerned about you dating again now."

"I don't know why. It was her idea."

"I mean, she's happy about it, of course, but she thinks we need to get a few things out in the open, in case you find yourself in a situation that, well, that you're not quite ready for. 'Cause when a boy and a girl, a man and a woman get together, things happen."

Nate turned from the desk, knocking a stack of essay papers to the floor, and sat up wide-eyed. "You mean sex?" He laughed so hard he started choking.

"You're not making this any easier."

Nate wiped a tear from his eye. If nothing good came out of his return home and the remainder of the school year to come, this one moment was worth it. "I can't help it. Don't you think I'm a little old for the birds and the bees talk? You missed out on that a long, long time ago."

"Do you mind? Let me finish. I've got things to do."

Nate apologized again.

"Look, sooner or later you're going to be alone with a girl and you're going to want to do it. You know what I'm talking about. We've all been there. But it isn't anything to be afraid of, not really. I want you to know how to handle it when the time comes. You can avoid a lot of embarrassment if you know what to do and do it right. Understand?"

So that was the point of The Big Talk. It was the Trojan Talk. Condoms. V.D. and all manners of The Clap. Oh, poor Charlie, Nate thought.

"I... Oh, hell. Here."

His father pulled a folded brochure from his back pocket and flipped it onto the bed. It landed upside down in front of Nate. "I want you to read that. And then if you have any questions, you can come to me and your mom. We'll answer them for you, okay?"

Nate bottled up his laughter until after Charlie shuffled from the bedroom and closed the door with a definitive thump. He was touched as much as he was amused to think his parents were so concerned about his sex life. He kept chuckling right up to the point he took the brochure and opened it.

Viagra. The little blue pill for erectile dysfunction.

Get a free trial today.

CHAPTER TWENTY-EIGHT

Scourge of the Vintage Rascal

It only took one look at Nicolette DuBois—a.k.a. Foxy Banker on WinkConnection.com—and Nate knew it was love at first sight. Just the sound of her name as it rolled off his tongue set his imagination soaring. It was a name right out of an Alfred Hitchcock movie. If Nicolette was half as good-looking as her profile picture, well, he couldn't wait to see her in person.

He loved the way she'd posed; a sharp navy business suit, arms crossed in a self-confident but casual way, with half-frame glasses perched at the tip of her nose and a pirate's smile. Nicolette had straight hair the color of light honey cut in a bob that was longer on her right side, and she winked at Nate from the computer screen, suggesting she would be all business in the boardroom with generous benefits in bed. Her online name was Foxy Banker because she managed a midtown Bank of America branch. Most of all, she was going to walk in the door any minute.

Tall, forty-five, divorced with no kids, Nicolette was a doer. She was still athletic after being an all-star hitter on the University of Santa Cruz volleyball team. Go Banana Slugs! She loved to sail the bay after getting a modest-sized sailboat in a major-sized divorce settlement from her dot-commer husband. She renamed it *My Husband's Dowry*. She had a yellow lab named Bonkers, and she loved to flirt in an unapologetic yet eloquent way. He prayed Festerhaven was going to love her. It was tricky setting up someone with a blind date when they had no clue they were being set up.

"I sure hope this one works out," Festerhaven said. "What are you? Oh-for-four now? Not even a second date." They sat on stools at a tall table inside the Almaden Lodge Bar. The fireplace was crackling even though the day had been mild. Nate tried to avoid the accusing gaze of the deer head mounted on the wall. Lanterns, antique snowshoes and poles dressed the pine walls. It was a yuppie ski lodge in the heart of the city.

"I have good vibes about this one," Nate replied. No way in hell he was going to tell FesterFace he had given a tryout to three other women who missed the first cut before suggesting that he join Nate to meet an online date. The worst was Samantha. She admitted her profile picture was a bit dated—Nate guessed by about fifteen years. Her hair was mostly platinum on one side, Julie-dark on the other, and she had a voice that was nasal and menacing. She could very well be a Disney cartoon villain. What in the world was Stanford thinking? He had plugged in all the traits that made him love Julie, and it had spit out Cruella de Vil, without the 101 Dalmatians.

So over the weeks he refined his search for Festerhaven's soul mate by siphoning information from him a few drips at a time and tweaking the profile. He tried to avoid being obvious while he learned about his taste in music, politics, books, movies, food and what he did in his downtime that didn't involve sports, his background and family and philosophy on life. Nate added every tidbit to the Stanford matchmaking program, or the VLM—Virtual Love Machine—as Nate had come to think of it. He spun it all into the Wink profile, improving it with every pass, to the point that he could see himself falling in love with the rascal if either of them had been the opposite sex. He was most interested in what FesterRascal wanted in his perfect mate. She was nothing like Julie.

Beyoncé's body. Greta Van Susteren's brain. Sara Palin's politics. Oprah's money and Betty White's sense of humor.

"Betty White?"

"Just got a soft spot in my heart for *The Golden Girls*. What can I say?"

It was a damned tall order, but Nate added the details as he mined them over the weeks and began arranging dates. Then, ping! He found Foxy Banker and they hit it off. Just as he had for Seth, he exchanged notes and winks with Nicolette, using Festerhaven's personality traits to woo the lady.

Festerhaven was surprisingly eager when he talked him into coming along on dates as his wingman in a mission to find Miss Right. Nate told him he wanted backup, a way to avoid being stuck alone with a loser, or an expert opinion to validate his good fortune before discreetly disappearing for the remainder of the night.

"I think you're setting the bar too high," Festerhaven said as he sipped scotch. "The first two were definite losers, but the last couple of gals? I'd have been all over them if it had been me. Like Stacey, the hot nurse, on that last date? I got along with her great."

Well, duh. *That's the point, doofus!* The fix was in, and while Nate worried that he might wise up, FesterEgo was too full of himself to see that he had much more in common with each date than Nate. If Foxy Banker was the one, all he had to do was step back and let Stanford's cupid algorithms take over. Stanford gave her a whopping nine-point-one. To Nate's way of thinking, that was soul-mate territory.

"The problem," Festerhaven said, "is you're out of your league. None of them seem like your type."

"Really? And what is my type?"

Festerhaven squinted at the ceiling of the bar. "I'd say a librarian. These gals you're shooting for, they'd break you down. Me? I could take them on and savor the challenge. Yeah, naughty and not too bright."

"Then help me out, here. That's not at all like Julie. I still don't see what you see in her."

"Low maintenance. I come and go as I please. She's fun enough. And there are times when being on autopilot with someone isn't so bad. Maybe you don't want to meatloaf *every* night, but they don't call it comfort food for nothing." It was a cringe-worthy answer, but Nate thought it was par for the course. Maybe he should get it over with and rat out Festerhaven come hell or highwater.

"But you said your ideal woman would be kid-free. That's not Julie."

"Ah, but you see, the daughter took care of that problem, didn't she? Moving to live with the cows, the gophers and rednecks in Texas. And what is it with you anyway?"

"Huh?" Nate could almost hear the trophy deer head on the wall clicking its tongue at him. Maybe they should move to that table on the other side of the room.

"You're likable on most days, but when you get out on these dates, you turn into a schlump. If you were my wingman instead of the other way around, I'd be getting second dates every time. And from there, who knows?"

Have another drink. Festerhaven was talking fast and loose tonight, more than Nate had ever seen before, and just delivered a big fat pitch that Nate couldn't resist. "You're crazy. So even if you were available, even if we remove Julie from the conversation," and Jules was never far from Nate's consideration, "they wouldn't look twice at you if I wanted to turn on the charm."

"Bet?" Festerhaven straightened his shoulders. "Twenty bucks." It had fallen into his lap; FesterChump couldn't resist the competition.

"You're going to lose this bet," Nate said. "But let's say for the sake of argument that you get a date with this Foxy Banker chick. Promise me you'll take the money but keep your pecker in your pocket."

"What do you care?"

Nate didn't see anything but curiosity in his face. "I don't. Not really. But it wouldn't be fair to Julie. I mean, we go back a long way, and unless you're thinking about breaking things off with her, play fair. You guys are getting married."

"But we're not there yet."

He had that right. It was a smidge of comfort Nate could use to rationalize what he was doing. This could be his last chance to keep them from reaching that point. When Festerhaven saw Nate scowling at him, he crossed his heart, held up two fingers in the Boy Scout sign of honor, hooked his pinky around Nate's and shook. He did everything except pull out a knife, slice their palms and press their wounds together in a pledge to be blood brothers. "Promise. You can even come along to chaperone."

Then Nicolette DuBois walked in. Festerhaven's head wasn't the only one in the room she turned. A full-figured short blond with hair down to her waist followed her. Nicolette's wingman, or wing-woman. He watched FesterFox study Nicolette like a connoisseur admires a fine car. She was a classic Porsche in a room full of minivans.

"If I don't get a phone number, I will be sorely disappointed, Evans," he hissed.

Her friend was Mary. She had a round face, deep dimples and a pleasant smile, cute enough to hold her own, but side-by-side, she was like an accessory that made Nicolette shine. If the good researchers at Stanford had any say in the matter, his "wingman" would fit Nicolette to a T. So he let Festerhaven have the first shot and offer them stools at the high table, pull his own next to her so that Nate was the odd man out next to Mary.

He had his role as the typical socially inept but lovable sidekick who fades into the background of the audience's mind as the hero puts moves on his mark. He even rehearsed it several times. He was taking Woody's advice to go all Guido and eliminate his competition for Julie's love, only in a way that didn't involve breaking kneecaps or cement shoes. The plan was simple even if pulling it off with little or no spilled blood would require the dexterity of a cat juggler. He had found Festerhaven a better match than Julie. Someone he would live happily ever after with if he could only get him to fall hard for Nicolette. He had already written the kind of things he planned to tell Julie when Festerhaven broke off their engagement.

Damn. There was a stuffed squirrel on the ledge above the bar. He held a large walnut in his paws and stared down at Nate with a tilted head, disapproving and disappointed in him. If Festerhaven played fair and let Julie down easy, Nate was going to be there to help pick up the pieces. Score one for Nate the White Knight.

The small talk was amazing to everyone but Nate. What a coincidence. Nicolette and Festerhaven had so much in common. Business professional? Check. Age within an acceptable window? Check. Athletic? Check. And the coup de grâce? She had season tickets to the 49ers.

Yep. These two were meant for one another.

Nate's attention returned to the table just as she grinned at Festerhaven and reached across to give him a fist bump. Festerhaven's gaze lingered on her before he pulled his eyes away from the cleavage Nicolette exposed as her silk blouse fell away from her neckline. Festerhaven offered to buy any extra ticket for a home game that she might have to unload. Nate watched her watch Festerhaven's glance dip and dawdle. Score one for the Foxy Banker.

"So what do you do, Mary, when you're not hanging out with rascals like us?" Nate asked.

"I'm a librarian." Of course.

And for fun?

"I like to read," Mary answered.

"What a coincidence, he likes to write," FesterSpoiler said and redirected the conversation by pointing in Nate's direction.

"That sounds…creative." Mary moved closer.

Nicolette pointed from one to the other. "He's a creative type, which I never would have guessed based on Nate's Wink Connection profile. He came across as fun, but in a button-down kind of way. Here we are for our first official Wink-and-Wine, and it turns out you're the buttoned-down guy, loosely speaking. Totally opposite of what I expected."

"Not so buttoned-down. I'd love to see your boat," Festerhaven told her. "Sailing the bay, that sounds like my kind of water sport. I've dreamed of having something small myself, but everybody says yachts can be a lot of work, and who has time when you're responsible for the future of thousands and thousands of kids?" The dork actually sighed. It was exaggerated but effective.

Nicolette, Mary and Matchmaker Nate gave Festerhaven a verbal hug. "Aww."

As they continued to talk, Nate had less to offer. He didn't need to compete with Festerhaven to be the most charming boy at the table. Festerhaven moved closer to Nicolette, confident enough to touch her shoulder now. Festerhaven didn't deserve Julie. Julie certainly didn't deserve to be hurt by this scuzbucket. His own experience with marital wife-foolery told him that if the dude was a cheater now, he wasn't going to stop after he married Julie. So in a sense, he was doing her a favor in a backhanded, sleazy way that he hoped to God and the squirrel on the mantle overhead that she would forgive him for if she ever found out.

The women excused themselves. Then Festerhaven waved a cocktail napkin in front of Nate's nose. It had a phone number scribbled on it. "Twenty bucks, my man. Pay up."

"It's too bad you're engaged to Julie." Nate pulled out his wallet. "You two hit it off. You don't meet someone like her often enough. She's special, don't you think?" Nate let that sit for three beats. "Okay. So pine tar moment."

"Pine tar?"

"Softball. We're teammates, right? Once you've swapped pine tar with a guy, you've got his back forever. I'm going to give you my advice.

I think you can do better."

"Better than what, her?"

"Better than Julie." Nate played his hand. It was a bluff but it was all he had. "No knock on Julie, but she's no Nicolette." He nodded at the far wall of the bar. "Nicolette is more your style. I like her a lot." He laid out his palms, balancing the best Julie had to offer on one hand, versus hooking up with Miss Right on the other. Julie was smart *enough* and was certainly pretty *enough*.

He told Festerhaven it was easy to see Nicolette was most everything Festerhaven had described to Nate as the qualities of the perfect woman. She was *enough* on steroids. "But more than anything, she's definitely warm for your form." Then he rushed to get in the kill shot. "Okay. Here she comes. To have someone like her after you says a lot about the man you are. I'm in awe, actually," Nate hissed. "You're a stud, no doubt. I'm saying remember that, as soon as you marry Julie, you take on her whole family as well. Overnight you're no longer the dawg-about-town who can attract a woman so hot as Nicolette. No, overnight you become Grandpa Russ. Grandpa."

Until then, Festerhaven merely stared off with amused tolerance, but he was sure Festerhaven cringed when he planted that seed, the image of a dismal future as Grandpa Russ.

"Think about it."

Nate could see the wheels turning, revved up further by Nicolette's perfectly timed stroke on the back of Festerhaven's neck as she reclaimed her seat and ordered another drink.

CHAPTER TWENTY-NINE
Jazz Night

The jazz music helped a little. The company helped a bit more, but Julie still hadn't shaken the blues. Mom had mixed up her medications again and spent the weekend in a stupor that Julie nursed her through. Tuesday, Tiffany said they were pressuring Joe to move out to Texas early, and she didn't know if they could stay in California until Julie's wedding, since Russell still refused to commit to a date. And Wednesday, speaking of dates…

"She seems nice enough," Carla said. "But I don't think she's quite right for Nate if you ask me."

"No one asked you, sweetie," Larry replied. "I like her. Though I'm not sure about those online dating sites."

Nate's date, Angela, was a quiet little redhead, pleasant and smart. "You know what they say about opposites attracting," Julie offered, but when Nate had walked in with Angela, Julie immediately found herself looking for flaws in the woman and in the relationship. That surprised and bothered her because it was none of her business. She couldn't help herself. She was happy that he had turned his attention to another woman. Sort of. Wasn't that what she wanted for him? She thought he could do better than picking up strangers through a matchmaking site. At least she could stop worrying about Nate showing too much interest in her.

Damn him.

Barbara Unger and Beverly Myers moved their chairs from an adjoining table in the Renaissance Club to join them.

"Seth and his band are pretty good," Barbara said.

"Not bad if you like that kind of music." Beverly gave her review. "But this is kind of fun."

Nate had rallied the staff to show up and support Seth and his quartet at the club. The music started a little late for a school night, but Julie thought why not go out even if Russell begged off. He was at some social event, a fundraiser, set up by somebody connected to two of the school board members up for reelection. It didn't sound entirely ethical, but he was good at that kind of thing. And if it helped him win enough votes to get the assistant superintendent's job, she was all for it. He had Superintendent Fox on his side, and he felt with a little face time with the right people, he could get the job offer before Christmas. That couldn't come soon enough. Russell had been getting testy. True, she might have had to neglect him a little lately. Mom had caught a flu bug that lingered for weeks. She and Tiffany had been spending a lot of time at home with her. Mom resisted any talk of bringing in a professional health care assistant, even part-time, who would chip away at her independence. Julie thought it was just a matter of time. She wished Russell could be more understanding, but he had a distant relationship with his own mother and was perfectly happy that she lived in another state. Julie had floated the idea that, while he was holding off setting a wedding date, and as soon as she no longer needed to spend so much time with Mother, she might move in with him. That would beat the Tuesday night and weekend visitations that had become their routine. Disappointing her again, he took it "under advisement" and suggested they could settle everything after the holidays. Another delay.

"So what's up with them?" Beverly said to no one in particular but watching Nate and Angela having fun in a dark corner of the room.

After showing up a little late, when Seth and the group were well into their first set, Nate made the introductions and small talk before he took his new girlfriend to a table near the rear, where the shadows were deeper.

"If I had a date like that, I wouldn't want a whole lot of light either. She looks better in the dark," Barbara said. That was unfair and Julie told her so.

Not wanting to be left out of a good catty conversation, Beverly offered her own assessment. "Well, if nothing else, Nate's a little old for her, don't you think? She's young enough to be his daughter."

Larry said, "Hey, I know I'm only a man, outnumbered here, too, but age shouldn't matter to us if it doesn't matter to the two of them. Am I right or am I right?"

"Wrong, as always," Carla patted his hand. "But then you are a man, and that's the same thing." She leaned over and kissed her husband.

Julie wished Russell could be there to see them. Carla and Larry clearly adored each other and weren't afraid to show it. Russell drew the line when he walked out of the house. Julie understood. It would be unprofessional to be overly affectionate at work, he had made that clear, though she wished he would drop his guard just once in a while. More often than not, it was Julie who instigated a smooch, a hug or holding hands when they were away from school. It was disappointing, but that was the way it was.

Not Nate Evans. She watched him make goo-goo eyes with his date over in the corner. They were laughing about something, again. It looked conspiratorial, something that they obviously preferred to keep to themselves. They were certainly having a grand time. They acted like a couple comfortable with one another even though Nate said they hadn't met before tonight. How much longer would it be before he took Angela's hand or kissed her in view of the group? Not long. He was like that. She felt a headache coming on, a good excuse to leave early.

Two songs later, the lovebirds rejoined the group, sitting across from Julie and Carla with their backs to the stage. She wasn't jealous, she didn't feel jealous, exactly, but it felt like an obvious attempt on Nate's part to show her that he had moved on. Angela was his proof. Julie had rejected him and now he was rubbing her nose in it. She thought he was better than that.

"So where did you say you met?" Beverly asked. "One of those dating sites?"

Nate nodded and gave Angela a knowing thumbs-up.

"Nate wrote the most romantic things. It was love at first email, practically," she said.

Julie steeled herself with a sip of wine. "Nate was always good at writing stuff, weren't you? Did he tell you we went to high school together? He could write romantic things even back then." What compelled her to say that? It slipped out before she could stop, so she rejected the temptation to advise Angela to not put too much stock in them, based on her experience.

"Of course, that was a long time ago," Carla cut in. "We didn't have email back then. Everything was done by carrier pigeon. Yep, it was a long time ago," she emphasized. Julie punched her knee under the table.

Angela giggled. The girl actually giggled. He had put a hand on her shoulder, nudging and shushing her. Something was up. He held up his hand, freezing the conversation, and shared an odd, almost conspiratorial glance with Angela. She giggled again.

"Do you hear that? Seth played this song for me in the band room a couple of weeks ago. He wrote it and I told him he had to play it tonight."

It was an interesting piece. Julie liked it. It made her feel lonely and hopeful at the same time. It was quite good.

Nate looked at Angela and said, "If I didn't know any better, I'd say he wrote that song just for you." Then he winked at her. Ugh. Julie thought that pushed the boundaries of sappy. If she hadn't been there to support Seth, and if she hadn't mooched a ride with Carla and Larry, she would've found an excuse to go home. She went to the restroom instead.

She was reapplying lipstick, sorting through her thoughts when Carla joined her.

"So what is it? You're not feeling a teensy bit jealous, are you?"

Should she deny it? It wouldn't work with Carla. "Maybe a little," Julie admitted. "I'm a little annoyed. One day he says he's in love with me, well, maybe not in so many words, and the next day he's got another woman on his arm. It feels like that was too soon and too easy for him if he actually meant what he said. That's the kind of thing he used to pull in high school all the time."

"Then get mad at him and get over it. What can you do? It's not like you don't have Russell."

They turned from watching each other, suddenly driven to check their makeup in the mirror, when a toilet flushed in the stall. They waited until they were alone again.

That was enough time for Julie to admit what was really bugging her. Considering that James never actually, formally asked Julie to marry him—that happened after she learned she was pregnant—and Russell surprised her with the engagement ring and the words, "Here, I bought this for you; I think it's time we made it official," Nate's offer to be her number-one option, the sincerity of his words, his voice and the look he gave her, was the sweetest, most eloquent and touching proposal Julie ever had. And she fell for it. He didn't mention the offer was only good for a week.

Nate was whispering in Angela's ear as they returned to the table.

She rubbed her temple and turned to Carla. "I think the headache is getting to me. Maybe it's time we head for home."

"Sorry to hear that," Nate said. "It's not too bad, is it?"

"Not terrible, but it is a school night."

"Can't you stay just a few minutes? It would be a shame to leave before we get Seth over to say hi. I know he'd really appreciate it."

She had to admit that was the reason for the night out. She didn't have to wait long. They cheered louder than most of the audience when the band stopped. "On that note," Seth said a strained laugh, "we're going to take a short break. Thank you." He was still a few steps from joining them at the table when he pulled up and his jaw dropped.

Nate stood and offered his seat to Seth. "Mr. MusicMan35, let me introduce you to Miss Angel Strings."

"What are you doing here?" Seth asked, moving closer.

"I came to hear you play music. That song you played, the one that goes"—she hummed a chorus line—"it's incredible. Did you really write it for me? Nate says you did."

Seth sat down next to this person called Angel Strings while Nate pulled up a chair next to Julie.

Leave it to Carla to take command. "Okay, kids, what's going on here?"

Seth looked at his lap, so Angela explained that Nate had written her notes on the dating site pretending to be Seth because Seth was too shy to write them. Wasn't that romantic? "Whenever I suggested we meet for coffee, he wouldn't, and I thought that was pretty weird because he kept writing me and I'd get this awesome email that was like reading a perfect piece of music. Finally, I wrote him back and told him to stop teasing me or go away, and that's when Seth confessed. He explained it all, that Nate had written those letters for him because he couldn't find the right words."

Nate said, "So naturally—and Carla, you'll appreciate this—being the busybody I am, once the cat was out of the bag, I jumped back into the middle of it and arranged for Angela to be here tonight. But we didn't tell Seth."

All eyes turned to Seth. Julie expected to find him squirming. That's how she would feel if she had been set up and it was revealed in such a humiliating way in public. But he was too busy watching Angela to notice.

"And how's that working out?" Larry asked.

Angela smiled at the group. "It's early yet, but so far so good."

Seth beamed. He was glad she came, and yes, he was kind of, sort of, definitely thinking about her when he wrote that song. Nate said so—you could believe it.

She followed Seth back to the stage, and he moved a small table to the front for her so they could watch each other during the quartet's second set.

"Aw. They're so cute," Beverly said.

"Nate, you make a good busybody," Carla said. "I couldn't have stuck my nose in their business any better."

"I've had a lot of practice lately."

That was mysterious both in the way he mumbled it and the way he dropped his chin and propped it in his palm on the table. She leaned forward and did the same.

"Good job, Evans," she whispered. Annoyed with herself, she stewed over her jealous reaction to what had been going on. How could she have let this turn into something so juvenile? Maybe it was Nate dragging her kicking and screaming back to their high school days. She was a teenager again, whapped by a jealous impulse simply because one of the cute boys she sort of liked was paying more attention to some other girl. Maybe she liked him more than she wanted to admit? Good Lord, that thought and the way it expressed itself sounded juvenile. Still, it wasn't as if she had jumped to the conclusion all on her own that Angela was Nate's date. He pushed her there.

Damn him.

"It's funny. And sweet. So this whole thing was a blind date you set up for Seth," Barbara said. "You had us all thinking she was *your* date."

"Why would you think that?"

"Why didn't you say something right away?" Julie asked.

He bit his lower lip and shrugged in a quick manner that could as easily have been a flinch. "Didn't occur to me, I guess. I wanted to get the two of them together, to surprise him, and I didn't think about how it would look. That's all."

Damn it. Nate was going out of his way to do something nice for their friend, and she made the gesture all about her. Her excuse of a headache was beginning to feel real.

"Besides, as neat as she is, Angela's not my type. Not even close."

Nobody said anything, leaving it up to Julie to ask, "So, Nate. Who exactly is your type?"

Instead of answering right away, he stood up and started clapping as Seth and the band took the stage. She heard him say, "My type?" And while the rest of the table's attention was on the musicians, he was looking at her. He tucked his chin against his shoulder and raised his eyebrows in a way that left no doubt he was making fun of her for asking the obvious.

You, better than anybody, Jules Cooper-Finch, know perfectly well. He didn't say it aloud, but the message was clear.

She looked back at him with as innocent a face as she could muster. She wasn't going to look away this time, though she knew she should, because it was the answer she wanted.

Damn him.

CHAPTER THIRTY
Jackpot

The phone was ringing when Julie stepped out of the shower. Naked and dripping, she grabbed a towel and went to the bedroom to check the caller ID, afraid that whoever it was this early had an emergency. She pouted at the phone. Carla could wait until Julie dressed. Fifteen minutes later, she stood at the kitchen counter checking messages on the phone with one hand while pouring her first coffee of the day with the other.

The phone vibrated in her hand to the bossa nova tune Julie had assigned to Carla's calls.

"I told you. It's an omen."

No hello. No *what are you up to?* Not even a casual *hey, it's me.* No, when Julie answered the phone, Carla launched into her omen theory.

"What's an omen?"

"The numbers never lie," Carla said. "Did you buy your lottery ticket yesterday?"

"Yes."

"Well?"

"I haven't checked yet. So tell me." Anxiousness crept up on her.

"Are you still playing the birthdays, yours and Nate's?"

"That was the point, wasn't it?" Yes, all through the weeks since Carla came up with her omen theory, and Julie planned to keep playing them until somebody won the jackpot.

"Jackpot," Carla said.

Julie tossed the coffee from her cup into the sink though she was still several feet away and missed badly. She could clean up the mess later. Better yet, she could hire someone to clean it up for her. Carla wouldn't joke about something like this. Well, she might, but not like this.

"Tell me. Tell me. Tell me," she pleaded. "We got all six numbers?"

"What, are you crazy? Of course not. I said it was an omen. Not a miracle."

Julie's breath returned to normal as she plopped into a chair at the kitchen table and watched coffee drip off the edge of the counter onto the floor. That's how she felt, too.

"Carla, what the…?"

"Oh. Sorry. But I was right. The first four numbers drawn last night? Your birthday and his birthday. It's an omen. You missed the Mega Ball by only one. If you had been leaning a bit to the left, maybe, you would've picked that one number lower instead."

She asked Julie if she knew what four numbers in the drawing was worth. Julie answered without hesitation, then suddenly ashamed that she kept those numbers in her head.

"Ninety-six dollars."

"Better than nothing. What's my commission?"

Carla stopped by Julie's office before lunch to apologize again. "I didn't mean to set you off like that."

Julie sniffed. "You almost gave me a heart attack, though. You did use that word. You did say jackpot."

Carla drummed her fingers on the edge of Julie's desk. "I meant Nate-wise. First he shows up here out of the blue. Then he makes it clear he's interested in you. Then you use your birthdays, like you were meant for each other, to win the lottery..."

"That was your idea."

"And a fine one it was. I should have played the numbers myself. What I'm saying, though, is you watch. He'll be somebody's Plan A in no time. There are worse jackpots to hit than having someone like Nate interested in you."

"Wishful thinking. On your part."

"Not yours?"

"Russell. Remember him? So there's nothing to think about."

Except there was if Julie wanted to be honest, she knew. There was nothing to feel guilty about, but it didn't stop her. Julie never did tell Russell about the notes Nate had left for her in her mail slot. She would have if Russell had only shown some interest, but that one was long forgotten. She did confess to Russell that after going for a milkshake with Nate and the others after school, she walked back to campus with him alone. But Julie waited until Russell was preoccupied with the Warriors' game on TV and it barely registered; he acknowledged it without taking his eyes off the screen. She definitely didn't tell him about how she asked Nate to recall their first kiss, or the truce she had with him after he made a pass at her. Well, it was more of a sweet, numbskull, unrealistic but not indecent proposal.

The worst part was that, when she added up all the things she didn't tell Russell, it made her fidgety when he was around and more critical of him when he wasn't. Take the other day, for example. She had found the cutest blouse at Nordstrom's over the weekend and only flinched instead of putting it back on the rack after her good sense was assaulted by the price. It made her look great, and she needed a little of that right now. First, he didn't even notice when she pranced into his office to show it off. Then when she called attention to her outfit, his compliment left her cold.

"I really like it," he said. "My mother had one that was a little like that. It looks much, much better on you."

It hurt when he said it. It infuriated her after the words smoldered all afternoon. Naturally, Nate made things worse when he stopped to chat as she was headed to Carla's classroom. She couldn't recall the conversation except for the part when he noticed the blouse.

"Is that new? Looks great. I'll bet you slayed around the office, and if you keep that up, you'll be giving Emma Lane a run for her money." Emma was the current most popular, prettiest-girl, prom princess and queen bee of the MHHS student body. She knew it was BS, but she loved that he said it.

When she hit the jackpot—as Carla put it—Carla suggested she take Nate out for dinner with the money. "He deserves something since you used his birthday. And what's my commission, again?"

She was still trying to decide if and how to tell him she used their combined birthdates on the winning ticket when they were sitting next to one another at the football game the following Friday. She didn't want him to get ideas about why he would figure into her fantasy of winning the lottery, but that became the least of her worries after the fool she made of herself that night.

Russell was late and Julie sat with the usual group of faculty. No one, not even Julie, had any reason to think it unnatural that Nate sat right next to her. Everyone laughed and cheered their heinies off. The Mt. Hamilton High Raging Poets even pulled out a rare win. Julie had a good time, so good through the first half of the game she never missed Russell. The Poets scored a touchdown, and everyone jumped, clapped and hugged the person next to them. For her, that happened to be Nate. And it was he, not Julie, who pulled away first, but not before he winked at her as if there was some conspiracy in it.

He said, "I like what you've done to your eyes. They look so mysterious in a fun kind of way. Nice."

"This? It's not much."

"You have those extra little thingies at the corners, that the really hot girls like to do. Do they have a name?"

"They're called wings." She added them just for fun after he compared her to Emma Lane, and after she found herself studying Emma's face in a chance encounter in the office. Until now, only Carla noticed. She didn't do it for him, but Julie liked the fact that, once again, he noticed the tiniest, albeit frivolous, effort to add a touch of spark to her appearance.

"They make your eyes younger. Or maybe that's the natural sparkle there." And then he turned away looking at…what? The scoreboard? The concession stand at the corner of the field?

It wasn't until Russell arrived that she felt guilty for flirting—yes, she had to admit it—flirting with Nate. Whatever spell he cast vanished and then she overcompensated. She went out of her way to pay more attention to Russell than she did to the game, slipping her arm through his, taking his hand in hers, sitting hip to hip and leaning into him when he made her laugh. She kissed him when the Poets scored again, and he was unusually receptive to her show of affection that night, considering they were in public. He wasn't embarrassed with the kiss, held her hand for no reason at all, and even put his hand on her knee, only to slide it higher on the inside of her thigh when he thought no one would catch him. He acted almost as if the others ceased to exist and they were alone, with the kind of attention that reminded her how complicated he was to love. Carla ribbed her about it after the game. She had noticed. Julie hoped no one else did, least of all, Nate Evans.

"You and Russell were so cute together I almost threw up," Carla said over coffee the following Monday.

"Was it really that bad?"

"Let's just say it was… well, let's just say it was."

Julie growled at no one in particular. "It's silly. It was nothing all that special."

"You could have fooled me. If I didn't know better, I'd say you wanted to score a point with Nate, show him that he shouldn't be so nice to you."

Julie got defensive. "You're crazy. Nate? Ha." Yes, she had a twinge of guilt, maybe, but she wasn't sending any message to Nate. She didn't think that was it. "I just wanted to let Russell know how much I love him. I owed him more attention since I've been spending so much more time with Mom lately and with Tiffany and her kids before they move."

"And spending time picking omen lottery numbers?"

Julie played with the ring and studied the diamond with little focus.

"You're not having second thoughts, are you?" Carla asked.

"I wouldn't call them that. Just questions."

"Sure. Like?"

"Things are a little crazy. Nate said he came back to teach here because it was like reliving the old days. But sometimes I think he wouldn't have done it if I wasn't here."

"You think maybe this is all about you?"

"He hasn't said that, exactly. But he makes it hard not to wonder what he was thinking before he showed up and started causing trouble."

"You call this trouble? You have two guys who are crazy about you."

"That's one too many."

They sat there, reading each other's thoughts. "Don't do anything to embarrass me, okay?"

"Okay. But what?" Carla tilted her chin lower and raised her eyebrows. Oh, she loved this, Julie knew.

"If the subject comes up, just happens to come up if you're talking with Nate, and you could find out if he really..."

"Really... what?" Carla was having far too much fun.

"If he knew I was working here and if that made a difference when he decided to take the job." Julie sounded tentative, her words soft and shy to her ear. The more she thought about it, the more she wanted to know how important she was to Nate. What was he thinking? What if she was reading too much into the attention he was giving her? The best solution, tried and true through the history of dating, the way she would have handled this if they were still teenagers, was to have her girlfriend talk to the boy and find out before she made a fool of herself.

"But you'd have to find out without being obvious. Oh, forget it.

What am I thinking? You don't have a subtle bone in your body. Just forget it." She turned and randomly picked at the files on her desk.

"I knew it. You still have a crush on him. Or is it just since he got back?"

She was intrigued, she admitted, but she would have to nip this in the bud. It was getting out of hand. The flirting was fun, and it was flattering. Unless she was going to break up with Russell—and there was little chance of that—she shouldn't encourage Nate anymore.

"That sounds sensible, but now you're curious. I am, too. We know Nate's hot for you. How hot? That is the question."

CHAPTER THIRTY-ONE

Free Falling

Trying to stay young was a pain in the ass. Or so Nate thought as Chelsea did the final rinse on his hair. He was seeing her every month for regular maintenance, a cut and color touch-up. She had convinced him to avoid going totally with the chestnut color of his youth, the one he had found on a box of Lady Clairol, and left a hint of gray at the temples. She said it was distinguished in a way that he'd have to beat off the women with a stick. She was nearly as good a liar as he was. He got only quizzical looks from the other customers, all ladies in various stages of cut, color and perms at Chelsea's Salon and Barber Emporium. Thank God they didn't call them beauty parlors these days, but finding a good, old-fashioned barber shop, manned by old guys with scissors and piles of outdated *Sports Illustrated* magazines on the table next to the waiting chairs, proved to be impossible, as impossible as getting through an entire Friday night high school football game without making a trip to the restroom every twenty minutes for bladder control through the second half. It was annoying, not only for the effort it required, but he was starting to identify with the old guys in those prostate drug ads that bombarded him on TV. At least he got a lot of exercise going up and down the stands, but the sore muscles in his legs reminded him all day Saturday what a pain that was, too.

And it was Saturday. After Chelsea finished with him, Nate went to the Barnes & Noble on Stevens Creek Boulevard. Christmas was coming, and he had a mind to spend what was left of his settlement with the Air Force on leather-bound notebooks for his students. Last week he decided to incorporate journaling into his classes, and he hoped that one or two fancy notebooks might actually get used without a class assignment. Maybe one or two might spark a creative thought; maybe one or two might plant a seed in a young mind and lead to a novel or a movie someday. The feeling of hope that came with being a first-year teacher was a natural high. You existed for the impact you would have on the future. That morning, it made the aches and pains of going back to school worth it.

He sat in the café of the bookstore sipping green tea. Hooray for the antioxidants. His mom would be proud of him until she saw how much artificial sweetener he used to make it palatable. He typed on his laptop, sending an email to his agent with an update on his story. He continued to steal liberally from his own experiences, adding details like the Friday night football games, chaperoning the fall dance and taking a spin around the dance floor with Julie to shock and amazement of the kids, and interacting with the students in a way that convinced him how, at its core, high school life hadn't changed much. The bigger problem was that even with as much fun as he was having, nothing was turning out the way he wanted. Jack thought sabotaging the relationship between the girl and her fiancé by setting him up with blind dates harvested online was promising and full of potential comic repercussions, but the fact that he didn't have a clue how the boy and girl would end up in each other's arms as the final credits rolled was a two-ton chunk of writer's block on Nate's head at the moment. Jack had mentioned it in passing to a couple of people of potential but wanted to know where the story was going, and so did Nate.

He finished an email full of excuses to Jack and an update to Woody, checked his favorite news sites, and responded to an email from Mary, the wing-woman for the blind date he had sicced on Festerhaven. Mary wanted to see him again, and to set up a double date with Nicolette and FesterFace. She dropped a vague line that Nicolette was interested in his friend as well. That was encouraging. He shut off his laptop and was in that netherworld when Julie walked in. He almost missed her, and probably would have if she hadn't noticed him first and waved.

"Hey, lady. Pull up a chair."

The bookstore and its café were unusually quiet for a Saturday; the weather was cold and miserable, keeping anyone at home who wasn't desperate enough to fight the Christmas shopping crowd at the mall. Julie sat down with a Frappuccino and bright eyes.

"This is a nice surprise," he said. "What have you got going today?"

"I'm on my own. I thought I'd do a little shopping." She said Tiffany had taken the kids down to see her in-laws in Hollister for the weekend. Russell was also out of town. Oh, yeah. He went down to Los Angeles to meet some college buddies and root for their Oklahoma University football team while it got the snot stomped out of it by UCLA. Even their friend Carla was gone for the weekend.

"Mom was doing really well and had a friend over for coffee when I stopped by this morning, so I decided to take a day for myself." She leaned back, deep into a brown leather chair in the corner of the coffee shop, and crossed her legs. She wore black stretch knit pants that flattered her figure and white rubber-bumper-toe tennis shoes. Her teal sweater was as shaggy as an unshared sheep and oversized to the point of hiding the rest of the lady's charms. "The only definitive thing on my agenda today is a nap."

Nate leaned forward with elbows on his knees in an identical comfy chair angled toward her. "Sounds perfectly boring in a good way." He pointed to the bag full of journals for his students and said that would be the highlight of his day. He asked her about her plans for the holidays. She had convinced her son to come down from Oregon and join them for Christmas at Mom's. With Tiffany and her family moving to Texas, this could be the last time they all got together for a while.

"I'm getting used to the idea of her leaving town. I think I'm okay with it now." But she talked with melancholy that nicked Nate's heart like a dull knife about her daughter and her grandkids and how much she loved them. Now they were moving. "It might as well be a different country," she said. She reached out and patted his hand. "Oh, God. I never thought I'd be one of those women who are defined by her children. But here I am."

"I'm glad you're here, for one."

She asked him why he never had children.

"I've thought about that a lot. The best answer, I suppose, is that when we got married, we were waiting for Valerie's biological clock to start ticking before we did anything about it. Either she never had one or turned off the alarm early in the marriage. We never tried."

"Do you wish you had?"

He shrugged. "She was convinced she'd be a terrible mother, and

I would never, ever dream of arguing her into something she didn't want. Not something that important."

Julie sat back in her chair—considering that, he supposed—and then she changed the subject. "You know, I've never been to one of our class reunions."

"Yeah. I kept thinking I'd see you there. You know what a sucker I am for that stuff." He asked what kept her away.

"You're going to think this is vain, or stupid, but I haven't gone to any because I haven't done anything interesting. I dropped out of Stanford after only one semester to raise the family. That's about it. When James died, I took first one, then another job, just to pay the bills. I hated both of them. I've never traveled anywhere. And then, since I've been working at the school, it's like I never got out. I never had anything worth talking about."

"Crap. You've raised a family. On your own, not to bring up a sore subject. Your kids are great, and you've got this job helping other kids get from here to college. You're a superstar in my book."

He could see the gratitude in her eyes. "You make it sound… You make me feel better. You were always like that. Gosh. We haven't talked like this since…"

"Since we were sixteen? I remember coming home from a Day On The Green Concert, and we sat on your porch until God knows what hour. Your mom turned on the porch light, and we stayed out there and talked."

Jules laughed. "And she started flicking it on and off, and we ignored it until she gave up."

She went on, but Nate's attention soared and he didn't register any of it. He imagined a shift, the first perceptible wave in a calm ocean before the tide turned. He imagined an opening where she might be convinced to dump FesterLoser. That would solve everything. Unless it was just his imagination.

"Do you know what the most exotic vacation I've ever had is? Disneyland with the kids. Look at you. You've traveled to other countries."

Some of them were interesting, but, "Wait a *min-ute*. You went with FesterFa.., uh, Russell, to Hawaii last summer."

My, the lady doth blush. She looked at her lap with rosy cheeks and a grin that sweetened her face.

"Well, until then. But that's not the point. You write great things. Things most of us without much imagination would never come up with."

Despite never really getting the love he wanted from the studios, Nate had his moments. And as bad as some of those movies were, they would long outlive Nate's personal expiration date. He had that going for him.

"I never got to live half the things I wanted to do, the kinds of things we talked about as kids. But you've gone out and done them."

She made it sound good to Nate. To think it had been only a few months earlier that the most exciting thing he ever attempted in his life, his botched suicide, failed badly. Thankfully.

"Why not start now? What's stopping you?" Nate waggled a finger at her, and Julie said, "Probably nothing."

She began to gather up the discarded napkins and empty cups. She was smiling. "Carla says the same thing. She is so much like you. Thanks for the attitude adjustment. I should let you go."

"What? So you can go home and nap?" Nate asked. "Screw the nap. That's for old fogies and people without a life. Remember what I told you a while back? I'm Peter Pan. I'll never grow up, and I can fly. Spend the afternoon with me and I guarantee if you don't feel more alive when I'm through with you, you are a lost cause." She hesitated. Nate expected her to reject the offer.

"Please?"

She appeared wary. The old Jules would have trusted him. She would have been all over the idea and ready to go.

"Okay. But this better be good, Buster."

Later, Julie threw her arms around Nate's neck, tossed her head back and said, "That was incredible. You were right. I've never felt anything like it." She had burst from the wind tunnel and tugged a pair of safety goggles down around her neck before leaping into Nate's arms. He used his hands to gently remove her helmet while basking in the closeness of her body. She didn't let go of him. "Wow. Just wow," she said.

They lingered on the deck next to a wind tunnel at the iFly Skydiving Center, an indoor skydiving simulator in Union City. He could have stood like that forever, nearly as thrilled as Julie had been in her five minutes floating on the air in the wind tunnel. At least he kept his feet on the ground. Nate had driven her to the skydiving center, doing his best to rebuff her curiosity as she peppered him about his plan every five minutes along the way. Her only moment of hesitation came as she paused at the front door, staring straight up at the five-story building. She was still flying high when they moved to a bench a few feet away afterwards.

"I don't know how to thank you,"

Nate thought about this. Dare he? This could be fun, or it could blow up in his face.

"You want to thank me? Here's what you do," he said. He turned a cheek to Julie and tapped it. "Plant one right there, sister."

"Is that all? Easy." She leaned in.

Nate's timing was exquisite. At the last possible moment before her lips reached him, he turned his head. Julie had, as he hoped, closed her eyes. She never saw it coming, and their lips met.

Julie jerked away, blushing. "You tricked me."

"Yeah. Now that's what I call living."

"So is this." And then she slapped him.

CHAPTER THIRTY-TWO

Sittin' on the Dock of the Bay

It wasn't much of a slap. He would have been disappointed if she let him get away with stealing a kiss without penalty. She had to defend her honor. It was strong enough to send a message yet coy enough to leave him guessing how serious she was. He took that as a good sign. Right now he was willing to hang his hopes on ambiguity.

Not counting the first five or six years of his life, it had taken Nate about fifty to fully understand he was never going to be the swiftest dinghy in the harbor. He considered himself a skosh above average in intelligence, but it seemed the rest of the world moved about one click faster. Nate was quick enough as a high school ballplayer to hit a fastball about one-third of the time, which gave him a batting average that, in the majors, would get you into the starting lineup. Life was different.

Now he understood that, in life, being a bit slow on the fastball for the other two-thirds of the time was barely enough to foul off most of what it threw at him. And then there were those painful times when he would whiff entirely. He had whiffed with his ex-wife in marriage, and Eppie Johnson was a screwball that kept him off-balance and frequently flailing. He had struck out with Julie because he had been swinging with his eyes closed. Maybe that was his problem—he could hit the fastball but women kept throwing him curves.

Add Nicolette DuBois to the list. Just when he had given up on her, he found himself loitering with her and Mary, waiting for Festerhaven. She had invited them to a Christmas party before the holiday break at the marina where she docked her yacht. She made it clear she was looking forward to seeing both of them with teasing innuendo that was unmistakably directed at FesterBoy. He had begun to worry this crazy plot to play matchmaker between Festerhaven and Foxy Banker would turn out to be a waste of time. If Festerhaven were to be believed, he hadn't had time to follow up after the "blind date" Nate set up. But Mary dropped a hint otherwise. Who to believe? That was a no-brainer; he knew what FesterLiar was capable of. But now, with Jules showing signs of interest and Nicolette firmly on team Russell, things were looking up.

My Husband's Dowry impressed him. When Nicolette talked of having a yacht, Nate had in his mind the movie version of a rich man's toy. He was thinking YACHT with a full crew and servants. Nate had seen motor homes on the L.A. freeway bigger than the *Dowry*. The ship in the neighboring slip dwarfed her. Her yacht was modest and cozy, not at all ostentatious, and that lack of flash appealed to Nate. Foxy Banker had good taste.

"Do you think Russell will get here soon?" she asked. Nate stood with her and Mary on the bay side of the dock that separated the boats. The party was happening behind them in the marina's clubhouse on a knoll above the docks. She sipped from a wineglass, each time wiping off the lingering raspberry lipstick that perfectly matched her boots. She wore a short-waisted leather jacket over a thick sweater, tight jeans and a straw cowboy hat tilted on the back of her head as if it was ready to slide off.

Nate said, "I can't imagine what's keeping him. He had to monitor some kind of emergency school board meeting. It should have ended long ago."

Simultaneously, he and she checked their phones. No Fester-Message. Music from a DJ's sound system floated down to them from land, a few people mingled on the dock between the boats, and several lounged aboard the *Dowry*, where Nate could see their faces through the port holes, laughing in the bright light and warmth of the main cabin.

They strolled along the wooden dock that rocked under their feet back toward land. The small talk turned to jobs and current events, both personal and of the world, anecdotes that made them laugh and empathize with one another over the clueless bosses they had to deal with.

"Speaking of Russell…" Nate said before assuring them he was kidding.

At one point, a good-looking guy, all ego and no clue, approached Nicolette and offered to buy her a drink. The joke was, of course, that the party had an open bar. The fact that she gave him the once-over as if tempted raised Nate's jealous hackles. He fended the guy off by mentioning how much Festerhaven was dying to see her again and wondered aloud what might be keeping him. Take that, you Old Spice-drenched Romeo.

Mary left in search of food and promised Nate she would return with a plate for him.

Over the next round of drinks, he picked several spots to praise

Festerhaven with left-handed compliments, trying hard to remember, and not repeat, the spin he put into the Vintage Rascal profile.

"Yes, he's something, isn't he?" Nicolette mused. "Just the other day, or maybe it was last week, we were talking about what he plans to do after getting his promotion."

"That may be what today's hoop-de-do is about. He'll probably come waltzing in here with the job in hand." The bright lights of the marina were behind her, putting her face in shadows that made it impossible to read. So he *had* been toying with Nate, and Mary was right. Multiple Festerhaven sightings could be a good sign.

Nicolette said she was surprised. "Then again, he probably didn't say anything because he feels a little guilty. After all, you and I met online and I was supposed to be your date, and yet here we are. You have Mary and I have Russell. Weird the way that worked out, huh?"

"Weird."

He might have explored the subject more, but Mary returned with two plates of grilled shrimp kabobs and Festerhaven on her arm.

"Look who I found wandering around up there," she said.

"Thanks for waiting, gang," he said. "You wouldn't believe the cluster-fuck I had to sit through this afternoon."

"So are congratulations in order? Is that what the board meeting was all about? You got the job, right? You are my new hero," Nate said, though the words were sour in his throat.

"We were wondering if we should have a bottle of champagne on ice just in case," Mary said.

"We'll have to keep it on ice a little longer. The board put things off until after the holidays." Festerhaven told them something vague about the dysfunction running rampant, keeping the board from taking action on the most trivial matters let alone something as critical as giving him the job that had, for all intents and purposes, already been offered. It was a lie; something about the glance Festerhaven gave him told Nate there was more to the story, and whatever it was had him pissed.

"I'm so glad you could make it." Nicolette drummed her fingers on his chest and let them linger as she handed him her glass. The spark between them was never more obvious, and it acted like a switch that turned on his charm.

Suddenly she was ravenous and took him to find the buffet, leaving Mary and Nate alone on the dock. Mary rolled her eyes and tilted her head at her friend's wake with the pained expression giving him the impression she had more than her share of time spent in her friend's shadow.

She was a quiet conversationalist, speaking in soft tones, joking with him and engaging him thoroughly. It made getting through the next hour bearable until he could get Festerhaven aside for a private chat.

"Those fucking assholes. You know what they did this afternoon? They fired John Fox."

"Superintendent Fox got fired? Just like that?" They stood at the very end of the dock and looked across the cove and over the narrow island that was a nature preserve separating them from the San Francisco Bay, protecting their harbor from the worst of the elements. The evening air smelled of saltwater, and Nate watched the lights of a jetliner on approach to Oakland airport on the opposite shore. What would this development mean to Julie's engagement? Festerhaven had used the job as an excuse to avoid setting a wedding date. Now that was in doubt. With the job in jeopardy, they could put it off indefinitely. Or they could be married next week. It worried him.

"Who knows for sure why they dumped him? Something about some consulting contract or two the district handed out to some company or two that apparently had some connection or two to Fox's wife. And maybe his father-in-law and Fox's sister, a dozen cousins and who knows who else."

"That sounds pretty bad." Nate morosely stated the obvious.

"You know what that makes me? Tainted. Fox was the one who handpicked me for his assistant super. I pulled my buddy on the board aside before I left to get the skinny and he said one of those assholes even used the word *toxic* during the executive session."

"Yowzer. What are you going to do now?"

"I'm not sure. The idea was to replace Fox when he retired in a couple of years anyway. Maybe we can accelerate that plan and get his job now. But that's for tomorrow. Tonight?" Festerhaven broke into a broad smile. "Tonight? I'm going to drink. And I'm going to get laid."

Nate toed the metal handrail to a ladder that rose from the water and curled over the edge of the dock. He leaned over. In the shadows on the water below, he could make out the nose of a rowboat tied to the pier. The rhythmic lapping of the harbor water was a nice counter to the sound of the party behind them.

"So when are you going to break the news to Julie?"

"What news?"

"Nicolette said you two have seen quite a bit of each other lately."

"She said that?" Festerhaven joined him at the dock's edge. "That wasn't exactly for public consumption but, yeah, a couple of times. Three or four. Five at the most."

"But what about your Boy Scout pledge, cross-my-heart-and-hope-to-spit promise? No hanky panky."

"What? And you believed me?" He grinned, big and phony. He was the Cheshire cat. The light from the marina made the white of his teeth stand out against the shadows on the dock. The bell on a buoy near the mouth of the harbor clanged, and someone shouted on an unseen boat several slips away. Sounds carried in the stillness around them.

"This thing with Nicolette, then. Are you just having fun or is this serious? Or is it going to get serious?"

"I think I'm in love."

"Lust."

"Yeah, there is that."

"Then you gotta do the honorable thing. Tell Julie you've had a change of heart. Break off the engagement. And it's not fair to Nicolette, either."

"Nothing in the rule book says a guy can't have it all."

Nate felt the shadow before he heard the voice. "Who's engaged?"

They turned to face Nicolette and Mary.

"Who's engaged?" she repeated. "To who?"

"Whom," Mary corrected.

"And whom is this Julie?"

"Who."

Simultaneously Nate and Festerhaven pointed to each other. "His."

FesterLiar told her it was nothing serious, babe. Babe? Nicolette had graduated from perfect stranger to babe. She looked at Nate and asked him if that was true. "Sounds serious to me."

Nate stalled. It depended on how seriously you define serious.

That was something of a moving target, wasn't it? It was a tough call. If he copped to the truth, Festerhaven being altar-bound, Nicolette would no doubt bail on him in a heartbeat. But lying wasn't much of an alternative. Just ask the crew on the movie shoot in Amsterdam that took him for every penny he had at the poker table. Nate was piss-poor at bluffing.

Before he could answer, Mary tugged at his elbow and led him away to a safe distance. Maybe it was the way sound carried in the night, maybe it was the decibel level of the lovers' quarrel, but it didn't take long for them to draw the attention of others on the dock. Nate turned his back.

"It's all my fault," he said. It had been pure folly from the start. He really should have thought it through.

"You can't blame yourself," Mary said. She laid a reassuring hand on his arm. "You only introduced them. There is no harm in that, right?"

If you only knew, Nate thought. Then the argument stopped, punctuated with a splash. Nicolette stormed past them, across the gangplank into the cabin of her boat.

"Oh, my goodness," Mary said.

They rushed to the edge of the dock in time to help Festerhaven climb off the top rung of the ladder, soaked from the top of his head to the tips of his loafers. He wiped the salty water from his face and flicked it at Nate, pointing his finger and growling. He stiffened his back, stood tall and walked past the party with more dignity than someone who had taken a dunk in the drink had a right to and went straight to the marina's parking lot.

Nate started after him but Mary held him back. Let him go and deal with it later. There was nothing they could gain from talking to him at the moment. A few minutes later, Nicolette emerged from the *Dowry* purses in hand. She glared at Nate as she handed one purse to Mary.

"Let's go. I've had enough of this."

Mary shook her head. She said she would stay a little longer, frustrating Nicolette, who stared at her, branding her a traitor. They watched her walk away until she turned for the steps to the marina house.

"Well, that was certainly exciting," Nate said.

"Nicki is one of my best friends, but it was bound to happen."

"What do you mean?"

"Let's just say they deserve each other. I could tell you stories."

Mary had a hand on his right arm. "I'm not sure I want to hear them," he said.

"That is unfortunate because they're pretty entertaining. But we can find other things to talk about on the way home. Nicki was my ride."

She focused on Nate with eyes so seductive she appeared to be a woman hoping for a good old-fashioned ravishing. Were her eyes blue or green? He couldn't remember. They started back toward the marina parking lot, and as they went up the steps, she asked, "You aren't engaged, are you? Or have a girlfriend?"

"Not even close," he replied. Not anymore. He had a sinking feeling that Festerhaven dashed his scheme with cold water the moment his butt hit the bay.

CHAPTER THIRTY-THREE

Another Bad Lang Syne

Carla had a way of making you do silly things. Some were more embarrassing than others. Some should never be spoken of outside the home. So New Year's Eve, Julie sat on Carla's sofa with a paper party hat on her head with bits of tinsel that dangled over her brow and into her eyes. She held a gold-striped party whistle like a cigarette between her fingers the way Lauren Bacall would in an old black-and-white film. Nate would be tickled that the image would cross her mind. But at the moment, she was of a mind to smack him. Or kiss him. She wasn't sure which.

Nate was complicating her life. He kept assuring her he was satisfied with their friendship the way it was. Then he deliberately cheered her up when she needed it most and took advantage of her when her guard was down, like that stunt at the skydiving center. Worse, he started invading her thoughts at quiet times during the day and making her restless at night. She wanted to smack Nate just for being there, and just for being Nate, because she had been thinking about him more than she should, and that wasn't fair to Russell. Once she recovered from her free fall at the skydiving trip, the pleasure it brought had her walking on eggshells around Russell. It was almost enough to make a girl wear yellow shoes so the yoke stains wouldn't show.

On the other hand, she wanted to kiss Nate because he was fun and unpredictable and he brought that out in her. She had forgotten what that felt like. Even the juvenile way he stole that kiss, and it was theft without a doubt, almost moved her to kiss him back just to see how he'd react. That scared her. They drove mostly in silence back to the Barnes & Noble, where he dropped her off at her car. He apologized and she forgave him, and even with the tension that followed her as she got out of his car, she was a happier person than when they'd met that morning.

Russell sat on the armrest of Carla's sofa slightly above Julie to her right. She looked up and then nibbled at the mouthpiece of her party horn. It was one of those moments when she was back to wanting to smack Nate silly because she had no right to think of him with Russell at her side. That was dangerous territory. On the drive back, Nate promised he would toe the line, keep a sensible emotional distance as well as a physical distance as best he could on a tiny school campus. That made Julie want to smack him for the past. Smack him for the present. And maybe one good one for the future, too, whether he would deserve it or not.

"How are you doing?" Russell laid his palm on the back of her head, then let it slip down, where he stroked the base of her neck. She tilted her head back to nuzzle his hand in response.

"Me? Just peachy." Julie laughed and blew her party whistle in his direction. It uncoiled with a toot, filled with her breath, and stretched up to him like a snake's tongue. Then she rested her arm along the top of his thigh and squeezed his knee. She looked at her new bracelet, a

Christmas gift from Russell. He brought it back from New Mexico, where he had spent the first part of the holiday with his brother and visited his mother. He skied Angel Fire, hit most of the casinos in the area and drove all the way to the pueblo in Taos to buy this little pixie turquoise bracelet from a Native American artist. It wasn't something Julie would have bought for herself, but he went to a lot of trouble. Russell left for New Mexico in a foul mood. The school board had fired the superintendent, and Russell couldn't do anything to help his own case for the job. Whatever he did or drank out there must have calmed him down. He came back in a better frame of mind, and his show of affection was a wonderful side effect. Julie had pressed him about a wedding date before his trip. She pointed out that Seth and Angela had decided on Valentine's Day, and they'd only known each other for three months. He promised to talk about it when he returned home.

They had dined that night at a New Year's Eve party at the Double-tree Hotel. It was scrumptious, but the band after dinner was loud, and the music had a new-wave edge to it that got everyone to their feet— the younger customers to dance and the fogies to head home early.

After pouring the champagne, Carla, bless her prying little heart, asked the question in Julie's mind. "So. Don't you think it's about time you kids set a wedding date? Seems like a great way to start off the new year."

Russell brushed the strings of tinsel from Julie's brow. "I don't see why not."

She waited for him to add something more. A little emotion would be nice. He treated the idea of setting a date with the kind of enthusi-asm she might schedule a vacation. Sure, it would be fun. Something to look forward to. Something you do every year.

Larry went to his study and came back with a calendar. Julie knew the best dates between the end of school and Tiffany's planned exodus to Texas by heart. She had a church picked out and brochures for places to hold the reception and others with definite honeymoon potential. She wouldn't have trouble convincing him to keep it a small affair, and Carla had a cousin who owned a catering business to handle that with a special family discount for Carla. None of which she wanted to share with Russell until he agreed to a date, just in case that seemed too pushy. But his months of foot-dragging and now that evening's tepid response led her to say something that, a few months earlier, she would have considered heresy. "Maybe we should wait until we find out how this shake-up with Dr. Fox is going to affect things. You might still get promoted. Whatever he did or didn't do shouldn't reflect on you. They'd be silly not to."

"The school board? Unreasonable? Surely you jest," Carla said.

"That's my girl," Russell said. "Always practical. Thinking logically. That's why we're such a good team."

Practicality had little to do with it. She wanted him to step up for her and he failed. She gave him an out and he grabbed it like a drowning man goes after a life preserver. She had been thinking recently that there was one other course. She was tired of being a part-time part of his life. If she couldn't pin him down to a wedding date that night, she was going to press him to live together. She would do that when they got home.

Russell went on, "But I say let them work their schedule around us. Or better still, let's not wait. Spring break, we can fly off to Las Vegas and find one of those Elvis preachers."

He was teasing, of course, and tipsy. Maybe it was the fact that they had been apart for nearly two weeks, but Russell was in great spirits. He was loose and a little naughty, slipping an occasional double entendre into otherwise innocent conversation. He fondled her knee or stroked the back of her hand, his fingers danced up and down her thigh, and Carla returned from a trip to the kitchen and caught him kissing the back of Julie's neck. That was the Russell she had fallen in love with.

They were gathering their coats shortly after midnight to the music of Carla's chuckle when Julie's cell phone rang.

Why Tiffany needed to call and wish her happy new year was beyond her. She could let it go to voice mail. Maybe it was cautious paranoia or intuition honed by years of waiting up and worrying for her children to get home safely at night, but she chose to take the call and make it quick.

The call was indeed quick. Julie listened for all of two minutes, asked clipped questions while fighting off tears. She kissed Russell good night and drove like a madwoman to the hospital.

Another Bad Lang Syne.

CHAPTER THIRTY-FOUR
You Can't Fool Mother

A week later, Julie stroked the back of her mother's hand. The hospital room's light was soft; overhead lamps had been dimmed for the night. Occasionally a staff member would glide past the open door, pulling Julie's attention away from the bed. Occasionally her mother patted Julie's hand and held it with their fingers interlocked. Occasionally she grinned.

"You'd better stick around. I'm not through with you yet."

"I didn't mean to cause such trouble," Mother said. "I thought it was just a little tumble." She had repeated that, apologizing over and over, sometimes with tears, in the week since she took her spill on New Year's Eve. Thank God Tiffany was there when it happened.

"Dr. Richards said today you're making good progress." The surgery to repair Ethel Cooper's hip had gone well. The doctor was more optimistic about recovery than Julie. Though he advised her to take a serious look at moving Mom into an assisted living center.

It was well past visiting hours. The first few nights she slept in the chair near the bed. Now she only needed to stay until her mother checked out for the night. Mom was having a good day, and even with the IV dripping painkillers into her system, she was more lucid than earlier that afternoon, when she slipped into a fitful snooze right in the middle of their conversation. Julie had taken the week off work and told Russell she planned to burn her sick days through the end of the month. It all depended on how much her mother needed her. Dr. Richards expected to send Ethel to a rehabilitation center for another week or two before she was ready to go home.

Her mother asked, "How is your father, dear? I'm sure this has been hard on him, too. They fixed up my hair today. Do you like it? I was hoping he'd come by so I could show it off to him."

"Very nice, Mom. But Daddy won't be stopping by." Julie flinched. A heart attack took Tony Cooper six years earlier. For all her eroding memory, this was the first time that Mother had resurrected her husband.

"Mom. You know that Dad is…gone."

Ethel sighed. "Yes, that's right. Sometimes I wish it wasn't so. So much that I forget. Or maybe I don't want to remember. I miss him."

"I do, too."

Ethel put on a happier face. "Well, dear. Tell me. How is that young man you've been seeing? As soon as they let me out of here, I think we should invite him over for meatloaf."

"Sure, Mom. We'll do that. Russell is doing well. He sends his love."

The hint of delight was gone in a blink of her mother's eyes. "Russell? Do I know Russell? Oh, of course. Mr. Principal."

"That's right."

"No, dear. I meant Nathan. That Evans boy. Didn't you tell me he's back? Aren't you seeing him again?"

"Only at school, Mom."

"Of course it's at school, where else would you see him? Do you have any classes together this year?"

Mom wasn't as lucid as she imagined. She must have thought they were students again. So Julie explained they both had jobs on campus. She saw him at school but wasn't going to be *seeing* him. "That's not going to happen."

"Oh, dear. Don't tell me he broke your heart again."

Julie felt her face flush. Maternal radar was a glorious thing unless it was *your* mother tracking *your* thoughts. Julie had spent too much time thinking of Nate over the holidays. Like her two-dollar splurge on lottery tickets each week, it had become a guilty pleasure that snuck in like a thief during quiet moments between worrying about her mother's health and all the tasks necessary to prepare for taking care of her in the future.

"Julie? Are you all right?"

"Sure, Mom. And Nate never broke my heart."

Her mother was losing steam. "If you say so, dear. I guess those tears had me fooled. Or I imagined it. It was so long ago; you were kids." Ethel closed her eyes and a smile crossed her lips. "I'm glad to hear that. Maybe we should invite him over for meatloaf. I love meatloaf."

"I'll work on that."

She didn't remember tears. She remembered buying a prom dress that she never got to wear. She remembered falling asleep on prom night, dateless, lying on top of her bed with the gown wrapped in her arms. She remembered trying to patch a shattered picture frame with glue and tape. The frame held a copy of the yearbook photograph that showed the two of them sitting close enough to be a steady couple that she had taken a ribbing for. Maybe there were tears. She had forgotten about tears.

"You know, your father really liked that boy. He was always so polite. Such a nice boy. Except…" Ethel opened her eyes and brought a hand to her mouth as if something jumped to the front of her memories.

"Except what?"

"Well, imagine if it had been your father who came home and found you two in your bedroom that afternoon. Oh, my, I was so embarrassed."

Julie let go of her mother's hand, leaned back and folded her arms across her chest. She couldn't work up a plausible way to deny it. "After all these years, are you telling me you knew? You knew all along? You never said anything."

"Of course I knew. But Nate was such a nice boy it was hard to believe."

"Take it from me, nothing happened." Julie patted her mother's hand. "You made sure of that. Your timing couldn't have been better to stop whatever was going to happen." She couldn't fathom how that episode had remained unspoken for so long. "And it made us think twice afterwards."

"That's why I let it go, dear. Lesson learned. It might have been different if you two had stayed together and I thought it might happen again, but I guess that wasn't meant to be."

"No, I guess not."

It had taken a while for Julie to make peace with prom night. In a way, it was hard to fault Nate. He had tried to explain it to her before the prom. He wanted to make a girl in a wheelchair happy. Eppie Johnson had had a rough life and deserved better, even if it was only for one night. It wasn't as if he had stood up Julie. He had never officially asked her to the dance; she simply took for granted what all of their friends assumed would happen. That didn't make the night any easier, but in wanting to give Eppie one night of happiness, he never thought about how he sacrificed Julie's happiness in the process.

"Your father. I was thinking about how he liked Nate because those two were so much alike."

"You're kidding. They weren't anything like each other. That's not how I remember Daddy. Nate is, I don't know, so full of life. Silly, sweet, irresponsible and unpredictable. Juvenile is a good way to describe it."

"Oh, you don't know what you are missing, Julie. Your father could be quite the stinker when he wanted to."

Julie thought about how little she saw of her dad. He worked tirelessly to build his accounting firm, only coming home for dinner and the solitude of his den in the evenings. That and to ground her every time she got less than perfect on any test or, Lord help her, a B on her report card.

"You came along too late, I suppose. He was so much fun when we were courting, and when we were married, young and poor. At some point he outgrew it. And he gave us a good life."

"That he did," Julie agreed. She loved her father, she was sure of that, but if there was a playful side to him, he rationed it through the years. Her date-night curfew was impossibly strict, but Tony Cooper believed that if a young girl hadn't had enough fun by eleven p.m., she wasn't going to have fun at all.

"You just get better, okay? We'll see. Right now you need to get some rest."

"I'm so glad you're here." She grimaced as she shifted her body to slip deeper into the blankets.

"I'll be here whenever you need me. Don't worry. We'll take good care of you."

"I know, dear. And I want you to know it's okay to take care of yourself, too."

"I'm not sure what you mean."

"Oh? Well, you're a smart girl. You'll figure it out. Take care of yourself." Her mother drifted away, nodding to the sound of Julie's voice. It was easy to dismiss her mom's words to the drugs or the creeping onset of dementia or exhaustion, but they worried her. Would she have anyone to take care of her when her time came and she was the one in the hospital bed? Tiffany had been with Mother when she fell, but how fast could she get there from Texas if Julie was in need? The prospect of that worried her, so she sat back and tried to not think of anything at all.

CHAPTER THIRTY-FIVE

The Kodak Carousel of Life

Julie took the least direct route home, sobbing at stoplights as she drove aimlessly across the valley and back. First it was her son, Daniel, who abandoned her to raise his family in Oregon, and then Tiffany and Joe announced they were moving, taking her grandchildren to Texas. Her father left them all behind when he died, and now her mother was going to die too. The doctor and the nurses assured her they were optimistic about Ethel's chance of recovering, but as much as she wanted to believe them, she couldn't find any room in her heart for hope that night.

Carla tried to be encouraging when Julie called her from the hospital. She said all the right things, but because it was exactly what Julie expected to hear, her sympathy had only a modest effect. Driving the streets of San Jose an hour later, she was just as sad as if the conversation never happened, but even if it had eased her sense of loneliness, she needed more. She needed a hug. From a man. One who would make her feel safe and loved.

But Russell wasn't home. That depressed her even more, and she didn't bother to leave a voice message when she called him. When the time came and she was on her own deathbed twenty or thirty years down the road, he probably wouldn't be there then, either, and she'd go straight to voice-mail hell. She was ashamed she would think that but angry with him nonetheless for not being there when she needed him most in the same way she was angry with her mother for growing old.

She put a kettle on the stove for tea when she got home. Reaching for the teabags in the cupboard, she knocked a stack of papers and envelopes off the counter. Julie began crying again, crushed by the weight of the present and fear of the future when she knelt on the floor to pick them up. They were all the bills, bank and credit card statements, insurance policies, financial information and attorney correspondence—the paperwork she had collected from her mother's home necessary to keep Ethel's life in order. Keeping Mom's life in order was going to be her job now while she was forced to watch her mother waste away in the grip of dementia.

Later she went again to the closet in Daniel's old bedroom full of keepsakes and searched for a plastic tub full of photos, slides and a carousel projector. The talk about her father at the hospital earlier that evening made her miss him more than ever. She carried the projector to her bedroom, pointed it at the wall from the corner of her bed and then doused the lights. The carousel hadn't been changed since the last time she used it years earlier for the reception after Tony Cooper's funeral. Daniel had done a great job of sorting and collecting the old family slides of her father's life from before Julie was born until about the time she got married. Daniel had even managed to get more recent pictures converted to finish the project.

Julie went through them slowly. Tony and his first motorcycle before he married Mom. Tony wearing a sombrero on their honeymoon to Mexico. Tony helping Julie as a toddler learn to walk across the living room. Dad and Mom dressed as a gangster and twenties-era flapper for a costume party.

Tears came back, but they comforted her this time. Her mother was right. The father in those earlier years, the one she had forgotten, was full of life. He really was Nate-like. The father she remembered was steady, reliable, loving but distant in a way that left her craving his attention and more grateful when she got it—like Russell. She ran the tip of her finger tracing the top of the slide carousel in its full circle.

That was life.

Two in one back then. Two men in her life now. One of them goofy, who made her feel loved, and the other one who made her feel grounded and safe. Good grief.

She continued reminiscing through vacations, Christmases and birthdays, with Julie growing up and Dad growing middle-aged. Then she came upon one of her favorite slides, a picture of her father straddling his motorcycle parked in the driveway. She had taken that one herself and guessed it was early in high school. Julie fingered the button on the remote control to move to the next slide when she stopped and drew a startled breath. How could she have forgotten? How could she have looked at that picture through the years without noticing the grinning, fuzzy-focused face peeking over her father's shoulder. Nate was sitting on the motorcycle behind Dad, but over the years he had become nothing more than a tree or a house or some other bit of irrelevant background to fill the scene. Now he was back. And she noticed. She pulled a pillow to her chest and leaned into her knees.

Tony and Nate had just returned from a ride around the neighborhood. It was Nate's first time on a motorcycle. She couldn't remember why he had been at the house that Saturday. Maybe it was a Sunday, but they mugged for her camera like best pals, thrilled to be together. Mother said that Tony had always wanted a son. For whatever reason, it never happened. Julie laid back on the bed and buried her nose in the pillow, amused by the irony that the picture suggested, if Nate had played his cards right, he'd never be Tony's son but he might have ended up being his son-in-law.

She tossed the pillow aside, its winter flannel fabric too rough and too warm against her face. She stopped smiling.

Prom night had been a disaster, but what she remembered more was the shithead Nate became afterwards. Some days she thought he was avoiding her. And on days when they were hanging out with friends, he wouldn't talk with her much and laughed less than he did with the others. She confronted him about it one time, and he mumbled an apology and looked into her eyes. What she saw was pity before he shuffled away. She wanted to forgive him. She would do anything to forgive him, but he wouldn't let her. And now it pissed her off.

Thirty minutes later, she was sitting at the IHOP across from Nate. It was near midnight, and she had been surprised that he was there to answer her call.

"I was writing," he said. He asked about her mother. That was sweet of him. She replied Mom was doing as well as could be expected and the prognosis was good. But she didn't call him in the middle of the night in need of a shoulder to cry on.

She asked how things had gone at school since they got back from the break. She was stalling, a little impatient, and didn't listen to his answer.

"Everybody misses you. When do you think you'll be back?"

"Huh? Oh. I'm not sure yet. As much as I can get away with, I suppose. It depends on Mom."

She sipped coffee. He wore the whipped cream from his hot chocolate on the tip of his nose. She swore he did that to make her laugh.

"Why did you turn into such a jerk after the prom?" Just like that, she ambushed him with her question.

He looked hurt. He sounded hurt. "Was I?"

"You were. Not to anyone else, but you were to me."

Her mother had asked if he had broken her heart "again." No, he hadn't, but she was beginning to worry he might. She wasn't about to start channeling the teenage angst she buried so long ago, but that night she needed to know why he did it the first time.

Nate put his hand on her arms that she crossed on the table like a barrier between them. He was surprisingly composed for someone hit with a question like that. He did flinch slightly at the tone of her voice, but seemed more amused than defensive, and answered easily as if it had happened only yesterday. He said, "For the record, yeah, I was avoiding you. But it wasn't like I was trying to be an asshole or stuck up or mean. Stupid? Yes, but never mean." He scratched his chin while she let the pressure to explain expand with the silence.

"I was crazy about you. Surely you know that," he said.

"Nice try. I wanted to forgive you for taking Eppie to the prom, but you treated me like dirt."

He thought about it and then answered with a slow, measured and rambling story of prom night. "Julie, I can't lie. I've had this very conversation in my head for going on forever, and more often than ever lately. It's crazy; I never thought I'd have a chance to sit here and tell you straight up, just like I imagined it. So here's the deal…"

Julie could see that, at the time, it might have seemed like a much bigger deal back then. She could also see how, of all the boys she knew, only Nate Evans was dumb enough to turn something the others might have bragged about into a reason to push her away.

Damn him.

CHAPTER THIRTY-SIX
Prom Night

Nate wore rented black. Eppie wore bridesmaid blue. The ballroom at the Sainte Claire Hotel downtown was dressed in gold. The lights were dim and the band only knew a smattering of disco. Disco was dead by then, and he was among those least likely to mourn its passing.

For a girl confined to a wheelchair, she had plenty of moves in her upper body to swing and fling and rock to the roll of the music. Sometimes Nate took the handles and spun her in circles across the dance floor. They had so much fun that, instead of being the odd couple out, they were the cool kids that the others wanted to dance near, and they formed small clusters of communal boogie.

Eppie predicted it would be a great night when he picked her up in his little beat-up Gremlin. The hatchback was perfect for carrying her wheelchair. Helping her in and out of the passenger side of the car was tricky, but the advantage was it required a kind of physical intimacy so close that he couldn't tell where his cologne ended and her perfume began.

Nate steered Eppie to a table during the first slow dance. She closed her eyes, her head swayed to the music and she had a mile-wide smile on her lips. He went to fetch punch, and she must have felt his return, because without opening her eyes, she beckoned him to bend close and then kissed him on the cheek.

"Evans, you really are the best thing ever. Thank you for doing this."

It was the third or fourth time she had said that in some form. "There's nothing to thank me for," he replied. He thought she was being too grateful. Embarrassingly so. He was having a good time and reassured her. "You make it sound like I'm doing you a favor. I've been looking forward to this."

"Just the same," she said. Then she tugged his jacket, pulling him close enough for another kiss. Lips this time.

Rocking with the up tempo was not a problem, but Eppie's wheelchair got in the way of a nice, romantic slow dance. It was during the medley of Styx/Kiss "Babe" and "Beth" that he watched Eppie's mood sink as they sat out the songs. Nate excused himself and took a break to cut a deal with two linemen from the football team in the men's restroom.

So he was prepared when Nancy Ashford took up a microphone and gushed as she announced the name of this year's prom queen: Eppie Johnson. It surprised no one, and he rolled her to the front of the dance floor to the sound of modest cheers. Eppie did the Queen Elizabeth hand wave and nodded like the royalty she was. Nancy put a cheap paper crown of gold on her head. As her Prince Charming, he also got one. Then the band began playing the ceremonial ballad while the other students cleared the center of the dance floor for the royal couple. Everyone was watching, gawking, he thought. The band played Eric Clapton's "Wonderful Tonight," a perfect song for dancing with full body contact, and she asked him to take her back to the table.

The football linemen he hired for two bucks apiece stepped up on either side of her and lifted her from her wheelchair. Nate sat down and they set her on his lap. The crowd clapped and cheered. Somebody whistled as he rolled to the center of the room. They had the dance floor to themselves, and he steered the chair in lazy circles to the rhythm. They surrendered to the music and the mood. Eppie held tight with her arms around his neck and head on his shoulder. He could feel her breath soft against his neck. She turned her head and their cheeks brushed. Nate knew there was a tear on hers, and the moment felt pure and right.

After the dance, they cruised from one side of the valley to the other with no particular destination in mind, not ready to let go of the evening.

She suggested stopping at a liquor store where her older brother worked nights and they could get beer without a hassle. He knew of a nice little opening on a short dirt road hidden in the Mirassou vineyard where they could watch the stars.

It turned out that Eppie's brother didn't sell Nate a six-pack of beer after all. He sold Nate a six-pack of Coke instead.

And a pint of Jack Daniels.

Nate laid a blanket down in the vineyard clearing where it sloped back toward the valley. They spent the rest of the evening staring up at the stars, spiking the Coke and sharing sips from the same can. The ratio of whiskey to soda increased with each one. He had a cassette deck in the car jammed by spaghetti of broken tape spilling from its mouth that he hadn't gotten around to fixing yet, so they tuned the radio to KLIV instead and relaxed as the DJ spoke to them and the music soothed them as it floated out the back of the Gremlin.

They talked a little, sighed a lot, and enjoyed just being. Eppie lay on her back, he was stretched out on his side with his head propped up by his elbow and the third can was empty when she said, "This is really nice, Evans."

"That's for sure."

She had one arm crooked beneath her head. Nate was gently stroking it between the edge of her short sleeve and her elbow.

"It's been perfect, I'd say," she said.

Nate felt warm and relaxed. He was carefree; the booze tickled his nose and relaxed him. He moved his attention to Eppie's neck and chin, and wondered if he could get away with moving his finger down and under her neckline, under her bra, teasing her with a touch on her breast. That would be enough to make his night.

He said, "A perfect night. Couldn't be better."

"Oh, I don't know." Eppie then took his hand and guided it to a spot above her knee under her hiked-up skirt. Nate was still contemplating whether this meant what he thought it meant, and if it really meant that, how to do it without coming off as an inexperienced jerk, when she patted her leg from waist to her knee and laughed to find Nate's hand where she left it.

"Don't tease me, Evans. It's up here." She drew his hand higher. "My legs may be worthless, but I'm not dead. I don't want to live like it."

CHAPTER THIRTY-SEVEN
Busted in a Bustier

"So what you're saying is, he cheated on you. That scum bucket."

Carla sat across from Julie at a long, black laboratory table strewn with notepaper, beakers, whiteboard markers, notepads, safety goggles and textbooks abandoned by students in their rush out of the last class on Friday.

"No. What I'm saying is, that's how Nate feels. He had this notion that, when he had sex with Eppie Johnson, he was being unfaithful to me." Julie had stopped by the school on her way to Mom's house to collect some things for Ethel's move to a rehabilitation center. After that, she would head back to the hospital for a few hours. Russell was already gone for the day when she passed his office; his secretary said he didn't come back from lunch.

Carla shrugged. "That's it? That's all?" She said it with an incredulous dash of drama. "That's the big kerfuffle that ruined your relationship with Nate? I am so disappointed."

"We never had a real relationship. We weren't going steady or anything close. That's what makes it so weird."

"He takes a girl to the prom and things go too far afterwards. They had sex. Nowadays too many kids think there's something wrong if they *don't* have sex. Though I guess it was a bigger deal back then. I thought so at the time. Didn't you?"

Julie ignored the question. "Let's face it, when you're seventeen, everything is a big deal in any generation. Anyway, he swears he once promised me that, when the time came, his first time and my first time would be our first time together. At least in Nate-speak, that's how he put it."

"Do you remember it? Did he really promise that?"

"Not in so many words. But we had a really close call two months or so before the prom. And that's when—"

Carla's eyes lit up. "Do tell," she interrupted. "So things between you were hotter than you've led us all to believe. I think I'm hurt. You had ample chance to say something. And nothing. Not even to your best friend."

Julie picked up a whiteboard marker sitting in front of her on the table and flung it in the general direction of Carla. "The point is, before it went too far, we got busted. By Mom."

"Your mother caught you?"

Yes and no. She told Carla how Nate scrambled out the bedroom window and they thought they had gotten away with it until Ethel told her, forty years later, that she knew all along. It seemed comical now. "A day or two later was when Nate gave me his "wanting to be first and only" speech. I thought he was asking me to go steady, but he wasn't. And when he started ignoring me after the prom we didn't go to, like we had broken up and he didn't want anything to do with me, actually what he was feeling... He was feeling guilty about having sex with that other girl and didn't want to face it. Or me, rather."

"And you're buying this now?"

"With anybody else, chances would be slim. But with Nate?" She shrugged and nodded with fatalistic resignation. What could she do? He was the only one she could think of who was naïve enough to see it as being unfaithful and dumb enough to let it come between them. "I have to say, it was sweet the way he apologized last night for it."

"Just a hundred years late."

Silence might be golden, but the quiet of a classroom that normally reverberated all day long with the chatter of students had a profoundly unique comfort. Julie sipped tea that Carla brewed on a hot plate behind her desk.

"I know what I have to do; I just don't know how I'm going to do it," she said. "But I surely don't need this kind of complication. It's too hard and I'm too old to put up with it. Do you know we sat and talked until nearly two o'clock this morning?"

"No wonder he dragged in here this morning like a whipped puppy."

"Yeah, well, I'm not feeling particularly frisky myself."

"So what are you going to do?"

"I'm scared." She said she was drawn to Nate, and the comparison to Russell couldn't be clearer. That comparison led her to think about all the little ways Russell cut her. Nate made it harder to ignore or excuse them. She had been doing too much of that.

She loved the way Nate was always upbeat and pulled everybody up with him. He was generous with compliments and was quick to help others in a quirky kind of way, pretending to be Seth in order to set up a blind date with the girl he didn't have the nerve to ask out about as goofy as it gets. That turned out to be not only fun but productive. They were getting married. And he told her he was in love with her in a way that made her want to believe. But.

"But he's a big risk. He's never been reliable in our history together. And now he's back with this crazy thing about living high school all over again. I'm afraid that maybe I'm just part of that and he'll be gone as soon as I break up with Russell. If I do."

The look on Carla's face was somewhere between amused and a superiority complex born in sarcasm. Julie pointed that out.

"You know I've never been totally sold on Russell. It's his weak chin, I think. And you know I've never thought it was a good match, at least ever since you told me he uses bacon-flavored dental floss."

"Floss aside, the point is, you can't go around trying to love one guy when you can't stop thinking about another guy, and thinking about the other guy all the time means you're not being fair to the guy you're going to marry, right?"

"Good lord, you're even starting to talk like Nate."

Julie sighed. "Yeah. Isn't that sweet?" The sarcasm was wasted on Carla.

"So I'm going to talk with Russell, tonight if I can. I need to see if he wants this marriage enough to stop dragging his feet."

"An ultimatum."

Julie nodded. "If he loves me as much as he says he does, we can live together until the wedding, and I can stop thinking about what it would be like to be with Nate instead. It would be settled. Nate would go away, and we could get on with our lives."

"That doesn't seem like the best basis to marry someone on. Aren't you listening to yourself?"

Julie said she didn't mean to sound so emotionally mercenary.

She was only making an argument for the practical, sensible choice. It wasn't the fun choice, though.

She called Russell before heading to the hospital and left a message, annoyed again that he didn't answer. That had been happening more frequently. With all the time she'd taken off work, Julie hadn't seen much of her fiancé lately. She needed to fix that as soon as possible.

She stayed late, watching television as Ethel drifted in and out. When she was sure Mom was asleep for the night, Julie clicked off the TV and headed back home feeling guilty for being preoccupied with confronting Russell. Alone in the confines of her car, she allowed herself to focus on her problem. What would she say? She pulled into a Chevron station and leaned against her car with her arms crossed while the pump filled her gas tank.

Julie watched the traffic light change and the cars pull away from a stop at the intersection. Everyone was headed home to families and husbands. When she climbed back into her car and switched on the headlights, they put a spot on a sign in the window of the convenience store. California Super Lotto Jackpot—Seven million! A mere seven million, she thought with a familiar twinge of disappointment.

"Somebody got lucky." Seven million meant somebody had won the jackpot in the drawing the night before. It wasn't Julie. Again. No, the closest she would ever get was the ticket she bought with Nate's birthday numbers. Close was nice. It was fun. It was exciting. But it was not a winner. Just like Nate.

She decided to drive by Russell's house and look for signs of life in case he simply turned off his cell phone. His car was in the driveway and there were lights on inside. He'd be happy to see her, she hoped, and that would make this easier. When the door opened, Julie found herself staring at a tall, gorgeous if disheveled woman in a bright red cowboy hat turned backwards on her head and cash in her hand. She wore a thick black collar, a rumpled robe that did little to hide the leather bustier underneath and tall stiletto heels so sharp they could spike a vampire's heart.

"You're not the pizza boy."

"No, I'm Julie."

"Oh. Well, it's nice to finally meet you. I'm Nicolette. Come in. Come in." The woman opened the door wider and turned.

"Hey, babe," she shouted. "It's not the pizza boy. It's the fiancée."

Julie stood there and glared at the woman.

"Oh, silly me," Nicolette the tramp laughed as she raised a hand to her perfect smile. "Really. Come in. I'll go untie Russell so you two can talk."

Fifteen minutes later, Julie was racing like a bat out of hell back home, keeping one eye on the rearview mirror, praying she wouldn't find flashing lights and a cop there. The aluminum baseball bat she had taken from the back of Russell's SUV in the driveway, the one that now leaned against the passenger-side seat of her car, rolled right and clanged against the door when she made a turn too quickly.

When she got home, she stripped naked and stepped into the shower. The water was as hot as she could stand, and she scrubbed her body as if that would wash away the filth of her relationship. She hated him more than anyone she had ever encountered, and her anger grew with the steam behind the curtain and swirled around her. She loathed herself even more.

How could she be so stupid? So gullible and blind? All it took was the right look, the right smile, the right touch in the right place at the right time and she was in love. She slumped into a sitting position against the back of the tub, dropping her head so that the hot water from the shower pounded the back of her neck. Worse, she had refused to see that their relationship had always been on his terms. That stung more than the jet of water against her cheeks when she raised her face. She had been lonely and he was the antidote. What she felt was love must have been desperation that turned her from a clear-eyed, intelligent woman into a dependent romantic pinning her future on a fraud. Good God, she was stupid.

She drew her knees in close and sat under the stream for a very long time. She had survived childbirth, and she had survived widowhood. She had survived the death of her father, the illness of her mother and the absence of her children. She assumed she would survive this, too. But as the water went from nearly scalding her to warm, then tepid to cold, she sat in silence and simply wanted to die and get it over with.

CHAPTER THIRTY-EIGHT
The Big Break

The rock, or lack thereof, was the first thing that he noticed about Julie Monday morning. The first thing, that was, after her smile, after her eyes that greeted him with numb sadness, after the swish of her skirt and the way the sunlight, which had finally broken through, kissed her hair. And that all came after the blue aluminum Louisville Slugger she had resting on her shoulder as she crossed the north quad near his English classroom. He thought she would be more intimidating if she could tap the head of the baseball bat in her hand like a prison guard with a billy club.

"Nice stick," Nate said when he snuck up beside her. Then he ducked to avoid being bopped as she spun at the sound of his voice. Her left hand, with fingers wrapped around the handle of the bat, was naked. It brought optimistic terror to his heart. Somebody got dumped over the weekend; anger stifled the air around her. It didn't take much to put two and two together and come up with five. Two people, two smashed headlights and one Foxy Banker added up to trouble. Nicolette must have forgiven FesterDick after the night she dumped him in the drink off the dock by the bay. Mary had even predicted it would happen on their drive home that night.

Nate took the Louisville Slugger and admired it. "You know, this is just like Festerhaven's Suzie Blue, his favorite bat."

"Really? Maybe that's how I wound up with it."

"Speaking of," Nate drew out the words. "Did you hear? Someone took a hammer or something to Festerhaven's car. Whacked the snot out of the headlights. You wouldn't know anything about that, would you?"

"Me? Why would you even think that? Hmm. I guess I should give Russell his bat back." She turned and walked away.

"So are you going to tell me about it?" Nate asked hopefully when he caught up to her again.

"No." Nothing more.

"Oh, come on. It might be helpful. If I can help."

"Not on your life. You're scum."

"Scum? What did I do?"

"You were born."

"Born."

"Male."

Julie pulled up quickly and lowered the head of the bat. Nate suspected the move was intentional because he walked right into it and yelped as the bat banged off his shin. "You can't help it. All men are scum."

Nate hopped on one foot and rubbed his battered leg. "Well, yeah. I guess it's in our DNA. If we weren't vital for the survival of the species, I'm sure someone would have figured out a way by now to wipe us from the face of the earth. And frankly, Jules, there are plenty of times I'd have a hard time making a case against it." Setting up the woman who could have been, might still become, his love and best friend for this heartbreak was one. That would surely be up there on the list of asinine male crimes and misdemeanors.

"Don't be so nice and agreeable."

"So you'll be less pissed off at me if I act like I couldn't care less."

"Just don't care so much. Okay? I'm not in the mood."

That was a stopper. He fought the urge to ask Julie what she meant. Had he crossed some unspoken line? Had Festerhaven mentioned him when whatever went down went down? He watched Julie walk away, hoping he was nothing more than scum by association in the fight between her and Festerhaven.

He could live with that.

He could recover from that.

He would spend the rest of his life doing right by her for it if she let him.

That afternoon, he stood up from his desk in the corner of his classroom.

"Okay, scribes, you can stop scribing. Time's up." He told the students to send their work to the assignment folder networked to the computer on his desk. "Make sure you have your name formatted properly on the unlikely chance I have to give you a byline. Homework for the weekend is two hundred words on one of your parents, grand-parents, siblings or dogs."

"Mr. Evans." Gabrielle raised her hand. Of course it would be Gabrielle. "What about cats? Can I write about my hamster? I don't have a dog."

"Miss Flores, you can write about anyone or anything that is living, breathing, eats, sleeps and poops. The goal is to write something about them that interests me. Remember, it's character development."

When the students filed out, Nate pulled out notes for the next class while he ran a hand over all the junk in the top drawer of the desk. He found his phone and checked his messages. All three were from his agent. Nate couldn't fathom what Jack would find so urgent that he'd spend half his day trying to reach him.

"Where have you been all day?"

"Jack, some of us work for a living. Wait, no. You wouldn't know anything about that, but that's okay. Really." Nate braced for another browbeating over his lack of production. He felt bad about wasting another week not adding to his story, but Julie's smile and a couple of busted headlights changed everything that morning. He could write that.

"You're going to thank me, Nate. Thank me big-time. I mean, big-time."

"Sure, Jack, sure." Nate laughed now. "The last time you said that, we got an advance that paid what? Enough for two hot dogs and a Big Gulp from 7-11. And even then, I had to give you your fifteen percent of one of those dogs."

"You're going to eat those words when you hear what I have to say, my friend, so don't piss me off. I sold the story for you."

"You sold *what*?" Nate knew damned well what. Jack seemed to think there was actual confusion there.

"The one you're working on now. Old guy gets crapped on by life and runs home to get mommy and daddy to kiss his emotional boo-boo. I pitched that *Cyrano* thing meets *The Sting* meets *Back to the Future* without the Delorean. She loved the concept. Have you found your ending for the story yet? Never mind, she doesn't need an ending yet. She says she's got history and trusts you."

Jack was talking a mile a minute now, and Nate suspected he might have some pharmaceuticals working for him. Nate had experienced Jack on coke once, and it wasn't a pretty sight. He could almost feel Jack's heart pounding through the phone.

He asked who "she" was, and why "she" didn't need an ending.

"I sold *Julie's Mulligan* to Tina Farnham's production company."

"*Diva Does Dallas, Peacock Blues* Tina Farnham? Emmy winner Tina Farnham?"

"She took a personal interest in the story once I got inside the gate."

"Tina wants the movie option?"

"She ran the story idea to Netflix. What's more, they want not only a movie but to follow it up with a pilot for a possible sitcom deal." He kept repeating "ka-ching!" And then threw out a figure, the money Netflix and Tina Farnham were putting on the table. Nate got up and drew a dollar sign on the white board at the front of the classroom, a big, bold, in-your-face statement of a dollar sign. It was the kind of money he always dreamed of. More importantly, it was the big break that dodged him all his life.

He knew Tina. He had worked with Tina before she hit it big. He hadn't talked to her in years. She's back. "How soon can we get the contract?"

Jack said Tina's people's people were working on it. "I showed them what you sent me, and they want to see more, but Tina wants that part. So we can finalize the details and celebrate when we get there at the end of the month."

"Here? What's going on?" Nate asked.

"Oh, yeah. Tina's going to be there, a bunch of celebrities will be, for a Silicon Valley charity fundraiser to fight global warming. Something about raising money to save penguins in the arctic by building giant ice-making machines or something like that. I have a ticket for you. In fact, Tina said she was looking forward to seeing you again. I didn't know you guys have a past."

"It's not much of one, trust me." Nate just left it at that; he didn't need to provide details suggesting there was more to *that* story.

"It's a week from Thursday. We'll go save some penguins, drink champagne and ink the deal Friday over coffee while we nurse our well-deserved hangovers. I'm setting up a breakfast meeting with Tina and her folks. We can get it done then. After we save the penguins. Do you have a tux?"

"I'll find one." Nate waited. He didn't know what to say. The irony of landing what finally could be the project to make his career at this particular moment stunned him. He had churned out so many words, fictional characters with their perfectly pithy dialogues, and all the plots Nate shopped while chasing his dream now felt so distant. Maybe Woody was right. When he started writing his story about finding Julie, he expected it would land on slush piles in producers' offices all over L.A. as usual. That expectation allowed him freedom to make it more personal than he would have written it otherwise and it put him in demand for the first time in his life.

Jack said, "Turn that crap you've been sending me into a formal treatment, and, for God's sake, when you write for Tina, put a lot more emphasis on the leading lady. Let's face it, that's all she cares about. It's what she's paying for. Total chick-flick."

"It's not a chick-flick. I don't do chick-flick."

"Well I sold it that way, do you want this or not? The way you wrote that Julie character. Cooper, right? This definitely turned into her story. Made it a lot better, too."

When did that happen? And either way, he should have changed her name before sending anything to Jack.

"Maybe we could rewrite and make *her* the one with the high school obsession. Well, we can fix that later. We're calling it *Julie's Mulligan*. Did I tell you that? The other characters are weird and funny, too. Keep it funny, okay? Keep Nat, the loser character. He's funny and that's the kind of shit you do so well."

"Yeah, I can do loser without even trying," Nate said, though the way this day turned out, with Julie dumping FesterCrud and getting a movie deal that exceeded even his wildest hopes, he smiled and started believing that was going to be a stretch from now on.

CHAPTER THIRTY-NINE

Hiccup

Anger was a funny thing. With people you cared about, it could be a moving target. It had cooled to a simmer in the week since Julie took the baseball bat to Russell's car, turning into disgust and a pain she assumed would eventually fade as well. She couldn't think of a single time in her life when she resorted to violence for any situation. She never even spanked her children no matter how much they deserved it.

"If I had known how good it feels, I would have hit something like that a long time ago."

Nate said, "Funny, I had that same experience not all that long ago. It's part of the reason I left So-Cal. You're a dangerous woman, Jules."

"And to think, Russell had the audacity to ask me to pay for the repairs. He didn't make excuses for being with that woman and he didn't ask me to forgive him and sounded pretty matter-of-fact about breaking up."

They were walking to the Dairy Barn. He had offered to buy her a milkshake after school every day that week. On Friday, the weather cooperated with one of those February days that practically begged people to move to California, clear and mild and two days past the last rain. The weather had warmed, and Julie had cooled down enough to take him up on the offer. Nate reached for the paper notebook and iPad Julie carried as they left the campus.

"Humor me," he said. Carrying her books like that was sweet and a bit unnerving. More than once, his hand brushed her hip as they walked. Julie didn't think it was entirely accidental. She elbowed him in the lingering way eskimos rub noses. That was intentional. Having him around had never seemed more comforting than right now. No matter that she had gone to Russell's house to serve up an ultimatum that could have led to her breaking up with him, what he did was inexcusable and it hurt. It hurt a lot.

She stopped, like slamming on the brakes the way Nate frequently did with her, and hugged him from the side with one arm. "Thanks for not being a jerk." Then she moved on.

They walked another block in silence, but it didn't feel awkward. By now, most of the adults on campus had heard some version of the breakup. She grew tired of dodging embarrassing whispers of support and pity. Nate was the only friend who didn't pester her every hour about how she was feeling, asking if she was okay, in that way people tried to comfort someone with a fatal disease or a dead spouse. He let Julie just be. She appreciated that and rewarded him by letting him back into the fringe of her life.

"I'm glad he didn't sic the cops on you," he said. "Although I'd guess that would only have called attention to something he'd rather not have to explain."

"That may be the only thing standing between me and jail. But then, it's still early. Check back with me in another week," she added with a weak laugh.

Nate held the door and she walked in ahead of him. Something about crossing that threshold made her open up, and she started talking about how angry she had gotten. It wasn't until she was describing the leather bustier- wearing bimbo in the cockeyed cowboy hat that she became aware of the blushing teenage girl taking their order. Nate didn't notice the cashier at all.

"Did you find out if she handcuffed him to the bed, or used a cord of some sort?"

She raised her voice slightly, for the benefit of the girl taking their order. That was fun. "She said she had to untie him." Thanks, but she didn't want a Chocolate Oreo and Peppermint milkshake.

"Milkshakes make everything better," he said.

She said he couldn't imagine how slutty the woman looked, and yes, a medium Pepsi was all Julie wanted. The cashier's manager moved closer, pretending to ignore them as she speculated on how uncomfortable that outfit must be in all the wrong places. Well, all right, make it a large Pepsi. Diet, please.

Nate nodded. "Especially the cowboy hat. Very painful if it's on too tight."

Julie got two looks from the opposite side of the counter and detected a layer of disappointment settling over the cashier and her boss as Nate led her to a table in the farthest corner of the diner.

"It's all so unbelievably cliché," he said. "To be met at the door like that. It's been used in more movies than that kid behind the counter has freckles. Bazillions. And I think I wrote half of them. Usually right around the seventy-minute mark in the movie. I didn't think it happened in real life, but no matter how much a producer called it lame and cliché, they always left it in because it sells popcorn. Wow. Who knew?"

She lamented she should have known about Russell. It must not have been the first time. She was so blind.

"Don't go there. The mistake is to beat yourself up over it. Better to beat up his car." He winked.

"I'm so embarrassed by that." Julie shook her head slowly. "I just snapped."

"Jules, you don't know snap. I know snap. I'm an expert in snappage. I could teach a class in snapology."

He was teasing her now, trying to cheer her up. It helped even if he was lying. "Right. You are the most easygoing, un-snappable person I know."

"You're right. I shouldn't have said anything."

He stirred his milkshake and she knew his mind had wandered off again. "What are you thinking? What's going on in there?"

"It's nothing. Forget it."

"No way. You brought up something; you can't take it back now."

Nate continued to stir, wrestling with whether to say more, while Julie watched and sipped her drink. He had pulled so much out of her with so little effort, could she do the same? "If it's none of my business, just say so."

Nate continued his mental gymnastics in silence before he picked up Julie's iPad. "They have wifi here." He poked, stroked and typed as he navigated the screen. "I would be the last one to make light of what you've been through. But I want to show you someone who really snapped his nut."

He handed the tablet back to her as a YouTube video rolled. "Isn't that the TV dog? Yes, I've seen this before," she said.

"You and three million others." He sighed.

Julie scrunched her nose. "Ouch! That poor little dog." She watched the scene play out. And when it was over, she asked, "But what does this have to do with anything?"

Nate moved around the table to the seat next to her and told her to play it again. He draped one arm along the back of her chair. That was nice. When the video reached the point where that poor sap crushed Ruffles the TV dog, Nate reached out and stabbed the screen to freeze the video. It was a bit fuzzy, but the crusher's face was unmistakably familiar. And at that moment, it was inches away from her own, deliberately absorbed with the image on her tablet in order to avoid her eyes. They sat there in silence. She studied his face, but even now, Nate had a sense of relaxed acceptance, calm as always.

Finally he said simply, "I jumped from a balcony."

"But why?"

"Oh. I was having a bad day."

"A bad day."

"A bad day. A bad month. A bad year, well, several actually. A bad life, I guess. That was the same day the Air Force blew up my home. I told you about that."

Yes, he had. Though every time he told it, he added more humor, until everyone at the school could laugh at his misfortune.

Now, he told her that, for reasons he didn't want to dwell on, he wound up at a party in the most depressed mood ever. "I took a pill that was supposed to make me feel good. You know those commercials for antidepressants that come with the warning they may cause suicidal thoughts? Believe it. I took something—Ecstasy, actually—and it is way stronger."

"Not to mention illegal," she cut in. Amazing, but as she thought about it, not shocking given his history of bouts with common sense the way other people fought off the flu.

"The doctor said it only heightened the anxiety I was feeling. Instead of making me feel better, it made me think there was no use in going on, so I snapped. I jumped. Seems suicide—I couldn't even get that right."

What in the world did you say about something like that? To someone like that. She wrapped her lips on her straw, thinking. Finally she nodded and said, "You're right. That is major snappage."

Using Nate's own words made him chuckle, but she wondered how he could treat something as serious as suicide so lightly. She didn't think at all when she bashed Russell's car; she acted on impulse. It couldn't possibly be the same, could it?

He moved back to his chair on the opposite side of the table. "What were you thinking?" Julie knew she sounded like a mother scolding her child for getting sick for eating crayons, and rainbow barf was not easy to get out of a beige carpet.

She reached out and took his hand. With gentle curiosity, she asked what made his life so bad. The way she saw it, his life seemed so successful and glamorous, better than most and way better than anybody she knew, but Nate shook his head. "Let's save that for another time. Another place. This isn't it. Besides, right now we need to keep you from doing any more damage to Festerhaven. We need to keep you out of jail." Julie pulled back ever so slightly as Nate reached out. He took her chin between his thumb and forefinger, drawing a smile from her.

He looked at her with lines at the corners of his eyes turned up, almost laughing on their own, and she couldn't help but look away. She hated when he did that, because she loved when he did. It was his flirty look, and she believed he saved it for special occasions. When they were young, he used it and the rest of the world melted away. God, she was such a…such a girl back then.

"You're trying too hard, Evans."

"What?"

"You know what. You are *not* getting out of this with just a look."

"What look?" His face was neutral except that the eyes were still dancing.

"*That* look."

"I didn't know I had one. Is it working?"

"It depends. What are you going after?"

"It's this. I have an idea of how to give you some perspective on this mess that may help. How much do you trust me?"

"I trust you totally—but only up to a point, that is. You're not going to suggest fake skydiving again, are you?" Julie felt something risky coming on. Nate had been right about the skydiving day and how a few minutes of thrill added color to her life.

He said, "If you thought that made you feel good, then how about this?" And what he suggested stole her breath away. She inhaled, forgetting about the straw in her mouth. It forced her to swallow quickly. Bubbles tickled her nose. Words failed her. Her response mortified her.

Hiccup.

CHAPTER FORTY

When the Stars Aligned

Nate had to drag Julie to his bed; she put up a good fight. He could have taken her in his arms and carried her across the threshold of the bedroom like a groom on his honeymoon. He could have hoisted her over his shoulder like a fireman escaping from a burning house. Instead, he hooked one of her arms around his neck and one of his arms around her waist to steer her across the living room. She was like a child who refused to surrender to sleep, wanting to stay up long past her bedtime even though she could no longer keep her eyes open. At one point, she stopped moving her feet, in a drowsy but playful mood, leaving Nate to lug her the last few feet with the toes of her socks picking up dust as they slid across the pine floor. While he'd hardly consider it the stuff of his fantasies, he hadn't held Julie this close, close enough to feel her heartbeat in his own chest, since their relationship was still in the minor leagues.

Julie stroked his hand after Nate laid her out on the bed and spread a thick quilt comforter over her.

"I'm sorry," she whispered.

He asked her what there was to be sorry about, but Julie only mumbled something indecipherable before drifting off. He backed out of the bedroom and softly closed the door. There was a guest bedroom in the beach house, but Nate pulled an overstuffed chair to the bay windows facing the ocean. The sun would be rising soon enough, and the morning fog would roll in, but it was still clear out there, and he decided he could sleep later. Like Julie, he wasn't ready to give up without a fight what could easily go down as the most perfect night of his life.

He was tempted to ask her a second time, just to prove he wasn't hearing things when she agreed to spend the weekend with him. No, he didn't dare press his luck. He made the offer thinking it would help Jules escape her heartache if only for a spell, and Lord knows he was an expert in that area. He didn't expect her to accept. Jack had arranged a weekend for him, getting the house so Nate could spend it writing in solitude and nudge him toward whipping out a full story treatment for Tina Farnham's company, Dangling Participle Productions. It was on a private cove between Santa Cruz and Capitola and belonged to one of Jack's friends of a friend of an associate of someone who knew someone who agreed to lend them the property for the weekend so that Nate could work without distractions. He was supposed to be alone, so having Julie along guaranteed he would be distracted, but he didn't care. Like sleep, he could catch up later.

They arrived long after sunset but the weather gods couldn't have provided a better, clearer, milder winter night than if Nate had hocked his soul to pay for it. He would have done it, too. And the forecast called for clear skies through sunset tomorrow, Valentines Day. Nate built a campfire on the beach. He and Julie formed a V above it lying in the sand on their backs, snuggled into separate sleeping bags with their heads side by side and their toes pointing to opposite sides of the cove. They talked without looking at one another, staring instead at the millions of stars splattered across the sky on a moonless night like a Jackson Pollack painting. For Nate, the drive over the pass had all the nervous energy of their very first date without the pimples. He tried too hard to be witty, and Julie laughed too hard at his lame jokes.

Conversation lapsed into long stretches of silence, silence that he might have ruined with random thoughts or mindless chatter in another setting. Ah, peace, vastly underrated these days. He let his weight and his worries sink into the sand and sensed Jules did as well.

Julie stared up and said to the stars, "I'm really glad you're such a screw-up."

"Should I take that as a compliment?" Nate let the waves fill the silence with their rhythmic wash on the beach as if they were saying to him, "Hush. Hush." It wasn't easy to take their advice.

She sighed a full-throated exhale drawn out like someone enjoying a back rub. "I still can't get it through my head. Suppose you had been successful, the suicide, I mean. That would be so awful. I just can't imagine."

"Hush. Hush," the sea said. Nate said nothing.

"Mmm. This is nice," Julie said.

He let his mind float. "I had a night like this—it was New Year's Eve, as a matter of fact—right after the marriage hit the rocks for good. Talk about a real shipwreck. So I jumped on the first plane out of Dodge, and I wound up with my butt in the sand under the stars and the sound of the surf washing out all the noise in my head along with those damned mariachis I could hear at the bar way down the beach. It was Mexico, and I felt like I had dumped all my troubles at the border. Millions of stars were out, just like this. In fact, I'm sure this is exactly the same sky. It hit me then. I realized how enormous the universe is and how small our problems are by comparison. I really felt at peace for probably the only time in my life."

"Until now?" There was hopefulness in Julie's voice.

"This? Nah." Nate let that hang between them as if the notion was ludicrous. Then he chuckled, "This is so much better."

Julie rapped the top of his head with the back of her hand.

"It didn't last, of course. It never does, but so what? It helped me at the time. I thought maybe this could help you now."

"Well, it seems to be working." Julie paused. "I wish we could stay like this forever."

"Jules, I would move heaven and earth to make it so. Move heaven and earth to make you happy." In a way, Nate felt as if he was halfway there.

"God, that is so sweet." Julie snuggled deeper into her sleeping bag and tucked the top layer under her chin. Wiggling as she did and shifting the sand beneath her in a way to get more comfortable brought her head closer to Nate so that he could almost feel the warmth of her cheek next to his. "That would be nice. Impossible. Impractical, but nice."

"To hell with being practical all the time. You need to learn to let go a little more. I mean, if buying lottery tickets is the big, decadent fun in your life each week, you need to up your game."

"Who told you that? Carla?"

"Carla and everybody else. But they all think it's cute. I do." He stopped her before she could defend herself. "Wait. Listen. You hear that? The waves. Listen. They're talking to us. They're saying"—he paused to time his words so they echoed the incoming surf—"hush. Hushhh."

And Julie listened. It was a long time before she said anything. "I get it—that feeling you had on the beach in Mexico. That's what I'm feeling."

"Don't fight it." Nate turned his face away from her toward the fire. The flames were gone but the driftwood refused to die out. It glowed a dull red and warmed his nose and added a flavor of charred bark to the salty ocean air. He thought if only Julie had been on that beach in Cancun with him, he'd never have come home.

He had rolled his head back and pointed her to one particular dim star in a small patch of black just below the Little Dipper. It was his star, he told her. His life was faint but unmistakable like the light from the star alone in a tiny spot of sky. "That bright one over there, surrounded by all the others? That's you."

With the fire dying out and the chill settling in, he suggested they move indoors and climbed out of his sleeping bag. He took Julie's hand as she awkwardly worked her way out of hers like a butterfly shedding her cocoon. He wrapped it around her shoulders and stood close behind her, watching the waves catch the starlight.

They turned back to the house, and it was on the last incline to its deck that Julie asked, "So. Have you remembered the first time you kissed me yet?" She bumped him playfully with her shoulder and lost her balance so that he had to catch her from behind, both arms wrapped around her and one hand accidentally cupping a breast. He let it linger longer than he should. She let him get away with it.

"You bet," he replied as they righted themselves. He had prepared for this, hoping he'd get the chance to show off. "It was on the field trip we took to Alum Rock Park in eighth grade, behind the gazebo with the sulphur water fountain. Ha! Take that. Didn't think I would. But I've known it all along. I was just messing with you last time."

"Well, you're messing again. You are so wrong."

"You're kidding."

"Nope. Strike two. You aren't even warm."

"Okay, back to the bench." He'd better hit the next guess out of the park. "I think you're making this up. But just in case, I'll give it more thought and get back to you on that one."

What followed into the early-morning hours was a pair of rambling dialogues. They were part confessional, a bit of reminiscing, and a truckload of discovery as they shared episodes from their life stories. At one point, Julie spoke slowly and chose careful words to explain how she dropped out of Stanford, got married before she was twenty and started raising a family. It wasn't the life she had envisioned.

Nate thought he was finally living the life he wanted. He had taken control for a change and made it real.

"Last time I asked, you said you wouldn't go back and change anything because of your kids. Cool enough. So now that they're gone and you're on your own again, what's on the Jules Cooper bucket list of things you wish you had gotten to do but didn't? Do you want more hot chocolate?"

"No. I think I'd want more than that out of life."

"I meant…"

"I know what you meant." She laughed.

He left her to think about it while he went to the kitchen to start another pot of milk and get cocoa mix from the cupboard. When he came back, she was stretched along the length of the sofa staring at the ceiling.

"If I could, I'd buy a motorcycle and ride it across the country."

That was a shocker. But it made sense as she explained.

"In one of those nights at the hospital, Mom and I were talking about my dad and how the only passion he had outside of work was his motorcycle, and the rides he used to take with a bunch of other people, mostly accountants and lawyers and such on weekends. Some days I think the only fun memories I have of him are riding with him on his bike when I was little."

"So I'll ask again. What's stopping you?" He went back to the kitchen to stir the milk barely simmering on the stove.

"Silly question. Those days are long past."

"They are not. Go for it."

"They are, too."

"Are not."

"Are, too."

Nate was enjoying it. They were like two children in a sandbox, squabbling for no reason other than for the fun of disagreeing. Tag, you're it.

Then he went back and stood in front of her with his hands on his hips. "Seriously, though. Stop making people drag you kicking and screaming to have a little fun. Do something big that makes you happy, just once before it really is too late. If that's a motorcycle, there you go. You could do it if you wanted. Didn't you say your son-in-law owns a bike shop?"

"He manages one. In *Texas* now, thank you for reminding me." She rolled onto her side and buried her cheek in the sofa's pillow. She talked to the floor. "But it hasn't been lost on me that maybe it's not coincidence that Tiffany married a guy who rides motorcycles the way her granddad did."

"See? It's in your DNA. I think you should do it. You could get a tattoo and wear a leather vest. Put a little vroom-vroom in your life."

She turned her head and gave him that childish, toothy smile and a dreamy, unfocused gaze. "I thought that's what we were doing this weekend."

Oh, that was the most perfect come-on he had ever encountered. Where had all this sexual tension come from? No matter, he was a boy who wanted to kiss her badly, and she was a girl badly in need of kissing, but before he could move, the milk on the stove hissed. It was bubbling over. He went to rescue it and reached for the metal handle of the pot without thinking. It burned his fingers and he spilled milk all over the stove when he dropped the pot. By the time he cleaned it up and went back to Julie, she was dozing.

Nate replayed their conversation in his head as he sat in the easy chair after putting her to bed. Sometimes he replaced her response to some topic they had covered with what he wanted to hear, or he replaced his own response with something he wished he had said instead. Sometimes he imagined dialogue on a topic they never approached. Mostly he sat back and enjoyed the afterglow of being with Julie when they said nothing at all.

When the first light of Saturday morning wrestled with the sky thick with fog, Nate got up and peered in at her. He heard her snoring, her exhales coming out in quiet puffs of breath. How perfect life would be if he could spend every night listening to her snore. Happy endings were a Hollywood myth, not impossible, but certainly rare in real life.

Still, Nate couldn't see any reason why he and Julie couldn't write one of their own. Then he went over to an antique rolltop desk against the pine-paneled walls in the opposite corner of the living room. A row of family portraits dating back to the wedding picture of a couple four generations earlier sat across the top of the desk. All those anonymous faces smiled down at Nate. He fired up his laptop and typed an email to Jack.

Thanks for the beach house weekend. Working hard on the story and it's perfect. Love triumphs. It's blockbuster.

CHAPTER FORTY-ONE

And the Waves Said…

Hush.

Julie leaned on a rail of the beach house deck with a mug of coffee warming her hands and the collar of her jacket turned up to protect her neck against the morning chill. The air was thick with the smell of saltwater and seaweed. She had gotten up to find Nate sleeping on the couch with his laptop still open on his stomach. He didn't budge when she draped a blanket over his knees and feet or when she fixed her coffee as silently as she could in the kitchen. She listened to the waves, and they were talking to her.

Hush.

Poor Nate. She had dumped what felt like a lifetime of insecurities, missteps and fears—real and imagined—in the hours between the campfire and sleep. Did she really make him carry her to bed?

She reached out her left hand as if to touch the incoming waves. She held it before her eyes. Steady, it didn't tremble anymore. She had trembled a lot in the days after discovering the truth about Russell. Anger, first, then uncertainty and nervousness kept her shivering through the week whenever she thought of him, when someone mentioned his name, and it came on strong every time she had to deal with him at work. Did she have a right to feel this calm now? It had only been seven days. Their exchanges at work had been cordially frigid in public, biting and bitter as a lemon when no one was looking.

Hush.

Nate was right. The ocean, the view, the comfort of a warm house and a weekend with a friend were working their spell. Maybe it was Nate. It wasn't as if she had shaken all the demons and weight that had seemed so heavy in just one week, but the tide was going out, pulling her troubles with it.

Oh, he would love that metaphor. It needed a sandcastle, though, and maybe a few seagulls skittering along the edge of the surf. She would suggest he use it in the story he was working on.

He was up and about as Julie made her way back through the living room on her way to the kitchen. The shower was running in the bathroom. She took inventory of food supplies in the refrigerator and cupboards. The pickings were slim. No fresh eggs, but frozen waffles and a toaster might be okay. She found a new box of Cap'n Crunch and some Pop-Tarts.

"I bet Nate would love those," she said. That seemed right up his alley.

She was feeding the coffeemaker with a fresh scoop when he came up behind her and slipped one arm around her waist. She stiffened. He didn't seem to notice, instead kissed her on the back of the head in a way that was insignificantly sensual before he turned away as natural as could be.

"Morning."

He stood in front of the food cupboard for a moment before

taking one of the Pop-Tarts packages. "You didn't see this," he said. "My mom would kill me, unless, maybe, if they had an organic kale flavor. Would you like one?"

"God, no. I've gone this long without. I'm on a mission to get through my entire life without ever having one of those cross my lips."

"Uh-huh. Now tell the truth. I'll bet you used to feed them to your kids, and I'll bet you snuck a bite or two, Mom. Don't lie."

"Well, okay. One or two nibbles, but only the chocolate ones."

"See?"

"But I ate them with my eyes closed, so that doesn't count."

Pastries toasted and coffee poured, she followed him to the living room, where he set his laptop aside and curled up on an edge of the couch. She sat on the opposite end facing him and pointed at the computer.

"Tell me more about the story you're working on. Are you really going to make a bazillion dollars on it like you said last night?" As she sipped from her mug, the coffee hit the sweet spot in her taste buds, the aroma intoxicated her, and she couldn't imagine wanting to be anywhere else that morning.

"Did I say bazillions? I meant hundreds. Well, maybe bazillions if we're getting paid in Zimbabwean dollars or pesos, considering the exchange rate and all that, but I don't think we're going to shoot this in Tijuana, so it'll have to be in plain old boring U.S. currency. Seriously, though, it's not huge by industry standards, but the potential is there to be as much as I've made on all my other scripts combined."

"Are you excited?" Silly question. He was already pumping his fist. Yessss.

"Do I look excited?"

"For you, a little reserved, I'd say," she joked. "But what about the story? Tell me more."

It was a story of redemption, he told her, of second chances and making good on them. And the hero was someone obsessed with the past.

"That sounds a lot like you."

"It is. And about moving back home at my age to do whatever the hell it is I'm doing. And I can thank the Air Force for it. If that hadn't happened, I would never have done something like this. Hitting rock bottom made me want to write about something that really matters. This is the most personal thing I've ever written. The parents, the school, even my crappy little Gremlin. It just feels right."

Julie played with her hair, curling the locks near her shoulder around a finger, and studied them. "Am I in your story?"

"Are you kidding? Without you, my dear Jules, I would have no story. It would have no life without you. You are the heroine, the queen bee. The very heart of the story. And I will thank you sincerely with all the other little people when I accept my Academy Award for best screenplay."

His eyes twinkled. It was such bullshit she couldn't help but laugh, but she was flattered that he would bother to even tease her that way, even in jest. It was the kind of joke that told her Nate wasn't putting her in the story. Good, she was uncomfortable with the thought of that kind of attention, fictional or not, though it was intriguing.

"Can I read it?"

"Not yet. I still need to write the ending."

They drove to Santa Cruz for crab cakes and smoked salmon at a gorgeous restaurant with huge windows facing a narrow harbor and a picturesque lighthouse on the point. When they got back from lunch, Julie was sorely in need of a nap. He took her hands in his and lingered at the door to the bedroom with a sweet, dreamy expression on his face. She was prepared with half a dozen ways to explain why she wasn't yet ready to add sex to the relationship even if she had agreed to spend the weekend with him. She needed time.

He winked, and then nodded silently before shooing her into the bedroom. Without a word, he knew what she needed and gave her space to heal on her own terms.

She changed into baggy sweats, unconcerned that Nate—single, attractive, goofy but sensual Nate—was on the other side of that door. She had just ended a relationship with a different man that cratered badly. She lay down and waited for sleep, but it apparently wanted to play tag instead. She drifted between wakefulness and drowsiness. It wasn't right to move so easily in love from one person to the next, if that's what she felt for Nate. You didn't just switch teams like that.

Who was she kidding? She had been moving in this direction since the first day after summer break, with Nate in Russell's office, and the way he brought up feelings buried long ago with just a look after they walked out. She knew all along those old feelings were rising to the surface. What would dating coach Dr. Rachel say?

"Get your ass in gear, girl," most likely. Or, more to the point, repeating the advice her mother had given her on that night in the hospital.

"Take care of yourself." Mother as a dating coach. Who knew?

She kicked off the blankets and padded into the living room. Nate was dozing on the sofa. She stood over the armrest and looked, upside down, into his face until he opened his eyes.

"Can I buy you dinner tonight?" she asked. "I owe you a dinner."

"What? For this? Don't be silly. You don't owe me anything."

"Oh, yes, I do. I won a small jackpot on the lottery, and Carla thinks I should buy you dinner because I couldn't have done it without you. It's the least I can do."

He closed his eyes, and with a sleepy sigh, he said, "Fine. I can't imagine how I did anything to make a difference, but if that's what you want…twist my arm. What did I do to deserve it?"

Julie leaned closer, her voice just above a whisper.

"Do you believe in omens?"

CHAPTER FORTY-TWO

Tootsie's Revenge

On the night of the great penguin charity gala, the boy in his tuxedo met the girl in her gown at her door with a corsage in hand. He escorted her to the waiting limousine, where they set out for the event. After forty years, prom night had arrived. They kissed. Love triumphed.

Send.

Nate stabbed the key on his laptop with all the cocky satisfaction of placing a winning chess move on the board. Checkmate.

It was Monday morning, and light was creeping through his bedroom window. He had worked through the night to write the ending to his story, dashing home after his weekend at the beach with Julie. He needed to wrap it up and get it to his agent in time for Thursday's gala and the contract meeting. His life had become a romantic comedy cliché. Wasn't that great?

The world stopped spinning, and the universe held its breath waiting for Thursday. He was touched when Julie explained over dinner Carla's "lottery omen theory" and their birthdays combining to be winning numbers. He invited her to be his date at the Penguin Gala.

They had survived the weekend at the beach house without having sex, agreeing that, for the time being, something, something, something and a couple of blah-de-dahs. He wasn't sure what he agreed to, he had trouble focusing on the details, but abstinence made the weekend more perfect. By the time he took her home on Sunday, there was a rising sexual tension between them that made the days that followed the longest week of foreplay he had ever experienced.

He was actually a little nervous about it. Throughout his sexual encounters before marriage, twenty-odd years of monogamy and a handful of interesting liaisons afterwards, the reviews—if you could trust a woman in the throes of passion and/or its afterglow—had always been good. Two thumbs up. Four stars. Even *Rotten Tomatoes* would give Nate's sex life a Certified Fresh, eighty-five percent approval rating, but he thought being with Julie would beat it all because, well, because it was Julie.

Nate went with flowers for Mrs. Cooper at the nursing home on Monday. On the way out, Julie mentioned she would be moving into her old bedroom at her mother's house for a few weeks of transition when Ethel returned home the following weekend and teased him with hints of consummating their teenage near-sex experience there.

Tuesday they lingered long after campus had cleared out for the day, walking hand in hand down the empty hallways. He pressed her against the wall in the space between two long rows of student lockers and "borrowed" a kiss. At the far corner, against the door to the biology lab, she pressed him and demanded that he pay it back.

Wednesday they sat across from one another at the Dairy Barn after school, ignoring a basket of soggy french fries on the table and laughing about the evil eye Festerhaven gave them when either one passed his office on their way out the door. Life was frosty around the admin building, but they had gotten whispered encouragement from most of the others.

"He is seriously pissed," Nate said.

"Good."

By Thursday morning, Nate was flying high. Tina Farnham loved the ending; she and her lawyers would arrive that afternoon from L.A. along with Nate's agent. Nate would wine and dine Julie at the gala to save the penguins and mingle with Hollywood celebrities and generous millionaires.

As a bonus, Festerhaven, who had been in a general snit ever since Julie found him with Nicolette and took out her anger on his headlights, became even snittier by the day, if such a thing was possible, as they transitioned from being just friends to a couple going steady while the campus staff watched and approved of the sweethearts.

So naturally, Nate's world was spinning in harmony with the universe when it jumped the tracks. An office aide stuck her head in the door to his classroom in the break after first period and summoned him to the principal's office. Nate rapped his knuckles on the secretary's desk as he strolled past; she shook her head with pity and sad eyes usually reserved for death row inmates and motioned for Nate to go right in. One of his creative writing students sat against the wall near the door and avoided his eyes. The woman with a June Cleaver hairdo sitting next to the girl, a woman oozing stress and anger, hit him with a glare that put a hitch in his step. She must be the girl's mother. Uh oh.

"So am I in trouble?" he asked Festerhaven after making sure the door had shut behind him.

"Of course. Why else would I want to waste my time with you?"

Nate waited.

"It seems Tynslee Butler has made some serious accusations against you."

Nate thought hard, starting with the most obvious and working his way to outlandish. Tynslee was a quiet girl, the kind easily ignored. She didn't say much, but when she did, it was worth listening to. Aside from a couple of instances when she stayed after class and pestered him with questions about how to become an actress in Hollywood, he had no extra-curricular contact with her. So any accusation of inappropriate behavior would be pure fiction, and that wasn't part of Tynslee's DNA, he believed.

"She says you've been showing adult films in class under the guise of teaching them who knows what. What have you been smoking? Are you crazy?"

Nate nearly choked on his own spit and had a coughing fit. When he recovered, he asked Festerhaven who was crazier. "Did she really say that?"

"One of your movies and the class assignment has Mrs. Butler upset. And now she's come down on my ass. And you know how I hate that." He left Nate standing and sat on the corner of his desk, dangling a leg so that his body angled away from Nate. "Would you tell me what this is all about?"

"You got me, chief."

He explained that he had held only four of his Thursday movie afternoons, and none involved what would be rated as "adult" films. "PG-13 at worst. And even then, Julie—Mrs. Finch—told me to cover my ass, so I had all the students get permission slips from their parents." Mentioning Julie's name was a mistake. Nate watched Festerhaven scowl. "I haven't used any movie that would be considered the least bit objectionable. So what is it that has her panties in a knot?"

"Did you have one of your sessions with a movie"—and there, FesterProsecutor checked a notepad on his desk—"a movie that promoted promiscuity and homosexuality?"

Nate was stunned. *Casablanca? The Wizard of Oz? Star Wars?* Hardly.

The principal brought Tynslee and her mother into the office and motioned for them to sit at the round table near the window that looked out over the front of the school grounds sloping down to the street. Nate's attention was drawn to the trophy shelf behind them, where, sandwiched between a couple of small medals and a handful of gold keepsakes, there stood a picture. FesterJock smiled at him wearing his softball jersey and pointing his bat, the same one Julie used on his SUV, at the camera. He thought it was appropriate for what he assumed was about to go down.

"Last month, Mr. Evans showed Tynslee this horrible movie," Mrs. Butler began.

He had to think. What was the movie?

"*Tootsie?* You're upset about *Tootsie?* That's a classic. Dustin Hoffman was nominated for an Oscar. Jessica Lange won one. It was the best movie of the whole of the eighties if you believe Roger Ebert, and I happen to think he walked on water."

"I am sick and tired of you movie people throwing your gay lifestyle in our faces. You have no business promoting that to my daughter, or anyone else, for that matter."

Nate protested. The movie not only didn't promote anything remotely gay, there wasn't a single gay character or issue in the story.

"Ha. The entire movie is about a man who likes to dress up in women's clothing. If I hadn't come across Tynslee's homework assignment, I'd have never known."

"Have you actually seen the movie, Mrs. Butler?"

Of course not. No surprise there.

"If you saw the movie, you'd know right away there is nothing gay going on. Heck, he even has sex with Terri Garr."

Okay, Nate thought, not a good argument to make in this situation. Damn. He plowed on, "Even so, you signed Tynslee's permission slip to participate in the movie class. So I can't see what the fuss is about on either level."

"I did no such thing. I would never approve."

All eyes swung to Tynslee, who stared out the window. She looked embarrassed, frustrated and guilty. Nate pitied her. He had half-heartedly checked all of the students' permission slips; everyone was signed and accounted for. He might have been a little more on guard for forgeries if he had any doubts about the movie. But *Tootsie*?

Nate asked Festerhaven for the slips he had turned in. They had to be in a file in the office.

"Uh, that's one more problem. It seems they don't exist. Mrs. Hernandez doesn't recall seeing them. If you turned them in, they've disappeared."

Disappeared? The way the principal sarcastically leaned on the word so hard was a message. He was making it clear they didn't "disappear" on their own. They both knew he had turned them in.

There was a good deal of bluster after that. Mrs. Butler demanded an apology, which she got from FesterSchmuck.

"Sorry," Nate said. "Can't do that." He was insulted not only for the attack on his judgment and his competence but the pure stupidity of the situation. Then the woman demanded his resignation. That was something Festerhaven seemed all too eager to accommodate before he ushered mother and daughter from his office with promises that it would be resolved satisfactorily.

"Can you believe that woman?" Nate asked.

He sighed. "Yeah, God help her. But what can you do?" Then he took a sheet of paper from his desktop and handed it to Nate. It was a letter of resignation.

"What if I don't sign it?"

"You would be doing me a favor. I'd fire you and that would give me a ton of pleasure. So don't think I'm the bad guy; it won't work."

In his anger, Nate's ears were burning, so he might as well go down in flames. "This has nothing to do with Tynslee or the movie. We both know that. You're pissed off at me. Me and Julie. You fucked up and you're taking it out on us. Pretty pathetic."

Festerhaven said he didn't like the fraternization between staff and teachers he had seen on campus lately. "I can't fire Julie. But you, you're still on probation. I don't need a reason to let you go immediately. Your ass is mine for the first year. Didn't you read your contract?"

Nate grumbled. He'd always been a big-picture guy. The details of contracts were best left to lawyers and agents.

Festerhaven said, "There's too much tension around here right now, and your presence on campus makes it worse. This will make my life easier."

"And what of Julie? This isn't going to make *her* life easier."

"No, I suppose not."

Then Festerhaven did something so surreal it appeared to Nate the whole thing played out in slow motion. He picked up his cell phone and began punching numbers.

"I'm having dinner with Nikki again tonight. Man, what a pistol she is. Frankly, I'd say I got the better end of this little trade. But you know? We were talking the other night about how lucky we were that we met because of you and that we seemed a better match than the two of you would have ever been."

"So?"

"We compared notes and realized how, on all the dates you dragged me to, I always got along with those women better than you. Nikki, Sarah the nurse and Wendy with the huge ta-tas. It seemed strange. And all of them from that dating website. When she showed me the profile you used, and the emails you sent her"—he pointed the phone at Nate and shook his head—"I couldn't have described me better myself. That's when we got on to you."

"You were an easy mark."

"That's a hell of a lot of trouble to get back at me for whatever. You set me up." Festerhaven punched one last button. Then the phone in Nate's pocket pinged with an incoming text message.

"So, Mr. Vintage Rascal, Nikki asked me to make sure you got this."

Nate fumbled with the phone. It repeated its alert, shaming him like a slap across the face. The text contained a picture of Nicolette, naked and lounging seductively on the bed with a sign between spread thighs barely hiding her charms. It read, "Love you, Nate."

"She takes a nice picture, don't you think? You should see some of the others. Maybe I should send a few to you, for old times' sake, before I send them to Julie."

Nate tried to stuff the phone back in his pocket, but it slipped out of his hand and clattered at his feet. He kicked it across the floor for good measure.

FesterAss said, "So I have my weaknesses, but this is all your fault. Now what do you suppose Julie will say when she finds out what a selfish prick you are? I'm ashamed of you. You've been toying with a woman I love."

"Love? I'm not the one toying with anyone around here."

"Julie. Me. Nikki. You're a real piece of work screwing around with everybody's lives, but today I'll cut you some slack. Julie doesn't need to know everything, right now at least, if you sign the letter. One of the campus cops will help you collect your things and walk you out."

Before he left the office, FesterGloater hit him with one last thought. "Nate, you went out of your way to break Julie's heart. That is really sick, my friend. Really sick."

CHAPTER FORTY-THREE
Tsunami

The Tina Farnham tsunami hit campus two hours later. Julie was doodling thoughts of Nate on a notepad when she should have had her nose buried in paperwork. She was worried. The word was Nate had quit that morning. He didn't give notice and walked away from the campus without so much as a good-bye. Nobody saw him leave; he was here one minute and gone the next, and nobody knew why. She tossed her pencil on the pad in frustration, bouncing it on its eraser head, and turned back to stare at the spreadsheet on her computer screen. He hadn't returned her phone calls or text messages. Nothing. Someone started a ruckus outside her office. She tried to ignore it but Carla leaned in.

"Whoa. You have got to see this. Whoa."

A half dozen visitors stood in a semicircle at the reception counter across from Mrs. Hernandez, the office manager. Julie recognized the woman in the middle of it all. Who wouldn't? The double doors to campus behind her opened with a rush and a new commotion. Students squeezed into the space, giggling, elbowing each other and snapping pictures with their cell phones. Nobody was taking charge.

"Tina Farnham. My goodness," Julie said. "What a pleasure. What a surprise. What can we do for you?"

The actress spun her sunglasses by one earpiece above her shoulder without saying anything. She motioned with a forefinger to a slender young man with dark hair parted in the middle and receding at the forehead at far too early an age. He wore a black T-shirt under a black linen sports coat, held his phone just above eye level, and did a slow pan of the office. "We stopped by to get a feel for the location," he said as he panned back.

"Location?"

"We had some extra time this afternoon, and we thought we'd drop by and catch up with Nate Evans here at the school," a woman behind Tina Farnham said. "We thought he could give us a brief tour." She stood on tiptoes to be seen over the actress's shoulder. She was also wearing black. In fact, they all dressed alike. Julie hadn't seen any collection of bodies like this since she sat in on a meeting of the high school Goth Club. Except for the missing nose rings and severe makeup, these people would fit right in. Only the woman herself added a splash of color with a red scarf draped across her shoulders.

Julie looked at her watch. "I'm not sure Nate is still here. Was he expecting you?"

No. They had expected to surprise him and "do a business lunch" after their tour.

She didn't want to explain he had resigned until she had her facts straight. Julie planned on making an early exit that afternoon; she had some serious primping to do before the gala, and she wanted to look her best when Nate picked her up. She turned to the office manager standing slack-jaw across the counter from the actress and working her mouth to gulp air like a goldfish. "Rosilla, would you get Mr. Festerhaven please."

A third assistant pushed a pair of large, black-frame glasses up from the tip of her nose and tapped the face of the iPad in her hand. "Rosilla. Got it. Secretary number one," she said. She shouldered closer to the actress to share her screen with Tina Farnham. She asked the others, "Sardonic aging single, or snarky mother figure? We could give her a few lines for comic relief?"

Someone else said, "Hefty and Hispanic."

"With an attitude."

"Could work."

Everybody had an opinion, but no one had an explanation for the commotion they had created. Julie watched Tina Farnham as the actress's eyes darted around the office while her entourage prattled. She smiled and waved at the students standing five rows deep at the door. Julie said, "Miss Farnham, I'm Mrs. Finch, one of the assistant principals."

"Finch? Assistant principal?" another of the actress's entourage asked. He was a skinny African-American with a face full of freckles. He scrolled the screen of his tablet with three quick swipes of the finger and said, "Okay. Cooper-Finch. Got it. Leading Lady Love Interest. Smart. Drab with undercurrent of sensuality, but serious to a fault."

"Suppressed."

"By life. Not her fault."

"I'm sorry?" Julie swiveled her head, trying to keep up with the voices in the circle.

Carla shouldered her way past Julie with a phone in her hand to stand next to the star. She stretched one arm out and slid the other around Tina Farnham's slender waist. "Really. If you don't mind. My husband will be absolutely tickled."

Julie saw frowns all around the Goth posse and it embarrassed her. They had failed to protect the star from this kind of intrusion. But the actress simply grinned, bent her knees and crouched enough to level her shoulders with Carla and posed for a selfie.

When the Kodak moment ended, Tina Farnham straightened and turned her attention to Julie. She took Julie's outstretched hand in both of hers. "Mrs. Finch. That would be Julie? Julie Cooper-Finch?"

"I haven't used 'Cooper' for a very long time, but yes. How did you know?"

"Love Interest," the entire group chorused.

"Whoa," Carla said. "Did you all practice that?"

"Play nice, Carla," Julie said through clamped teeth.

The three young people armed with iPads tapped and swooshed in a race to find their response. "Carla. Last name TBD. Sarcastic Sidekick. Petite but feisty."

"She'll get all the zingers," the young black man who had been pushed aside by Carla's rush to get her picture said. "I can write that one in my sleep."

Carla snatched his tablet before he could stop her. "Does it really say that here?" She deftly turned her back to prevent the man from recovering it. He made two halfhearted attempts to reach around Carla and then shrugged to his boss.

Tina Farnham said to Julie, "The way Nate wrote you, I was expecting someone much more drab. Oh."

"What does Nate have to do with this?" Julie figured it was all about the story he had sold, but watching this group and hearing their confusing references to each of them and debating various characteristics was like watching a foreign film. A lot of drama, too much posturing, and the dialogue she heard didn't make sense.

"Miss Farnham. Welcome to Mt. Hamilton High." Russell blew in and cleared a path up to the actress. The man at Julie's left leaned behind her and whispered to the iPad woman.

"Principal, right?"

"Must be," she replied. She checked her tablet. "Obstructionist bureaucrat, arrogant, antagonist. Villain."

"Boy, he looks the part."

Julie raised a hand to her lips to hide a smirk. "He is the part," she whispered. She felt like a conspirator, even if her role was still vague.

It was at that point that a man with a tired face and a bald head stepped up from where he had been hanging behind the crowd. "If someone could track down Nate for us, please. Tina, I told you we shouldn't drop in unannounced like this."

Russell glared at her in a way that made Julie feel like she was to blame. "Nate has already left for the day. He's gone." Russell looked at the faces of his staff members before settling on her. "He won't be back today, I'm afraid. He resigned this morning."

Julie's heart sank. The pieces were starting to fit together.

The bald man shook Russell's hand. "I'm Jack Hewitt, Nate's agent. You all know Miss Farnham, of course. And these are, well, they're her staff. Miss Farnham is producing the story Nate has written about this." He circled his finger to indicate the Mt. Hamilton High universe.

"Nate's been writing a story? About us?"

"He didn't say anything about it," Julie lied. Her heart felt like dead weight and she couldn't swallow. He had talked with such joy and enthusiasm about the story over their beach weekend. He mentioned that it was Tina Farnham's company buying it, and hoped to introduce them at the charity ball that night, but he never told her he planned to quit the school and leave them all behind when the deal was done. Why else would he have left without a word?

The agent looked past them all, distant and distracted, and he started a grin. "See, Tina? Nate captured this place perfectly. Am I right? Baby boomers will eat it up."

"Inspired," Tina Farnham agreed. "It could have been so mundane, but this is funny and pathetic at the same time. You're all so…"

"Funny and pathetic?" Carla asked from a chair near the wall, where she sat scrolling through the black assistant's tablet.

"Adorable. I love you, each and every one of you people."

"Wait. I hear the Mouse squeaking. Beef up a version with a couple of hip-but-wholesome teenagers, and we could sell it to Disney."

"Ka-ching!"

"Excuse me." Julie backed away. She went to her office, leaving the door ajar just enough to keep an eye on the scene outside. Once again, Nate didn't answer his phone. She left a voice mail, short and terse, demanding a callback ASAP. She threw her cell phone at the mouth of her handbag and missed. She stood, arms crossed, tapping her foot. Nate wouldn't have done all this just for the story. She couldn't believe that. Research? Inspiration? If that's all it was, then what did that make last weekend with the snuggles and the kisses? Was that research, too?

She wasn't going to cry. She was not going to cry. Just in case, Julie reached for the large box of tissues on her desk. She kept it filled for the tear sessions with girls who needed comfort and advice from someone older than their peers but not their parents. Usually it was about boys or the isolation of not being a part of the crowd. Sometimes they needed tips on how to explain to Mom and Dad that community college might be a more realistic goal than a Harvard scholarship. Her box of tissues didn't discriminate between tears that were justified and those brought on by exaggerated angst.

Julie collected herself and went to the door. She bumped into Tina, who was reaching for the knob just as Julie yanked the door open.

"Mrs. Cooper-Finch, thank you for giving us your time this afternoon. I know this created quite a stir. But Hollywood does that. It is craziness incarnate, right? But, believe me, it would have been worse if word leaked ahead of us that we'd be here today."

"Life has been crazy enough around here lately. But you took it to a whole new level." Julie meant it as a jab, but the actress only smiled.

"We better move along. It seems we have half the school swarming around now." Then the actress closed her eyes and inhaled, exhaled and repeated the process.

"Are you all right?" Julie asked.

"Oh, yes, Julie. No, Tina. Tina Cooper? Well, we can settle on the name later. Tina Cooper-Finch? No, that's not working." When she reopened her eyes, she said, "I was feeling the part. And you know what? I like you, Tina."

"You don't even know me. And my name's Julie."

"We'll have to fix that, of course. Yes. I believe I do know you. Nate captured your character very well. I can do that character, and I can see why the hero would move heaven and earth for her. It's a cliché line, I know. But if we get Ryan Gosling to play the part of the hero and say Nate's line the way he wrote it? Women in the audience will cream their panties. Pardon my French. It just works."

"It sure does." It sure did last weekend. Did he write about that? Moving heaven and earth for this Julie-Tina-character? God, she was so stupid. Nate had scripted the weekend, and she played right into his hands.

"Have you ever considered acting? Either that or you must really enjoy what you do. You have a gift. It's real. It's in your eyes. There is fire in your eyes."

If she only knew. Nate had used them. Suddenly Julie was in no rush to get home, and as much as she had been looking forward to their evening among the stars at that celebrity fundraiser, she had no appetite for caviar, champagne and making nice. An hour later, she was still trembling with anger as she walked to Carla's classroom. Surely she hadn't let Nate do this to her again, getting her to fall for him when he was only having fun.

Carla sat at her desk reading from an iPad.

"Still here? I thought you'd be home by now. What did Nate say?"

Julie shook her head. "He's not answering his phone. I haven't heard back from him."

"When you do, all I can say is 'oh boy.'"

Julie asked what that meant and then shifted her eyes to the slender tablet propped up against two large science textbooks in front of Carla. "Say, isn't that the iPad one of Tina Farnham's assistants had?"

"Yeah. In the confusion, this, um, got misplaced."

"Misplaced? The last place I saw it was in your hands. You were looking at whatever it was they had there about us."

"It's not as if I stole it. Exactly. It sort of never found its way back to that nice man. You can give it to Nate and he can return it, but I've been reading this story he wrote for them. I think you should, too. There is a lot of good stuff here."

The way Carla said that, with irony thicker than molasses, touched some dread-inducing nerve in Julie. "Good stuff in a good way? I hope."

"Kind of intimate if you ask me. You're not going to like it."

CHAPTER FORTY-FOUR

A Thorny Situation

A rose thorn cut across high on Nate's cheek, just below his left eye, leaving a sliver of a wound deep enough to draw blood. He raised an arm to fend off a swipe from the opposite direction and then, with both arms, protected himself from being bashed on his head. Julie was using the bouquet he brought as a spiked, though admittedly sweet-smelling, cudgel.

"So you'd move heaven and earth, would you? I don't know about heaven, mister, but this is what pain feels like on earth." She held the roses in both hands and swung at him again from her doorway. Nate rushed Julie from the porch. He wanted to hug her. He wanted to comfort her. But first and foremost, he wanted to stop her from bashing him. She backed away to slam the door in his face, but Nate was too far into the house by that point. She wheeled and stomped down the short hallway and into the living room, tossing the flowers against the wall.

Nate knew when Julie opened the door that things were worse than he feared driving over to her house. He had tried to convince himself that his sudden departure would go largely unnoticed as long as FesterButt kept his mouth shut. He had promised Nate at least a day. If he hadn't left his goddamned phone on the floor of the principal's office, he would have called Julie. He would have had some advance warning. They didn't give him the time to say good-bye to anyone on campus, just pack up his stuff, and Bob, the campus cop, escorted him out and around the back of the building, keeping an eye on Nate until he drove away. He considered calling her from his mother's home phone but decided to wait, knowing they would have the evening together to talk about it.

He showed up in his tuxedo, and she was wearing a baggy sweat-shirt and blue jeans. He was carrying roses; she was carrying a grudge. Her face was as hard as a botched Botox job, and her jaw clenched as she took the bouquet and battered him with it. Their date to the gala that, to Nate, had become the prom they had missed out on the first time around, was doomed.

Nate followed her as she stormed ahead. Julie shook both hands in the air, furiously, as if she had washed them in contaminated water and then found she had no towel.

"You bastard!" She liked that one, Nate noticed, because as she vented her anger, she used it a lot, along with *liar, stupid*, and *asshole*. But when she skidded to a stop in front of him, hands on her hips, and said, "Fuck you," Nate knew he was really in trouble.

She went to her purse on a credenza near the kitchen, turned and threw something. He used his elbows to protect his head as he ducked and knocked it to the floor. He recognized his cell phone. Festerhaven must have loved blowing the whistle on him.

It was one of the few times that words failed Nate. Words were, after all, his life.

"I can't do this. I can't do this again," Julie said. "I can't go from hating you one day, kissing you the next, and then being ready to kill you. On. Off. On again. Back and forth and never serious. Just like school. The same thing, over and over and over. How could I be so stupid?"

He never meant to lead her on. He was just a stupid kid back then. He should have asked her to go steady long before the senior prom. Maybe as early as grade school, but certainly by the time they were old enough to date. He hadn't thought it through; he just wasn't ready to grow up. For the first time, he could see how it might have looked that way to Jules. It must look that way again.

"And to think, I convinced myself you had changed. You have, but in the worst way. You were deliberately using me this time. I wouldn't have figured it out yet if Tina Farnham hadn't shown up at school this afternoon, looking for you, but you had already left by then."

Tina Farnham did what? Why hadn't anybody told him? Oh. His phone, right. Sitting there on the floor at his feet now. He noticed the screen was cracked. That took some serious anger. "Believe me. There was nothing deliberate about it." It was a weak excuse. What would be the best way out of this mess?

"They told us all about the story you wrote. You. Me—and by the way, I am not frumpy and repressed the way you made me out to be. Russell. Carla. All of it. All of your Hollywood friends are laughing at us. When you said you were writing about *your* life, coming home and living like a teenager again, I didn't think this is what you meant. I read what you wrote. The worst part, you have been messing with my life. You went out and stole my boyfriend. You deliberately ruined our relationship so you could have a good story to sell. You stole the man who loved me. Russell confirmed it, too. He told me all about how you and that woman set him up. Did I say fuck you yet? And I want you out of here. Right now." She sputtered with tears on her cheeks and pointed to the phone, cracked and lying at his feet like roadkill. "And those disgusting pictures."

Julie moved a step closer, closing the distance between them. She pointed her finger at Nate. "In all the years we've known each other, all the disappointments, this has to be the worst."

"Just hear me out." He should have seen Julie would find out what he had done to sabotage her relationship and been ready for it. He was so concerned about her being heartbroken when Festerhaven broke off the engagement, he didn't stop to think about what would happen when his role in that shit hit the fan.

Julie shook her head. "You ran away rather than face me after your fling with Eppie Johnson. You ran away from your marriage. You ran away when life got hard, coming back home to live this fantasy of yours, pretending to be a teenager again. And now that you've gotten what you need out of us, out of me, you quit and you're running away again."

That was unfair. He might be a relationship wrecker, but he wasn't running out on her. He didn't run away to college. She had a boyfriend and he had a scholarship down south. "I came back after school let out for the summer, but guess what? You were in such a rush to get married, you had dumped me like a hot potato the moment my back was turned. We were only eighteen, for God's sake. And as for my marriage? My *marriage*? You want to know how shitty that ended?"

He was seething now. *Take a breath. Let it go.* He bit hard, swallowing the details, he was losing it and they badly wanted out. He might tell her later; he might never, but this wasn't the time. "You don't know diddly about my marriage. I worked at it harder than anything in my life and stayed with it long after its expiration date." He began pacing. "How could you be so smart and so blind at the same time? I didn't quit this morning, the man who loved you—as you put it—fired my ass and had Bob the cop kick me off campus. He didn't tell you that part, did he? Why did he want to get rid of me like that? Yeah, he wanted to screw me for proving what a bastard he really is, but this was the only way he could get back at you. He couldn't stand the sight of you being happy. And you were going to be happy while I was around."

He told her she didn't deserve to settle for Festerhaven. "I never told you what a dickhead he was because I didn't want to hurt you. He went out of his way to do it. That's the man who loved you. And for the record, that woman you found him with? She wasn't the first. Probably not the second or third, and she wasn't going to be the last."

He wished he could shove that last bit back into his mouth. It tasted like shit coming out, and he felt even worse as he watched her stiffen.

"You are a liar."

"No, I am an idiot. But don't blame me because you couldn't see Festerhaven for the cheating asshole that he is. Is that what I ruined for you? He was doing that without my help. Wake up and smell the frappuccino, babe."

"Great. Even if it's true, you went out and helped him. And now you want to excuse what you did telling me you fixed Russell up with another woman to save me? You did this all for my benefit? How dare you think you know what's best for me and then try to run my life. I don't need rescuing. At least not your kind."

"I did it out of selfish desperation. It was either that or be forced into shopping at Bed Bath and Beyond to find you a wedding gift, watch you go off and marry the wrong guy *again*, and spend the *next* forty years of my life wishing I had done more."

Julie stepped even closer; her dark eyes were boring painfully into his. What happened next, Nate could have scripted. Julie swung her right hand, flat-palmed and aimed at his face. He knew it was coming but surprised himself at how easily he caught her wrist and stopped it several inches from his jaw. And he did it without flinching. Then he pulled her body against his, so close he could feel her passion through his skin. He was Rhett Butler and she was Scarlet O'Hara. Cue the music. Her anger would fade, but passion would engulf them. Julie's chin tilted up, defiantly daring Nate to kiss her. So he did.

Or so he tried.

In the next part of the scene, something Nate had never written and couldn't anticipate, Julie pulled a ninja move on him. She rammed her knee into his groin and stomped the heel of her shoe into his foot. Nate made a mental note—never get into a tussle with a woman who aced her self-defense class at the YMCA. Damn, that really hurt. Julie put a leg behind his knee, tugged his arm and threw him over her hip to the floor.

Or so she tried.

Julie had neither the strength nor the balance to make it work, and they both wound up sprawled, Julie on her stomach and Nate on her back.

"Get off me."

Nate took his time. He was laughing. He didn't care if that only made her angrier. It couldn't get any worse. It couldn't get any more ludicrous. He offered her a hand up, but Julie put on her sulk face and backed away, scooting butt and heels away from him on the floor.

"Jules, I love you. I have always loved you. I have loved you since we were this high." He held a palm toward the floor at his knee.

"Wrong. You're not in love with me. And I was stupid to think so."

"That's not right. And it's not fair. You don't know—"

"This is pathetic. This homecoming story you dreamed up, trying to rewrite the past? Second chances, isn't that what you said on the beach? It was a lie to use me. Shut up," she said. It was a bark. And then she stared up at him, putting her arms around her knees.

She slapped his hand away when he tried again to help her off the floor. He didn't mind this time. She stood up without him. Julie didn't get it. Worse, she didn't want to get it. "I am going to count to ten. I want you out of here by the time I get there. If not, I'm calling the police."

She started counting. One. Two.

"Jules, you can't treat me like a child."

"If the sneaker fits… Three. Four."

Shit. He hated to slink away, but Julie wasn't about to turn and face him.

"Five. Six."

He stomped to the front door in what he thought was a defiantly tactical retreat. He scooped up the bouquet of roses and slammed the door on the way out. Then he stewed on the front porch.

Nate plucked a single rose, pounded his fist on Julie's front door and then barged in. She came out of the kitchen as Nate approached, wiping a tear from her eye with the back of her sweatshirt sleeve. Then she rubbed the eye with her finger as if she were merely trying to get rid of a speck. She turned her face away and held up a palm in that speak-to-the-hand stance. Nate grabbed it and folded her fingers around the stem of the rose. He held her hand in his.

Nate let go of his anger. He softened but spoke in a measured, determined tone. "You can go on hating me from now until whenever. I didn't come here to write that damned story. That just sort of happened and things got out of hand. That's been my whole life. I let things happen and they get out of hand. It's so rare that anybody gets a second chance like the one I had, and I fucked it badly. You'd be goofy to give me a third chance, but that's for you to decide. I didn't leave everything I had, such as it was, to come here and rewrite the past."

"Okaaay." Julie dragged out the word, unconvinced and waiting for more. "That's sure what it looks like. What are you trying to do?"

"I'm trying to rewrite the future."

CHAPTER FORTY-FIVE
Tina Rides Again

Friday morning it was the talk of the campus. Nate had resigned and wouldn't even finish the school year. He was moving back to L.A. to write a movie about them for Tina Farnham. He came. He conquered. He slunk away.

Reaction was mixed.

Barbara, the English and drama teacher, was frustrated.

"I've called Nate three times now," she told Beverly as she nuked a breakfast burrito in the lounge microwave. Julie wanted to ignore them as she squatted behind the open refrigerator door. She was tired. She was grumpy. She hadn't slept last night. She was clearing the collection of last month's leftovers from the bottom shelf of the refrigerator so the staff would have room to grow mold on a new month's worth of neglected lunches.

"What did he say?" Beverly asked.

"He isn't answering. I'm only asking to audition for a part. I'm sure he could arrange something. After all, I've covered his classes more than anyone else."

"And nobody could play you better than you."

Seth Naylor was disappointed.

"Angela and I were going to ask him to be our baby's godfather."

"You're pregnant? So soon."

"Not yet." He blushed. "But we're working on it."

Students admired him. The office staff envied him, and Russell refused to talk about him, except to say "that son of a bitch" as he slammed a file of paperwork on the top of her in-basket.

As for Julie, she loved him. And it hurt.

Second lunch period, she passed the fountain, where, at the start of the school year, she accused him of not growing up. She was on her way to Carla's science classroom, and she decided that while it might be true Nate hadn't changed over forty-some years, she wondered what that said of her for falling back under his spell and loving it. She should be stronger than that.

Carla had called, insisting she had to come over for a cup of coffee in her homeroom. Julie had given her the full story after Nate left the night before, and she couldn't imagine what more Carla had to say. Now, suspicious curiosity hit her as she reached for the doorknob. Carla could have waited until the end of the day, but no, she had to see her right away.

And, "Whoa!" was all Carla said when Julie pressed for a reason.

She paused at the door and collected herself just in case. Damn him. If Nate was in there with Carla, using her to get to Julie and make his lame case again, and if she was helping, out of some misguided attempt to nudge them toward reconciliation, then Julie would be out the door faster than...

"Oh."

Tina Farnham stood with Carla and the young, black, freckled fellow from her entourage. Carla was pouring coffee from a pot she had pulled off the stand over a Bunsen burner. Tina used a fingertip to pull her sunglasses down to the tip of her nose. "I think we need to talk," she said.

Carla winked at Julie as she explained how she had "found" the young man's tablet. When he called the office trying to locate it, someone put him in touch with her. "DeSean said he would swing by and pick it up. And look at this; he brought a friend with him."

Julie pointed to the iPad on the edge of the table. Tina's assistant was drumming it with his fingers. Julie apologized for causing trouble, though she didn't want to call it theft. She doubted Carla would feel the need.

"I told them we read what Nate wrote about us," Carla said.

"We shouldn't have. That was rude and unforgivable." And so typically Carla, she thought.

The actress offered her own apology for the stir their unannounced arrival on campus caused the day before. That was where the whole mess started. "But that's neither here nor there. I thought you could tell me something about Nate. The poor boy was absolutely suicidal last night."

Julie felt a lump in her throat. "Suicidal?"

"Positively."

"Positively," her assistant echoed.

"In fact, Nate would hate me if he knew I was here today. But"— Tina sighed—"we may never see him again."

"Why? What's happened to him? He hasn't tried to, you know, do it again, has he?" A wave of nausea swept over her like nothing she had felt since those bad oysters she ate at Charlie's Crab Crate and

Sushi Bar. Nate had assured her that he had moved on from the things that troubled him enough to attempt suicide, and he sure acted like the happy, goofy, irreverent, irresponsible, troublemaking Nate she knew. Could he have been too proud to admit he was still harboring suicidal thoughts? She could have handled their fight last night a little better. Sure, he was a jerk, but he was a sensitive jerk. Now it was her fault this time. Visions of YouTube videos and squashed dogs and pathetic little puppy paws trying to escape from under Nate's broken body flashed in her mind.

"Do what again?" Tina asked with a blank face. "Nothing happened that I know of, although he must have had one heck of a hangover."

The panic faded, but her breathing took its time returning to normal. She was disgusted with herself for even thinking it and disappointed that she could forget how angry she was at him.

Tina told Julie that she had a long chat with Nate after the fundraiser. It was a smashing success, raising money to build super-industrial icemakers for the penguins in the arctic.

"I'm pretty sure penguins live in the *Ant*-arctic," Carla said. "You know, the South Pole?"

"Whatever. We raised over three million. Everybody wants to jump on the ice wagon now. Struck a real blow against global warming and for saving those little rascals. Wherever they live."

"I'm glad everything is working out for you," Carla said. Julie appreciated the sarcasm in Carla's voice. The girl had her back.

"Did you know that most penguins mate for life? I didn't. I learned that from him last night. We had a little party after the gala up in the suite. Nate showed up late, missed the gala but stayed late and we talked until, I don't know, dawn. We haven't done that for a very long time."

Curious. Nate and the actress, did they have a history? "He's very good at that. Talking till dawn. You've known him for a while?"

Tina ignored the question, leaned on one elbow and drew circles around the rim of her cup. "I would like to be your friend. Do you prefer Julie? Or Jules? He kept calling you that. When he wasn't talking penguins last night. Can I call you Jules?"

"She won't even let *me* call her that," Carla grumped.

Julie climbed onto a stool on the opposite side of the table from the actress. She leaned forward, confused, certainly curious, but not all that angry with her. It wasn't her fault. Nate was the one who had hoodwinked them.

"Miss Farnham. Tina. I don't know what it's like down there in your world, but I don't appreciate all the pretending. Nate shouldn't have lied to all of us about what he was up to. He used us. Worse, he manipulated people and he ruined things, relationships and lives, and, well, just about everything. He did it so he could have this great story to sell. I don't blame you for buying it, but he treated us like a bunch of puppets on a string. Do you know what that feels like?"

"Every day, Julie. Welcome to my world."

"And talk about selfish."

"He said he really did set your boyfriend up with another woman. Until then, I thought he made up that part for the script. Frankly, I think he could have run with it a bit more."

"That was the funniest part, if you ask me," DeSean said.

"Nobody asked you." Carla elbowed him.

"Are you in love with Nate?" Tina asked. She put both elbows on the countertop now and leaned in, staring at Julie through the blue flame of the coffee Bunsen burner.

Carla and DeSean leaned in from their corner of the table so that the four heads created a huddle.

"Yeah, I'd like an answer to that, too," Carla said.

Everyone stared at her as if her answer carried the weight of the world. She knew the answer, but the answer was complicated. She could let them guess. "That's personal. Are you?"

Julie's lips worked halfway to a smile. It was nothing more than a joke that rolled off her tongue with little thought. She was kidding.

"Yes. At least I would be if not for you."

That was awkward. Everything skidded to a halt.

Carla coughed. "DeSean, how would you like to see our espresso machine in the faculty lounge? It's really something. Maybe you can help me figure out how to make it work."

"I don't drink espresso."

"I don't, either. And bring that notebook of yours."

What was the actress thinking? Tina didn't answer; instead she pushed her sunglasses up on her nose over her eyes. They hid what Julie assumed was a condescending look. The actress cocked her head, confirming it. "Let me tell you a story."

"Is this going to wind up in your movie, too?"

"Of course not. Well, then again, I can see where it might be useful. No, probably not." Then she explained to Julie how she had met Nate on the set of a film they were shooting in Aspen. "Nate was just another one of the staff writers, an extra pair of hands on the script. A nobody, really."

But he caught her eye with some perfect insight for Tina's character during a brief script meeting. It might have been the fact that

Tina was playing a newly divorced character and Nate was still dealing with his wife issues and the breakup of their marriage. "The things he wanted to add touched me. Right here." She tapped her heart. Tina said she was single again, between her second and third marriages, or was it third and fourth? No, definitely second. Their meeting turned into a long lunch together, followed by dinner the next night, and a night together that turned into a six-month relationship.

"But when I suggested we move in together, he wasn't interested. Well, he *was* interested. Who wouldn't be, with me? But just the same, he said he wouldn't."

They had one of those long, rambling conversations that lasted all night and revealed too much information.

"I know *that* feeling," Julie said.

"That boy can talk up a storm. What it came down to, and the reason he didn't want to set up house with me, was dealing with his divorce made him realize he was in love with a girl he'd known all his life. Oh, he loved his wife, but he never forgot the girl."

A composition notebook sat on the lab tabletop an arm's length from Julie. She pulled it close, opened it and studied the blank page as if it would give her the answers to a critical midterm. This was life and she was afraid she might flunk.

Tina stated the obvious. "He was talking about you. All those years ago. After reading his script, I knew it the moment we met, Jules."

She stood, staring at Julie from behind her dark glasses before picking up her purse. "I've got a plane to catch. Better go." She moved toward the door. "In the corner of my office, there is a stack of scripts and story pitches, project proposals and the like about this high." She held her palm just below her waist. "Most are pure drivel. But the writer in each and every one would give their eyeteeth, their first born, abandon their spouses, and some would even crawl across hot coals to have their movies produced. It's the nature of the business. This was Nate's chance to break out of the pile. It's the stuff of dreams. And what does he do? He throws that fat opportunity back in our face."

"What do you mean?"

"Nate skipped out on our meeting to sign the contract. He refused to even negotiate with us for a better deal. No sale. No deal. No movie. I talked to his agent. Jack says he doesn't want anybody to have it. Maybe he was still drunk. Maybe it was the hangover, but I think it's because you threw him out last night. Jules, I like that he calls you that, what he wrote wasn't just any old story. It was moving. It was beautiful. It was a love poem. For you."

"For me?"

"That's why I came here. I thought you ought to know. You don't look like you have any magical powers, but you sure cast some kind of spell over him. What's your secret? I might need it for my next husband." The actress had gone off the deep end. It was all far too dramatic and probably made up. But she was okay with that. It was soothing in a B.S. kind of way.

"I gather you want me to talk with him. You want me to convince him to give his story to you." Julie was insulted. These people would do anything to get what they wanted. Crush people and break hearts in the process? Who cares?

Tina Farnham paused after opening the classroom door. She took the sunglasses from her face. Disgusted. "Give me a bit more credit, please. No, that ship has sailed. Wouldn't touch it now. I'm doing this because Nate is my friend, still one of my favorites. I may not have thought twice about this story if it came from someone else. But from Nate? It was the story that, when we were together, I would have wanted him to write for me. About me. He's in love with you and you know it. You're too smart not to. No, I'm here helping out a friend, maybe two friends if you'll let me. What you kids do from here is your business."

By Sunday morning, she still hadn't decided what to do about Nate. She spent the weekend going back and forth. Pulling weeds in the backyard on Saturday, she wanted to do the safe thing. The practical thing. She would let him go on his merry way and avoid getting emotionally caught up with someone as unpredictable as him. In the shower, the water was hot and the soap was unusually sensual as she lathered her body with her bare hand instead of a washcloth. Why not take a little risk?

Because it wasn't sensible.

Would you rather be sensible and lonely or shoot for the moon and enjoy the ride?

She tried to ignore the battle in her head as she walked home from the Happy Yen Mini Mart under a partly cloudy sky and air that smelled like spring was around the next corner. A small, rectangular and unmarked brown box greeted her at the base of the front door when she got there.

She opened it at the kitchen table, and there were two items inside. The first was a sheet of binder paper on top with a note from Nate, asking her to meet him after school. No place and no time. Nothing more.

The second item was a navy blue piece of fabric. It wasn't until she held it up that she recognized it, a sweater that brought her to tears and made her laugh. The fabric was coarse, but the sentiment was sweet, and it melted her heart in a way only Nate could.

Pinned to the lapel, a scrap of paper with a clumsy script meant to resemble a child's handwriting:

Our first kiss.

CHAPTER FORTY-SIX
Into the Sunset

By the following Friday, Nate had confessed it all to Sister Sam. Samantha. She taught seventh grade science at St. Christopher of the Cross Catholic School. She was the only nun on staff these days. Back in his day, sisters ran the joint. You couldn't launch a decent spitball without hitting one. The current principal, Mrs. Kennsington, assigned Sister Sam to monitor him as long as he was going to hang around the front steps after school and make sure he wasn't a pervert. He couldn't blame her, but convincing the principal took quite a bit of doing on Monday afternoon.

Mrs. Kennsington didn't really believe it was all in the name of love until he walked her down the hallway lined with sixty years of class photos, stopping near the end and pointing to the mug smiling from the third row of portraits, second from the left.

"That's me. And that's Julie Cooper. She's going to meet me here after school."

Four days later, he was still waiting.

Sister Sam was thirty, though she looked ten years younger. It was the fresh face and freckles, he decided. Nate twirled a white carnation in his hand. He liked Sister Sam. He never had a problem with the nuns when he was growing up, but he never saw them as real people. They were all born a hundred years old with a no-nonsense attitude. They knew everything, so they liked teaching and they were all at least seven feet tall. Samantha Jean, on the other hand, was once a little girl, had parents and siblings, still liked to roller-skate around the playground when no one was watching, and she stood a shade over five feet tall. They talked a lot over the course of the week. She even had a semi-serious boyfriend in high school, so she could relate to Nate's plight.

The playground had fallen quiet, parents had fetched all their students, and there was no action left in the school day. "It looks like it's safe to leave me out here now, and I'm sure you have better things to do than babysit me. I might stick around a little longer."

Sister Sam asked if he would be back on Monday. Nate said he would, as well as Tuesday and beyond. "As long as it takes."

Samantha said she would stick around, too, another half an hour. "I'd hate to miss something." So they talked about stuff until the shadow of the cross on the building's gabled roof crept across the sidewalk and headed into the street. They turned their heads at a *putt-putt-putt* approaching. Julie *putt-putted* and sputtered to a stop with a last-minute lurch at the curb on a scooter. It was one of those Vespas you saw people riding along cobblestone European streets in the movies. And it was pink.

"Is that her?"

"Yes, it is."

"Cool ride. Cool color. I'll be going now. This is going to make a great story for the gals at the convent over dinner tonight. Email me an update, promise? Good luck."

Nate met Julie at the bottom of the steps.

"I was in the neighborhood," Julie started. "I got your note. I wondered if you would still be here."

"Seems I can't let go of the past. Or maybe it won't let go of me."

"Like a dog with a bone minus all the slobber."

"Clever, Cooper."

Julie tapped his shoulder as she slipped around him on her way up the steps, pausing on the first one. "For me?" She took Nate's carnation. "The last time you handed me a flower, a thorn bit my hand. It was bleeding when you left."

"Sorry about that. I didn't mean to hurt you." Nate said it naturally and then recognized how much it meant in the grand scheme of his screw-up.

"It's okay. That scratch under your eye is looking pretty good now. Who would have thought roses could be so dangerous?" As she made her way up four more steps to the top, she said, "I guess we wounded each other." Julie laid a hand on the railing, turned and gave him a sideways glance, a hint of a smile and pointed the flower at him as if it were a magic wand. He swallowed hard. It was déjà vu all over again.

"You know, these steps have always been special for me," she said.

"You, too?" Nate was feeling the heat now. He rubbed one foot against his other ankle hard. He wanted to make sure this wasn't one of his fantasies. No, it was real, for sure. And he felt like a kid again. He watched her drift from one side to the other. Then she looked down at him, tapping the flower in her palm, and said, "Our first kiss. You finally remembered."

"I never forgot it. Not really."

"It was here on the steps. Fifth grade. The Christmas pageant?"

"We came out here to get cupcakes from your mother's car after the play. You were dressed like Mary."

"And you were Joseph. And you kissed me. On the lips, before we went back inside."

"And that snitch David Cox ratted us out to Sister Mary Constance. Boy, did she let me have it."

Julie nodded. "I got the lecture about what nice girls do and don't do."

"I blocked it out for years, emotionally scarred, because it was such a painful experience."

"Kissing me?"

"No, that I beat the snot out of David for ratting me out to Sister and got three raps on the knuckles with her ruler and a week of detention."

Nate moved to the top step and sat down. He studied the sky and the street. Julie sat down beside him.

"Thank you for coming," he said. "I was sure you would, then I started to worry that I screwed up again."

"It was touch-and-go there for a while. I'm so tired. I'm tired of being alone. But I'm still not sure about this. About us. Too many times we had moments like this. I don't know why I should think it will be any different this time."

Nate wanted to tell her about his déjà vu and dreams of pretty little raven-haired loves on the steps before he was old enough to know love. Better to save it, if this was going where he hoped, and bring it out when they were old and gray and time validated the inevitability of their soul mate-ness.

"I've been thinking all week. What exactly did you mean, you know, that cute little line you dropped about rewriting the future?" she asked.

"It's like this. Go ahead and laugh if you want. Let's agree that I've always had a part of me stuck in the past. That's not so crazy, but where it gets crazy is that there were times when I would think of you and I could force myself to believe that if I only wished for it hard enough, if I meditated, ruminated, or even opiated really, really hard, I could go back in time and fix things. Things like us. Sometimes, when I was really down, it actually pissed me off that I couldn't make the impossible happen."

"That's when you decided to get professional help?"

He wasn't sure she was kidding, but whatever. "So I came home, thinking I would build this wall and live in the past as much as I could until I felt better."

"And you're sure you don't need therapy?"

"Ah. I may have been living in the past, but I always stayed in the moment. I knew the difference, but it made me feel better. Then it was weird the way things fell into place with the job at our old school and you being there. Like it was meant to be. I thought that would be enough. But that first day I saw you was when it really all came into focus."

"And what was that?"

"Not only was it stupid to pretend I could recreate the past, but I didn't really want that. I had this incredible second chance at convincing you to give *me* a second chance, and I was going to do everything I could to keep from blowing it again. Does that make sense?"

"In the way only you could. So why did you have to write about it?"

"It's what I do. I dream; I write; I wanted to write about us."

"But that's what makes no sense. You had the chance to achieve something you worked for, that you dreamed of all of your life, and you turned them down when they were ready to buy it."

"Yeah. Funny. It was our story through and through. We were living it, but if it wasn't going to have a happy ending, I didn't want to make one up just to please them, and I didn't want them tacking on some stupid ending that wasn't real. Then it wouldn't be our story anymore. And it seemed like the story was going to end exactly the same. Nowhere good."

Nate crossed his arms and leaned forward against his knees. He tilted his head and, with closed eyes, drank in the late-afternoon peace.

"What are you doing?"

"Savoring this for a memory I'll want to pull out thirty or forty years from now. God, it's a shame we don't learn when we're young to stop and smell the roses. No matter how hard you try, you have to put some history between yourself and a special moment to understand how great it is."

Julie stood. She went to the scooter, lifted the seat and pulled a ball of navy fabric from the storage compartment. He stood and followed her to the sidewalk. She offered it to him. The sweater was worn and faded St. ChrisCross blue. A gold patch with the school's initials covered the left pocket. On the breast, next to the top button, his note, *Our first kiss*, pinned to it.

He hesitated, took it in his hands and then pushed it back to her.

"I want you to have it."

"I'm still not sure it's the right thing."

"Take it for now. Keep it until we break up."

"How can we break up when we're not together?"

"We will be if you wear my sweater. I know it doesn't fit and all that. But I'm asking you. To, uh, you know, go steady?"

"Until we break up? That could be ten minutes from now."

"Or it could be ten years, or never."

She held the sweater to her chest and dropped her chin, thinking. Deciding. She buried her nose in the fabric. "It smells musty. I don't think anyone would tell you to stop and smell the polyester."

"What? You've never heard that before? I'm thinking of having a T-shirt made with that saying. Stop and smell the polyester."

Julie kissed him lightly on the cheek. "Okay," she said, and returned the sweater to the compartment under the scooter seat and picked up her pink helmet. She drummed her finger on it, looking at Nate with more light in her eyes than he had seen before. Studying him.

"Your story. Have you figured out how it ends yet?"

Nate shook his head. "No clue."

Julie put on her helmet and straddled the scooter. She patted the seat behind her. "Come on. I could use a chocolate milkshake right now. Maybe something will come to us."

"I can't ride with you," Nate said.

"Why not?"

"Because it's so…so pink. Your scooter is pink."

"It was your idea. Remember when I said I always wanted a motorcycle but that I was too old to do something like that? I'm younger than that now. You're the one who said I should stop being afraid to live. So here I am, living the dream."

"Your dad might be proud, but that's not a motorcycle. I've had lawn mowers with more power than that."

"Are you coming, or are we having our first fight?"

Nate climbed behind her and wrapped his arms around her

waist as she started the scooter and settled in. She asked Nate if Tina Farnham would still want the story.

"She'd lap it up."

"Then we'd better get busy on it." Julie revved the little bike twice and let it settle back into a steady idle. She turned her head and raised her voice. Over her shoulder, she said, "One thing, though. Your character Julie? She's way too wimpy. She needs more spine."

"Got you."

"And a tattoo."

Credits

I have to gratefully start out with thanks to Will Vitales, (Mt. Pleasant High School class of '76), who sparked the initial idea for this book with a lively discussion at our high school reunion by asking "Would you go back and do it again?" Thanks to my once-upon-a-prom date Laurie Ameln Louie (MPHS-'73), who inspired the direction it would take over dinner at Applebee's a few days later. Kudos also to Carla Gunnels (MPHS-'74), high priestess of the alumni Facebook group and all the classmates there who helped resurrect memories and acted as my de facto focus group for various plot twists. Go Cardinals! A special shout-out to Elizabeth Loyd Almeida (MPHS-'76), who shared many details, some intimate, about finding her soul mate Dave through online dating even though I twisted it for nefarious purposes in the book. WinkConnection.com wouldn't exist without her.

As for the grownups, thanks to Mrs. Martha Guerrero, current principal at Mt. Pleasant High School, for a day on the old campus, and her generosity of time to explain how things work in high school now. Thanks to Mr. Fred Matalone, my former teacher who shared with me what it was like to be a teacher both in the '70s and today. Thanks to Angela Smith for her editor's eye and unconditional support of my fiction, to Corina Carrasco (MPHS-'74), who provided the last coat of copy polish, and to Caroline Tolly, the editor who helped me put this into a coherent form. Last, but not least, thanks to my wife Kim who, after forty years and counting, greets my every bad idea with a roll of the eyes, a heavy sigh, and encouragement: "I guess it's all in the execution."